Both Ends of the Circle

Both Ends of the Circle

Nell Finnemore

Matador
9 Priory Business Park,
Wistow Road, Kibworth Beauchamp,
Leicestershire. LE8 0RX
Tel: 0116 279 2299
Email: books@troubador.co.uk
Web: www.troubador.co.uk/matador
Twitter: @matadorbooks

ISBN 978 1800463 936

British Library Cataloguing in Publication Data.
A catalogue record for this book is available from the British Library.

Printed and bound in the UK by TJ Books Ltd, Padstow, Cornwall
Typeset in 11pt Sabon MT by Troubador Publishing Ltd, Leicester, UK

Matador is an imprint of Troubador Publishing Ltd

For Erica

Chapter One

1968

They didn't normally shop in Rackhams but for once Becky and her mother strode confidently through the big swing doors and made straight for the escalators, bypassing the counters full of over-priced cosmetics, staffed by immaculately made-up assistants who thought nothing of people who couldn't afford to blow a week's rent on a pot of face cream. Becky's eyes widened as the escalators glided them up through floor after floor of half glimpsed displays: glamorous evening attire, luxurious furniture, impossibly expensive cutlery and china, until they eventually reached their destination – the department dedicated to school uniforms.

Becky had expected the place to be teeming with other children, perhaps even other girls getting kitted out for Eleanor Vaux Grammar School for Girls, but they were the only customers. A library-like hush lay over the polished wooden counters and the ranks of neatly labelled drawers behind them, the sobriety unrelieved by a pair of headless dummies, one clad in the uniform of St Thomas Aquinas Boys' School, the other representing Dame Elizabeth Cadbury's netball squad. A long pelmet ran all around the back wall, displaying the ties and badges of every grammar school in Birmingham. It was like entering an exclusive club to which passing the eleven-plus afforded right of entry. Becky took in an audible breath.

A middle aged woman in a black skirt and cardigan advanced from the furthest end of the counter to ask: 'Can I help you?'

On the very rare occasions when they had entered Rackhams before, perhaps to admire the magnificence of the Christmas decorations or to 'see how the other half live,' this enquiry had invariably been met with an almost guilty denial, but today Becky glowed with excitement as her mother replied, 'I've come to get my daughter's uniform for Eleanor Vaux.'

'Of course,' the assistant nodded and smiled. It was as if years of experience had given her a special insight, Becky thought, so that the moment they had appeared at the top of the escalator, the woman had known instinctively that she was marked down for Eleanor Vaux.

While Becky's mother produced a much folded copy of the school uniform list and a stump of pencil from her handbag, the Rackhams lady retreated to the banks of drawers, withdrew one of them completely and placed it on the counter top. The uppermost item in the drawer was an identical list mounted on a piece of stiff card and underneath it Becky could see that the drawer contained Eleanor Vaux ties and scarves, all neatly folded. An involuntary shudder ran down from her hairline.

'I always suggest we work our way outwards,' the lady was saying. 'Which means we start with the navy blue knickers. Will that be five pairs, one for each day?' She was reaching for another drawer as she spoke.

'Two pairs.' Becky felt herself redden as her mother's voice cut in quickly. 'Minimum two pairs. That's what it says on the list.'

The assistant only checked momentarily before asking, 'Do you know the waist size?'

The split second's hesitation was just long enough for a powdering of ice to settle around Becky's heart. They had fallen at the first hurdle. The assistant knew them now for the pretenders they were – people who could not afford five pairs of navy knickers – people who had to hide behind the 'minimum' escape clause.

The assistant produced a yellow tape and measured Becky's waist to establish the size of knickers. After the knickers came the starchy white blouses. Then the school skirt. Becky could hardly take her eyes off the stack of brand new clothing mounting on the counter, blazer, mackintosh, sweater, science overall, games skirt, airtex blouse, the roll call of garments went on and on. She tried not to notice the tightness about her mother's lips as the time for payment approached. Suppose all those careful calculations had failed to ensure that she had the right amount of notes folded inside her purse?

At last the tie – the coveted silver, blue and black tie – was placed on top of the pile.

'Will you be taking a school scarf?' The woman's hand hovered over the drawer, her fingertips skimming the pale blue and silver stripes.

There was a pause while Becky's mother consulted the list. 'Optional,' she read aloud. 'No thanks, we won't bother with a scarf.'

Becky's eyes pricked with tears. She blinked them back. She mustn't let the woman behind the counter see. Come to that she mustn't let Mum see either. But as they took the escalator down to the next floor, their purchases folded into large carrier bags bearing the Rackhams logo, her mother hissed: 'What's the matter with you?'

'Nothing.' Becky wanted to dig in her pocket, where she thought she might have a paper tissue, but her hands were full of bags.

'What *is* the matter,' her mother demanded more loudly.

'I just… well, I thought… I was going to have a school scarf.' Becky's voice trailed away into a miserable warble as a little sob chased unbidden after the words.

'For goodness sake! Stop that snivelling. You're showing me up.' In spite of this warning her mother's voice rose in direct proportion to the colour in Becky's cheeks as they made their way between the perfume counters. 'Do you know how much you've just cost me? Ungrateful, that's what you are. Do you think money grows on trees? You heard how much that little lot came to. And is that good enough for you? Oh no! I want a school scarf,' she affected a childish whine.

'Sorry Mum.' Becky edged through the doors and out into Corporation Street, wondering if a smack was imminent, but her mother's hands were – like her own – fully occupied with their purchases. In any case her mother was moving from anger into the adjacent neighbourhood of righteous self pity.

'There's me with hardly enough left for our bus fares home and you want a school scarf. What's a school scarf anyway? Just some gaudy bit of material for you to lose. I don't know what you want one for. You never normally wear a scarf. Bloody snob school.'

Becky said nothing, keeping her eyes focussed on her feet and the cracks in the pavement. She was stung by the accusation of snobbery because it was true that she had only really wanted the scarf for show. Partly because it would have looked so grown-up and partly because the secondary moderns didn't go in for them.

Her mother seemed to relent a little. 'They're optional,' she said in a kinder tone. 'So a lot won't have them. You'll see. Come on now. I want to get the five past bus. Frank's coming round tonight, so I don't want to be late.'

*

Just over an hour later Becky was in their tiny living room, watching the smoke from her mother's cigarette as it formed a pale, undulating spiral staircase to the ceiling. The cigarette had been left propped in the ashtray and Becky could see that if it did not receive some attention soon, the ash would reach the lip of the ashtray which would overbalance the smouldering end so that it would probably fall onto the carpet.

'Mu-um,' she called half heartedly, but her mother was out of earshot, getting ready for Frank, humming to herself, even while she pursed her mouth to apply lipstick.

Frank was due at half past six. Becky glanced at the clock, adjusted the cigarette to a safer angle and retreated to her own bedroom. In doing so she had hoped to avoid Frank when he arrived, but at the sound of their door bell her mother called: 'That'll be Frank. Go and let him in.'

It was useless pretending not to hear, so Becky descended the stairs to the front door of the flat as slowly as she dared, hopping back as she opened the door, just in case Frank got any ideas about greeting her with a kiss.

'The young princess herself,' said Frank. 'How's everything with you today, young lady?'

'Very well thank you,' mumbled Becky, as she trotted back up the stairs, taking care to keep a couple of steps ahead of him.

Frank was Mum's new friend and although Becky didn't like him much, the good side to it was that he seemed to make Mum a lot happier. Frank was a tall man with wide shoulders, a broad body and long thin legs which gave him an appearance of being top heavy. His Brylcreemed hair was an indifferent shade of orange and he had pink, freckled skin. He was much given to touching Becky, leaning forward to squeeze her knee when he made one of his not very funny jokes, or patting her on the head or shoulder in passing. A couple of times he had grabbed and squeezed her hand and on the previous occasion when he had arrived to take Mum out, Becky had been pretty sure that he was going to kiss her goodbye, only she saw it coming and moved smartly out of reach. Frank's hands always felt warm and damp against her skin, making her feel as if he had left an invisible stain which she wanted to wash off. While Becky didn't like any of this, she didn't say so or flinch away for fear that Mum would accuse her of being rude.

She led him into the sitting room where they stood awkwardly in the cramped space between the furniture. Becky dared not return to her bedroom lest leaving Frank on his own be construed as bad manners. She asked if he would like a cup of tea but he said no, which ruled out any legitimate escape to the kitchenette. A moment or two of awkward silence ensued before her mother appeared in the doorway, handbag on her arm ready to go out.

'Hello Frank,' she said. There was something very silly about her expression, Becky thought. It was as if her mother was trying to convey the impression that Frank's arrival was a nice surprise, which was daft when they all knew that he was expected.

'Now Becky,' her mother turned her attention away from Frank for a moment. 'You be a good girl while I'm out and don't answer the door to anyone.' She leant forward expectantly and Becky obediently puckered up and kissed the proffered cheek. Her mother reciprocated, leaving a ruby smudge of lipstick. To Becky's horror, her mother then reached into her bag and brought out a cotton handkerchief which she dabbed against her tongue and applied to Becky's face, while Becky wilted in embarrassment. Frank laughed which only encouraged her mother to rub the dampened handkerchief more vigorously than ever.

'Say bye-bye to Frank,' her mother instructed, catching Becky's eye and making a very obvious jerk with her head.

Colouring scarlet Becky thrust out a hand, keeping a deliberate distance between them as she had seen people do in formal situations on the television. 'Goodbye, Frank,' she said.

Frank, pretending gravity, shook the extended hand while her mother gave an exasperated laugh and said, 'What on earth…'

'Have a good time,' said Becky, retrieving her hand the second Frank's clammy grasp had loosened.

She watched them downstairs and waited on the landing until she heard the outer door close behind them. After that she opened the door opposite the living room and darted up the stairs hidden behind it. Although she wasn't really supposed to go into her mother's bedroom without permission, she often did when Mum went out. She really liked the attic bedroom with its secret stairway hidden behind what looked like no more than a cupboard door. The attic window looked out into the branches of the tree which grew outside on the pavement and the walls were papered in a pattern of faded pink and red cabbage roses, which Becky thought passably romantic. It's like a bower she told herself. She wasn't absolutely sure what a bower was but it seemed to go with roses.

Becky would have liked to have had the attic room, but Mum said she needed it because she had a double bed and the other bedroom – the one with the narrow sash window at the back of the house – only had space for a single bed and a wardrobe.

'We could probably squeeze a little table in there – and a chair,' her mother had said of Becky's room, when they first came to look over the place. 'Then you'll have somewhere quiet where you can do your homework. You'll have homework to do, once you get to the big school.'

Becky liked the idea of a chair and table, whose introduction would turn it into a study-bedroom, she thought, or even a studio. A studio certainly, if there was to be art homework. It was art at Eleanor Vaux, not painting, which was what it had been called at junior school. At Eleanor Vaux they had proper art rooms with sinks and everything, not like junior school, where the paint pots had to be taken into the cloakroom for washing out and monitors spread newspaper across the same desks that were used for everything else.

They had seen the art rooms on Interview Day during a tour of the school. There were all sorts of special rooms at Eleanor Vaux. Rooms for geography with maps all over the walls and a music room with special stands to put music on and a piano – not an upright piano like the one at junior school – but a big piano with a flat top so that the person playing could look out over it like the pianos you saw people playing on the television. There were science laboratories with rows of test tubes and a room full of cookers and kitchen equipment. It was like a different world. Exciting and scary all at one go.

They had moved into this latest flat just before Interview Day. It was the upstairs part of what had once been a single dwelling, but these days there were two front doors inside the porch: one belonging to Mrs Wilkins who had the ground floor and the other leading to their flat. Their front door opened straight onto a flight of stairs which were very dark even in the middle of the day and smelled of boiled cabbage and disappointment. At the top of the stairs the windowless landing was always sickly yellow in the glow of a naked light bulb.

Becky realised that before the house was chopped into flats all the upstairs rooms must have been bedrooms...

except the bathroom of course. The bathroom was still a bathroom and Becky's little room at the back was still a bedroom, but the other two rooms on that floor had become a sitting room and what the landlord called a kitchenette. Becky wasn't clear on the exact difference between a kitchen and a kitchenette, though she thought perhaps a kitchenette didn't have a fridge. There had been a fridge in their last kitchen but here there was just a gas cooker, a stainless steel sink unit and some cupboards whose doors had been clumsily painted in a greenish-mustard shade. They were supposed to be sliding doors but although they were only lightweight hardboard they didn't move very easily – sometimes in jerks and sometimes not at all.

During the eternity of the summer holidays Becky had the flat to herself while Mum was out at work. Sometimes she crept up the attic stairway to indulge in games about castle turrets and hidden chambers and sometimes to secretly apply Mum's lipstick. Otherwise she mostly sat on her own bed, reading. She kept her library books on a long wooden shelf in her bedroom, which was held up by the same sort of heavy metal brackets as the ones under the kitchenette shelves and like them was painted with thick mustard gloss. Becky liked to think of it as her bookshelf although it had other things as well as books on it (the little table and chair had yet to materialise and there was nowhere else to store anything except in the wardrobe). That summer she had mostly been reading school stories full of characters called Flavia and Imogen, who wore gymslips and said things like, 'How jolly' and 'What a good wheeze'. She didn't suppose anyone at Eleanor Vaux would really talk like that.

Just six more days, she thought, before I find out for myself.

*

The first day of term finally dawned warm and sunny. Even in the relative cool of the early morning, Becky found the full regalia of skirt, blouse, tie, sweater and blazer unexpectedly oppressive. The white collar was stiff against her neck and the blazer weighed a ton. At least the weather meant that she would not have to explain the absence of a scarf. She hoped in vain to find another girl in an Eleanor Vaux uniform waiting at her stop, but she was the only one and although she took care to sit in a vacant double seat when the bus arrived, none of the girls who got on wearing Eleanor Vaux uniforms took up the unspoken invitation and when they all surged off at the school stop none of them fell into step with her, all of them either walking separately or joining up with people they already knew.

On Interview Day they had entered the grounds via the main school gates but this morning someone had erected a portable blackboard and easel alongside the main gates. On the blackboard someone with very neat handwriting had written: *First year pupils use lower gates.* A chalk arrow underneath the lettering pointed the way.

The lower gates were not so grand as the main gates. They were just plain metal gates without the Eleanor Vaux coat of arms in fancy painted metalwork – or the motto *Contendere et Vincere* – whatever that meant. Entering through the lower gates only served to magnify how unworthy she was. She wanted to turn and run but instead

Becky drew in her breath and followed the stream of other girls along the lower drive, past the rose beds and the bicycle sheds, past the gymnasium windows, past the frosted glass of the toilets until she came to a set of double doors where another blackboard, this time propped on a chair, indicated with the words *First year pupils* and another arrow, where the newcomers should enter.

Inside these doors there was a sort of lobby with a notice board facing the doors. *First year pupils find your name in the form lists and assemble in your form rooms.* Three large sheets of paper had been pinned beneath this instruction, each headed with a room and a form number and an arrow pointing to right or left. Below each arrow was a typed alphabetical list of names. At sea in a silent world of chalk arrows and written instructions, Becky stood in the lobby and wanted to cry.

Another lone girls who had been walking a few paces ahead of her on the drive was standing in front of the boards. She turned and spoke shyly. 'I'm in IR. My name's Charlotte Young so I'm always at the end of lists. What's your name? I'll help you look.'

Overjoyed at being spoken to by an apparently friendly human being Becky said, 'I'll be at the top. Rebecca Addison… There,' she pointed as she spoke. 'I'm in IH. Room 22.'

'Oh.' Charlotte Young sounded gratifyingly disappointed. The arrows indicated that IH and IR were in opposite directions.

'Perhaps I'll see you later,' Becky ventured.

'Good luck,' said Charlotte Young, giving Becky a half-hearted smile before she set off to find IR.

Becky followed the direction indicated by the IH arrow, going through a set of swing doors and along a deserted corridor. The shiny soles of her new black shoes echoed off the stone floor. The sound seemed to bounce around the walls and ceiling, following her like a rattling drum beat, noisy as her heart. She passed toilets, changing rooms and the door to the gym, before the corridor turned at right angles and she found herself next to a deserted classroom. For a panicky moment she wondered how the rooms were numbered. How would she know when she had reached Room 22 – the home of IH? Then she saw the small metal plates painted the same dark red as the doors, which made the numbers rather difficult to decipher. That first empty room was number 23 so the next one must be number 22.

There were already three people in Room 22. Becky could see them through the glass panes in the classroom door. She sensed at once that the two girls sitting in front row desks already knew each other. She guessed that they had probably come from the same primary school and would not welcome her intruding into their conversation. The other girl was sitting in the last desk of the row alongside the windows: the seat furthest away from the door. Her face was almost hidden by the book she was reading.

Becky opened the door and stepped inside. The two girls at the front glanced in her direction but didn't stop talking. The girl at the back didn't raise her eyes. Becky hesitated then walked to the back of the room, choosing a seat next door but one to the reader. She was conscious of her shoes beating out a tap dance and when she sat down her chair scraped loudly against the floor. She felt an acute sense of loneliness. Perhaps no one would be friendly.

Perhaps no one except Charlotte Young would ever speak to her for her whole time at Eleanor Vaux. Perhaps she wouldn't make a single friend. And now she stopped to think about it she wasn't really sure if she could remember what Charlotte Young looked like. She might not be able to pick her out even if their paths ever did cross again, which seemed unlikely in that vastness of rooms and corridors which from her recollections of Interview Day seemed to go on for ever.

Looking down at the surface of the desk she saw that someone had carved *DIZZY* on it, probably with the point of a compass and near the hole for the inkwell someone had fashioned a neatly shaped heart around the name Paul, so long ago that the word was almost lost in the grain of the old dark wood.

A sound from across the room told her that another girl had entered, but when Becky glanced across she saw that the girl had slipped into a desk near the door and begun to rummage in her satchel without looking up. Three more girls came in shortly afterwards and they also chose to occupy desks on the corridor side of the classroom. It seemed as if no one wanted to sit near her. She took a sidelong look at the reader in the corner. She had a thin, elongated nose and her hair was in blonde plaits, which fell forward and skimmed the desk each time she turned a page. Becky wished she had thought to bring something to read. She undid the stiff buckles of her new satchel, inhaling the leather smell of its interior while checking the contents of her pencil case. A yellow one bought at Woolworths. Crayons, pencils, fountain pen, compass and protractor were all present and correct.

She was just wondering how much longer she could pretend interest in her plastic protractor when a girl with a round face and blonde hair entered the room, hesitated and then walked decidedly to the back, taking the desk between Becky and the girl with her nose in her book. Not liking to stare at the newcomer Becky looked straight ahead at the blackboard. It was clean and expectant, like the shiny faces of the girls who kept on appearing at the door, hesitating and then finding themselves a seat. Becky counted thirty desks in the room. Five rows across and six seats in each row. As more of the spaces were claimed, buzzes of conversation began to flit about the room on butterflies' wings.

Becky jumped when the blonde girl tugged her blazer sleeve. Turning she found her next door neighbour grinning at her in a friendly way.

'If we're going to be in the same class we'd better introduce ourselves,' the girl said. She had a smile in her voice and enthusiasm in her blue eyes. Her blonde, shoulder length hair was drawn back off her face by a bobble on top of her head and because it tended to curl, the ends flicked up where it met her shoulders. 'I'm Nicola. Nicky, for short.'

'I'm Rebecca. Becky for short.'

There was a brief silence while they continued to smile at each other. Then Nicola turned to the girl on her other side. 'I'm Nicky and she's Becky,' she said, in her bright, friendly way. 'Who are you?'

Becky marvelled at her courage. The book looked quite grown-up. It wasn't a children's book, you could tell from the cover.

'I'm Paula,' said the sophisticate, laying her paperback face down on the desk. She did not after all, seem unduly perturbed by the interruption.

Sensing that the others were looking to her, Nicky said, 'I came from Roseberry Hill Primary, but there's only one other girl coming from my school and her name was on the list for IP. I wasn't really her friend anyway,' she added by way of an after thought.

'I've only just moved from Erdington,' said Becky. 'It's on the other side of town. I don't know anybody.'

'No one else came here from my school,' said Paula. 'So I don't know anyone either.'

'Well never mind,' said Nicola, cheerfully. 'We all know each other now.'

Whenever she remembered the moment, even many years later, Becky could still recall the sense of relief. It was as if Nicky had taken them both by the hand. None of them had to be on their own anymore.

Chapter Two

1979

The Chinese waiter with the John Travolta hair cut came to clear away their plates. They had chosen the restaurant in Cannon Street not only because the food was good, but also because it offered a cheap 'Business Man's Special' at lunch time.

'You're going to be fine. You'll be perfectly O.K. meeting loads of new people,' Becky was saying. 'Look at our first day at school. I was completely bowled over by your confidence. I've never forgotten the way you introduced yourself and took charge of us.'

'Confident? Me?' Nicky laughed. It was a quieter sound than it had been in their IH days, but still infectious. 'Crikey Becka! I was always the giddy one. You had all the ideas, all the get up and go.'

'Well you were pretty confident that first day, when you just bounced straight in and asked my name. I didn't dare speak to anyone at all.'

'Not any more,' said Nicky. 'Ten years on you're Miss

Independence and I'm subservient to my marriage vows. So... where he leads... I follow.'

An awkward flicker passed between them. Becky appeared to be on the point of saying something, changed her mind and returned instead to the safety of Memory Lane. 'You just epitomised an Evie for me, that first day. You had everything going for you. Right down to your school scarf.'

'You and that bloody school scarf,' Nicola was half incredulous. 'I can't believe you're still going on about it.'

'Everyone had one except me.'

'Becka if you'd had one you wouldn't have worn it. How many detentions did you get for being caught without a tie?'

'*Not* the point.' Rebecca laughed in her turn. 'I wanted one. Everyone else had one and I wanted the option of not wearing mine.'

'Everyone else did not have one...'

'Well it felt like they did.'

The waiter approached to ask if they would like anything else. The two course 'Business Man's Special Lunch' didn't include coffee.

Nicky said, 'I have to go, Beck. I'm meeting Mark off the train.'

At the mention of Mark there was another flicker, this time noticeable enough to generate a slightly awkward pause. Nicky reached down and began pleating the table cloth while Becky asked the waiter for the bill. Once he had left them again she became serious. 'Nicky,' she tried unsuccessfully to initiate eye contact. 'Are you really sure you want to go?'

The pleating became more urgent, less even. 'Of course I'm not *sure*.' Nicky's gaze remained focussed somewhere beyond the far wall of the restaurant. 'Who would be? I mean, anyone would feel a bit nervous… going to live in a new country, where they don't know anyone. I know I shall miss my family and my friends and then there's my job… but I can't put my career ahead of his. I mean Women's Lib is all very well but I'm the one who'll be giving up to have babies, so naturally his job's got to come first…'

'Not necessarily,' Becky began earnestly. 'Since the '74 Act came in…'

'Spare me the party political broadcast, Beck.' Nicky attempted a smile. 'Besides which Philadelphia's not the other side of the world you know. Well yeah – O.K. then it is – but I shall come back sometimes. We get our return air fare paid once a year.'

'And what about the other stuff – between you and Mark?'

'That's all over,' said Nicola, firmly. 'You know he's promised it won't ever happen again.' She couldn't quite manage to meet Becky's eye.

'I wish,' Becky began, but she stopped as Nicola's hand unexpectedly closed over hers. 'Don't Becka. Don't spoil our last lunch together. He's my husband and we've got to work things out.' Our last lunch, she thought. Only the two of us. Another unspoken source of sadness. Something still too raw to speak of on an occasion such as this.

Becky was silent. In spite of their long friendship, Nicky had erected No Entry signs on every avenue which led to the subject of Mark.

Nicky released her friend's hand and reached under the

table for her bag, looking down so that she wouldn't have to see the way Becky's lips came together. She knew that Becky was on her side, but just now she wasn't helping. If Becka loved someone the way she, Nicky, loved Mark, then Becka would understand. In real life everything didn't always turn out exactly as you wanted it to be. Sometimes you had to compromise. Even when it meant accepting the stinging humiliation of Mark's unfaithfulness.

'I'll get the bill,' Becky said abruptly, standing up and hurrying across to the cash register beside the entrance, before Nicky could protest about paying her share.

That was another difference between them, Nicky thought. Unlike Becky she would never go to the till before the bill was brought to the table, just in case it was the wrong thing to do in a restaurant. It was all very well for Becky to talk about her self confidence on the first day at Evie's. Everything had been different then, with different rules. In adult life when other people broke the rules it wasn't necessarily them who got punished.

The first spots of rain were starting as they left the restaurant, forcing them to make a hurried parting: Nicky to meet Mark at the station and Becky going back to her office. Our last Thursday lunch together, Nicky thought. I'll never find a friend like Becka in Philadelphia.

*

Three days later it was still raining. Nicky watched the drips falling off the leaves of the lilac which grew alongside her parents' kitchen window. It had been there as long as she could remember, flowering faithfully year on year.

'I had lunch with Becky on Thursday,' she said, holding her half eaten biscuit over the kitchen sink so as not to make crumbs. It was my last lunch with Becky before we go, she thought and this is my last Sunday lunch at Mum and Dad's.

Her mother was putting the Yorkshire pudding tin back on the top shelf in the pantry and did not hear. The two women were alone in the kitchen, taking their time over the final stages of the post lunch clear-up. Mr Christie was in the living room watching the football and didn't want to be distracted by idle chatter. Dennis, the Christie's middle son, was out in the garage showing his new car to Mark and Michael the youngest brother, had gone upstairs to do his homework. It was just a normal Sunday lunch like any other. She must not think of it as anything special. Must not allow herself to get upset.

Mrs Christie emerged from the pantry. 'It doesn't know when to stop, does it?' she said in a falsely cheerful voice as she looked out through the rain-streaked window panes. Nicky's mother was much given to making pointless remarks about the weather to which she expected no response. Knowing perfectly well what was really in her mother's mind, Nicky felt a stab of guilt, which isn't fair, she thought. It isn't my fault that I can't make everyone happy. Sometimes you couldn't be a good daughter and a good wife. Taking a cue from her mother she temporarily avoided the thing in both their minds, saying instead: 'Has Michael decided which universities he's applying for?'

Mrs Christie's brow puckered over the question. 'Ooh, I'm not sure, love. I think he's still sorting all that out with the school. You'll have to ask him. Somewhere in London is favourite, I think.'

Nicky finished her biscuit and flicked the remaining crumbs from her fingers into the plastic washing up bowl, where they began to expand damply.

'I shall miss him when he's gone,' Mrs Christie said, refolding a tea towel and hanging it over the rail on the back of the door. 'I suppose our Dennis will be next… and you won't be popping round anymore.'

'You'll be free of us all,' Nicola said brightly. 'You'll have the house to yourselves for the first time in over twenty years. Then you'll be able to come over and see us. Have a holiday in America. How about that?'

'Well,' said her mother. '*That's* something to think about.'

It was another of her mother's pet phrases: one she employed when confronted by ideas which were almost beyond her ken, like the moon landings and the idea that babies could be created in test tubes. She had never been in an aeroplane. The family went to Minehead for their holidays. There had once been some desultory talk of Spain, but Mr Christie hadn't fancied the idea of the foreign food and Mrs Christie didn't fancy flying.

'We've picked out the wallpaper for the living room,' her mother said. 'Your dad's going to start on it next weekend.'

Nicola recognised the tactic. 'It's not so expensive to fly to America as it used to be,' she said. 'And once you get there you can stay with us, so it'll be all found. Taking everything into account it probably wouldn't work out any dearer than a fortnight in Minehead.'

Her mother half turned away as if engaged in some imaginary task by the pantry door. 'It's a nice stripe, a Regency Stripe it's called in the book. In Sage Green.'

Mark appeared at the kitchen door.

'We'd better be getting off,' he said. 'There's still lots to do at home. Are you ready, Nicky?'

*

He was a good looking lad, Mrs Christie thought, after they were gone. A nice looking chap, who was a good provider. A girl couldn't ask anything more than that. Of course his job had been almost too much of a good thing really; taking the pair of them off to America any day now. Well – another six days to be exact – and she could be exact almost to the minute. She had never imagined her daughter living more than a few miles away at most… and now Nicola was going to America. Of course you had to pretend to be pleased for them. But sometimes she caught herself wishing that Nicola had ended up with a more ordinary sort of chap, with an ordinary job. Then again there weren't the jobs like there used to be. With all these redundancies, she had to remember how lucky they were that Mark had got a job at all, even if it was taking them so far away. Some people said financial pressures were one of the reasons that so many young couples weren't staying together these days. Of course youngsters didn't stick at things the way people used to. Mrs Simms down the road's daughter had split up with her husband only last month. Mrs Christie hoped she had managed to bring up her three better than that. Marriage was something you stuck at through thick and thin.

From somewhere above her head the sound of Michael's stereo burst forth. An American voice singing something about a telephone. She recognised it as one of Michael's favourites. An unconscious smile appeared on her face. 'He's very clever is our Michael,' she would confide in neighbours. 'All his teachers speak very highly of him.' She always used the possessive 'our' when talking of her children. She knew it was a bit common, but it just slipped out. Well... she had never been one for putting on airs and if people thought she was common so be it. She knew she wasn't anyone special, but at least she could be proud of her children. Dennis had done well for himself getting that job at the garage. He'd always been car mad. Nicky had a lovely house and a smashing husband and how many people could say their daughter and son-in-law were going off to live in America? As for Michael, he would probably do better than any of them. Ever so clever his teachers said he was.

Chapter Three

1968

Mr Sinton was the only male teacher at Eleanor Vaux who never wore a collar and tie, having managed to persuade Miss Forster, the headmistress, that a tie would become entangled in the strings of musical instruments and was therefore detrimental to his teaching methods. Mr Sinton had a somewhat eccentric appearance: a shiny bald head trimmed with a half circlet of white, collar length hair, button eyes behind round spectacles and a long indoor coat, patched at the elbows. Miss Forster's reservations about the potentially subversive tendencies of a man who wore a purple polka dot dickey bow at parents evenings were only slightly mollified by the way Mr Sinton sustained the fine musical traditions of Eleanor Vaux, organising both the school orchestra and the senior choir (the junior choir was the province of his underling, Miss Healey). Fortunately Mr Sinton had never fuelled these anxieties by confiding in Miss Forster that he cared less for pushing up the size of the music 'A' level class, than that the girls who came into his orbit might have their lives opened up to the possibilities of Mozart, Beethoven and Vivaldi.

On this early October morning he had abandoned the prepared lesson about time signatures, thrown open the music room windows and allowed Elgar to flood out across the hockey pitches where it was absorbed into the sunshine of the Indian Summer.

'Music of the English countryside,' he announced, sweeping across the room with his coat billowing behind him like a magician's robe. 'Close your eyes and listen. Imagine yourselves flying high above the fields and hills. See the landscape opening up beneath you. The trees, the rivers and streams…'

He scanned their faces as he spoke. Some were on the edge of giggling, others were concentrating too hard, missing the point and one or two were as expressionless as puddings, but he noted approvingly the way Rebecca Addison's face was alight. Helen Staveley sitting two rows behind her looked much the same. Those two were not down on his list of girls who played instruments – well perhaps they should be.

At the end of the lesson as the class was moving out, he called them to one side. 'You girls aren't on my list of musicians,' he said. 'Would either of you be interested in learning an instrument?'

'I used to play recorder at my old school,' Helen ventured hesitantly.

'Well why aren't you coming to the junior recorder group?'

'I didn't know if I was good enough, sir.'

'Well come along, come along and give it a try next week.' As Helen scuttled away, half elated and half terrified at being picked out, Mr Sinton turned to Rebecca. 'How about you?'

'I haven't got a recorder.'

'Well have a think about it. If you're interested ask your parents to buy you one.'

Becky stayed silent, scrubbing one foot against the floor while the sock on that leg started to wriggle down.

Mr Sinton decided further encouragement was needed. 'Did you enjoy the music we played today?'

'Yes sir,' she said, fervently wishing to be released. At this rate he was going to make her late for next lesson.

'I don't suppose you have many records like that at home, do you?' Mr Sinton spoke gently, without considering the harshness of the implication.

'No sir.'

'Well you can borrow any of the music department's records you know. I shall need a letter from your parents to say they have given permission and undertake to pay for any breakages,' he paused, full of unwitting cruel kindness. 'But I'm sure you would be very careful with anything you borrowed.'

'Yes sir.' Becky was now in a positive dither lest he make her late for French. She guessed that Nicky and Paula would wait for her outside the music room, but the rest of the class was long gone and they had to get right across to the other side of the building.

'Well think about what I've said and have a word with your parents. Off you go now to next lesson.'

'What did he want?' Nicky asked, as they broke into a curious gait which avoided the 'no running' rule, but was barely quantifiable as walking.

'He wanted to know if I'd like to learn to play recorder or borrow some records.' Becky didn't slacken her pace. The corridors were already almost empty of the torrent of girls which flooded into them at the end of every lesson and coursed along until swallowed up for the beginning of the next.

'Are you going to?' asked Paula.

'No,' said Becky. 'We're going to be ever so late. Thanks for waiting.'

*

The day had been unseasonably warm but by tea-time it was cool enough for the kitchenette window to steam up when cooking commenced. Becky was sitting at the Formica topped kitchen table with her maths homework in front of her, concentrating too hard to notice that the bubbling noise which had been emanating from a pan of potatoes for some time, was growing steadily more impatient. She continued to search for the common denominator of thirty fourths and sixteenths until there was a sudden explosive burst of hissing, at which point Becky leapt up from the table too late to stop scummy, boiling water pouring over the edge of the saucepan and all over the top of the cooker.

Her mother chose that moment to appear. 'Bleedin' ell! Didn't I tell you to watch those spuds didn't boil over. I was only gone a couple of minutes. Honestly… the one thing I ask you to do…'

'Sorry Mum. I was doing my homework.'

'Doesn't stop you looking at the spuds every now and then, does it?'

'No.' Becky began to gather up her books. The table would be needed for them to eat on and anyway now that Mum had appeared she was sure to start talking and Becky found that common denominators needed her full attention.

'Mum?'

'Yes?'

'You remember how you said I could have a little table in my room, for a desk?'

'I didn't say could. I said might. Do you think I'm made of money?'

'No. Sorry.'

The boiling potatoes had filled the kitchenette with steam, so when Becky carried the books into her bedroom she slid the bottom sash up an inch, admitting some cool air together with the sound of birds against a background of distant traffic. She thought about the music Mr Sinton had played for them. It had been like a magic spell, the way he had made them close their eyes so that they could soar above the countryside like birds themselves. She closed her eyes and tried to recapture the moment, stretching out her arms like wings, but one hand hit the wall and anyway she couldn't remember enough of the music.

'What *are* you doing?'

Becky jumped. She hadn't realised that she'd left the bedroom door open. Her mother went into the bathroom, shutting the door behind her without waiting for an answer.

The next question came out of the blue over the sausages, mashed potatoes and cabbage.

'What did you do at school today?'

Becky chewed as slowly as she could to play for time.

The first thing that came into her head was Mr Sinton's music lesson, but it would be no good saying anything to Mum about flying, which would be dismissed as barmy. Nor could she mention the idea of a recorder because that entailed expenditure. The absence of a record player in their household rendered the loan of records an unsuitable topic too.

Becky emptied her mouth. 'Nothing much,' she said.

'Nothing much,' her mother echoed with a sour laugh. 'You could have gone to the secondary modern and done nothing much and a lot more cheaply too. You must have done something. What was that homework you were doing?'

'Maths.' Becky seized the cue gratefully. 'We had maths this afternoon and Miss Mislet gave us homework. We're doing multiplication of fractions. If you get two different sorts of fraction you need to find the common denominator…' she trailed off. Her mother was pushing some left over cabbage and mash to the side of her plate and did not appear to be listening.

Seeing that Becky had stopped talking she said, attempting a joke, 'Common denominators. I didn't think they had anything common at that school. Well you obviously understand what it's all about, so you'll have done it in no time and be able to clean that mess off the cooker where you let the potatoes boil over.'

Becky opened her mouth to protest then closed it again. It was no use saying that it wasn't her night for the washing up. Arguing was just a quick route to a back hander.

'I know it's not your night but you'll do it for your old mum, won't you?' She gave the child a conspiratorial wink. 'I've been hard at work all day and poor old Cinderella has to get her reward sometimes.' She stood up and carried her plate across to the sink before continuing, 'Yes Cinderella, you *shall* go to the ball. Be a love Becky and get all this sorted out while I get ready.'

Becky hadn't realised that her mother was going out. She wondered if Frank was coming round to pick her up, hoped he wasn't and then felt guilty because assembly that morning had been all about loving one's neighbour, which according to Miss Forster meant not only Mrs Wilkins who lived downstairs, but someone like Frank as well. From the sink she caught glimpses of her mother flitting between the bathroom and her bedroom. She could smell the perfume her mother had sprayed on from the atomiser she kept on her dressing table – a little china trinket, with a bulb you squeezed to make the perfume squib out. Mum was wearing her pink nylon petticoat – the good one which hadn't been singed – and once her face was done she wriggled her way into a black dress which sat tight across her hips.

'Hook me up at the back, will you? That's it. Now be a good girl. Don't open the door to anyone or stay up too late. Got to run.' She kissed the air somewhere an inch above her daughter's hair, picked up her coat and bag and disappeared down the stairs.

As the front door slammed shut Becky ran up into the attic to watch the departing figure out of sight. A drift of discarded clothing lay across the double bed and perfume lingered near the door.

'Well *I'm* going out on Saturday,' Becky said aloud, half in consolation half in triumph.

*

Becky had been in a fever of excitement ever since Nicky had issued herself and Paula with invitations to tea. On the day itself Nicky met them at the bus stop as promised, so that she could walk with them to her house. 'Doesn't it seem funny,' she said. 'Seeing each other out of school uniform? Golly Paula, your hair looks lovely.'

Paula, whose plaits had been liberated into a shimmering cloak which fell half way down her back, blushed pink.

'It looks just like a Tudor lady off one of those Jean Plaidy books you're always reading,' Becky agreed.

Becky thought it was a tea fit for the Gods. Mrs Christie had laid up the front room table with a lacy white cloth just as though they were grown-up, important visitors. There were egg and cress sandwiches, followed by cake which Mrs Christie had baked herself. After tea they cleared the table and played Monopoly and after Monopoly, Nicky brought some of her books downstairs and they began to talk about reading. Paula seemed to have read more books than both the others put together.

'I'm going to be a writer,' she confided. 'So I have to read a lot. Every spare moment really.'

'Are you?' Nicky's blue eyes opened wide. 'I don't know what I'm going to be. I hope I'll be rich though. When I was much younger, ' (it would never do to admit that it was just last year) 'I used to have a Sindy doll and I had Sindy's car. You know – the red open top sports car. I'd love to have a car like that in real life. Although I'd have to learn to drive and that might be quite difficult.'

'One of the sixth formers is having driving lessons,' said Becky. 'I saw the car coming to pick her up while we were in science.'

'How can she be having driving lessons in school time?'

'I don't know. The sixth form can do all sorts of things. They don't have lessons all day. Sometimes when they haven't got lessons they make coffee in their common room.'

The sixth form and its mysterious activities seemed such a gulf of years away as to be an impenetrable enigma.

'Have you done all your homework?' asked Nicky.

'I have,' said Becky. 'That history took ages.'

'I haven't started mine,' said Paula. 'I was reading this great book and I had to finish it. It's called 'The Golden Rendezvous' by Alistair McLean. You can borrow it, if you want.'

'Thanks,' said Nicky. 'But I haven't finished the last one you lent me yet.'

'I will,' said Becky. 'I've finished that Chalet School book and I don't need to do the reading Mrs Rollins set us for English, because I've already read 'Treasure Island' twice. I wish we were doing a book I haven't already read.'

'I don't,' said Paula. 'It's useful doing a book I already know. I hate it when she asks the class to read bits out loud. People ruin it by droning and some people read as if there's a full stop at the end of every line, so I keep 'Treasure Island' open on the desk as if I'm following it and have the book I'm actually reading down on my lap.'

When Nicky finally escorted her visitors to the bus stop, Paula said: 'I'm going to ask if you can both come to tea at mine next Saturday.'

The cool October breeze penetrated Becky's pink cardigan. If Paula got permission to invite them, then by inference it would be her turn to play hostess the following weekend. Nicola's house was a three bedroom semi and her mum put a paper doily between the fruit cake and the plate. Paula always seemed to have enough pocket money to keep replenishing her supply of paperbacks at five shillings a throw. Tea in their kitchenette – even supposing Mum agreed to it at all – was not an edifying prospect.

In spite of these gloomy misgivings she was looking forward to telling Mum about the fruit cake and the Monopoly. Sublime. That was the word to describe it. (A jolly good word she had come across in an English lesson and adopted for her own.) Not that she intended to tell Mum that tea at Nicola's house had been sublime, because that was sure to get Mum ratty. If Becky ever said anything about other people's things being particularly nice, Mum always managed to interpret it as her saying that their own things weren't good enough and that inevitably led to a lecture about how ungrateful she was. No. She would just tell Mum that it had been nice. (Even though Mrs Rollins, who taught them English, said you should never use the word nice in conversation or compositions if you could possibly think of anything else to say.)

Her eagerness to relate the adventure of tea at Nicky's was defused when she turned the corner and saw Frank's car parked outside. She found Frank and her mother sitting side by side on the settee in the living room.

'Been to your friend's?' asked Frank. 'That's nice. Did you enjoy yourself?'

'Yes, thank you.' Becky hovered in the doorway, wondering how soon she could legitimately escape to her room. 'We played Monopoly after tea. Paula had Mayfair and Nicky landed on it and got absolutely wiped out.'

'I like Monopoly myself,' said Frank. 'Haven't played for a good few years now.'

'Pop the kettle on for a cup of tea while you're standing there Becky,' her mother said.

'No, no.' Frank started getting to his feet. 'Becky's only just got in. I'll make it.'

'I'll make it,' said Becky, almost sprinting into the kitchen. What's Frank doing, going into our kitchen and making tea? she thought crossly. We haven't known him five minutes.

*

Sitting in Paula's bedroom after tea the following Saturday, with the sky darkening outside and the wind gusting through the trees in the garden, Becky couldn't stop thinking how lovely it was. There was a window seat with a cushion running all along it, covered in the same flowery material which had been used to make the curtains; a proper book case for Paula's books and on the bed what looked like a doll, whose full skirt turned out to be a hiding place for Paula's nightie. A nightdress case, Paula called it. Becky imagined how happy anyone must be, to go to bed every night in a palace like this.

Paula had showed them all her secrets: the hidden drawer in her musical box, the locked diary her godmother had given her last Christmas, which she hadn't got round to writing anything in yet and the hidden ledge under her bed where she kept the torch she used for reading under the bedclothes.

Becky had already invited the others to come to tea

with her the week after next. She felt that she ought to say something to prepare them for how different it would be to their homes, but she couldn't think of how to begin. To her surprise Mum had agreed to the idea at once, only suggesting that they postpone the invitation for a week so that it coincided with the Saturday nearest Becky's birthday. 'Then it can be a birthday tea,' she suggested.

At this point Frank had chipped in and said why not take the girls out to the pictures, have tea afterwards and then he would run them all home in his car to save anyone needing to get the bus after dark. Mum had looked a bit hesitant at first but then Frank said it would be his treat, at which Mum had looked really pleased and said: 'Ooh Frank… you are good.'

Becky was so thrilled by the idea that for once she didn't even mind Frank being part of the package. Mum seemed to be as excited as she was herself and kept coming up with new ideas about what they should have to eat. 'Pickled onions,' she said. 'Those special ones with the white skins. Cocktail onions they call them… crisps as well… and cheese and pineapple on sticks.'

Becky couldn't resist imparting some of this appetising information.

'It sounds like a party,' said Nicky.

'It's not a party,' said Becky. 'It's just a birthday tea. We haven't got room for a party. We live in a flat. Just a small flat.'

'I've never been in a flat,' said Paula. 'What's it like, living in a flat?'

'It's just like living anywhere else,' said Becky. 'Except that we don't have much space.'

'In the meantime, what are we going to do *next* Saturday?' asked Nicola.

'I don't know,' said Paula. 'You can come to mine again if you like. Mum won't mind.'

'Or...' Nicola paused, as if building to a suggestion of some magnitude. 'We could go into Kings Heath together and look around the shops.'

This sounded like a very grown-up adventure and just the kind of thing a trio of Eleanor Vaux girls ought to be doing on their day off.

'I think that would be all right, said Paula.

'I think I would be allowed to,' said Becky. 'After all I shall be twelve the week after next.'

Chapter Four

1979

As the 50 bus made its stop-start progress along Moseley Road, Becky's thoughts were all of Nicky. She would be part way across the Atlantic by now. High above the water, just a minute silver speck if you happened to be looking up from a ship, as the plane passed overhead. She wondered how Nick was feeling as she headed into unknown territory, going off to a country she had never even visited, which was going to be her home for the next few years at least. If only… She pulled herself up short. No use thinking of if onlys. During the last few days she had thought of little but Nicky's departure and their subdued, almost strained, last lunch together. 'And then there was one,' she said to herself.

She got off at the Bull Ring in a kind of daze, half wondering what she was doing there. She worked in town Monday to Friday. Why on earth come into town on her day off as well? 'It's because you've got nothing else to do,' her inner voice twitted her. 'And no one to do it with.'

What had Nick called her? Miss Independence? On a

whim she went into a travel agency and began to look at the brochures for coach holidays. She was due some time off and there must be plenty of cheap breaks available in September. Cheap-ish anyway. It would have been lovely to go to Paris or Rome or even a Spanish beach, but she couldn't really afford that – not with the premium for a single room – so she settled for a long weekend in the Lake District. She had never been and the photographs of lakes and mountains looked more appealing than the pictures of Welsh castles and West Country cream teas. She had to pay in full because it was only a couple of weeks away and even as she was writing the cheque, she knew deep down that the whole thing was a bad idea.

*

'Going on your own?' squeaked Margie, the receptionist, when she broke the news at work on Monday. 'Crikey! That's a bit brave, isn't it?'

'It's an organised coach trip to the Lake District, not a one woman hike through sub-Saharan Africa.'

'Oh… a coach trip. You'll be chatted up by a load of wrinkly old men. Don't forget to brush up on your bingo and community singing.'

'It isn't that kind of coach trip,' Becky attempted dignity. 'The coach just takes you to the hotel in Ambleside. After that you can do whatever you please.'

'Not much *to do* up there, is there?' asked Margie. 'Wouldn't you have been better going somewhere a bit more lively? How about Blackpool or one of those Club 18-30 holidays?'

'I can't think of anything I'd hate more. I just want some peace and quiet and a bit of a break.'

'Well you won't get it by joining a pensioners' knees up.'

In spite of her protestations to the contrary, when Becky stood on the forecourt of the coach depot, having manhandled her suitcase on and off the bus to save on a taxi, she swiftly realised that she was the youngest person there by several decades. The other passengers all seemed to be travelling in pairs and they eyed her curiously, as she stood in line to have her case put into the luggage compartment. Telling herself that she didn't care, she bagged a double seat half way down the bus and rummaged in her bag for 'The Cement Garden' which she had begun in bed the night before and not found particularly engaging. When they eventually got underway she glanced out of the window from time to time, but while the bus was pounding up the M6 there was very little to see. The couple across the aisle unpacked a little picnic, complete with pale pink paper napkins which they spread on their knees to catch any stray crumbs. A smell of egg and cress sandwiches crept into her air space, making her wish that she'd had the foresight to throw more than a packet of crisps and a Penguin biscuit into her bag.

After the stop on the motorway – a queue for the ladies of course, followed by an indifferent cup of coffee – she gave up trying to read 'The Cement Garden' in favour of a newspaper, but the headlines seemed to be as depressing as her novel. She felt tired and dispirited and wished she had stayed at home.

Even their arrival was less than propitious. The famous

Lakeland scenery which had tempted her north was obscured by low cloud and the hotel in Ambleside felt chilly as they stood in line with their luggage, waiting to be issued with keys to their rooms. Nor was Becky heartened to learn that her room was on the top floor, which meant lugging the suitcase up four flights of stairs. When she finally got to her door and flung it open, the room was so small that the door bounced straight back off the side of the bed and all but hit her in the face. However when she stepped across to the window she found that the weather was lifting and beyond the roof tops she could see hills – mountains even – appearing and disappearing behind wisps of clouds which floated around them like a series of gauzy veils. It was beautiful. Miles of amazing countryside which was hers to explore for the next three days. She remembered how she had always coveted her mother's attic bedroom and decided that in spite of its limitations, the little room on the top floor was a good omen after all.

*

Dinner turned out to be more of an endurance test than she had anticipated. The waitress put her at a little table by herself, which she was glad about in one way because the snippets of conversation she could overhear did not sound particularly edifying, but at the same time she felt conspicuous on her own. Some of the other guests did bid her, 'Good evening,' in passing, but no one attempted a proper conversation and some of them favoured her with smiles which she interpreted as pity for this strange, friendless girl who had to travel alone.

It was the first meal she had eaten out since her farewell lunch with Nicky. Not much of a send off, she thought – the 'Business Man's Special' at a city centre Chinese – but Nicky had insisted that she didn't want any fuss. 'I'll only get upset,' she'd said. 'We both will.' Which was true. It had been a difficult meal. So many things that neither could bring themselves to talk about. Wounds too raw to explore in the emotionally heightened atmosphere of Nicky's imminent departure. Now she was here, waiting to order, waiting for food, waiting between courses, there was suddenly too much opportunity to think about those things. When she ate at home she invariably propped a book up on the table – often one of her legal text books – but here she had observed the polite convention of not reading at the table, which left her with nowhere to look and nothing to focus on but the very things she did not want to dwell upon. She decided that good manners or not, tomorrow she would bring something down to read at the table. Not 'The Cement Garden'. Maybe there would be a bookshop in Ambleside where she could get something else?

She had trouble getting to sleep in the unfamiliar room and then woke several times during the night. In the early hours she crept out of bed, slid the curtains aside and looked out. The sky had cleared and was peppered with stars, quite unlike anything she had ever seen at home. It was amazing and beautiful. Surely it must mean that something good was going to happen? She shook her head at her own superstition. Life had taught her that you had to make your own luck.

As soon as breakfast was over she set out to explore, deciding to leave the shops and ferry for later, in favour of following a finger post which pointed to Jenkin Crag. Who was Jenkin, she wondered, and what sort of view might his crag offer, supposing she got to it? She had only been walking for a few minutes when a group of serious hikers overtook her, stomping along in heavy boots, some wearing waterproofs, all of them carrying rucksacks. She had already noticed a lot of people around the town wearing proper walking boots with thick woollen socks. Some of them had gaiters, waterproof trousers, anoraks, the whole regalia. It made her feel a bit underdressed in her jeans, sweatshirt and trainers. Well it was not as if she was planning to do any serious mountaineering. She would just follow the path for a bit and see where it took her. If it started to get difficult she could always turn back. All she wanted was to reach a nice view.

Unfortunately the path almost immediately led her into a thickly wooded area from which views were in short supply. The shale underfoot soon gave way to mud and Becky had to hop from one tree root to another, in order to keep her increasingly muddy trainers from sinking in ankle deep. She considered turning back but it appeared to be lighter up ahead and that implied a thinning of the trees and surely once she came out in the open she would be looking down on the lake? However when she climbed a little further, she found that although there were breaks in the canopy, the trees surrounding her were as dense as ever. She paused in a small clearing to weigh up her options. The path was not particularly difficult now that she seemed to have got past the worst of the mud and if she climbed a little bit higher she must surely emerge onto the open hillside. It seemed a pity to give up now.

She began to climb again. It was much steeper than it had been at the beginning, but she was rather enjoying the challenge until a large stone to which she had confidently entrusted her full weight slid sideways, taking her foot with it and depositing her onto the track. Her foot twisted sideways under her as she fell, the pain of it sharp enough to make her cry out.

She lay completely still for a moment before struggling into a sitting position. She had thrown out her hands to save herself and holding them out in front of her, she saw that she had taken some skin off one palm, which was bleeding. Stay calm, she told herself. The sight of blood always makes things seem worse than they really are.

Yet even in those first seconds while she considered her hands, she knew that they were not the real problem. She rolled down her sock and looked at her ankle. There was no obvious injury but trying to flex it made her feel sick.

I have to stand up, she thought, otherwise I might be here all night. Apart from the posse of walkers who had overtaken her at the beginning of the path, she had encountered no one else. It took several minutes to pluck up the courage, but eventually she managed to drag herself upright by leaning on a boulder and then using a nearby sapling to steady herself. However when she attempted to put any weight on her right foot, the pain surged through it so that she had to lift it off the ground at once and clutch the sapling, steeling herself against the awful possibility that she might be about to faint.

Now what? She had never been much good at hopping, not even on flat ground and this was clearly not hopping terrain. It was so awful it was almost funny. She started to laugh then started to cry. After a time she lowered herself back to the ground and for the first time since leaving the hotel, she checked her watch. It was only mid morning which meant that no one would miss her for hours. Even if they did miss her, no one would know where to come and look for her. She knew that there was something called the Mountain Rescue, but here in the woods she would hardly qualify for anything so grand as that. Perhaps if she waited a while her ankle would stop hurting and she would be able to walk on it? Then again, she was getting cold… either that or the shock of the fall had sent her shivery. Whichever, it was probably better not to sit still. The only solution seemed to be to work her way down the path on her backside and that wasn't going to be easy. She located a clean tissue in her pocket and bound it round her scraped hand in order to keep dirt out of the raw patch, then began attempting to make her way down hill, not much more than a couple of inches at a time. Progress was slow and awkward and it was no use thinking about what it was doing to the seat of her new jeans.

It took some time to gain the small clearing where she had paused earlier. Here she dragged herself onto a patch of reasonably dry ground and considered her options. When she was climbing the path had seemed obvious, but now that she was facing in the opposite direction, Becky realised that there were several openings between the trees, all of them leading down the hill and none of which was definitely identifiable as the route she had originally come up. Did it matter so long as she was going down? All ways must lead back to Ambleside, surely? But suppose they didn't? Suppose she got completely lost?

She must not start blubbing again because that was just pathetic and getting her nowhere. If only someone would come… At that moment she thought she heard a voice somewhere above her. Even as she gathered herself to yell for help she heard the distinctive clumping vibration of boots on the ground and caught sight of two figures coming down the path. Two tall young men were swinging down the slope, as easily as if they were walking down Corporation Street.

'Hello! Having a rest are we? Crikey… what's happened to you?'

Now that help had arrived, Becky found herself almost incoherent with relief, only managing to blabber out something about missing her footing and hurting her ankle, before she found to her embarrassment that tears had sprung into her eyes again.

'O.K. Better let us have a look. Now then… don't worry. I won't hurt you.'

As the one with auburn hair, who was slightly the taller of the two crouched down and looked at her ankle, Becky noticed almost subconsciously that he had a Brummie accent. 'It's a bit swollen,' he said. 'But I don't think it's broken. Here Ed… you have a look.' As he straightened up, Becky got her first proper look at his face and discovered that he was handsome. His dark haired companion was not half bad looking either. Suddenly everything seemed a lot better than it had been a few minutes ago. What were the odds, not only on being rescued, but on the rescuers being a couple of good looking blokes? It was fairy tale stuff and for a second or two she half wondered if she was hallucinating.

Ed agreed that the ankle was probably just twisted.

'Better not try putting any weight on it,' cautioned his friend. 'If you take my rucksack Ed, I'll carry her down. Piggyback would probably be easiest.'

Becky began to protest that if they could just support her she could probably manage to hop, but this was brushed aside. 'It isn't wide enough for three abreast. I'll carry you. It isn't very far.'

As Ed helped her onto his companion's back, Becky said: 'I don't even know your name.'

'Sorry. I completely forgot the etiquette of rescuing someone off the hillside. My name's Sean and this is Eddie. What should we call you?'

'Becky.'

'Brummie aren't you?'

'Yes.'

'That makes three of us then.' He hitched her further up his back. 'That's right… hang on round my neck. Where d'you live?'

'Kings Heath.'

'I'm from Great Barr and Ed's from Kingstanding. Right then, we're all set.'

*

Becky was wary of magic. No good ever came of getting romantic and star struck, but all the same it was hard not to be swept off your feet when a knight in shining armour (or hiking boots and a cagoule which these days came down to almost the same thing) not only carried you on his back, but insisted on driving you to a distant A&E in order to get your ankle checked out and then offered you a ride back to Birmingham in his car the following day. Sean insisted that he had been planning to cut short his trip anyway (Eddie stayed on to camp with the group of friends they were holidaying with) and even if Becky didn't really believe him, she had ceased arguing around the time when he first proposed to give her a piggyback down the hill.

Chapter Five

1968

'Paula are you out of bed yet?'

'Yes Mum.' Paula tried to slide her feet over the side of the bed in order to avoid this being a complete fib, but the blankets were still tucked in and while she was wrestling them from under the mattress her mother's accusing face appeared at the bedroom door.

'You're not up at all. Come on or you'll be late.'

Paula mumbled something non-committal while trying to pull her nightie down, because her mother was still standing in the doorway looking straight at her.

'Do you want me to get your clean vest and pants out?' Her mother was already moving towards the chest of drawers without waiting for an answer.

Paula would have liked to say that no, she just wanted her mother to go away, but that would have been too cheeky so she struggled free of the bedclothes and pretended to be putting something into her satchel while her mother laid out the underwear.

'Haven't you got your satchel sorted out for school? If I've told you once I've told you a hundred times, you must get yourself organised the night before. You don't have time to do it now. You should be out of your nightie and getting dressed.'

'It's done now,' said Paula, grabbing her underwear and heading for the bathroom.

In the bathroom she bolted the door and ran water noisily, pretending not to hear the voice which followed her along the landing issuing directives to hurry up. Pulling off her night dress she stared at her chest in the mirror. She couldn't detect any sign of growth at all.

It was Monday and therefore gym, which meant the humiliation of the showers. It was by far the worst ritual of the week. First you stripped off all your clothes, not knowing where to look but at the same time just knowing that everyone else was looking at you, then you ran through the tiled corridor where fixed shower heads sprayed jets of water from either side. The water might be anything from stone cold to boiling hot. There was no way of knowing what the temperature would be until your skin encountered it because talking was forbidden and any girl who squealed at an encounter with icy water was sent back for 'being silly'. Nor was there any question of standing under a jet and making sure you actually got wet all over. You just raced through getting wet wherever the shower happened to hit you while Miss Leopold, the P.E. teacher, stood watching and sometimes singling people out to go through again because she said they hadn't showered properly, but really just for spite. There was no question of removing the sweat or dirt accumulated in the preceding lesson, because there wasn't any soap or even pretence at washing. Back in the changing room you scrambled into your clothes as fast as you could without bothering to dry yourself, partly because the bell had already gone (Miss Leopold seemed to delight in making everyone late for next lesson) and the more so in desperate haste to cover yourself up. This too was accomplished under Miss Leopold's eye as she stood imposing at five foot ten in her tracksuit and whistle, watching everyone get dressed.

At the beginning of the year only a handful of girls had been wearing bras but by half term the numbers had increased significantly. Nicky had appeared sporting a 32AA, which she said felt funny at first where it did up at the back. Paula examined her own chest every day and felt increasingly desperate. She had heard Gail Foster and Deborah Reed joking about people who still wore vests, whom they referred to as the vestal virgins and now Becky said she was getting her first bra at the weekend.

The only way to get out of showers was to be having a period. Miss Leopold kept a register and if you were having a period she marked it in her book. You could only be excused if your mother had written a note, so you couldn't fake it. This ensured that the onset of menstruation was as publicly notched up as was the wearing of a bra. Paula had a terrible fear of being last. The end of the first year would come and she would be the only girl who had neither experienced periods or a bra. She would be singled out as a freak.

It was hard to believe that before starting at Eleanor Vaux she had actually imagined that P.E. would be rather exciting: a chance to try hockey which she had only read about in school stories, to say nothing of getting to go on the trampoline in the gym. The first lesson had been a huge disappointment because instead of changing into their brand new games skirts and aertex shirts, they had been instructed to lay out their entire P.E. kit, right down to the regulation navy shoe bag complete with initials embroidered on it in pale blue silk, while Miss Leopold undertook a positively militaristic inspection of everything.

The second lesson – which Paula had assumed could only be better – turned out to be even worse. Everyone was required to strip down to their navy knickers in order to be weighed and measured. Coming from a mixed primary school where changing for P.E. had been nothing more than exchanging a pair of plimsolls for one's shoes, Paula was unprepared for the experience of standing almost naked in front of twenty nine classmates. Each girl stepped up in turn and their height and weight were called out by Miss Leopold for her sidekick Mrs Grenville to note down in the same book where Miss Leopold kept a register of menstrual excuses. Poor Kay Fenton, the biggest girl in the class, had looked as if she wasn't far off crying when her weight was shouted across the room. P.E. lessons had started badly and gone steadily downhill…

At breakfast when she and her mother were alone at the table, Paula said: 'Will you buy me a bra, Mum?'

'Well of course I will when you need one.'

'Can't I have one now?'

'Don't be silly Paula. You haven't got anything to put in a bra yet. You probably won't need one for ages. These things run in families and neither your grandma or I have ever had much of a bust.'

Paula met the others at the school bus stop as usual

and they walked the last leg together, heads bent against the wind. Occasional icy rain drops stung their bare knees and every so often Becky put in a hop to haul up her socks. Becky had cried off the expedition to Kings Heath on Saturday because her mother had unexpectedly announced that she was taking Becky into town, to buy her a new dress for her birthday.

'What's your new dress like?' asked Nicky.

'It's brown with a sort of black swirly pattern on it and buttons all down the front.'

'Mini skirt?'

'Of course. What did you two do in Kings Heath?'

'I got a lipstick,' said Paula. 'It's called Orange Tango. I'll have to be careful not to let my Mum see it or she'll go all freaky. She thinks I'm too young to wear make-up.'

'I bought a record.' Nicola paused for effect. She had never bought a record before and thought it almost qualified her as a teenager.

'Which one?'

''Lily The Pink' by The Scaffold.'

'I've heard that on the radio,' Becky said. 'It's quite good.'

'I want a transistor radio for Christmas,' said Paula. 'So I can listen to Radio One in my bedroom. Mum and Dad won't have it on downstairs. Honestly they're such old fogies.'

'My Mum likes Englebert Humperdink.' Nicky spluttered at the thought. 'Can you imagine!'

'My Mum probably doesn't know who Englebert Humperdink is,' declared Paula. 'She is really, totally behind the times.'

As they entered the lower gates the rain began in earnest and although they broke into a run they were soaked by the time they dived into the cloakroom where they had to plunge into the dripping jungle of bigger girls hanging up their macs and negotiate an obstacle course of umbrellas propped open to dry, until they reached the row where the first years had their pegs. The dampness invaded registration. Gloves and scarves were steaming on the radiators and little pools formed under desks where wet feet fidgeted while Miss Harrison took the register before telling them to line up for assembly. Only when the whole school had marched into the hall did Miss Forster walk out onto the platform to announce the opening hymn. When the last notes had died away the headmistress signalled with a majestic, palms down descent of both hands that they could be seated. This morning the hall floor was not only cold but also damp where numerous pairs of feet had marched into place across it, but everyone dropped obediently at the signal and listened to Miss Forster reading something about Gladys Aylward. After the reading and the moral lesson to be drawn from it came the sign (palms upward, movement reversed) for everyone to stand. Prayers were next and then another hymn during which a number of hands made nervous explorations to ascertain whether there were embarrassing damp patches on the backs of their owners' skirts.

Then it was time to sit down again for the notices. Monday morning notices always concluded with the detention book: the weekly naming and shaming of all those who had been put into detention the previous week. This week the list included Charlotte Young of IR. There were a few hastily suppressed gasps from the front rows, where the first years sat. It was inevitable that someone had to be the first in their year to get a detention, but that didn't stop it being the talk of the form room as books were collected for first lesson.

'What did she do?' asked Becky, but no one seemed to know for sure. Bad marks in a test, someone said, or maybe talking in class.

First lesson on Monday was English. Everyone liked Mrs Rollins, who was neither fierce nor unkind and who today kicked off the lesson with some exciting news: 'Some of you may know that there is a new film of 'Romeo and Juliet' and it is coming to the Scala Superama a week on Saturday, so I have booked a block of seats. I know you won't be starting Shakespeare until next year but this is a golden opportunity and I strongly recommend you to join the school party. One of the things which makes this version so unusual is that the director, Franco Zefferelli, has chosen a girl of just fifteen and a boy of seventeen to play the leading roles. In Shakespeare's original Juliet is a young girl, just entering her teens…'

Mrs Rollins' enthusiasm was contagious and at the end of the lesson the whole class jostled to put their names down.

'I don't know if I'll be allowed to get the bus into town on my own,' Paula said doubtfully.

'Go on,' urged Nicky. 'Put your name down. We'll meet up and go together. Then you won't be on your own.'

In spite of Nicky's confidence on the matter, Paula continued to entertain doubts. The 'Romeo and Juliet' trip was uppermost in her mind when she walked home from the bus that afternoon and she intended to ask permission first thing, but when she turned the final corner she saw Auntie Lena's car parked outside the house and her heart sank. Of all the tedious friends and relations who might decide to drop in, Auntie Lena held a particular dread, because she was Mum's old friend from school and therefore an Evie (Paula called her Auntie Lena because she called all her parents' friends uncle and auntie).

After letting herself in at the kitchen door Paula took as long as she dared to drape her damp mackintosh over a chair in the hall, but there was no respite before her mother's voice came from the sitting room. 'Is that you Paula? Come in here. Auntie Lena's here.'

'You know it is and I know she is because we all saw each other through the front room window as I came up the path,' Paula muttered under her breath. 'Just coming,' she said, more loudly.

'Hurry up. What are you doing?'

'I'm taking my shoes off in the kitchen. They're wet.'

Ophelia appeared at the kitchen door and came to weave around Paula's legs, tickling them with her soft fur while pointedly eyeing her empty saucers by the kitchen door. Having removed her shoes Paula picked the cat up and cuddled her close. Ophelia did not approve of that sort of familiarity and wriggled until Paula placed her gently back on the black and white chequer board floor at which Ophelia allowed herself to be stroked, purring softly. The good thing about Ophelia was that her love was conditional on things you could easily deliver, Paula thought. Any fool could open a tin of cat food.

'Come on Paula, where are you?'

'I'm just getting a drink.'

She slopped some milk into a glass, not forgetting to put some in Ophelia's saucer. Not daring to risk a fourth summons she took her glass of milk into the sitting room and perched reluctantly on the edge of the chair nearest the door.

'Well,' said Auntie Lena, the moment Paula entered the room. 'How are you liking it at Eleanor Vaux?'

'Very well thank you.' Paula's tone was wooden.

'She loves it, don't you?' her mother said enthusiastically. 'She's been longing to go, ever since she was about seven years old. Thank goodness she got a place. She would have been so disappointed otherwise.'

'Well of course she got a place.' Lena laughed. 'She's your daughter after all.' She turned back to Paula. 'I expect you've already made some friends. Well of course you have. I'm sure you made friends on the very first day.'

'I did actually,' said Paula.

'Paula's made lots of friends,' her mother said. 'She's off to a birthday party on Saturday.'

'Not a party,' Paula demurred, but they weren't listening.

'Do you remember that day just after Paula was born when I came to see you in the nursing home? I looked down into that crib and I said then she was a little Evie.'

'As if it was yesterday. Mind you it sometimes doesn't seem all that long since we were there ourselves.'

'I expect your mother will have you practicing on the tennis courts in the spring.' Lena turned back to her friend's daughter.

Here it comes, thought Paula, the bloody Senior Shield.

'Your mother and I partnered each other and won the Evie Senior Shield for tennis two years running. It had never been done before: the same pair winning two years on the trot.'

'And our record still stands,' Paula's mother sounded shrilly triumphant. 'When we went to look around the school I checked the board in the entrance hall. Never the same names twice except in 1943 and 1944 – Lena Marchant and Jean Prentice.'

'Are any of your new friends good players?' Lena asked Paula.

'I don't know. We don't play tennis this term.'

'Of course not. How silly of me. Though I thought it might have come up in conversation.'

Not likely, thought Paula. Do you think I go round telling people that my mum won the tennis shield God knows how long ago?

'So,' said her mother brightly. 'What *have* you been up to today?'

'We had English,' said Paula. 'And Mrs Rollins is organising seats for the film of 'Romeo and Juliet' at the Scala a week on Saturday. Can I go please? I've put my name on the list.'

'Of course you can go.' Her mother shot Lena a satisfied look.

''Romeo and Juliet',' said Lena. 'One of my favourites. Do you remember in lower fourth when Squiffy Hamilton…'

Sensing her opportunity Paula stood up, still cradling her empty glass and started edging towards the door. 'I've got to start my homework,' she said.

Her mother inclined her head in a sort of nod of

dismissal while at the same time making a gesture, its meaning embarrassingly obvious to Auntie Lena, to indicate that Paula's milk had left a moustache on her upper lip. Blushing hard Paula left the room. The cat was lurking in the hall. Paula picked her up and carried her upstairs. 'It's all right for you Ophelia,' she whispered. 'You never have to go before The Inquisition.'

Chapter Six

1980

'I had a letter from Becky this morning.'

'Oh yeah. Did she have anything interesting to say?'

Nicky noticed the way her husband didn't look up. She had always suspected that he did not really like Becky. 'She's got engaged. To that chap she met on holiday. The one who rescued her when she twisted her ankle. Isn't that romantic?'

'If you say so. I hope he knows what he's letting himself in for.'

'What do you mean?' she asked rather sharply.

'Oh well… nothing really. I just think she'd be a bit of a handful, Becky.'

'Meaning?'

Mark was already tired of the subject. He walked over to the T.V. and flicked it on. 'She's always seemed to me as if she likes her own way, that's all.'

Not like me, Nicky thought. I'm a pushover. Maybe that's why you married me? Aloud she said, 'Is it 'Dallas' tonight? Do you really think someone's going to shoot J.R.?'

'That's what everyone says.'

'I'm making coffee, would you like some?'

'Please.'

She thought about the letter while she brewed the coffee. Becky was obviously head over heels and yet she had such a funny way of putting things. *I know it's love, but I can't trust it,* she had written. *I'm so happy that I feel something must go wrong…* She supposed that Becky must mean she kept on expecting to wake up. It was something of a fairy tale after all. What were the odds against going out for a walk, tumbling down and being rescued by an unbelievably handsome guy (there had been a photograph in a previous letter) who just happened to live in the same city as you did, was single and therefore up for grabs?

She had been irritated by Mark's comment that Becky might be 'a handful', but she could understand what he meant. Becky was dead set on having a proper career and getting married probably wouldn't change that: she hadn't put in all those years of studying just to give it all up and have babies… And it was true that she liked to have her own way, but that was only because she was used to being independent.

Mark's voice floated through from the next room. 'Hey Nick… Do we have any Bassett's Double Chocolate left in the freezer?'

'I think so.'

'Be a sweetie and lob some into a dish for me, will you?'

Nicky crossed the kitchen to check on the ice cream situation. More than half a year in America had still not fully accustomed her to the novelty of having ice cream available in the house whenever she wanted it. Hardly anyone she knew at home owned a domestic freezer, but here it seemed to be the norm. She amused herself with an oft replayed dream of showing her mother around the flat, opening up the freezer to display three or four exotic flavours of ice cream, maybe taking her to the market to choose from all the amazing stuff on offer there (although never any of the egg custards or dripping cakes that she had so loved back home). The truth was that she knew that her parents would never come over. It wasn't just the cost of the air fare, but the thought of being in an aeroplane for hours and hours. Well maybe if not her parents, then perhaps Becky and Sean might come to visit. Between them they probably earned quite a lot, or would do when Becka was a fully qualified solicitor. And they would have the spirit of adventure which her parents lacked.

When she handed Mark his dish of ice cream she said: 'Wouldn't it be nice to invite Becky and Sean to come over and stay with us after they get married?'

'Yeah I suppose so... if you like.'

'Try not to sound so bloody enthusiastic.'

'Come on, hon. I'm trying to catch the news here. I wasn't really listening. Of course you should ask whoever you want to come over, although I'm not sure about having some guy we've never met to stay.'

'But Becky is my best friend and Sean will be her husband.'

'And I'm just saying we've never even met the guy. Suppose he turns out to be hell on wheels? Suppose... oh I don't know... suppose he steals from your purse or burns the apartment down.'

'As if Becka would marry someone like that!'

'I know I'm being extreme. What I mean to say is that we might not like him. *I* might not like him, which would be damned awkward if we were all cooped up in the apartment together every night for a week. All I'm trying to say is that we should at least meet him first, maybe when we go back this summer and then we can decide whether we both like him enough to have him in our home for a few days, O.K.?'

'I suppose so.' She went back to the kitchen and returned with his coffee. 'I'm going to write straight back to congratulate her. I'll use the table in the kitchen so I'm not distracted by the T.V. Will you call me when 'Dallas' is coming on?'

'Sure. And don't go issuing any invitations we might regret,' he called after her.

She collected her airmail pad from the dresser drawer and sat down to compose her letter, but after writing the address and a few initial lines of congratulation she came to a halt. She supposed that Mark was right about checking what Sean was really like before rushing into inviting them to come over, yet at the same time, now that she had envisaged the invitation it seemed the obvious thing to extend it and she felt that its absence would dominate the letter. The dream of showing her friend over the city had faded before it had time to flower. It would be so great to have someone over here that she knew. Specially now...

She had decided to say nothing to Mark until she'd had a test. There had been a couple of false alarms before and it was no use getting worked up about nothing. She knew he was dead keen to start a family. He had told her several times that the company approved of having family men on the payroll, his healthcare insurance would provide the very best of maternity care and anyway he'd always said that that he wanted them to have children. If only she felt more sure of herself. If she was right then she wouldn't be able to fly home in July like they had planned. She told herself that she badly wanted a baby but at the same time the responsibility of caring for one was quite scary. Most girls relied on their mothers and sisters and friends to come and help out in the beginning… A hollow fluttering seemed to rise up through her abdomen, making her feel as if she wanted to be sick. Was that what it felt like to be pregnant? Or was it just butterflies brought on by the thought that she *might* be pregnant?

Chapter Seven

1968

Three days after Mrs Rollins announced the 'Romeo and Juliet' trip, Miss Harrison dropped a bombshell at form registration. 'We appear to have a thief in our midst,' she said, gravely. 'Two purses have been stolen from within this classroom.'

The announcement was greeted with gasps of surprise. In truth Miss Harrison herself had been reluctant to acknowledge the presence of a pilferer in her form. When Kay Fenton claimed that her purse had vanished on Wednesday morning, Miss Harrison had been inclined to ascribe the loss to Kay's own carelessness. However when Alexandra Dunston's purse was reported missing it was an altogether different matter. Alexandra was a sensible, well organised girl, whose father was a lecturer at the university, to say nothing of being a prominent member of the P.T.A. Unfortunately Alex had not noticed that her purse was gone until the end of the school day, by which time it was too late to do anything about it until the whole form was assembled next morning.

After outlining the circumstances of the case Miss Harrison embarked on a little speech about the expectations of honesty and the shared values which bound the whole school together. As she spoke the form mistress scanned the thirty anxious faces before her, paying particular attention to the countenance of Rebecca Addison. She knew that it was the normal schoolgirl reflex to blush as soon as a theft was mentioned, but there was something about the way the girl couldn't meet her eye which convinced Miss Harrison that here was someone with definite knowledge of the missing money and she knew from the address in the back of the register that the girl's family were not from the ranks of the better off. After winding up the homily with a final word or two about trust, Miss Harrison instructed everyone to sit still while she undertook a thorough search of desks and bags.

Miss Harrison made noises of disgust at the messiness of Paula Morrison's desk and confiscated chewing gum from Adele White's satchel, but she made no progress whatsoever in tracing the missing purses. She was particularly thorough when she reached Rebecca Addison but a minute examination of her belongings failed to throw up anything which connected her to the theft.

Conscious that the weight of suspicion had fallen upon her, Becky felt as if she might crumble to red-hot dust while Miss Harrison searched her things. The feeling took a long time to subside and was worsened by the fact that she didn't get a chance to speak privately with her friends until morning break. Once they were on their own in the quad she said urgently: 'You know those purses that were stolen?' When the others nodded in assent she continued:

'Well I think I know who took them. Yesterday morning I saw Joanne Embury by Kay Fenton's desk. I thought she was putting something into Kay's bag – maybe a book she'd borrowed or something like that – and I never thought about it when Kay said her purse had disappeared because you know how Kay is always losing things? Well this morning when Miss Harrison started going through everyone's stuff, I saw Joanne take something out of her desk and stuff it up the front of her school jumper when she thought no one was looking. I don't know what to do about it. Do you think I ought to tell Miss Harrison?'

Nicky's lips were pursed into a donut of surprise. Paula said doubtfully, 'Telling's not very nice... but I suppose it could be vital evidence.'

'It might be,' said Becky. 'But suppose that wasn't what Joanne was doing in Kay's bag? I don't want to get her into trouble if it wasn't her. And what's worse I'm sure Miss Harrison thinks it was *me*.'

'In that case I think you probably ought to tell,' said Nicky. 'Although it isn't a very nice thing to do.'

'I'm not really sure what I saw,' said Becky. 'I mean not 100%.' (They had recently been doing percentages in maths.)

'Perhaps you should confront Joanne,' suggested Paula. 'If she admits it then you can go and tell Miss Harrison with a clear conscience.'

'Or better still,' said Becky. 'She could go and own up herself.'

'Suppose she refuses to own up?' Nicky regarded the others doubtfully.

'If she admits it us then we can give her the choice, either she tells Miss Harrison or we do. I think that's probably the best thing. Will you come with me?'

'What?' asked Nicky. 'To tell Miss Harrison?'

'No silly. To find Joanne Embury.'

'All right then.'

Since their arrival at Eleanor Vaux the IH pupils had formed various friendships and alliances. Alex Dunston and Norma Whitfield, two clever confident girls who had something to say on every conceivable subject and had arrived from their primary school as established best friends, had been elected IH form captains. The sporty girls seemed to hang together, while another group were united by an interest in the junior choir. Adele White, the only black girl in the class, had become bosom friends with Veronica Nicholls who was universally acknowledged as the class joker. Until now it had never occurred to Becky that Joanne Embury did not seem to belong to any particular group. Joanne was not an especially noticeable girl in spite of the auburn hair which might have made her stand out. She never said very much, never put her hand up in class or volunteered for anything. In P.E. she neither shone nor encountered Miss Leopold's ridicule for being among the slowest or least graceful. It was not that Joanne was an odd or unlikeable girl, merely that she was so quiet and inoffensive that it was easy to overlook her altogether.

At the end of break they found Joanne in the form room, extracting books from her desk in readiness for their next lesson. She was alone as usual. Becky walked straight up to her. 'Can I talk to you?' she asked.

Joanne looked up with an expression of suspicion and surprise. 'What about?'

At that moment the bell rang. 'I have to talk to you,' Becky said urgently. 'Meet me at the start of lunchtime in the cloakrooms.'

'O.K.' Joanne, still looking wary, watched as Becky headed for her own desk at the back of the classroom.

Unless it was raining, form rooms were always locked five minutes after the bell which signalled the start of lunch. Whereas Miss Forster was very keen on the beneficial effects of fresh air irrespective of the outside temperature, her pupils were equally keen on avoiding it. When they were not eating in the dining room, girls tried to escape the necessity of wandering about outside by holing up wherever they could find a private nook or cranny within the building. The cloakrooms were a particularly popular location in which to hide out, though liable to be cleared every so often by prefects doing a sweep of the building.

As soon as the lunch bell sounded Becky, Paula and Nicky hurried to the cloakroom, where they spent a couple of minutes nervously awaiting the arrival of Joanne Embury. The moment she appeared the quartet withdrew wordlessly into the ranks of navy blue mackintoshes, to a position where they were out of sight of the corridor. At this point Becky turned to Joanne and asked without preamble: 'Did you steal Kay's purse?'

'No I didn't.' Joanne looked indignant. A deep flush began to spread outward across her cheeks.

'I saw you go into her bag yesterday morning.' Becky found that her own cheeks were burning fiercely although she didn't know why. 'And while Miss Harrison was searching today, I saw you hide something up your jumper.'

'I didn't steal the purses.' Joanne's face had reached a

more fiery shade of red than Becky had previously thought it possible for human skin to achieve.

Nicola said, 'If you don't own up Becky will have to go to Miss Harrison and tell her what she saw.'

Joanne swallowed audibly.

'It would be better if you told the truth,' said Paula, with what she hoped was sufficient gravity.

'I didn't steal the money,' Joanne said, adding after a moment: 'I was just borrowing it.'

The others were so completely floored by such a ridiculous fib that for a moment none of them could say anything, so Joanne continued: 'I was going to give it back. I planned to put the money back in the purses and hand them in to Lost Property on Monday. I thought everyone would just think the purses were lost. And that's what they did think when it was just Kay's purse.' Joanne paused as if to emphasise the reasonableness of this. 'Only when Alex's purse disappeared as well, Miss Harrison made a big song and dance about it.'

'Well *two* lost purses in one day *is* a bit much of a coincidence,' said Paula.

'I was going to pay the money back... honestly.' Joanne's hazel eyes went from one face to another, full of mute appeal.

'Then why take it in the first place?' asked Becky.

Joanne swallowed audibly again. 'I wanted to get a place on the 'Romeo and Juliet' trip,' she said. 'But my mum said she couldn't give me the money until Dad gives her the housekeeping on Friday night and it would be too late by then because the money had to be paid in today.'

Paula looked incredulous. Nicky's expression softened. Becky nodded without realising she was doing it.

Nicky said: 'What about Kay and Alex? If you took their money then they wouldn't be able to pay for their places.'

'Of course they would,' said Joanne, her tone implying that Nicky had just said something extremely stupid. 'All they had to do was tell Mrs Rollins they'd lost their money and bring some more in today. Which is what they did. Kay Fenton's family have got pots of money – they went to Spain for their holidays – and Alex Dunston lives in a great big house near the university.'

'But you can't just steal from people because they have more than you do,' Paula objected.

'I've never done anything like this before,' said Joanne. 'And it wasn't stealing. I was really careful about who I borrowed it from. Only please don't tell. I'll be in ever such trouble if you do.'

'Well,' said Becky, thinking hard. 'Will you swear a solemn oath never to steal – or borrow without asking – again?'

'O.K.' Joanne said rather too easily. 'I swear.'

'And you're going to give the money back?' asked Nicky.

'Yes. I'll do it on Monday like I said.' As an afterthought she added, 'Perhaps you could help me. You could distract them while I'm slipping the purses back into their desks. To save handing them in at Lost Property.'

'We can't get involved,' Paula blurted out. 'If you get caught everyone will think we were in on it from the start.'

'Hang on though,' said Nicky. 'We'd be doing a good thing by helping her put right a wrong.'

'And I wouldn't get caught,' added Joanne. 'I'd be really quick.'

‘We’d better think about it,’ said Becky. ‘We’ll have to get a move on now. It must be time to join the queue for dinner.’

No one invited Joanne to tag along with them but then again none of them said she couldn’t. After they had collected their trays and were leaving the serving hatch, Joanne cleared her throat and said nervously, ‘Can I come and sit with you?’ And that – as far as any of them could ever remember afterwards – was pretty much how Joanne came to be the fourth member of their group.

Chapter Eight

1982

None of the shoppers in Kings Heath High Street seemed to be looking where they were going. Becky's progress was continually checked by pushchairs, meandering groups of kids and the wheeled shopping bags favoured by pensioners who had no thought for other people's ankles. She had almost reached Sainsbury's when she saw a familiar figure.

'Mrs Christie,' she called out.

When Nicky's mum turned at the sound of a familiar voice, Becky was shocked by the change in her. It was as if someone had taken a pale grey eyeliner pencil and etched worry-lines all over her face. She looked smaller than Becky remembered and the way she was huddled in her nondescript coat and headscarf she gave the impression of wishing that she were smaller still. All the same she managed a smile when she saw who was calling. 'Hello Rebecca,' she said. 'How are you?'

'I'm very well thanks. How about you?'

'Oh I can't complain. I'm just doing a bit of shopping.'

Mrs Christie spoke slowly, as if talking was something she needed to gear herself up for.

'And how is Mr Christie?'

'He's still looking for a job. He isn't getting anywhere with it.' The words slowed almost to a standstill: 'He won't accept that he's not going to get another job… not at fifty five. There's too many younger men available.'

Becky was about to say something bright and optimistic but Mrs Christie's face stopped her. Instead she asked: 'Have you heard from Nicky recently?'

'I get a letter every couple of weeks. I expect she still writes to you too?'

'Yes. Not as often as that of course.'

There was an awkward pause.

'How's Michael getting on?' asked Becky. Michael had always been a sure-fire winning topic, so she was disconcerted to see Mrs Christie's face crumble into an expression of even deeper distress.

'He's doing very well for himself. Finished university now. He got a very good job at the end of it. He's been taken on with a firm in London.'

'Oh,' said Becky sympathetically. 'I expect that means you won't see so much of him…' The older woman's face made her stop.

'He doesn't come home anymore. Cut himself off from us he has since Dennis… Nicola will have told you about our Dennis?'

'Yes… yes she did. I was really sorry to hear about it.'

'We've tried to keep it quiet,' said Mrs Christie, speaking mechanically, like a child reciting a well-learned lesson. 'But Michael's afraid it'll damage his career if it gets out. A brother in prison…' she dropped her voice, so that the word prison almost slipped unheard onto the damp pavement. 'That sort of thing doesn't do you any good when you want to be a barrister.'

Becky was about to say something else but now that Mrs Christie had cranked up the momentum to speak, it wasn't easy to stop her.

'The neighbours all know of course,' she went on bitterly. 'At least it can't touch Nicola and Mark. They're too far away. I go and see him in prison.' She raised her eyes to meet Becky's and there was an unexpected spark in them.

'That's very brave of you,' said Becky. 'It must be very difficult.'

'He's my boy.' Mrs Christie shifted her handbag onto her other arm. 'I have to go on my own. Norman won't come with me. He says we must have gone wrong somewhere – brought our Dennis up wrong – but he wasn't treated no different to any of the others and they've done all right?' Her face appealed for confirmation.

'Of course it's not your fault,' said Becky.

'I don't think he meant to do anything wrong. Not really wrong. It was just paperwork, that's what he said. It wasn't like he was hitting old ladies over the head or breaking into people's houses. It was just something that happens in the motor trade. When you think of the things that go on these days, I can't believe they've sent my Dennis to prison over some old log books or something. There's not a day goes by I don't think about it.' She fell silent as if the spring which had enabled her speech had finally wound down.

'Would… would you like to come and have a cup of tea

somewhere?' asked Becky, feeling shamefully relieved when Mrs Christie shook her head and said that she had to get on.

They were on the point of parting when Mrs Christie suddenly had another thought. 'And what about you, Becky love? Aren't you getting married soon? I'm sure Nicola said something about it in her letters.'

'That's… not happening now. We broke it off. Broke up.'

'Oh dear. I am sorry to hear that. You've always been such a pretty thing. I thought you would have been snapped up long ago. Still… you're not much over twenty five. There's plenty of time yet, isn't there?

'Remember me to Nicky, won't you?' Becky said. 'Next time you write to her.'

'I don't write to her,' said the older woman flatly. 'I send cards and that… on their birthdays and such like. I don't have the education to write lovely long letters like she does. I never know what to say. She knows I like reading her letters though. She knows I'm always thinking about her.'

The memory of this conversation replayed itself in Becky's head as she stood waiting for Joanne barely three weeks later, standing only a hundred yards or so from the spot where the chance encounter with Mrs Christie had taken place. Nicky's mother had looked very low that day. Should she have detected something? Was there anything she could have done? Small comfort that everyone who knew Mrs Christie must be thinking these same thoughts, sharing that nagging self doubt and all the time wondering at the level of despair which must have driven the poor woman to take her own life.

Joanne's hair enabled Becky to spot her from some distance away. In deference to the occasion Becky was wearing a suit the colour of wet slates over a shirt of paler grey silk and when Joanne approached, Becky noted that she too had adopted funereal black trousers with a black velvet shirt, although the fringed scarf draped about her neck and shoulders was striped with silver, pink and purple.

'Hi.' Joanne gave her a quick hug. 'Have you been waiting long? I was afraid my train was going to be late. We sat for ages just outside the station.'

'It's O.K.' Becky reassured her. 'We're in plenty of time.'

As they set off together in the direction of the church, Joanne said: 'I was a bit surprised they're having it in a church. I thought the church was funny about suicides.'

'I thought so too. I think they might be giving her the benefit of the doubt. You know... saying it could have been an accident... that maybe she didn't really mean to do it.'

Joanne looked surprised. 'But I thought from what you said on the phone that it was definitely suicide?'

'Oh no doubt at all. I mean she swallowed a whole bottle of pills... but I think... you know... to be kind to the family... Anyway thanks for coming up. I just felt it was something we could do for Nick.'

Joanne nodded. 'It must be absolutely awful for Nick. Being so far away and not able to get home for her mother's funeral.'

'She said in her last letter that Mark had the chance of a permanent contract out there. It was only going to be five years originally.'

They had already reached the church.

'Do we go inside or wait out here?' asked Joanne. 'I can't remember what the form is at funerals.'

'Go in I think,' said Becky.

In spite of this they continued to linger on the path, reluctant to eschew the warm, sunlit world of trees and traffic in favour of the chilly vault like interior beyond the porch.

'How's Ant?' Becky asked.

Joanne's face visibly lightened. 'Busy as ever of course. As if the day job wasn't enough there's the night school classes twice a week and after Christmas the framing course starts.'

'Framing?'

'Professional picture framing. It's all part of the long term plan. We're going to raise every penny we can and get a little gallery somewhere – preferably a tourist honey pot – Cornwall maybe. We wouldn't just sell our own work, we'd hang other people's too and if Ant could earn some extra money doing framing for local artists that would help make it viable.'

'Sounds great,' said Becky. 'Is it risky?'

'Starting your own business has always got to be risky,' Joanne said. 'On the other hand working for yourself beats hell out of teaching or designing stuff for that bunch of Philistines at Canterville Cards.'

Becky digested the news of these plans rather sadly. While it probably represented a marvellous scheme for Jo and Ant, a move to Cornwall would take them even further away from Birmingham and being tied by the demands of running a business would mean Jo had even less chance – or perhaps even more of an excuse not – to come up and visit her parents and that meant in turn that she and Becky would have even fewer opportunities to get together.

'Better go in I suppose,' said Becky.

Joanne preceded her, a slim figure in her black trousers with a pair of narrow heeled boots adding a valuable extra inch to her height. They slid into an empty pew surrounded by uneasy shuffles and whispers which bounced off the high ceiling like small, soft balls of sound, undulating endlessly around the cavernous stone nave.

'Ant's going to do the practical things like the framing and I'm going to look after the books,' Joanne continued their conversation in a low murmur. 'Which means another night school class.'

'I can't imagine you ever volunteering to do maths.'

Joanne grinned. 'I wasn't really all that bad at maths. Actually I've got a lot to thank Miss Mislet for. It was her who spotted that I couldn't see properly and got my mother to take me to the optician. I didn't have my glasses till half way through first year if you remember.'

'I'd forgotten. Was that Miss Mislet?'

'Yes. She must have noticed me peering at the board. Do you remember poor Sue Farrell, that girl with the lisp? She used to say Mith Mithlet.'

'Of course I do. She was in my French set. She used to get in a terrible knot, trying to pronounce things.'

'I was reading an article the other day, ' Joanne said, thoughtfully. 'Did you realise that the year we started at Evie's was the same year Martin Luther King was assassinated? It was also the year the students rioted in Paris and Enoch Powell made his rivers of blood speech. Basically this article was saying that all sorts of awful things were happening everywhere. In Vietnam and Czechoslovakia… you name it … and the irony was that the best selling record of the year was 'It's a Wonderful World'. The funny thing is,' Joanne continued. 'I don't really remember any of those things. I suppose they must have been in the papers and on the news, but back then the only really important things were the things happening at home and at school.'

At that moment a collective awareness seemed to run through the congregation, silencing all conversation. The cortege had arrived. As the procession entered the church Jo inclined her head close to Becky and whispered: 'Poor old Nick. First a miscarriage and now this.'

Becky had been wondering what would happen about Dennis. As he came into her line of sight she assumed that he must have been let out for the day on compassionate grounds. He was walking a pace or two behind his father and his brother, perhaps accidentally or perhaps Becky thought, at their insistence. Three men in dark suits. No female presence in the front pew at all. We're here for you, Nick, Becky thought. We're here for you. She formed the words, hard and deep in her mind, as if this act of concentration could send them skimming many miles across the ocean until they reached Philadelphia, where it must be about six in the morning and Nicky must be awake and thinking about what they were doing here in Kings Heath.

The service was brief and dignified. By concentrating hard they both managed not to cry. The sunshine seemed almost blinding as they walked out of the church. After the hushed tones in church their voices sounded artificially loud.

'If Mark's job is made permanent,' Becky said. 'I don't suppose they'll ever come home except for holidays.'

Joanne asked abruptly: 'Do you think Nick's really happy?'

Before Becky could answer Dennis appeared alongside them. 'Thanks for coming,' he said. 'You will come back to the house won't you? Then I'll see you when we get back from the crem.'

There was no time to reply before he had to move on. Joanne turned to face her friend. 'I really don't have the time Becka. I promised to go and see Mum and my train goes at three. I hardly ever go to see her. The line I take is that if Ant's not welcome, then I'm not welcome either.'

'It's all right,' said Becky. 'I'll go back to the house. I've taken the afternoon off work anyway.'

It was several years since she had been inside the Christie's house but very little appeared to have changed. There was a cold buffet laid out on the table in the front room and it stabbed her heart when Becky realised that she recognised the table cloth as the one Mrs Christie had used that first time she and Paula had been invited to tea. She had held it together during the church service, but the sight of the cloth brought her unexpectedly to the verge of tears. Several neighbours of the kind who invariably cut the ham sandwiches for funerals had taken charge of the catering and after one of them had offered her a glass of sherry which she declined, another had furnished her with a cup of tea. The china was mercifully unfamiliar, perhaps loaned for the occasion. Drinking the tea, pale and horribly milky though it was, gave her something to do. She did not recognise anyone else but felt that she had implied a kind of promise to Dennis and would therefore have to stick it out until the family got back. Once that happened she could have a quick word, say how sorry she was and leave.

In the meantime she stood looking at the photographs on the sideboard, some of which had appeared since her last visit to the house, including one of Nicky and Mark standing at the church door, newly married and a big one which seemed to dwarf all the others, of Michael in his gown and mortar board, holding a roll of paper to represent his newly awarded degree. Alongside these were some much older photographs which she could remember from years before. There was that one Nicky had always hated – the black and white studio pose – with Baby Michael in his matinee jacket and romper suit, flanked by Nicky and Dennis, she wearing a kilt and a knobbly home-knitted jumper and sporting Shirley Temple curls, while Dennis sat in light coloured shorts which showed off dimpled knees and wearing a jumper which matched his sister's. Nicky's face was alight with an angelic smile but Dennis had a mischievous grin on his face. He looked a right little devil even then, Becky thought.

When she turned away from the photos she saw that a woman of around her own age had come into the room and was trying to catch her eye. The woman seemed vaguely familiar and when she spoke the face suddenly slotted into place. It was a woman who had done some temping at work to cover for a receptionist on maternity leave. 'Hello. It's Rebecca, isn't it? I thought I recognised you.'

'Yes and you're Linda, aren't you?'

'That's right.' The newcomer lowered her voice as if

inviting Becky to join her in a conspiracy. 'Isn't this awful? *Ever* so sad. Are you a relative?'

'No,' said Becky. 'A sort of family friend. I was at school with Nicky.'

'The daughter.' Linda nodded. 'I thought she might have come over for the funeral.' There was a hint of disapproval in her tone.

'It's very difficult to get flights at short notice,' said Becky defensively. 'And very expensive. She and Mark had already used up their flight vouchers for this calendar year. And anyway, she hasn't been well.'

'Oh… yes… well I didn't mean anything,' Linda said hurriedly. 'I don't really know her… the daughter.' She lowered her voice and inclined her head again in the attitude of one sharing a confidence. 'I didn't really know *her* either. Only I wasn't doing anything today so I came down to help my mum with the food. Mum and Dad live a few doors down. They only moved here about six years ago so I've never lived here. In fact I don't know the family at all really.'

'It's very good of you to help,' said Becky.

'Well… it's the least you can do. I mean… It's *ever* so sad.' Her tone lifted. 'Anyway… what are you doing with yourself these days? Did the wedding go off all right? Any sign of tiny feet pattering?'

Becky stared at her blankly.

'You got engaged just before I left,' Linda prompted.

'We didn't get married,' Becky said. 'We broke it off.'

'Oh I am sorry. Have I said the wrong thing?'

'No, no,' said Becky quickly. 'It doesn't matter and you weren't to know. Excuse me,' she added, moving towards the door. 'I must take my cup into the kitchen.'

'That's all right.' Linda seemed equally grateful to terminate the conversation. 'I'll take your cup. I've got to go and help keep the washing up under control.'

The rest of the party returned from the crematorium soon afterwards. Mr Christie made straight for his usual armchair but Dennis glanced around the room, caught sight of Becky and came straight over. 'Thanks again for coming,' he said.

'It's nothing,' said Becky. 'She was always very kind to me, your mum. She always made me welcome.'

He nodded. 'Our Nicky's friends were always round,' he said. 'But you more than any of them. Do you remember that time you made a load of stuff for Mum's birthday?'

Becky did remember, but just like the table cloth and the snapshots on the sideboard she felt that talking about it might be too much to bear. A lot of memories were crowding in on her – times when they had been all together – happier, simpler times. Pulling herself together with an effort she said: 'I wondered if you would be able to come.'

'They let me out for the day,' he said. 'I'll be out on licence in another few weeks anyway.'

'What will you do when you get out?'

'I'll be all right. A mate's fixing me up with a job.' He grinned as he caught the flicker in her expression. 'Don't worry, it's perfectly legit. With a bit of luck he'll help me find a flat as well.'

'You won't come back here to live?'

'You must be joking.' He jerked his head in his father's direction. 'He blames me for what happened. But it wasn't me. It was him. She was invisible to him. Just someone who did his washing and fetched him his meals. As for that little tow rag,' his eyes darted across the room to Michael and back. 'He never came to see her from one year's end to the next.'

Becky didn't know what to say. While she was listening to Dennis, she had been noticing how like Nicky he was in appearance, the same round face, the same smile, which Dennis gave her now, half heartedly at first and then more as if he meant it. 'Life has to go on,' he said. 'I loved my mum dearly and I'm going to miss her. I don't want to sound heartless, but in a few week's time I have to come out and pick myself up and get on with my life.'

'No one could deny that,' Becky agreed.

'You haven't got married or anything have you?'

'No.'

'I don't suppose there's any chance of a date when I get out?'

For the first time since she had entered the house, the clouds cleared and Becky almost burst out laughing. Keeping her face straight with some difficulty she said, 'I don't think so Dennis. It would be just too weird. I'm sorry but to me you'll always be Nicky's little brother.'

Chapter Nine

1968

Joanne handed the purses in at Lost Property on Monday, telling the prefect on duty that she had found them on the netball courts. The fact that they had reappeared with the original contents intact inclined Miss Harrison to ascribe the whole episode to some kind of misguided practical joke.

As for Becky, by Monday morning she was on such a high after her birthday treat that she had all but forgotten Miss Harrison's unworthy suspicions of her. The day had been wonderful from first to last. She had worn her new dress, they had all enjoyed 'The Jungle Book' at the cinema and Mum had done such a lovely tea that she thought the others probably didn't even notice the various shortcomings of the kitchenette where they sat to eat it. Mum had even provided a cake with a pink and silver frill around it and the words *Happy Birthday* iced on top.

There had been one potentially awkward moment when Nicky said she had brought 'Lily The Pink' and Becky had to explain that they hadn't got anything to play it on, but luckily Frank chose that moment to produce a large rectangular parcel from behind the settee. This turned out to contain a game called Frustration, which was very much like Ludo but played on a special plastic board with a pop-o-matic dice. They had all seen it advertised on the television and knew it was the very latest thing.

When Frank finally drove Paula and Nicky home he let Becky ride in the car too and on the journey he persuaded them to sing 'Lily The Pink' which they all knew off by heart, joining in himself in a funny voice which made them all laugh. Paula and Nicky said 'thank you for a lovely time,' at least twice to Mum and then to Frank and really seemed to have enjoyed themselves.

'They seem like nice girls,' Frank had said on the drive back to the flat, which made Becky feel proud to have such good friends.

By half past nine that night (which was Becky's usual weekend bedtime) Frank had still not gone home.

In the weeks which followed her birthday Becky noticed that whereas at one time Frank had always taken her mother out somewhere, now he quite often came to hang around the flat, sometimes not going home until long after Becky was asleep. She wondered what he and Mum found to say to each other for so long. It wasn't as if they were always talking to each other about madly interesting things when she was around. Not talking to each other the way she and Paula and Nick and now Joanne did. They had so much to say that break and lunch time and walking to the bus stop together was never long enough. Sometimes they even missed the first bus on purpose just so that they could carry on talking.

The 'Romeo and Juliet' trip had provided one of their endless topics of conversation. The anticipation kept them going for weeks in advance and the reality lived up to all they could have wished for. The Scala Superama was fabulous, according to the breathless account which Nicky's mother received later. It had an illuminated canopy which jutted out across the pavement almost as far as the road, the underside of it covered in lights which sparkled against the winter afternoon sky. The vast foyer was a red carpeted paradise of glass and chrome, leading into an even vaster auditorium, which had deep velvety seats and matching curtains which parted silently to reveal the biggest screen they had ever seen.

Nicky had not entirely followed the plot of 'Romeo and Juliet' because people kept making long speeches which she didn't altogether understand, but the costumes were just beautiful: as if the characters on the covers of Paula's Jean Plaidy books had come to life. And it didn't matter if she couldn't follow all of it because she was only a first year and couldn't be expected to understand everything that went on in a grown-up film. You could tell it was a film meant for grown-ups, not only because it was Shakespeare which you didn't start until second year, but also because when Leonard Whiting got out of bed you could see his bare bottom. She didn't mention *that* to Mum.

On the way home from the cinema she had got into a friendly argument with Paula about whether Leonard Whiting was more handsome than Michael York. Nicky had said she liked Michael York best, but Paula said you weren't supposed to like Michael York best because he played Tybalt who was a baddy.

'I wish I could play Juliet,' said Becky, dreamily. 'Only you need long hair. You could do it Paula.'

'No I couldn't. I'm no good at acting.'

'Anyway,' Nicky said. 'Her hair's not the right colour.'

'Don't be daft,' said Becky.

'Well Olivia Hussey's hair is nearly black.'

'There's nothing to say it has to be,' said Becky. 'Juliet's hair can be any colour only it has to be long.'

'Mrs Rollins said she was only fifteen when she made the film,' Joanne said. 'That's not really much older than us.'

'Did you see her bust in that low cut dress?' asked Paula, more than a shade enviously.

'Just think,' said Becky, in response to Joanne. 'In three years time that could be one of us.'

*

Within a week of the cinema visit Olivia Hussey and her excellent bosom were all but forgotten. As first years they had been unaware that Eleanor Vaux held internal exams towards the end of each autumn term and were jolted by the news the exams would start the following week. This fearful state of affairs took over as the main topic for discussion in the cloakroom, which had become their regular lunch time haunt ever since Joanne had discovered a way to avoid detection by crouching behind the coats hung against the wall and pressing oneself as flat as possible. So far no patrolling prefect had spotted the way some coats appeared to have bunched up or even sprouted feet.

'Annette Maudesley's older sister told her that the

teachers read out everyone's marks, so the whole class know who's come bottom,' said Becky. 'I just know I'm going to be bottom in everything.'

'It'll be all right,' said Nicky. 'My mum said, "Just do your best." What did your mum say Jo?'

'Nothing,' said Joanne, from her post by the exit where she was poised at the ready to alert the others if they needed to dive behind the coats. 'I haven't told mine we're having exams.'

'My mum keeps on mentioning how she used to come top in geography,' Paula said. 'I know *I* won't come top in geography. I don't need geography anyway because I'm going to be a writer.' She pushed at a couple of coats until they swung to and fro, stirring others on the adjacent pegs until she had managed to set off a chain reaction all along the row.

'Never mind,' Nicky said. 'It'll be Christmas soon. We'll be able to go round to each other's houses in the holidays. You as well Jo. We'll have a real laugh. Remember when it was your birthday Becka and we sang 'Lily the Pink' and your dad joined in...'

'He's not my dad,' Becky said quickly. 'He's just a friend of my mum's.'

'Oh.' Nicky looked extremely uncomfortable. 'Sorry Becka.'

'Don't tell anyone, will you? That I haven't got a dad.'

'Of course not,' Nicky said.

'We won't say anything,' said Paula.

'I sometimes wish I hadn't got a dad,' said Joanne, then seeing the other's faces she added quickly, 'I won't tell anyone.'

'Miss Harrison said she'll be giving us the timetable for exam week tomorrow.' This from Becky.

'What did she mean about allocating our seats?' asked Nicky.

They found out the following day. During exam week every form was paired with another form from a different year and the two forms shared their classrooms, with girls from each year seated in alternate rows to guard against cheating. IH was paired with IIIV whose form room was next door. Seats were allocated alphabetically, so the first eighteen girls on the IH register, which included Becky, Nicola and Joanne, all had desks in Room 22, while Paula found herself among the nervous little company of twelve first years who were forced to enter the alien third form territory of Room 23.

On Monday morning Becky watched from her allocated position near the form room door as Paula and her fellow evictees left to take up their appointed places next door and thought that Jean Plaidy's Tudor heroines could scarcely have looked more terrified when en route to the scaffold. The little column of IH exiles was replaced by a dozen members of IIIV who ambled in as if they owned Room 22 and were liable to kick aside any first year rash enough to get under foot.

On the Friday afternoon before exam week a member of IIIV who had been selected for the neatness of her handwriting, had inscribed all the special instructions pertaining to exam week on the blackboards in her own and IH's form rooms. All over the school each form room had undergone identical preparations as if for some sacred festival. Now as Miss Harrison progressed around the room, laying the first exam papers face down on the desks, Becky carefully re-read the long screed covering the black board. She already knew it off by heart but when she came to the final words: *Any cheating or suspicion of cheating will result in disqualification* she shivered at the awful finality of it. Just suspicion – you didn't actually have to cheat. If Miss Harrison so much as *suspected* you of cheating that would be it. Disqualified. Disgraced. It was terrifying.

The actual exam – once they were allowed to turn over their papers and begin – was not nearly so bad as she had feared. It was the geography paper and the first question merely asked them to identify various symbols found on an ordnance survey map.

Windmill, Becky wrote, *church with tower, contour line.*

So far, so good.

When they compared notes afterwards even Paula thought there might be grounds – albeit limited – for optimism.

The third year exam papers mostly lasted longer than those set for the first years, so while the third year got to work on Latin, first years were allowed an extra half an hour of silent study before their papers were given out. Becky had immersed herself in the comfortable familiarity of 'Anne of Green Gables'. She could see that Rowena Abbott – who sat immediately in front of her – was poring over her maths book, but it had not occurred to Becky to look through her maths books. Either you knew how to do it or you didn't. Then she realised that Miss Harrison's eyes were on her. She stopped looking in Rowena's direction and concentrated hard on her book but she could still feel Miss

Harrison looking at her. She looked up again and this time her eyes met Miss Harrison's which made it even worse, because now Miss Harrison knew that Becky knew she was looking at her. Cheeks burning like fire, Becky tried but failed to focus her thoughts entirely on what was happening in Avonlea School.

Why was Miss Harrison watching her? Had she seen her looking at Rowena's book? And even if she had, surely that couldn't be classified as cheating when the exam hadn't even started? But was it *suspicion of cheating*? That was all that was needed.

Soon afterwards Miss Harrison gave the pre-arranged signal and the first years stood up as silently as they could and walked to the front of the room where they placed their books in three neat piles below the blackboard, before returning to their places. When Becky – the only girl carrying anything other than a maths book – added 'Anne of Green Gables' to the pile, she passed close by Miss Harrison who said in a low voice, 'You're very cool, Miss. It will be interesting to see *your* marks.'

Not understanding this at all, Becky returned to her desk in a state bordering panic. While the maths papers were distributed she kept her head down, not daring to look anywhere except at the blank back page of the exam paper.

'Begin.'

She turned the paper over and the printing wouldn't come into focus. She was convinced that Miss Harrison was looking at her but she dared not look up to find out. She breathed in the smell of the duplicating ink from the paper, mingled with the stale, sweaty smell of the desk lid.

She must calm down. Maths wasn't hard really. Nothing to be frightened about. She took a deep breath, shut her eyes, opened them again and began to work.

She was so engrossed that she jumped when the silence was broken by a clattering sound as someone's ruler hit the floor. Becky didn't dare turn around but she could see the third year in the adjacent desk glaring over her shoulder, trying to identify where the noise had come from. Rattled, Becky went back to the problem she was working on. She had come out with such a funny answer that she knew it must be wrong. She would have to go through it again and check her working. She reached a more satisfactory solution at the second attempt. Raising her head a fraction as she turned over a page, she realised that Miss Harrison had crept up and was now standing immediately beside her. Becky's hand began to shake so hard that it made her writing wobbly. This was it. She was about to be denounced as a cheat. It was so unfair when she hadn't done anything wrong. For a moment she thought she was going to be sick, but then she looked down at the place where Miss Harrison's brown lace ups had been and saw instead a patch of scuffed, dusty floor. Miss Harrison had moved silently on. She was saved.

*

By the time school returned to normal there was only a week and a half to go until the holidays. French was the first result for IH and just as Annette Maudesley's sister had foretold, the exam papers were handed out in reverse order with each girl's position in the class together with the percentage she had achieved read out for everyone to hear.

Deborah Reed was the first name called and she walked to the front to collect her marked paper, trying to look as if she didn't care. Joanne blushed very red at number twenty seven, although as she said later, she had not really expected to do any better. 'I'm hopeless at French.'

Nicky and Paula tied at twenty first. 'Lucky you were in separate exam rooms,' Becky said. 'Or they might have suspected you.'

Mrs Pritchard went on up the list, fifteen... fourteen... Becky already had her feet turned towards the aisle in constant expectation of her name being called next.

Ten... nine... Becky began to think she had been forgotten until: 'Sixth with 78% Rebecca Addison.'

Becky stumbled to the front to collect her paper, all but tripping over the various satchels and bags which littered the aisle, in her haste to retrieve her paper and get back to her seat.

'Well done,' Nicky mouthed, across the aisle.

'Fifth with 81%, Annette Maudesley.'

Annette sat immediately in front of Becky and as she returned to her seat she whispered, 'We'll both be in top group.'

'What did you mean Annette?' Becky asked as they packed up their books at the end of the lesson. 'About being in top group?'

'After Christmas we'll be put into sets for French and maths,' Annette said. 'They work out the whole year's marks then divide us up into three sets, top, middle and bottom, depending on how we did in the exams. After that we have French and maths lessons in our sets instead of our form groups.'

'We'll be split up,' said Nicky, horrified.

'Only for maths and French,' said Annette.

History results came next. Nicky was mortified to discover that she had got the bronze age and the iron age all mixed up. Joanne and Paula were relieved to find they had done a lot better than in French. Becky was positively astonished to find she had finished eighth. Norma Whitfield and Alex Dunston came first and second and looked as though they thought it was no more than their proper entitlement.

'My mum and dad aren't going to be very pleased,' said Paula.

'But you came tenth. Tenth's not bad,' said Joanne.

'Tenth's good,' said Nicky. 'I've only been twenty first and seventeenth so far.'

'It's English that's the really important one for me,' said Paula.

In her heart of hearts Paula was very worried about English. The paper had started off with some grammar and punctuation questions followed by a comprehension exercise and finally an essay. The essay choices had been *A Memorable Holiday, A Surprise Package,* or an opening line *The river flowed silently beneath the castle walls...*

Paula had chosen the final option, embarking on a tale with a dozen characters and masses of description about the river, the castle and the town below it in which she had become totally absorbed until after covering eight sides of paper her flow had been abruptly halted by Mrs Venables saying, 'Pens down,' at which point Paula had realised with horror, that not only was the kidnap of the heroine and the quarrel with Bold Sir John left unresolved, but worse still she had not allowed time to read through any of her answers. Even as she waited for the paper to be collected a spelling mistake glared up at her from the very first line of the topmost page. Now the moment of truth was near. Mrs Rollins waited for everyone to settle down in their seats before handing back the pile of marked papers on her desk.

Nicky was fourteenth, her best result yet. 'An interesting essay Nicola, well done,' said Mrs Rollins, who had managed to say something encouraging to everyone.

Joanne was tenth. Paula glanced around the room, trying to remember who had yet to receive their paper back apart from herself and Becky. Alex and Norma of course... Annette Maudesley was called out at ninth... Adele White was eighth. Paula began to pray. Mrs Rollins must have liked her story. She had surely written more than anyone else?

'Seventh Paula Morrison.'

The knife of disappointment stabbed deeply.

'Sixth Norma Whitfield.'

Norma stood up, pulling a face at Alex. Only sixth her expression said.

'Fifth Rowena Abbott... fourth Veronica Nicholls... third Renata McFarlane.'

Alex and Norma were seen to exchange knowing looks.

'Second Alexandra Dunston and first Rebecca Addison.'

Momentarily stunned Becky couldn't move, but there was Mrs Rollins smiling expectantly and holding out her paper while Alex and Norma were turning around in their seats, staring in blatant disbelief.

Paula fought back tears, reminding herself that she mustn't be jealous.

Mrs Rollins spent the rest of the lesson going over the paper. Paula could afford not to listen because she hadn't actually got any questions wrong, merely squandered marks on the spelling errors which littered her paper. Mrs Rollins's red pen was all over it, making the sheets look like a series of badly bandaged wounds from which blood seeped in every direction.

Noting how quiet Paula was as they were changing for hockey, Nicky said, 'Your mum and dad will be pretty pleased with seventh, Paupau.'

Paula nodded, pretending to concentrate on her boot laces. She couldn't begin to explain that the English result was the one which mattered for her, not her parents.

'Come along, come along. Put on your bibs. You all know which positions you are playing.' Miss Leopold stood in the doorway, watching impatiently as the pile of yellow and red bibs were collected and tied on. 'Is everyone here? Two laps around the pitch to warm up, then get into position ready to bully off.'

A biting wind was blowing across the playing fields, carrying with it an occasional whiff of cottage pie from the kitchens and making the nets billow out at either end of the pitch. Paula kept her back to it while she finished tying on the yellow bib with LI on it. She knew Left Inner was a position Miss Leopold allocated to people who weren't very good. She was supposed to keep up with the attack and pass the ball out to Becky on the wing, but mostly she never got near the ball and when she did she couldn't hit the wretched thing anywhere in particular. At least Miss Leopold had allocated her a bib. As there were only eleven places on each team, when everyone was in school it left eight people to suffer the ignominy of being left to practice beyond the touchline, dribbling hockey balls up and down to each other until Miss Leopold stopped play and swapped people in and out. People like Gail Foster and Debbie Reed were never swapped in and out because they were good at P.E., whereas people like herself or Nicky often were, which although shaming did provide some welcome relief from trying to keep up with the game and getting hit by other people's sticks or the wretched ball.

Having started the game off, Miss Leopold vanished indoors as she often did on these colder days, leaving the game to proceed under a darkening sky. After about five minutes the red team claimed a goal which the yellow team disputed as off side. A noisy argument ensued which was silenced abruptly by an irate whistle from the touchline.

'What do you think you are doing, IH?'

Miss Leopold's lungs had been specifically designed to be heard across the width of several sports pitches. As Joanne once said, she could easily have moonlighted as a fog signal in the Channel.

'Why have you stopped playing? This is a hockey lesson not an opportunity for a chin wag.'

'We've scored a goal, miss,' Gail ventured.

'Then get back to the centre again, don't stand about gossiping. If I come back out and find anyone is standing about instead of playing, I shall be handing out detentions.' With that Miss Leopold headed back to the games teachers' changing room, where she hoped the kettle would be on the point of boiling.

A few minutes later it began to rain. If it started to rain during a hockey lesson Miss Leopold sometimes let them off, but this was far from guaranteed. All over the hockey pitch people exchanged worried looks. After Miss Leopold's last pronouncement no one dared to stop or attempt to harness group opinion.

The rain turned to sleet and still Miss Leopold did not return. Mud coated their boots and splattered grittily up their thighs. Nicky tried to turn too quickly and slid over on the wet ground. When she got to her feet it looked as if someone had run a giant paint brush down her right side, leaving a broad streak of brown. There was even mud in her hair.

Then Annette Maudesley fell over too and when she got up the girls nearest to her could see that tears streaked her muddy cheeks.

'We should all go in,' Becky said. 'This is crazy. She can't give us *all* a detention.'

'Yes she can,' Paula said. 'She could give us form detention.' Privately Paula was entertaining an awful vision of them playing on forever. Condemned to some sort of unending hockey hell – or at least being stuck out there until they were missed by Miss Mislet, who would be expecting them for the first lesson immediately after lunch.

Miss Leopold finally emerged from the building just as the electric bell heralded the start of the lunch hour and gave a single long blast on her whistle. Thirty bedraggled figures trudged off the pitch and into the changing room, leaving a trail of mud in their wake. Miss Leopold had disappeared to turn on the showers, returning to glower at the damp, shivering group, as they struggled to unfasten sodden bib strings and boot laces with frozen fingers.

'Why on earth didn't you come inside you idiots?' she

stormed. 'Have you seen the state of the pitch? It's so badly cut up, I doubt if we'll get any more play on it this side of Christmas.'

No one spoke. A sound – possibly a sneeze – came from one corner, but nothing more. It was more than anyone dared to answer back.

Chapter Ten

1982

Becky sat at the table with the writing pad in front of her, unable to decide how to begin. She had been mulling over her reply all day without coming to any sensible conclusions and even now, sitting in front of the blank sheet of notepaper, pen poised above the top right hand corner she still hesitated. Ought she to include her address or not? Sean's letter had been forwarded via her old address. She had only paid for the mail to be sent on for six months, which meant that quite soon any letters which went there would be binned. Without the new address he would not be able to contact her at all. Well that was what she wanted wasn't it? For him to be completely excluded from her life. How could she begin to forget him if he kept on initiating contact like this? (But how on earth could she ever forget him anyway?)

Then again it looked rather pathetic not to include an address – bizarrely secretive – and besides which he could still easily track her down because he knew where she worked. So she wrote the address, put the date underneath and got as far as *Dear Sean* before it struck her that perhaps in providing her new address, he might think that she was signalling her willingness to receive more letters in the future, irrespective of whatever she said within the body of this one. Perhaps she ought to ignore his letter altogether? But she knew that she couldn't do that. Leaving the letter unanswered was too cruel and contemptuous... and anyway he would only write again, thinking that perhaps she had not received the first one.

I am sorry for the delay in replying to you (Yes – that was good – businesslike – the sort of phrase she might dictate at work) *but your letter had to be forwarded on to my new address.* She must cut short the fatal temptation to tell him about her new house, curb her pride in becoming an owner occupier – albeit with a millstone of a mortgage round her neck – and resist at all costs the encroaching tide of might-have-beens, the thought that instead of only one signature on the dotted line, only one person choosing the furniture...

I have read everything that you have written very carefully, but none of it alters the fact that there can be no future together for us. I honestly feel that prolonging any kind of contact between us will only lead to more pain and I think it would be better if you did not write to me again.

A vision of him rose unbidden in her mind. She saw his expression as he recognised her handwriting on the envelope and his face falling as he read the contents of her reply. She blinked then took a deep breath, telling herself that she was not going to cry, because what the hell would that achieve? How to finish? Going straight to *Yours sincerely* would be unbelievably blunt and cold. And now all the wrong phrases began to chase one another through her mind, deadly combinations like *I will never forget you* and *I will always love you* so that she had to put the pen down on the table, lest the hand holding it became as treacherous as her thoughts.

With love, Becky. There – she had written it. It meant nothing after all… it was no more than what she put on her Christmas cards, even the ones she wrote to people she seldom saw or scarcely cared about. She slid a matching envelope out of the stationery set, folded the single sheet, slipped it inside and sealed it quickly before she could change her mind.

Chapter Eleven

1968

Paula knew that her parents would start discussing her report the moment she went upstairs to bed, so as soon as she was in her pyjamas she moved into position, sitting on the third stair down with her bare feet resting lightly on the fourth stair. The third stair from the top was Paula's regular listening post because if anyone emerged unexpectedly through the sitting room door she could make it from there onto the landing in a single movement, before anyone had time to look up and see her.

She was distinctly chilly in just her flannelette pyjamas. There was a radiator in the hall but it was always set at a low temperature – even in December. It would be warmer in the sitting room where the gas fire supplemented the luke warm radiators: but not too warm, because a current of colder air flowed in from the hall and the connecting door between the hall and the sitting room was never fully closed. The Morrisons were firmly convinced that warm, enclosed rooms were a breeding ground for germs. Putting on an extra layer was considered a far more healthy (and economical) option than turning up the central heating. However this desire to keep air circulating was useful from Paula's point of view, because her mother's high, clear voice always travelled readily up the stairs and even her father's gruffer mumblings were usually audible, providing the wireless wasn't on too loud.

After reading her report neither parent had openly complained or criticised. It might have been easier if they had, because a discussion of that sort opened the way to mounting a defence: to repeat as Joanne had very reasonably pointed out, that not everyone could be top. Eleanor Vaux wasn't like primary school where a significant proportion of the class were not very clever and could therefore be counted on not to do well in tests. At Eleanor Vaux all the people who couldn't pass their eleven plus had been weeded out, which made the competition much tougher. Or am I just making excuses? Paula wondered, miserably. Perhaps I'm just not clever enough.

If only her parents could be a bit less interested. Jo said her father hadn't even bothered looking at her report. According to Jo, he'd put it on the mantelshelf unopened, saying that he would look at it later, whereas her parents had seized on the thin brown envelope as though it contained a cheque from the football pools. Then of course when they actually read the thing they'd exchanged a look which Paula knew all too well and her mother had put on the brave little smile she used in moments of disappointment and said, 'Seventh in English, darling, that's very good,' but not as though she really meant it. She might as well have said, twenty first in French Paula, what a useless child you are, Paula thought, bitterly.

The instant she reached her post on the stairs her suspicions were confirmed. Her mother was already in full flow: '...obviously some sort of problem. It may be to do with the teacher not bringing out the best in her. It looks as if the school have realised that because they've put her in the middle set for French. Now that clearly shows they know her exam result wasn't a true reflection of her abilities, because coming twenty first out of thirty would normally mean the bottom set.'

In fact Paula knew that this placing was entirely due to some execrably poor marks in IR, which had just pushed Nicky and herself into the middle third of the marks achieved by the whole year.

'Will she have a different teacher after Christmas?' This from her father.

'Yes.' There was a pause, presumably while her mother consulted the report. 'It will be a Miss Hardiker after Christmas. This Mrs Pritchard who took them last term must be having a different group so we can probably expect things to improve under a new teacher.' After another short silence her mother's voice came again. 'It's the maths I worry about. Maths is so important. We don't want Paula languishing in the middle set and falling behind.'

'I don't suppose...' Her father's voice was drowned out by someone moving some unseen object in the sitting room.

'Perhaps we could write to the school asking them to review their position.' Her mother was talking again. 'Paula ought to be able to cope with work in the top set.'

Ophelia appeared suddenly beside Paula, making her jump violently and clap her hand across her mouth to stop herself shouting out. Indignant at not receiving a friendly welcome, Ophelia gave a couple of loud meows which drowned out her father's reply, so all Paula heard was: '... earn her place.'

'Is that Ophelia upstairs?' said her mother. 'I don't want her getting onto the beds. I'd better fetch her down...'

Paula did not wait for any more, springing from a sitting position onto the landing and half rolling, half crawling into her bedroom, watched somewhat contemptuously by Ophelia who clearly considered it a singularly undignified method of exiting the scene.

They mustn't, they absolutely mustn't start writing letters to school, asking to have her moved into a different set, Paula thought. Everyone would get to know and that would be just too embarrassing. Besides which she wouldn't be able to manage in top set. She just wasn't clever enough, that was obvious from the exam results.

Chapter Twelve

1983

The mirror image of the bedroom looked like a stage set at the beginning of a play: artificially neat, brightly lit, with a window through which the audience could see a backdrop of lighted apartment blocks, while somewhere offstage a distant police siren wailed, so that the audience would know it was an American play. And what of the character standing pensively centre stage in a garish, ill fitting costume? Well perhaps it was a comedy?

Nicky turned away from the mirror in search of her shoes. The reflection was too depressing for words and could not be improved by anything she had time to accomplish in the ten minutes before the cab was due. The red dress had been a hideous mistake. One of those nightmare, desperation buys chosen principally on the basis that it fitted. Nor was it any use pretending to herself that she didn't know the dress would have been a size eighteen if she'd bought it in England. In part she blamed her failed attempts at pregnancy. She had only ever made it as far as three months, but it had been a wonderful excuse not to care and American portions provided a lot of scope for a hungry, pregnant lady.

'Are you ready, hon?'

'Nearly.'

She fumbled with the strap of her right shoe and tried not to hate that Mark called her 'hon'. He never called her 'love' anymore because it didn't suit his shiny new transatlantic persona. He called his dinner jacket a tux and talked about moving out of town to a house with a yard. While she had become bi-lingual, saying boot in the privacy of their own apartment and trunk when communicating with the world outside, Mark had taken on board the whole thing, even using these American words when they went home 'on vacation' to England.

She reminded herself that she must not think of England as home. The States was home now. If everything had gone as expected, Mark's original contract would have been finished by now, but the promotion had changed everything. The goalposts had shifted so far that Mark was talking about applying for American citizenship. This also made her feel uneasy. It was not that she didn't like America. Mark was right (as usual, she added loyally) in saying that it represented golden opportunities for the good life. It was not, as she reminded herself for the third time in the past half hour, that she was unhappy here. But becoming an American instead of being British somehow felt like a scary, irrevocable step. President Reagan's Star Wars programme swam nervously around the back of her mind. Not that it mattered much where you were on the planet if that backfired, she supposed.

'Cab's here.' A touch of impatience in his voice. 'You look nice,' he added as she stepped into the hallway; but she knew he couldn't possibly mean it. She looked terrible... she knew she did. That awful red dress made her look like a frumpy forty-something.

I'm not twenty six until next week, she thought desperately.

'Now try to remember,' Mark said, as their cab headed into the traffic. 'Valerie Ondrokov is the one who's got a kid with leukaemia. You remember Valerie? Very tall and slim with red hair? Her partner, Fred, is head of my number three section so it would be really good if you could offer to get involved in some fund raising.'

As they got nearer and nearer to the hotel where the reception and dinner were being held, Nicky felt the familiar sick fear rising from her stomach. She knew that she was not a good company wife, in spite of devoting herself to the role full time. She ought to be more like Marcie, who was married to Vince, who played racket ball with Mark once a week. Marcie was an excellent company wife who always remembered everyone's name, entertained with aplomb and was stick insect thin with a superb bone structure, probably inherited from her Eastern European forbears.

I'm just a pudding from the West Midlands, Nicky thought.

It would have been easy to hate Marcie if only she hadn't been so nice. Marcie always made you feel at ease, stopping to chat and never making you feel as if you were a boring no-mark. That was one of the things Marcie had tuned to a fine art. She circulated and talked to everyone (well everyone useful at least) and each person felt that she was interested in them.

The thing is, Nicky thought, it's much easier for people to think of something to say to me because they can always fall back on asking something about England (she had lost count of the number of times that she had explained just where Shakespeare's birthplace was in relation to where she had grown up) whereas she had run out of things to ask about living in America. If you still hadn't found out those things after living there for four years you just came over as a klutz.

She spotted Marcie as soon as they arrived, looking calm and poised and talking with a guy from J division. Nicky would have liked to make for the familiar safety of Marcie's company but the way was blocked by Bob and Dora, people she half recognised from previous company gatherings.

'Hello Mark, hello Nicola. Good to see you both.' Bob was an ex-college football player and everything about him was huge, including his smile. After a further exchange of pleasantries, Bob said, 'I see you Brits did real well at the Oscars. Richard Attenborough must be a pretty happy guy right now.' He pronounced it 'Attenburrow' with the emphasis on the 'ow' at the end.

'It must be a great film,' Mark said. 'We'll have to make time to see it.'

Nicky desperately tried to think which film they were talking about. She knew that Richard Attenborough had taken to directing films, but at that moment all the name would conjure up in her memory was watching black and white films on a Sunday afternoon, kneeling on the hearth rug with Dennis while men in duffle coats battled through the Atlantic, fighting a war which she was now learning had been won by the Americans.

Fortunately Bob and Dora decided that it was time to circulate. When they moved aside Nicky caught sight of the woman who was standing just behind them. She was wearing an almost backless black dress, which showed off a long, narrow expanse of pale golden skin starting at the nape of her neck, where her blonde hair had been swept up on top of her head and tapering down to her waist, where her dress came just high enough to keep within the boundaries of good taste. The woman happened to turn at that moment and favoured them with an immaculate smile. Nicky had become familiar with the standards of American dentistry but the woman's teeth were almost too perfect to be real.

'Nicky, this is my assistant Bettina. Bettina… meet Nicky, my wife.'

The head to toe appraisal was over in a fraction of a section but Nicky saw it and burned crimson, the shade of her face clashing with the shade of her dress.

'Of course. I would have known you anywhere from the photo on Mark's desk.' Bettina extended a manicured hand. 'How lovely to meet you at last. Mark talks about you all the time.'

*

Two days later when she returned home unexpectedly early from her Spanish class, Nicky discovered them in bed together. If the Spanish Class had not been cancelled that day she might never have found out that her husband was having an affair with his assistant. She certainly would not have discovered them in – or more accurately on – the bed together that particular afternoon. Only a series of chances: the illness of her teacher, the decision to come straight home, the snagged finger nail which had sent her straight down the hall to get an emery board – these inconsequential things had all piled one on top of another and led to her standing in their kitchen, leaning against the refrigerator door, hot and cold, angry and sad, all at the same time.

She heard the bedroom door open and close, swiftly followed by the front door. For a moment she thought he had gone too – sneaked silently away with his mistress – but then he appeared in the doorway. He was tightening his tie, so returning to work for the afternoon evidently figured in his plans.

She stared at him saying nothing. Incredibly he said nothing either. Their mutual silence was so loud that it blanked out every other sound. The refrigerator, the building site across the street, everything.

She watched him as he finished getting dressed, the hands that had lately been delving in Bettina's crotch now used to check the buttons of his shirt, the angle of his tie. The pink tip of his tongue ran swiftly around his lips, upper then lower. Tasting her, she thought. Tasting her salty, sweaty, skinny little body. Then she realised that he was going to say something. It seemed to happen in slow motion, as if there was a time lapse between the words leaving his mouth and reaching her ears.

'We can talk about this later.'

That was all he said. He could have been referring to anything or nothing. Then he was gone. She was frozen in a state of disbelief. He could have said so many things. Sorry… that was the word uppermost in her mind. Yet now she came to think about it she was not entirely sure that hadn't been the word she had used: the single exclamation which had escaped her lips when she'd opened the bedroom door and stumbled in on them.

Sorry. Oh… so sorry. Have I disturbed you in the act of screwing my husband? How very thoughtless of me.

She tried to move but got no further than the breakfast bar where she sought support by leaning on one of the stools. Once they were over the initial surprise what a wonderful laugh it would give them: the look on her face as she caught sight of them, followed immediately by her embarrassed, apologetic exit, as though in interrupting she had committed an unforgivable breach of good manners.

I ought to have kicked her skinny ass, she thought.

Permitting herself to think along this enraged – if unlikely – line made her feel better. Drinking her own anger was like a tonic. She stopped leaning on the stool and marched defiantly down the hallway into the bedroom.

They hadn't even bothered to straighten the bed.

'I ought to cut his balls off,' she said out loud.

The reflection in the mirror seemed to be cheering her on.

'If it was the first time…'she began.

The reflection looked wise and understanding.

'It's the fact that he doesn't even think he has to apologise.'

The reflection's eyes followed her as she opened the top

cupboard where the suitcases were kept. Take the lightest one, the reflection seemed to advise. And better stop looking at me while you put your things together. Otherwise you'll see how sad I am and that will make you cry. Just get on with it. Take what you need. Think how lucky it is that you're up to date with the laundry.

It took surprisingly little time to pack the case and carry it out into the hallway. When she went back to get her coat she noticed the silk tie that she had bought him for Christmas, lying over the chair back where he had discarded it the day before. She picked it up and tried to rip it but it was too well made. The nail scissors on the dresser made a mess of it, but it was a time consuming business.

She caught the challenge in the eyes of the reflection. Pathetic. You can do better than that. She extracted the contents of his wardrobe in armfuls. He had always had expensive tastes in clothes. She found that the drawers could be pulled out completely and tipped wholesale onto the bed and the floor. His cologne proved inadequate to the task because it came out of the bottle far too slowly, but the happy thought that she had only yesterday paid a visit to the market supplied fresh inspiration.

The ketchup came in a much larger size than the British version. The bed soon began to look as if some brutal revenge involving a chain saw had recently taken place. Then a splodge of ketchup hopped up and hit her cheek and the reflection caught her eye. Mustn't mess up the clothes she was wearing. Once she had taken everything off she was able to throw herself into the business with renewed enthusiasm. The reflection in the mirror joined in vigorously, a naked dervish, capering wildly in the snow storm created when packets of pancake mixture and desiccated coconut were tossed high into the room. It waved its arms like a frenetic cheerleader as she flung the eggs, each of which splattered in turn against the window pane. A couple missed and hit the drapes instead... Miss Leopold had always said she couldn't throw straight.

When all the readily scatterable, pourable ammunition had been exhausted, Nicky stood in the doorway to survey the devastation. It was the most spectacular declaration of independence that Philadelphia had seen for some time.

'Revenge is sweet,' she informed the dishevelled figure in the mirror. 'And so,' she added, licking her fingers and dropping the empty container, 'is maple syrup'.

She showered, washed and dried her hair. It was amazing how much water escaped all over the bathroom floor when you didn't bother with the shower screen. Then she emptied all the towels she could find into the bath, turned on the taps and tossed in everything else that was lying around. Mark's electric shaver teetered desperately on an island of heaped towels before being engulfed by the tidal wave created when a potted palm went in. Her attempt to write *BASTARD* on the mirror using toothpaste was a dismal failure. Toothpaste was obviously a medium which required a lot of practice to master and she didn't have time for that. She turned off the taps before leaving. Mr Hegelmeyer on the floor below would be upset if the tub overflowed through his ceiling.

When she got into the car she began to shake, victim to the aftershocks of an emotional earthquake. In spite of having a licence she did not drive very often and it took all her will to hang on to the wheel and watch the traffic.

Thank goodness she didn't have far to go. As she turned south on 176 Helen Reddy came onto the car radio. *...I am strong, I am invincible...*

'Damn right I am,' Nicky said aloud.

At the airport she parked the car, paid for short stay, then dropped the keys into the trash. The business with the tickets and passports was something Mark had always taken care of and she approached it nervously, expecting unseen complications where none existed. She gulped at the amount to be set against the credit card. She had never signed against such a big amount before. *I am strong, I am invincible...* she glanced up anxiously, afraid that she had said it out loud, but the woman on the desk gave no sign.

After checking her suitcase, she drifted over to sit near the windows. It was a bright, sunny day. The silver speck of an approaching plane captured her attention. She thought about her mum, remembering her thinly concealed anxiety at the prospect of her daughter flying across the Atlantic. To her mother flying anywhere had represented a big deal. Mum could never have envisaged that a day would come when she, Nicola, would just go down to the airport and catch a plane to London, almost as easily as she had once caught a number 11 bus.

Come to that, Nicky thought, even as recently as this morning, I wouldn't have thought it possible either. But that had been this morning... before the Spanish teacher took sick.

Chapter Thirteen

1968

As Miss Forster addressed the school in their final assembly before Christmas, Nicky reflected on what an eternity had elapsed since the uncertainty of their first day. Three months down the line it felt as though they had been at Eleanor Vaux forever. It was funny she thought, how much humans changed in the first bit of their lives. First you were a baby, then a little child starting in the infants, then you turned eleven and went to secondary school which put you into a different age group overnight. At some point in the unimaginably far distant future you would leave school altogether, transforming instantly into the grown-up you were going to be for the rest of your life. Weird really. Hard to imagine and still a very long way off, like looking at something through the wrong end of a telescope. She ceased contemplation of these great mysteries in order to give her full attention to Miss Forster, who in contrast to everyone else was somehow failing to give out the impression that she was full of seasonal good will.

Although her staff and pupils were aglow with festive spirit of one sort or another, the truth was that Miss Forster did not really like the last day of the Christmas term. There was altogether too much excitement in the air. It engendered the sort of atmosphere in which girls got giddy and did foolish things. The early afternoon was the best part of the day, for this was traditionally the time when the whole school processed down to St Michael's Church, where they packed into the pews for the school carol service. In these Godless times Miss Forster doubted if the huge Victorian barn of a building was ever full to capacity except for this one annual occasion, when the carols which the entire school had been practicing for several weeks beforehand were performed, not for parents or onlookers but for their own joy and satisfaction... oh and for God of course.

The sound of six hundred carefully rehearsed, predominantly female voices always stirred her emotions. By tradition the service always closed with 'Adeste Fidelis' which all pupils from the second year onwards knew by heart and sang out with a vigorous certainty, whether they took Latin or not. For Miss Forster it was the highlight of the musical year: a moment which bound the whole school together, staff and pupils alike united as one and singing their hearts out. Mr Sinton, in his capacity as head of music, had once suggested that the format of the carol service be changed but she had soon put paid to that idea. Traditions like 'Adeste Fidelis' were worth preserving. Mr Sinton had no proper sense of what was appropriate. Only that morning she had been forced to tell him to remove a tinsel wreath which some of the girls had persuaded him to wear on his head. Ridiculous man.

The girls always went straight home from the church, but the staff returned to school for a little end of term gathering in the staff room. Miss Forster anticipated this with considerably less enthusiasm than the carol service, in spite of the fact that the staff party had originally been her own initiative and she still personally provided the funds which paid for the refreshments. In earlier years the staff had been extremely appreciative but the old, familiar faces were starting to disappear. Dear Miss Tinkler had been claimed by a retirement bungalow at Exmouth last summer, while Betty Philpotts who had joined the school just before it was evacuated in 1939, would only be with them for one more Christmas. The old guard were being replaced by a new generation. A generation who far from appreciating the end of term get together, gave the impression that they might be thinking it was all rather a bore… even that a second glass of sherry might be expected.

Chapter Fourteen

1968-9

As soon as all the Christmas presents had been opened Joanne experienced the sense of anti-climax which inevitably pervaded the rest of Christmas Day. There was still the food of course. The aroma of slowly roasting turkey had been tickling their nostrils since the moment they woke up and perhaps because of this her father seemed to be in a very good mood. He had the television on and was watching some children in a hospital, being given their presents by someone dressed up as Father Christmas.

'Look,' Brian stopped putting plastic pigs into the barn of his newly acquired, hardboard farm and pointed at the television. 'Father Christmas.'

'That's right son.' His father expertly flicked another bottle top across the room, before pocketing the bottle opener and refilling his glass. 'He's given that little lad a toy farm just like yours.'

Her mother came in from the kitchen, wiping her hands on her apron.

'What time's our Sonia coming?' asked Joanne.

At that moment they heard Sonia's key in the front door and Tex began to bark and dance about out in the back garden, where he had been expelled for the day to stop him jumping up and getting mud on everyone's good clothes.

'You must be psychic,' her mother said. 'That's her, now.'

Although Jo's older sister Sonia did not live with them anymore she still had her own key. She had moved out almost a year ago and now lived with their mother's sister, Auntie Maggie, who hadn't got any children of her own. Ostensibly this had been to shorten the distance Sonia had to travel to work but Joanne knew very well that wasn't the real reason.

'Merry Christmas everyone.' Sonia came in and kissed them all in turn, including Brian who twisted away and wiped his cheek on his sleeve afterwards.

'Now there's only Mary and Sid to come and we'll be all set.' Their mother paused, a slightly troubled look in her eyes. 'I hope we're going to have enough. Is that another bottle of beer you've opened, Harry?'

'What's it to you? There's plenty left.'

Joanne affected a deep interest in the manicure set her Auntie Pat had sent her.

'Is that a farm, Bri?' Sonia's question was overloud. 'Coo… look at all those animals you've got there.'

'Well, I just thought – you know – Sid always likes a few beers and we don't want to get down them too fast or there might not be enough.'

'Leave the beers to me and stop your bloody nagging will you?'

From beneath pale orange lashes Joanne watched her mother retreat into the kitchen without saying anything more. She began to breathe a fraction more easily. Sonia caught her eye and gave her a limp smile. There was a short silence. The man in the Santa suit was persuading hospitalised children to sing into his microphone with dire results.

'What a load of bloody rubbish,' her father burst out. 'You'd think if they were going to put something on the telly they'd come up with better stuff than this.'

None of them spoke. They all knew that he was on the cusp of a dangerous mood. Silence however, was not a safe retreat.

'Cat got your tongues? I suppose *you* think it's all right? You only ever want to watch rubbish.'

'We're not watching it Dad,' said Sonia carefully. 'It's you who's watching it. Why don't you turn it off, if you don't like it?'

'Don't back talk to me young lady.' He moved forward in his chair as if on the point of rising. 'You might be nearly eighteen but don't think you can talk to me any way you feel like it.'

'I was only saying that none of us are watching it.' Sonia was clearly trying to keep her voice free of anything which could be construed as either anger or fear. 'And why not turn it off if you don't like it.'

'Don't tell me what to do you cheeky little bitch.' As her father made another move toward the edge of his chair, Sonia slid further back into hers in a perfectly synchronised movement. 'I've told you before, when you pay the licence you can decide what we have on.'

Joanne slid the zip which ran around three sides of the

pink and white plastic case holding the manicure set to and fro, as if intent on discovering how a zip worked for the very first time. In the distant hospital ward, a freckle faced boy was telling Father Christmas a knock knock joke.

'I'm not trying to tell you what to do. I don't care what you have on the television.' Sonia's voice rose. 'I've only been here five minutes and you're picking on me already.'

'Well if you don't like it you'd better bugger off to your auntie's then, hadn't you?' her father sneered. 'You got off there smartly enough as soon as you'd got a few bob coming into your pocket. Anything rather than give me and your Mum some housekeeping after we've kept you for sixteen years.'

Sonia looked despairingly from her father to her siblings and back again.

'Go on,' he said. 'What are you waiting for?'

Sonia stood up. To Joanne, she said, 'I've brought some presents. They're in a Woolworths bag in the hall.'

'Don't go.' Joanne wasn't sure if she had spoken aloud or not and if Sonia heard she made no sign. Joanne heard the front door close behind her sister just as their mother reappeared from the kitchen to announce cheerfully: 'That's the sprouts ready to go on,' then ask in a completely different tone, 'Where's our Sonia?'

'Gone back to your sister's.'

'But what about her dinner?'

'Your sister'll give her some dinner. She won't go without. Spoilt rotten that girl is. She'll be ruined at your sister's. Well she needn't bring any trouble home here. If it hadn't been for your ruddy sister, she would have had to stay here where we could have kept a proper eye on her. But oh no! Your sister said she could go and live there. And she couldn't wait to bugger off somewhere she can have her own way all the time.'

Something in their mother seemed to snap. 'You drove her away.'

Joanne's fingers froze on the zip. She noticed Brian, steadfastly stacking plastic hay bales into the trailer parked in his miniature farm yard; he might have been deaf for the amount of reaction he was displaying.

Their mother's voice cracked into sobs as she retreated into the kitchen. 'You drove her away. Just like you've driven her away today.'

Their father leapt out of his chair, slamming his glass down so that the remaining beer churned like a small, angry ocean, full of brown, foamy waves as he followed his wife into the kitchen.

'Come on, Bri,' Joanne said quickly. 'Let's carry some of our new things upstairs out of the way.'

The voices in the kitchen were cut short by the crash of something heavy falling, intermingled with the sound of crockery smashing on the quarry tiled floor.

The television screen in the corner was filled with smiling nurses singing 'We Wish You A Merry Christmas'.

'Come on,' Joanne repeated. 'You take the cowboy game. You're not playing with that just now. I've got the Spirograph.'

On their way back downstairs they encountered their mother in the hall, holding one hand up defensively and aligning herself so that they couldn't see her face. Before anyone could say anything the door knocker sounded a brisk rat tat tat.

'It's Sid and Mary,' her mother said. 'You'll have to tell them I'm not well.'

The hearty 'Merry Christmas' froze on Sid's lips as soon as he caught sight of Joanne's small white face.

'Mum's not very well,' she said. 'She's had to go to bed.'

'Oh dear me,' said Mary. 'I am sorry to hear that.' She exchanged a look with her husband and in that moment Joanne knew that they knew. Not that anyone would say anything, but everyone knew just the same. Uncle Sid was Dad's brother. How could he not know?

Her father emerged from somewhere in the back of the house.

'Hello Harry,' said Sid. 'Joanne's just been telling us Amy's not very well. Sorry to hear that. Perhaps it would be better if we didn't stay.'

'No, no… Amy wouldn't want that. The dinner's nearly done in any case. Young Joanne can finish things off if you'd just give her a hand Mary. Mind you she's a bit clumsy. She's just knocked some dishes on the floor and broken the lot. Run along Joanne and clear them up and then we can have our lunch… Now then Mary… get your coat off. What do you want to drink?'

*

Frank turned up shortly after Becky and her mother had finished their Christmas dinner. When he kissed them both and wished them 'Happy Christmas', Becky noticed the odour of beer and tobacco hanging around his head like an invisible halo that had slipped a bit.

'Now then Becky,' he said in a particularly hearty voice.

'You go into your bedroom for a few minutes and keep the door shut. No peeping now. You don't want to spoil the surprise.'

Becky departed with as much good grace as she could muster, although it was cold in her bedroom and the window was running with condensation because Mum had been using the oven most of the morning to cook the chicken. Not that Becky wasn't used to the cold. She often sat on her bed wrapped up in the eiderdown, so that she could read undisturbed by the clatter of the television. It wasn't really the cold she minded so much as Frank ordering her about.

Unlike Mum's previous men friends who had mostly been content with just picking Mum up to go out to the pub or the pictures, Frank had somehow become involved in their lives. Lately Becky had sensed a sort of campaign to get her to like Frank. Mum thought she was being subtle – forever drawing Becky's attention to instances of Frank's kindness – while Frank himself tried too hard to be nice and to make her laugh, when quite honestly she would far rather he had just left her alone. There was something faintly embarrassing about these efforts. Not just embarrassing but also futile, Becky thought, because they don't *really* care what I'm thinking or feeling.

From her room she heard footsteps on the stairs and muffled laughter. She hoped it wasn't some sort of practical joke at her expense. She crossed the room to the window where she rubbed her hand across the pane, sending a cascade of drips chasing one another down to the wooden frame which was showing signs of black mould again. All the back gardens within sight of her window were damp and deserted. People didn't do things in their gardens in the winter. Specially not on Christmas Day, when if the television was to be believed people all grouped together wearing paper hats and pulling crackers, neither of which had been in evidence at their Christmas dinner table, though Mum had strung some paper chains and balloons across the living room. Frank had got in on that as well. Luckily he had turned out to be quite good at blowing up balloons. Becky was forced to admit to herself that he occasionally did have some uses.

'Becky.' Her mother's voice came from the living room. 'Becky… you can come in now.'

Feeling absurdly nervous, Becky entered the living room hesitantly, stopping short when she saw Mum and Frank standing side by side, grinning like a pair of village idiots. They were standing between her and the window, looking furtive and over excited and pleased with themselves all at the same time. Frank was holding out a small flat square parcel, wrapped in green and red Christmas paper.

'I've got you a present,' he said. 'Go on… take it,' he added, as Becky hesitated. 'It won't bite you. Can you guess what it is?'

'It feels like a record,' Becky said doubtfully as she received the gift into her hand.

'Aren't you going to open it?' Mum's eyes were shiny, as if she was going to cry.

An awful thought hit Becky like a splash of cold water down the neck of her frock: Frank must have forgotten they hadn't got a record player. It was going to be awfully embarrassing when he realised that he had given her just about the one thing she wouldn't be able to use. The parcel was secured with white tape, overprinted with holly leaves which had rather splodgy berries. Becky peeled it away as slowly as possible, putting off the awful moment of truth. As she folded the paper aside she saw that it was 'Lily The Pink'.

'It's number one! It's Top of The Pops!' said Frank, doing his best Jimmy Saville impersonation.

'Thank you,' said Becky, wondering what on earth she was supposed to say next.

'Now then,' Frank seemed to be having trouble keeping still. 'What do you need to go with a record?'

Becky stared at him dumbly.

Stepping to one side, Frank made an expansive gesture towards the table he had been standing in front of. 'Dah da-ah! A record player.'

Becky couldn't say a word.

'I think we've forgotten our manners,' Mum began, but Frank would have none of it.

'She's just excited that's all,' he said. 'Here we are Becky. Come and see how it works. This is the knob to turn it on...'

Becky stood alongside him while the record was carefully balanced at the top of the central pole, with the restraining arm laid across to hold it flat. Then Frank showed her how to move the smaller lever to 45 which made the turntable rotate and then the other lever which sent the record flopping down onto the turntable and then the lower arm glided across, dipping down and down as if it was searching blindly for the edge of the vinyl before finally settling onto it with a whispered crackle. As if by magic the voices of The Scaffold came charging out across the living room.

Having no other records they played 'Lily the Pink' nine

times in succession before everyone agreed that it would be in order to turn the record player off for the time being. Meanwhile Frank sat on the settee with his arm around Mum and Becky was for once prepared to forgive him, even though it was embarrassing to see grown-ups carrying on like that.

Later on Mum went into the kitchenette to cut them all slices of Christmas cake to have with a cup of tea. While she was out of the room Frank said: 'I reckon we get on all right… you and me… eh Becky?'

Caught completely off guard she didn't know what to say.

'I think a lot of you. You know that don't you?' Frank sounded a little less comfortable.

'Yes,' said Becky, deliberately not looking at him. 'That's why you bought me the record player. Thank you.'

'No need to thank me again,' said Frank. His customary heartiness seemed to have deserted him. Becky wondered what on earth was coming next. 'I'm very fond of your mum, Becky,' he continued. 'And she's very fond of me. That's why we'd like to make a nice home together.' The words were starting to come out faster now, as though having finally got to the meat of the issue he wanted to get it over with as soon as possible. 'Would you like that? We could have a nice house somewhere. You needn't change schools. We wouldn't want you to change schools because you're doing very well. Your mum's ever so proud of you. That report – phewee – I wish I'd had reports like that when I was your age.' Receiving no response he went on: 'We'd have a spare bedroom so your friends could come and stay the night. And a garden so's you could sit out and sunbathe in the summer, how about that? What do you think, Becky?'

Afterwards, she couldn't remember exactly what she had said. Just that she supposed it would be O.K. or something grudging like that. Something not very enthusiastic really, considering he had just given her the most expensive present she had ever received in her life. Frank hadn't seemed to mind though. He had accepted her response just as enthusiastically as if she had thrown her arms around his neck and acclaimed him for the long lost father she had never known.

Much later, when she was lying in bed, Becky thought over what Frank had said. It would be really exciting to invite a friend to stay the night. She didn't often invite her friends round to the flat because there wasn't really room for them. Mind you… it was even more noticeable that Joanne never invited any of them to her house. At first Becky had suspected that Joanne was ashamed of where she lived, perhaps because it was small and pokey like their own flat, but one day they had ridden past Jo's house on a bus and it just looked ordinary and about the same size as Nick's. Becky had concluded that it was another of those mysterious things it was better not to ask about.

Anyway… once Mum and Frank found their new house she would be able to have friends round all the time. It wasn't clear exactly when this happy state of affairs was coming to pass. Frank had referred to the matter as if they were all three involved in some pleasant conspiracy, while her mother spoke vaguely of it happening after some 'things' had been sorted out and Becky knew that grown-up 'things' were another area of life where it was generally better not to ask too many questions.

Old people were funny she thought, as she dozed

towards sleep. The way Frank put his arm round Mum! You had to be young to be properly in love like Romeo and Juliet. She couldn't imagine Frank shinning up onto that balcony just to get a few more minutes with Mum or taking poison because he thought she was dead.

Frank did not appear again until one afternoon at the very end of the Christmas holidays. Becky chose her moment carefully, waiting until she knew that her mother was going to be out of the room for several minutes. She knew that Mum didn't like cats but her hunch that Frank wouldn't know that seemed to be confirmed when Frank responded to her innocent sounding enquiry by saying that he couldn't see why she shouldn't have one, which she interpreted to be as good as him saying that she could have one once they moved to the new house. Perhaps there would be more advantages to Frank living with them than had originally met the eye.

The new term began next day. It felt funny to be going into maths without the others and Becky wavered in the doorway, looking for a friendly face from IH. It was all right for Alex and Norma who just took a pair of adjacent desks in the front row as usual, but apart from them hardly anyone from IH seemed to have made it into the top set. It was a relief to spot Adele White smiling shyly and indicating a vacant desk next to her. Adele's best friend Ronnie was down in middle set (and without Adele's homework to copy was quite likely to slide down to the bottom set after the summer exams).

Paula's parents had been up to see Miss Harrison about Paula being in Set 2 and Miss Harrison had reassured them that all the groups did exactly the same work, so there was no question of anyone being left behind. The girls would all be up to the same point at the end of the year, she said, so if Paula did well enough in the summer exams she could move up a set without any problem. As everyone was doing the same work, Becky couldn't see why they had to be in sets at all. The most likely explanation seemed to be that being put in a lower set was a sort of punishment for not doing well in the exams, which seemed unfair because not everyone could come top.

The Christmas holidays soon became a distant memory. In the second week of term it snowed heavily. Half a dozen huge snowmen appeared on the hockey pitch and outdoor P.E. was suspended in favour of country dancing in the hall. Some days they were let out of school early because all the buses had stopped running and they had to trudge home through falling snow. Six inch icicles hung from the guttering outside the gym and everyone's coats bore the daily evidence of snow ball fights. A thick foliage of frost decorated Becky's bedroom window for days on end and at night she huddled beneath the eiderdown with a hot water bottle and wondered how long it would take Frank and Mum to sort out their 'things'.

Chapter Fifteen

1969

'Now don't go getting into any mischief,' Mrs Christie said from the doorway of the front room.

'We won't, Mum,' said Nicky. 'Bye bye. Have a nice time.'

'Come on Vera,' urged her husband. 'We don't want to hold everybody up.'

'They're up to something,' Mrs Christie said as her husband finally closed the front door behind her. 'I never saw four faces looking so much like butter wouldn't melt.'

'Well there's nothing you can do about it now. You shouldn't have let her have the other three round if you can't trust them.'

'They're usually all right.' Mrs Christie sounded doubtful. 'Of course we've never really left them together on an evening before.'

Mr and Mrs Christie seldom went out together in the evening but this was a special occasion: a works outing to a country pub which had a skittle alley. There was a coach laid on, the price of the ticket included a chicken in a basket supper and for Mr Christie it had the added bonus of killing two birds with one stone because it was his wife's birthday next day.

Nicky watched her parents down the path then cried: 'All right everyone into the kitchen!'

The plan to prepare a surprise Sunday tea as a birthday treat for her mother had been hatching for almost a fortnight. Pocket money had been pooled to buy the necessary ingredients, which three innocent faced conspirators had smuggled into the house when they arrived and within a few minutes of her parents' departure, Nicky and her friends were all engaged in the tasks they had worked out previously.

Paula, who had been detailed to follow a recipe for fairy cakes, was the first to encounter a problem. 'The butter's rock hard,' she said. 'It just won't mix with the sugar.'

Becky, who had volunteered to cut sandwiches, was experiencing similar problems and had already pulled holes in two consecutive slices of bread. 'I think it needs to be warmed up a bit,' she said.

Nicola and Joanne were combining their efforts to make a trifle but this was not going according to plan either. The seemingly straightforward task of cutting up a swiss roll and placing it in the base of the dish had rendered their fingers and everything else they touched uncomfortably sticky and now they were having a dreadful struggle trying to open a tin of mandarin oranges.

At this point Dennis walked in. 'What are you doing?' he enquired.

'Buzz off Den. It's a surprise for Mum and you mustn't say anything.'

'What's it worth?'

'It's worth not having your nose crushed up against the pantry door for a start,' said Nicky. 'Now hop it.'

'Can I have that bit of swiss roll?'

'Yes, yes, anything only go away,' said his sister, handing him the last remaining piece of cake with one hand while giving him a shove in the direction of the door with the other.

Dennis moved as far as the doorway where he stood cramming the swiss roll into his mouth so that the jam smeared across his chin.

'Oh no,' squeaked Becky as she almost dropped the butter dish onto the lighted gas ring. 'Now it's gone all runny and I think I've burned my fingers.'

Joanne looked at the remains of the butter doubtfully before saying, 'I expect it'll be all right. Can you do this tin, Nick?'

'I'm no good at tins,' Nicola said. 'Can you do them Paupau?'

Paula turned from her cake mixture and considered the proffered tin opener for a moment. 'The one we've got at home isn't like that,' she said.

'I'll have a go if you like,' said Becky.

Joanne handed the implement over and Becky took a turn with it. In order to lever the cutting blade of the tin opener around the top of the can it was first necessary to force the spiked tip of the blade into the lid of the tin. Becky placed the can of mandarins on the draining board and brought the point of the tin opener down several times in quick succession, but although she made dents in the top of it, she failed to penetrate the tin.

'What we need,' said Jo. 'Is something to hit it with.'

'Shall I fetch Dad's hammer?' Dennis asked impassively from the doorway, wiping his jammy hands down the sides of his shorts as he spoke.

'No. Just shut up and go away,' said Nicky.

'We could use the rolling pin,' suggested Joanne, who privately thought the hammer sounded quite a good plan, but was reluctant to concede points to a mere eight year old.

Nicky found the rolling pin and Joanne held the tin opener upright on the tin of mandarins while Paula hit the top of the tin opener with the rolling pin. The resultant impact sent the tin of mandarins shooting off the draining board. It landed heavily on Nicky's foot before bouncing away against the base of the stove. It was impossible to decide whether the top of the tin had sustained further damage or not, though an additional dent had now appeared in one side of it.

'This is ridiculous,' said Nicky, crossly. 'I don't know how Mum manages this thing. There's nothing for it we'll have to use the hammer.'

Dennis sped off to fetch his father's hammer from the shed without being asked. Paula's first hammer blow glanced off the tin opener and made a small concave indentation in the rim of the tin. The second missed altogether and made a horrible crashing noise on the draining board. At the third blow the tin lid finally submitted and juice oozed through a small slit in the top. Scenting victory, Nicky forced the blade of the opener into the slit and jerked it up and down so that a jagged tear began to appear across the top of the can.

'You're supposed to go round the edge,' Becky said.

'I'm trying but it won't go where I want it to.' Nicky spoke through clenched teeth as she wrestled the tin opener up and down.

Eventually she achieved an irregular serrated hole which was large enough to release the mandarins onto the swiss roll.

'You know these sandwiches?' said Becky. 'Do you think we ought to keep them in the fridge? I mean it's a whole day until they're going to be eaten.'

'We can't keep them in the fridge. If we do Mum will see them and then it won't be a surprise,' said Nicky. 'Tell you what,' she added after a moment's thought. 'We could balance another plate over the top of them and put them in the bottom of my wardrobe. That's the nearest thing we've got to a fridge.'

They were startled by a shriek from Joanne who had caught her thumb on the raw edge of the empty mandarin tin. Becky dropped the slice of ham which she had been about to lay across some buttered bread and Paula put down her bag of flour so hard that a puff of it blew up and hit her nose.

'Look out Jo!' exclaimed Nicky. 'Don't bleed into the trifle.'

'Cor. It looks just like the chimps' tea party in here,' Dennis remarked from the doorway.

'Go away!' shouted Nicky. 'Go and watch the telly. Isn't 'Dixon of Dock Green' on or something?'

Joanne's cut did not appear to be particularly deep but her thumb was reluctant to stop bleeding, so at Becky's suggestion they wrapped it in a tea towel which enveloped her entire hand. At least that meant no one could see the blood, but with Joanne wounded and temporarily out of action preparations continued more slowly.

Nicky kept eyeing the clock anxiously. She had only managed to wheedle permission for one friend to actually stay overnight (they had played scissors, stone, paper for the honour and Joanne had won) so the others had lifts arranged to collect them at nine o'clock and everything seemed to be taking much longer than they had expected. Operations on the trifle had been temporarily suspended while they waited for the jelly to set, so Nicky helped Paula wash up in the wake of her cake making. Paula seemed to have used an awful lot of equipment to make a dozen fairy cakes. Some of mixture seemed to have found its way onto the table and there was a pale dusting of flour on the floor. At least Dennis had lost interest and gone off into the living room which was something to be thankful for.

'What's that smell?' asked Joanne suddenly.

'Oh no!' Paula flung open the oven door – an operation she should have considered at least five minutes before. 'They're burnt.'

'Never mind,' said Nicky in her most encouraging voice. 'There's still time to make some more.'

'But what shall I do with these?' asked Paula as she surveyed the blackened tragedy of her evening's work.

Everyone exchanged looks.

'We can't just put them in the bin,' said Joanne. 'It'll be a dead giveaway.'

'I know,' exclaimed Nicky. 'We'll bury them in the garden.'

'Cremated and buried…' murmured Becky.

'It's all right,' Nicky continued. 'Don't panic. Now your sandwiches are finished Beck, you and Jo can go and bury the first lot of cakes while Paupau does another lot.' She turned to Paula, 'You'll be much quicker this time… now you've got the hang of it.'

Paula regarded her with serious doubt.

'And I'll do the blancmange for the trifle,' Nicky continued. 'It's dead easy. It tells you how to do it on the packet.'

At the second attempt Paula's cakes were given no opportunity to go awry. Repeated opening of the oven door may have contributed to a somewhat flatter shape than was normal, but at least they were not burnt. It was now the turn of the trifle to give trouble. Although Nicola's blancmange was ready to go on top of it, the jelly showed no sign whatever of solidifying.

'Perhaps it needs longer to set,' suggested Becky. 'What did it say on the packet?'

'I don't know. I've buried the packet under loads of peelings in the dustbin so that Mum won't see it. And I can't give it any longer,' wailed Nicky. 'We haven't got much time left. I'll just have to put the blancmange on and hope for the best.'

'Is the jelly supposed to come over the blancmange like that?' asked Joanne, a couple of minutes later.

'I don't think so,' said Nicky, miserably.

'Don't worry,' said Paula. 'You won't see any of that once you've put the cream on top.'

In order to give the trifle the best possible chance of sorting itself out they turned their full attention to icing the fairy cakes. A miscalculation with quantities meant that not only was the icing extremely runny, but there was also a lot left over after the cakes had been covered. Dennis appeared in the nick of time and was provided with a spoon.

'Phew,' said Paula, pausing to push her hair out of her eyes and leaving a smear of pink where her cochineal coated fingers had made contact with her face. 'We're nearly done.'

'But look at the time,' said Becky. 'Frank'll be here in a minute. I'll just cover these sandwiches with a spare plate and then they can go upstairs with the cakes.'

It took several minutes to clear out the bottom of Nicky's wardrobe and the resultant space looked as if it had not seen a duster for some time.

'Careful,' said Paula. 'Don't let the bottom of that dress drag on the fairy cakes. The icing's not dry yet.'

The others had been gone for some time before Nicky and Joanne tackled the final layer of the trifle. The blancmange had acquired a reassuringly leathery surface and only jiggled slightly on its cushion of watery jelly. When it came to opening the cream Nicky was standing no nonsense from the tin and fetched the hammer straight away. The base of the tin opener had acquired a slightly flattened look, but she thought that with a bit of luck no one would notice. Only a relatively small hole was needed before the cream came blobbing out.

Joanne licked a finger which had got cream on it during the operation of transferring the contents of the tin into a jug and said: 'It's not very sweet, is it?'

Nicky tried an exploratory taste and pulled a face. They decided to add sugar which while it sweetened the cream, gave it a somewhat gritty texture.

'It's not very thick,' said Joanne. 'I'm sure it's not supposed to be runny like this.'

'Of course it isn't,' said Nicky. 'What on earth's wrong with it?'

They tried stirring in more sugar but this had no discernible effect on the consistency.

'This is all wrong,' said Nicky, suddenly tired and dispirited. 'The top of the trifle is supposed to be smooth and creamy, not thin and crunchy.'

'We need to disguise it,' said Joanne.

'What? You mean put it in a trilby hat and dark glasses?' Nicky giggled in spite of her momentary gloom.

'Suppose we mix something else in with the cream to make it seem thicker.'

'I was going to put glace cherries on top for decoration,' said Nicky. 'I suppose I could mix them into the cream instead.'

'Well they won't sit on top of this anyway,' Joanne said, after two experimental cherries had drifted to the bottom of the jug. 'So you might as well mix them in.'

They found some walnut halves in the pantry and added those for good measure before spreading the resultant mixture over the top of the trifle.

'Mum's trifles don't look like that,' said Nicky. 'But I suppose it will be OK.'

The trifle was carried upstairs to join the rest of the feast in the wardrobe before the girls put on their night things and pretended to have been in bed for hours.

At the bus stop on Monday morning the others couldn't wait to hear how the surprise had been received.

'Mum was really thrilled,' Nicky reassured them. 'She

said to thank you all and that it was one of the nicest surprises she's ever had. Dad was a bit funny when he first saw the trifle. He said, "whatever's that?" but Mum said it was trifle done in the modern way and he had to keep up with the times. Wasn't it lucky that we managed to do it in the modern way, completely by accident?'

Chapter Sixteen

1983

Nicky tried to telephone her father from Heathrow but there was no answer. He must have popped out to the shops for something. She tried again when she reached Euston Station but there was still no reply.

There was plenty of room on the Birmingham train and she managed to get a block of four seats to herself, spreading her belongings out on the table in order to discourage any chatty soul looking for a travelling companion. She felt thirsty but she wasn't sure how much a cup of British Rail coffee would set her back and she had used up most of her small cache of English money getting from Heathrow and buying her ticket for the train. Nor did she know how much she ought to allow for the bus fare from town. It was ages since she had travelled on a W.M.P.T.E. bus but a taxi was out of the question.

She was dog tired. Every few minutes her eyelids drooped and she had to force herself awake. In different circumstances the sight of blossom covered trees and the extraordinarily green fields rushing past the train windows would have lightened her heart, but Nicky could not entirely believe in it. Any moment now she might wake up and find herself back in Philadelphia. And maybe it would be better if it had all been a dream. A lone long haul plane journey provided a lot of time to assess what a mess you had made of your life. If you assumed, optimistically, that you were going to last long enough to get a telegram from the Queen, then by twenty five you were already at the quarter way mark.

And what have I done with the first quarter of my life? Nicky asked herself. Big fat nothing. Since going to America she had become no more than a person called 'Mark's wife' and now even that role was gone.

By the time the train pulled into New Street Station the sky had become overcast. Nicky tried to cheer herself up at the first sight of the Rotunda. People might think it was an ugly, flat-topped salt cellar of a building but at least it symbolised home. On the station concourse she hesitated over ringing the house again. She didn't want to give her dad too much of a shock by turning up unannounced on the doorstep, but then again she was going to be there in under half an hour and every minute of delay prolonged the endurance test of the journey. Struggling with her suitcase and a handful of loose change, she tried the number again and found it was engaged. Blow it. Never mind... at least that meant he was in.

The bus still left from the same place it always had. She got a seat downstairs and sat looking out of the window, noting the things that were different and the things that had not changed. At least she had Mum and Dad's to go back to. She still thought of it as Mum and Dad's, even though Mum had been dead for nearly a year.

It might take her a while to get a job and sort out her life. She didn't like to think that she would be sponging on her dad, but then again he would probably be only too pleased to have someone there to do the housework and the cooking for a while.

She did not see anyone she knew on the walk from the bus stop to the house, which was a blessing because she didn't feel like explaining what she was doing there, walking along the road in the middle of the day, suitcase in hand and no husband. The suitcase seemed to have acquired weight since she'd set out with it the day before. It had become necessary to transfer it repeatedly from hand to hand and it was such a relief to put it down that she almost dropped it on the step when she reached the house. As she rang the bell she felt herself sway forward, giddy with thirst and exhaustion.

Dad never normally hurried himself to answer the door so she was surprised when the shadow of an advancing head and shoulders appeared almost immediately in the frosted glass panels. The latch clicked and the door swung open to reveal a complete stranger: a heavily built woman with short, iron grey hair in a cauliflower perm. She was wearing a floral printed dress beneath a calamine pink cardigan and the sort of sensible, rubber soled slippers which no woman under fifty would contemplate.

The two women stared at one another.

A host of thoughts raced through Nicky's head. She even double checked the number on the door although she knew there was no mistake.

'I'm looking for Norman Christie.' As she spoke she looked past the stranger into the hall. The wallpaper was the same. The old-fashioned, unframed mirror still hung in its usual place.

The older woman didn't smile. She stared harder at the visitor as though trying to see through her. 'Are you Nicola?' she asked doubtfully.

Nicky's throat emitted a dry rasp of confirmation.

'You'd better come in,' said the woman. She stood aside so that she could shut the door once Nicky had stepped into the hall, but then sidestepped smartly so that she preceded her into the living room. 'We've got a surprise visitor Norm,' she announced. 'It looks as though she's come to stay.'

Her father looked up from the paper he had been reading. He was occupying his usual chair but wearing a rust coloured pullover which Nicky didn't recognise.

'Nicky!' he exclaimed.

'Hello Dad.' She gave him a hug, conscious of the cool gaze of the woman who had let her in. 'Dad, I'm sorry to barge in. I tried to ring you from the airport but there was no answer.'

'Ah... well...' Her father looked momentarily shifty before he said, 'We probably weren't back by then. Me and Vi were having a couple of nights away. One of those Golden Rail Bargain Breaks to Brighton. Very good value out of season. We've only been back in the house just over an hour. What are you doing here, love?'

Nicky hesitated. She wished that the woman called Vi would stop looking at her. Not staring exactly, just looking as though she had you pinned to the spot like a moth on a lepidopterist's board.

'I've left Mark,' she said. 'He'd got another woman… and it wasn't the first time. I've decided to leave him for good, Dad. I'm going to get a divorce.' She paused expecting the word divorce to bring the ceiling crashing down, but nothing followed her announcement except a short, awkward silence. 'I was hoping I could stay here for a bit,' she continued more tentatively. 'Just until I get myself sorted out.'

'Well of course you can, love,' her father said, but Nicky caught the way he glanced doubtfully at Vi as he said it.

'You must be parched.' Vi addressed Nicky for only the second time. 'I'll go and put the kettle on. Then I'll make up the spare bed.'

'It's all right,' said Nicky. 'I'll sort my bed out. I know where everything is.'

Vi pressed her lips together in a clear token of displeasure.

'Better let Vi look after it,' said her father. 'She's moved a few things around. She'll know better than you where to lay her hands on stuff.'

'Well I'll just put my case upstairs then,' Nicky said. 'I need to use the loo anyway.'

She almost stumbled on the stairs. There was a sense of unreality about the whole situation. She dumped her suitcase on the landing while she went into the bathroom. The toothbrushes huddled side by side in the mug together with the feminine toiletries on the shelf (Vi was evidently a member of the Avon Lady's regular clientele) confirmed that her father no longer lived alone.

She tried to think when she had last had any direct communication from him. He never wrote letters of course, but she had called him from Philly every so often and he had never so much as mentioned this Vi person. The effort of trying to work it all out made her feel dizzy again.

When she had splashed water on her hands and face and dried herself on a peach coloured towel that she did not recognise, she collected her case from the landing and pushed open the door of her old bedroom. Here another shock awaited. The furniture had all been moved aside or shipped out altogether, supplanted by a sewing machine table and a dressmaker's dummy. Any attempt to make up the bed would have involved moving several lengths of fabric, a couple of cardboard boxes and a large polythene bag full of pale blue wool.

She turned at the sound of footsteps behind her. It was Vi.

'Was this one yours?' Vi spoke in a neutral voice. Carefully neutral, Nicky thought. 'We use the one next door for visitors now.' She indicated the room which had once been Michael's.

Nicky nodded, not quite trusting herself to speak as she shifted her case into the room which had once been Michael's. She decided to seize the bull by the horns. 'I hadn't realised my Dad had… er… anyone living here with him. I'm sorry…' Then she stopped. I'm not sorry, she thought. What have I got to be sorry about?

'I expect he would have got round to telling you soon,' said Vi. 'It's not always easy with grown-up children.' She did not speak as one who was seeking any understanding or sympathy, merely as if stating a bald fact. 'There's nothing wrong with it,' she added. 'We're both widowed. He's fifty seven and I'm fifty eight and we're old enough to know our own minds.' She gave Nicky a look as if inviting her to argue the point if she dared.

'Of course not,' said Nicky. 'I mean... yes... no... There's nothing wrong with it at all. We all have to live our own lives.'

'I'll go down and pour out the tea then,' said Vi.

When Nicky managed to get Dennis on the telephone, she discovered that he had been aware of Vi's residential status for two weeks. 'I dropped in to see the Old Man and there she was,' he said.

Nicky had chosen to make her call while her Dad and Vi were out shopping. She noticed that although her father had never accompanied her mother on shopping trips, Vi apparently expected and received his assistance in this sphere. 'How long has she been here?' Nicky asked.

'I don't know. She can't have been there all that long.'

'Well how long? When did you last come and see him?'

'Oh... I dunno. A couple of months ago... maybe a bit more.'

'Den,' she said reprovingly.

'Hey. Come on Nick. You didn't exactly drop in every other day yourself. Anyway you know me and Dad don't get on.'

'What did he tell you about her?'

'Nothing much. Her name's Violet Davies. They've known each other for years and years. She and her Old Man used to drink at the club where Dad used to go for his pint on a Sunday lunchtime. Her Old Man died about three years ago... Surely you must have found all this out yourself if you've been living there for three days?'

'They don't say anything about it,' said Nicky. 'They

just sort of behave as though she's been here forever and the way they are – the way she is – I feel sort of awkward asking anything. Dad says next to nothing and I keep expecting her to say that it's none of my business. They keep mentioning someone called Andrew, who I think must be her son, but I don't feel as if I can just come out and ask who they're talking about. It's hard to explain but it's really awkward.'

'It might not be a permanent thing,' Dennis suggested. 'They might be having a bit of a fling.'

'It looks pretty permanent to me,' said Nicky, thinking of the general re-arrangement of everything from the kitchen utensils to the sewing emporium where her bedroom used to be. 'She's even moved the photos that Mum always kept on the sideboard.'

'Dad told me that he'd cashed in his endowment policies,' Dennis said. 'That's how they keep affording these trips to York.'

'What trips to York? It was Brighton they told me.'

'Well I dunno. They'd just got back from York the day before I called in,' said Dennis. 'The Old Man made a point of telling me. Said his motto from now on was "Enjoy It While You Can". I think his point was that I needn't think anything of his would ever be coming to me, which is fine because I never did anyway.'

'Crikey,' said Nicky. 'If he's cashed his own policies in that must mean there's nothing left of the insurance money he got when Mum died.'

'Who cares?' said Dennis. 'It's his money. You'll be all right won't you? You'll get something when you divorce Mark? I tell you what, if that bastard ever comes anywhere near me he'd better watch himself.'

'I always thought you liked Mark.'

'Maybe I did but you're my sis.'

It engendered a warm feeling to think that at least one person was on her side. Even if it was Dennis, whose uses were probably confined to blacking Mark's eye for him. But when the call was over it was Dennis's other words which lingered uncomfortably: They've known each other for years.

A subsequent call to Michael took on a very different complexion. The existence of Mrs Violet Davies was a complete revelation to him. 'She can't be living with him,' he exclaimed, in what Nicky took to be a mixture of amazement and something verging on puritanical disapproval.

'Well they're both old enough to know their own minds,' said Nicky, stopping short when she realised that she had just echoed Vi's own justification.

'They haven't said anything about getting married have they?'

'No,' said Nicky. 'But it's barely a year since Mum died.' Barely a year. It echoed around the room. The presence of another woman in the house so soon after her mother's death had pulled her up short. It conjured all sorts of bad tasting, bitter thoughts.

'He hasn't mentioned a will, has he?'

'What?'

'A will. So long as he doesn't marry the woman and he doesn't change his will, we'll be water-tight.'

'Michael,' she said, not wanting to understand but knowing perfectly well: 'What do you mean?'

'Got to safeguard our interests, Nicky. That house must

be worth eighteen thousand now. It's not a king's ransom split three ways but it's all we're going to get so...'

'Michael,' she interrupted. 'For God's sake! He's only fifty seven.'

'So? He isn't getting any younger. He might go on for another thirty years of course. And I hope he does... obviously... but we don't want any complications.'

Nicky could feel herself getting crosser by the minute. 'You can't expect Dad to stay on his own for the next thirty years, just to protect what you see as your inheritance,' she said.

'Of course not.' Michael's tone was as smooth as treacle. When he spoke again his secretary would have recognised the tone he used for not very bright clients, who couldn't be expected to understand the finer nuances of their case. 'No one says he's got to live on his own. I'm just saying he may need to remember where his obligations lie.'

'As far as I'm concerned,' said Nicky. 'His obligations are to himself. He and Mum did their best for us when we were their responsibility, but now it's up to us to make our own way in the world.' The irony of this struck her even as she spoke when here she was, using her dad's phone, freeloading bed and board, because she had nowhere else to go.

'Of course, of course.' Michael was still using a syrupy tone. 'All I'm saying is that we have to take care Dad doesn't make any rash decisions which might lead to us losing out... because I'm sure he wouldn't want that.'

It was unbelievable she thought, that Michael, who had been supported through sixth form and university, who had in fact ridden the parental gravy train a good five years longer than his brother or sister and who now had an income they could only dream of and an expensive address in London, was still looking to wring every ounce of what he considered his due from his parents.

As if from afar she heard Michael say: 'What you need to think of now is your own immediate situation. My firm only undertakes criminal work but I'm sure I could soon sort you out with an excellent divorce specialist. Mind you, I think you should consider taking proceedings in the U.S.A. A good, shit hot divorce lawyer could really take Mark to the cleaners over there.'

'Actually, I've decided to get some advice locally,' said Nicky. 'I'm going to talk to Becky in the first instance. You remember Becky? My friend from school?'

'Well personal recommendation can be very useful. Has she been divorced recently? I didn't realise she'd got married.'

'She's not married,' said Nicky. 'She's never been married. She's a solicitor.'

'Who? Becky from school? I thought she left when you did and went into some office job with an insurance firm or something.'

'She did,' said Nicky. 'But after that she got a job in a solicitor's office, took all her exams and she qualified last year.' There was an unmistakeable note of pride in her voice at her friend's achievement.

'Oh… I see,' said Michael.

'Anyway,' said Nicky, 'I mustn't keep you. I expect you've got work to do.' In addition to which she didn't want Dad and Vi to come back and find her on the phone. It wasn't that her dad would mind her using the phone, but

Vi had that way of looking at her which made Nicky feel guilty: as if Vi could read her thoughts and would suspect that she had been bitching to her brothers.

After Nicky put the phone down she wandered into the kitchen but there was nothing for her to do there. The formidably efficient Vi had already done everything, including peeling the vegetables in advance of their dinner. Retreating upstairs to Michael's room she glanced around the time warp posters and tried to raise a smile. She was surprised that Vi hadn't got round to taking them down. They looked tired and faded, particularly the one of Kate Bush which had a big tear in it. For a moment she toyed with the idea of taking them down herself but it seemed an imposition to interfere with someone else's room.

A wave of hopelessness engulfed her. No wonder Mum had killed herself. That was what you did, when you'd got nothing left. A visit to the Jobcentre the day before had been a sobering experience. She had worked at Gaskells right from school until they went to Philly and she knew that they would give her a good reference, but no one seemed to care about good references or even a fistful of decent 'O' levels anymore. What employers wanted now was relevant experience. Mostly experience of working with computerised accounting systems that she had never even heard of. Gaskells had been slow to embrace new technology and it had all been about to happen just as Nicky was leaving. She had only been out of work for just over four years but it might as well have been forty. It seemed as though the whole world had moved on and she had somehow been left behind.

I'm unemployable, she thought. I'll have to scrub floors

or something. Although even that probably required a Diploma in Mop Manipulation these days. I'm a nothing, she thought. Paula and Jo went on to university to make something of themselves and Becky fought her way up from zero. Whereas I just settled for being a wife and mother and I couldn't even get that right. Tears trickled down her cheeks at the thought of two gory, harrowing miscarriages.

Mum had made sure of things. She had taken a whole bottle of aspirin. She wouldn't have suffered. She had just fallen asleep and never woken up again.

There had always been a supply of aspirin in one of the kitchen cupboards, along with the indigestion remedies and cough mixture, the Andrews Liver Salts and Vick Vapour Rub. Unless of course Vi had moved them, just like she had moved everything else. Displacing each lingering shred of the previous inhabitants, erasing all evidence of her mother and herself as if they had never been part of the picture… but surely there would still be some aspirin in the house. Maybe it was still where it used to be.

She took the stairs slowly, observing her descent in the hall mirror: fat, yet hollow eyed, like some cruel caricature of her former self. As she passed the telephone it started to ring but she only hesitated for an instant. There's no point answering it, she thought. It won't be for me because hardly anyone knows I'm here.

The front room door stood open and as she passed by she noticed a straggling spider plant hanging from a hook driven into the ceiling, held in some tasselled monstrosity of a plant pot holder. Another of Vi's improvements no doubt.

The telephone seemed to ring more loudly. Its note so

persistent that it got right inside her head. She would have to silence it, just in order to think straight. She lifted the receiver and brought it up to her ear like an automaton.

'Hello. Can I speak to Nicky, please?'

'It's Nicky here,' she said, rousing as if from a bad dream.

'Nick, hiya. It's Becky. I got your message. Sorry I couldn't ring back straight away. What's up?'

Chapter Seventeen

1969

The start of the summer term involved yet more expenditure. IH were to begin cookery lessons and this meant obtaining a flat-bottomed plastic basket to be used for transporting ingredients to school and the finished culinary article home again. Unfortunately cookery was timetabled on the same day as the other new endeavour for the term – tennis. Struggling onto the bus equipped with the unwieldy cookery basket, a tennis racket and a satchel, Becky was only thankful that she did not play violin in the school orchestra.

During the Easter holidays the white lines of the hockey pitch had faded until they were no more than a ghostly reminder in the grass, overlaid by a newly marked athletics track with a rounders pitch in the centre. All the netball hoops had all been moved to one end of the courts, where they stood lonely and neglected like a group of miserable, one-legged triffids and each of the courts had sprouted iron posts which supported ancient tennis nets.

Frank had paid for Becky's racket. It was not a very expensive one but at least it looked shiny and new. Jo's racket was a hand-me-down from her sister Sonia, whose secondary modern had fortunately played tennis. Previous to Sonia's tenure the racket had been owned by the girl next door, whose parents had bought it for her when she started at a grammar school in 1958. It was kept in a heavy wooden press which was held together by screws and wing nuts at each of the four corners. It took an embarrassingly long time to extract the racket from the press, spelling out the antiquity of the object for everyone to see. All the new presses had a hinged central bar which opened the press to release the racket in a single movement.

Becky's racket only had a blue plastic zip-up cover over its head. Alex Dunston said it was absolute death to a racket, not to keep it in a proper press. 'It'll warp in no time,' she said.

Alex had a white tennis skirt and a white shirt with a delicate edging of pale pink around the collar. You were allowed to wear tennis whites if you had them and Alex – who played at a club – naturally did. Norma had therefore persuaded her mother that tennis whites were an essential item of kit and by spending almost every day of the preceding holidays in the park with Alex she could now play passably well. They looked like a pair of swans among all the other blue clad crows at the start of the first lesson.

There was a third girl in the class who had tennis whites but no one knew it. Paula had stuffed her tennis skirt and white tee shirt right to the bottom of her gym bag and put her currently redundant hockey boots on top of them. She had decided that whatever happened Miss Leopold must not cotton on that she could play, because then she might be picked for the first year team and that would mean extra practices which ultimately meant more showers and more humiliation. If necessary she would muff every shot.

Miss Leopold arrived for their first session armed with boxes of balls, but she didn't give any of them out. Instead she made everyone hold their rackets in front of them, because she said the first thing they needed to learn was how to hold their rackets properly. Once this preliminary knowledge had been imparted Miss Leopold showed them how they should draw back their racket to hit an imaginary ball and then do something called following through. When everyone had a go at this, several people managed to clobber their neighbours and it began to look as if tennis might turn out to be as dangerous as hockey after all.

Eventually Miss Leopold told them to get into pairs and stand one on either side of the nets, four to a court. One partner was to put their racket on the ground and throw the ball for the other person to hit it back. This of course pre-supposed that everyone could throw the ball with sufficient accuracy that it went over the net and landed somewhere reasonably close to their partner's racket.

'Throw to her forehand,' Miss Leopold barked, as Nicky tossed the ball up and Becky ran forward, flailing hopelessly as the ball bounced past. Out of the corner of her eye Becky saw a missile struck by Kay Fenton whistle dangerously close to Miss Leopold's unsuspecting rear. At least someone has managed to hit one, she thought.

On her way home, Becky reflected that tennis had not turned out to be nearly so much fun as she had hoped. However, she would have to be careful not to express those sort of sentiments to Mum, because she mustn't appear ungrateful for the tennis racket. When she let herself into the flat she was surprised to see that her mother's summer mac was hanging on its peg by the front door. Mum didn't usually arrive home until well after she got in from school.

'Are you there, Mum?' she called as she mounted the stairs.

'In here.' A muffled voice came from the sitting room.

Becky dumped her cookery basket, satchel and tennis racket in the kitchenette as she passed. She found her mother slumped on the settee, face blotchy and eyes red with crying. She had a handkerchief clutched in one hand and there was a newspaper lying alongside her.

'What's the matter, Mum?'

Her mother opened her mouth to speak but instead of words, strange mewing sounds came out, followed by loud sobs. She made as if to lift up the newspaper then dropped it again, still sobbing hopelessly.

'Please don't cry, Mum,' said Becky. 'What is it? Shall I make you a cup of tea or something?'

Her mother shook her head and appeared to make a monumental effort to regain control. She held out her free hand and Becky took it, kneeling at her mother's feet and clasping the damp hand between her two smaller ones. Her mother dabbed clumsily at her face with the handkerchief and noticing how wet the hankie was and how red her mother's eyes and nose were, Becky realised that she must have been crying for some time.

'Don't know how to tell you,' her mother struggled to get the words out as a barrage of sobs threatened to overwhelm her again. 'Lunch time edition of the 'Mail'...

someone brought it into work... had to come home... can't bear it...'

Becky squeezed the hand tighter. It was all she could offer. She could feel her own eyes filling up in spite of not having the foggiest what it was all about.

'Terrible accident.' Her mother's voice sounded as though it was coming out through a gravel filled tube. 'Lorry pulled out... not his fault...'

The intimation of something terrible sent a tear spilling down Becky's cheek.

Her mother couldn't look at her. Instead she looked down at the front page of the newspaper as she whispered, 'Frank's dead.' The words sent her into another frenzy of weeping. Becky relinquished the hand so that they could hug each other. The instantaneous guilty knowledge that she had never really liked Frank made her cry all the harder.

After a while Becky made a pot of tea but her mother could only manage half a cup and left untouched the greyish rock bun, extracted from the little hoard in Becky's cookery basket. As it grew dusk it was Becky who put on the lights and made more tea, hovering like a nervous shadow in case she might be needed.

'Would you like something to eat, Mum?' she asked much later, but a shake of the head was the only reply.

Becky consumed the remaining rock buns alone in the kitchenette. Then she felt ashamed. How could a decent person feel hungry at a time like this? To assuage her conscience she washed everything up and tidied the kitchenette thoroughly. Then she remembered her maths homework and did it at the table. She could leave the geography because it did not have to be handed in until

Friday. She made another pot of tea and carried a cup into the sitting room, where an earlier offering still sat untouched on the table next to the record player. Becky's eyes prickled when she thought of Frank and his Christmas surprise. The lights were on but the curtains had not been drawn. The clock said it was after ten. Her mother sat in an untidy heap at one end of the settee. Her head had fallen sideways and Becky could see that her eyes were closed. The steady sound of her breathing denoted sleep. For a second Becky wondered if she ought to wake her mother so that she could go up and sleep more comfortably in her bed, or perhaps fetch a blanket and lift up her feet to make her more comfortable. In the end she decided that it would be better not to risk disturbing her at all.

She was just going to creep away when she spotted the newspaper. It was still lying on the settee. If Mum were to move her arm it might catch on the paper and the resultant rustle might wake her up. Silent as a ghost Becky tip toed across the threadbare carpet and gripping the paper firmly between her finger and thumb she slid it clear of the settee and stole back to the kitchenette, where she spread the paper out flat on the table. The front page was dominated by the headline *Fatal Accident – One Man Dead.* There was a picture underneath showing a tangle of metal, which Becky realised with a sick feeling was all that was left of Frank's Cortina. The report said that a lorry had come straight out into the traffic. Two cars had been involved, Frank's and another one. The other car driver was badly injured and in hospital. The lorry driver had escaped with cuts and bruises. It was thought that his brakes might have failed.

It isn't fair, Becky thought.

She read on towards the bottom of the column. *The dead man is Frank McMahon, age 38, of Tile Cross. He leaves a wife and two sons.*

Becky read it again because it couldn't be right. She hadn't even known his other name was McMahon. He had always been Frank... just Frank. And how could he possibly have two sons and a wife? He belonged to us, Becky thought. He was going to live with us. Any past unease at this prospect was entirely subsumed by her resentment of these interlopers.

She sat for a long time in the kitchenette before going to bed. She left the sitting room light on for Mum, just in case she woke up in the night and couldn't remember where she was. It took Becky a long time to get off to sleep and when she did it only seemed like moments until she was woken by an alien sound. She lay rigid under the covers, waiting for it to come again. The light from the hall came in through her half open door, painting a wedge of the carpet in colours that stood out against the monochrome shadows which swathed the rest of the room.

The sound came again, a dreadful keening noise like a wounded animal. Trembling, Becky slid out of bed and peeped into the hall, where everything looked just as usual. The sitting room door was open and she could see that the light was still on in there. The sickening whimper came again. Becky crept as far as the sitting room door, from where she could see her mother sitting head in hands. As she hesitated her mother let out another low, mournful howl. Becky returned silently to bed and tried to block her ears with the bedcovers.

Chapter Eighteen

1983

As Nicky watched her old friend working at the table she thought it was almost like turning the clock back to when they were at school together. Only the surroundings were different. Nicky was sitting in one of the armchairs in Becky's living room with her legs folded under her, cradling a mug of tea. The room was minimally furnished in neutral fawns and creams with relatively few pictures or nick-nacks, though the pine bookshelves were crammed with volumes of every shape and size. The books notwithstanding, the entire contents could have been disassembled and packaged for transfer in a matter of hours. In spite of the financial security she had achieved Becky still habitually travelled light.

A self confessed workaholic, there were few evenings when she did not haul some files out of her expensive, brown leather brief case and spread them out on the table. Nicky couldn't decide whether her friend was so career orientated because she was a truly driven, ambitious woman or whether the achievement of goals and the compulsion to achieve still more had become an inescapable consequence of using work to fill a void in her personal life. It hadn't always been like this, Nicky reflected. She could definitely recall a time when Becka still had an active social life: there had even been an engagement.

As Becky half raised her head before almost instantly returning to her work, presumably having recalled the word or phrase she had been seeking, Nicky cast her mind back to the question of the brief engagement. Sean... that had been his name. Sean was a blank space in the story. Someone Becky had met, fallen in love with and then just as soon discarded... assuming it had been her and not him who had called the engagement off. It had all happened while she had been in America, so her knowledge of Sean amounted to no more than a faded snapshot and a few lines in a series of letters.

One particular line returned to her now: *I have never been so happy...*

She remembered writing to congratulate Becky on her engagement and then hearing not much later – surely not in Becky's very next letter? – that the engagement was over. After that it seemed as though relationships or romance of any sort were completely off Becky's personal agenda. There had never been any mention of a boyfriend after Sean. Nor had Becky ever really explained what had happened. Though Nicky was curious, it had been a difficult thing to ask about in a letter and since she had been back home the subject had never come up.

Becky glanced up at her and smiled. 'Penny for them?'

'I was just thinking that here we are, two spinsters of the parish. No romance in our lives...'

'You're not exactly a spinster of anywhere. Besides

which romance is dead,' Becky said cheerfully, screwing the cap back onto her pen, then stacking her paperwork together with an air of finality. 'It's all about sex these days.'

'Surely you can manage a bit of romance first, before you get round to the sex?'

'Aah… you mean the preliminaries of the date? The bit where you get taken out to dinner and bored senseless with his job, the boasting about his penis extension car and if you're really lucky the magical moment when he whips out his groovy, up to the minute pager to show you how it works.'

'You old cynic, you!'

'My dear you haven't been single in the eighties yet. Believe me the rules have all been changed. No…' Becky paused for a moment. 'I suppose that's not fair. I'm sure there really are some nice men out there. Men who belong to some lost tribe of true romantics and can still sweep a girl off her feet at twenty paces, but I just don't get to meet them. Most of the males I come into contact with are either miserable little tow rags who're up before the bench for breaking and entering, or middle aged business men who leer and ask if they can call me Rebecca, while hoping I'm going to get them off a speeding charge. As for my fellow solicitors, I'd actually begun to hope that I'd finally heard the last of those dreadful showing each other our briefs jokes and then I got hit with one again just last week, God help me.' She had been packing everything neatly into her briefcase as she spoke and finished the operation by closing it with a snap.

'Isn't there anyone nice where you work?' prompted Nicky.

Becky laughed again. 'Jonathan and Charles are both married, darling Gerry is gay and lives with a very sweet companion called Barry. Mel is Jewish and terrified of his mother. He would never dare make a pass at me, still less take me home to meet the matriarch. Tony is not my type to say nothing of being an absolute swine with women and Julian is just out of university and still wet behind the ears.' She paused to draw breath. 'What about your place of work?'

'They're all women in my section,' said Nicky. 'You wouldn't catch a grown man working for those rates of pay. The only men I meet are Mr Goddard, the accountant, who's married with three children and that geeky bloke with glasses who emerges from the inner sanctum of IT whenever someone's computer goes wrong.'

'To hell with men,' said Becky. 'Let's open a bottle of wine and celebrate the fact that it's Wednesday.'

'Actually it's Tuesday.'

'All the better. Bugger. I was thinking of court tomorrow and got a day ahead of myself.'

Nicola laughed. It was her old infectious giggle and Becky noted it with approval, because it was good to see how readily Nick laughed these days. She was a different person to the pallid, despairing woman of a few weeks ago.

'Come and stay with me,' Becky had suggested, on learning of the awkwardness of living alongside Vi.

'I couldn't do that,' Nicky had protested. 'For a start off I couldn't pay my way. I haven't got any money.'

'So what? Look at all those Wagon Wheels you used to share with me at break time *and* the roast chicken flavour crisps. I never had any money in those days. Then there were all those meals your mother provided when I was starving in my various garrets. Anyway you can be my guest and guests don't pay. Pay me something when you get a job.'

'But that's the thing,' Nicky had protested. 'I seem to be virtually unemployable.' But she had accepted the invitation and coached and encouraged by Becky had managed to get a job in the purchase ledger section of a building supplies company. The money was peanuts but Becky continued to find excuses for not accepting any rent and covertly supplemented their consumables, so that the shared shopping bill did not cut too deeply into her friend's inadequate pay packet.

The truth was that although far too determinedly self sufficient to acknowledge it, Becky rather liked having someone around. The fact that the someone was Nicky made it even better.

Chapter Nineteen

1969

'Are you going to tell Miss Harrison about Frank?' Paula asked.

They were sitting at the edge of the playing fields, close to the wire netting which separated the athletics field from the tennis courts. Paula, Becky and Jo were finding daisies with long stems so that Nicky, who had the least badly bitten nails, could turn them into daisy chains. The plan was to transform the daisies into four circular wreaths which could be worn on their heads in afternoon lessons, until they were instructed to take them off. The Daisy Chain League was a secret society dedicated to enigmatic acts of disobedience. It had been invented by Ronnie Nicholls after she had been given a detention by Miss Hardiker for wearing the wrong shade of brown shoes. So far membership was limited to a few trusted confidantes in IH and a handful of IR sympathisers.

'I can't say anything to Miss Harrison,' said Becky. 'It's not as if he was my dad or anything.'

'Will you have to go to the funeral?' enquired Joanne. 'My mum wouldn't let us go to my nan's funeral. She said funerals are no place for children. Of course it might be different for you because you *are* twelve.'

'I don't know what's happening about it,' Becky said. 'I hope not. I don't want to go – not really – because then I'd have to explain why I'm not in school.'

The others nodded. Frank not being Becky's father made everything very complicated. When Colleen Bell's pet rabbit had died she got her proper dues in public sympathy, but people who did not fit in as fully qualified members of your family or family pets were presumably a different matter.

Becky thought that the others had been splendid about Frank when she had confided in them at the bus stop that morning, greeting the news with exactly the right combination of regret and excitement. All four had experienced the same sense of creepy enthralment at the thought of having travelled in the ill fated Cortina with Frank and after listening anxiously to Becky's account of her mother's inconsolable desolation, were united in agreement that mindful of the lengths to which grief stricken lovers were prone to go, Becky had done exactly the right thing in hiding the aspirin and the sharp vegetable knife under her mattress before leaving for school that morning.

The news of Frank's demise had temporarily diverted Paula's mind from the miserable time she'd had at home the night before. It had begun at the tea table when her mother started quizzing her about the wretched tennis team. Paula had immediately assured her parents that the tennis team had not been mentioned. It was only the first tennis lesson, she said and Miss Leopold had just been working on everyone's forehand.

'And what did she say about your forehand?' asked her mother.

'Nothing,' Paula said truthfully, not adding that Miss Leopold had not been given the opportunity to pass comment, because Paula had taken care to be the throwing half of a partnership with Joanne. However the knowledge of her hidden tennis whites weighed heavily on her conscience and perhaps this generated some uncertainty in her replies, because her mother kept returning to the subject of the tennis lesson in the way that she always harped on anything when she thought Paula was holding something back.

Worried that her parents might still be musing on matters relating to the tennis team and fearing they might attempt something awful like writing to Miss Leopold about it, Paula had taken up station at her listening post immediately after she had supposedly retired to bed. After listening to a lot of boring, grown-up talk about the neighbour's privet hedge and an advertisement in the 'Radio Times' for reclining chairs, Paula was not surprised when the conversation turned – just as she had expected it would – to herself. She had anticipated the topic to be tennis, but instead the discussion took a wholly unexpected turn which made her nibble the end of one plait in horror.

'I found one of Paula's notebooks when I was putting the garden seats away,' her mother said. 'It was out by the sundial so I brought it inside in case it got rained on. Do have a look. She seems to be writing one of her stories. It's absolutely priceless.'

Pinpricks of horror raced all over Paula's limbs. Immediately before tea she had been composing a torrid love scene, in which Colonel Strathhugo forced his attentions on Lady Gladiola. If her parents looked at the latest pages she would die… always presuming that they didn't kill her first.

She heard her father mumble something, then there was some laughter after which he began to read aloud: '*The colonel* – that's not how you spell colonel to start with – *the colonel's moustache* – dear me can't spell moustache either, *was like a bristly toothbrush. Leaping down from his equine steed, he said, Don't be* – what's this word? Frittered? *Don't be frittered, sweet lady*,' more muffled laugher, '*I am come to your rescue*. Lady Gladioli? Surely not? *Lady Gladiola almost swooned at the sight of this excruciatingly handsome newcomer* – Good God Jean! What sort of fearful rubbish are they teaching her at Eleanor Vaux?' Then he laughed again.

Paula was almost crying with mortification and could barely hold back from running downstairs to seize the precious notebook. She was furious with herself for having left it lying around for her mother to find. She had been hiding her stories for some time now. When she had been much younger she had often read them aloud to her parents, but the time came when she could read well enough to glance up from the page, catch the amused glances and sense the patronising tolerance. How dared they laugh at her like that? When she was as famous as Jean Plaidy, with a row of novels on every library shelf, that would show them.

*

From the windows of the staff room Mrs Venables could see at least a dozen first year pupils separately engaged in grubbing up daises from the athletics field. 'What is this fixation with daisy chains among the first years?' she asked of Miss Pentland, who had just turned on the staff room kettle for a post lunch cup of tea. 'Is it something they've picked up in art or drama, d'you think?' As a science teacher Mrs Venables had an instinctive mistrust of airy fairy subjects like art and drama and was inclined to ascribe any sort of offbeat fads in school, to be as likely as not due to their pernicious influence.

'I think it's just the time of the year,' said Miss Pentland. 'At least it's not as bad as that craze for red hair we had in '53… or was the red hair earlier than that?'

'The *paper* flowers craze is the one I remember,' Miss Mislet joined in. 'Every lesson I seemed to catch some wretched girl making the things under her desk when she ought to have been working. To say nothing of another three or four wearing the silly things twined into their hair.'

'I had IH for first period after lunch yesterday,' Mrs Venables grumbled. 'I had to tell half the class to take daisy chains off their heads. There's no place for that sort of thing in a chemistry lab.'

'I actually think it's rather charming.' Mr Sinton was ambling across the room on his way to his personal refuge in the corner. 'I got them to sing 'Nymphs and Shepherds' and 'Where the Bee Sucks'. The little garlands of flowers added a delightful pastoral effect.'

Mrs Venables and Miss Pentland exchanged looks.

'It will be summer exams before we know it,' said Miss Mislet. 'That will settle them back down.'

Chapter Twenty

1984

Nicky had spent almost an hour with Gerry, the partner at Becky's firm who was looking after her divorce. It was awfully depressing, she thought, as she made her way downstairs to leave the building. She was too preoccupied to notice the presence of anyone else in the foyer until it was too late and she had cannoned into Clive Aston. She recognised him at once from a charity event that Becky had hauled her along to just before Christmas and blushing scarlet began to stumble into an apology, but he got in first.

'I am so sorry, Nicky. It is Nicky, isn't it?'

'Yes. Please don't apologise, it was totally my fault. I wasn't looking where I was going.'

'That makes two of us. Look… I only called in to drop off some papers. I insist that having trodden all over your feet the very least I can do is take you for coffee. '

'Oh… but you really don't need to do that,' she said feeling inwardly glad that she had put on the smart, chocolate brown skirt and jacket which she had bought for job interviews.

'I insist. You haven't got to be anywhere else have you? No? Well that's all right then. We'll cut through the Bull Ring and pick up some cream cakes from Druckers,' he said. 'Then I'll take you on somewhere much nicer for coffee.'

Nicky soon realised that it was just as well she didn't need to be anywhere else, because the next thing she knew Clive's car was speeding out of Birmingham along the Alcester Road, giving her the slight sensation of being kidnapped. It was a dark blue car with cream coloured, leather seats. She didn't know anything about cars but she could recognise that this one must be worth a lot of money. Then she saw the house he lived in and the car fell into context.

'I promised I'd take you somewhere nice for coffee,' he said. 'And I never break my promises.'

They drank their coffee in a conservatory which looked out across his garden towards the open countryside. The January sun was already sinking, a great orange ball which almost appeared to be balancing on the topmost black branches of three ash trees that marked his western boundary. Small pockets of frost still lay in parts of the garden, glittering and picturesque when viewed from the centrally heated comfort of the house.

'You can't beat Druckers for cakes,' he said. 'But you can't beat Cliveden for comfort. It's the name of the house,' he added, perhaps thinking that she had missed the plate alongside the front door. 'Like the stately home. Although I suppose it should be Clive's Den, really.'

'It's very nice,' she said, conscious of the inadequacy of the expression. 'Have you lived here long?'

'About eight years give or take. You live with Rebecca don't you?'

'At the moment,' she said, thinking that he must have either recalled something she had said during their previous encounter, or else had done some homework since meeting her which was a distinctly flattering possibility. 'I'm getting divorced. I expect I'll look for somewhere of my own once the divorce is finalised.' It was brave talk but she knew that this was starting to look like an increasingly optimistic notion. She didn't earn anything like enough to start a mortgage and she did not qualify for a council flat. Private renting fell into the categories of too squalid or too expensive for serious contemplation.

'Miserable business, divorce,' he said, 'whatever the circumstances. Been there done that. Got the tee shirt.'

Oh dear, she thought, now he's going to start telling me about his divorce. People were like that when they knew that you were getting divorced too. Wanting to wallow in shared misery. To her relief he started to talk about the house instead and how he had recently transformed one room into a fitness centre.

She guessed that he was older than her though she couldn't tell by how much. He had little crows feet at the outer corners of each eye, which far from making him unattractive gave him a look of shrewdness, suggesting someone with a wide experience of life who knew his way around. His eyes were blue and his blonde hair looked natural as did his tan. Sure enough he broke off from the subject of running machines to mention the swimming pool at his villa in Spain, before returning to the subject of his quest for fitness on the rowing machine which was installed somewhere in the house.

'I've lost some weight over the last few months,' Nicky said, 'but I still need to lose a bit more.'

'You shouldn't,' he said. 'You look lovely as you are. I can't abide skinny women.'

She knew that she ought to resent the faintly proprietorial tone, but the compliment was irresistible.

'Look at that,' he said. 'The sun's gone below the yard arm. Or in this case below the tree tops. It must be time for a drink.'

It was true. She looked across to the ash trees and saw that their topmost branches were now etched blacker than ever against the deepening orange disc.

'What do you say we open a bottle of wine now and later on I'll arrange to have some Chinese food delivered?'

Taken by surprise, Nicky hesitated only for a moment. 'Thank you. That sounds very nice,' she said. 'I'd better just ring Becky though, to let her know that I won't be home for dinner.'

'Of course. Use the phone just through here.'

As she dialled Becky's number, the absurd thought ran through her mind of how cross her mother would have been with her. Getting into a strange man's car and going somewhere without even knowing where he was taking you, was a sure fire way of getting yourself raped and murdered so far as her mother had been concerned.

Oh well, she thought, having left a message on Becky's machine, at least they'll know where to start looking for the body if he murders me. As for the other part she had pretty much assumed that a bit of consensual sex was an implied part of the equation, once opening bottles of wine at half past three in the afternoon had been mentioned. The thought half aroused and half scared her. It was certainly an unexpected way of spending her day off.

She found him in the kitchen where he had already uncorked a bottle of red wine. The kitchen was beautifully fitted out, with woodwork stained dark green, shiny red tiles on the walls and pristine black marble worktops. It was also extremely tidy which Nicky thought might be explained by his predilection for take-aways.

'Do you like to cook?' He must have noticed the way she was looking around.

'Yes,' she said.

'Are you good?'

'I'm passable,' she said, modestly.

'I do a great chilli,' he said. 'I suppose you learnt a lot of new dishes when you were out in the States.'

He *had* done his homework, Nicky thought. She took a gulp of wine before answering. 'One or two. I learnt how to do blueberry stuffed French toast, which let me tell you is just heavenly.'

'You'll have to make it for me sometime,' he said. 'I must say Nicky that you strike me as a girl who could cook up a storm in all sorts of ways.' He reached out and touched the side of her cheek. It was little more than a caress but enough to turn her face towards him, so that he could kiss her. She hadn't expected a move in this direction quite so quickly and a phrase of Becky's about romance being dead flashed through her mind. The line had been corny but it was a splendid kiss, measured and enticing and very appealing to someone who had been starved of kisses for many months. She offered no resistance when he moved in to kiss her again.

'Have you ever been in a jacuzzi?' he asked and when she shook her head he said, 'There's one upstairs. Come up and you can try it out.' He spoke as casually as if he was no more than offering to buy her an ice cream at the pictures.

Nicky hardly knew what to say. Things were moving much faster than she had anticipated. He took her by the hand and began to lead her out of the kitchen. 'Bring your glass,' he said, when she showed signs of leaving it behind. 'You should never go in a jacuzzi without a drink.'

He led her upstairs, managing the stem of his glass and the neck of the bottle in his other hand. At the top of the stairs he opened the door onto an impossibly huge bedroom. It was more like a film set than something you'd expect to find in somebody's house, she thought. A massive four poster bed sat on a raised platform and at the opposite end of the room there was an arched opening beyond which she could see a low wall of blue tiles surrounding an enclosure which looked from a distance rather like a kiddies paddling pool, but turned out to be the sunken jacuzzi bath.

After placing their glasses and the bottle on the blue tiled surround he started the taps, releasing a gushing Niagara of water. Then he turned back to Nicky and began to unbutton her shirt, kissing her and running his hands slowly over every inch of her and although she had a terrible feeling that this was all part of a well practiced routine, she was equally conscious of an insistent pulse between her legs and a strong urge to kiss him back. And why shouldn't she indulge herself with a little fun? It was probably all wrong to be influenced by the hedonistic temptations of a jacuzzi in luxurious surroundings but hell… when was she ever likely to get the chance again?

Although he did not appear to be monitoring the water level he seemed to know the precise moment to pause and turn off the taps. He must have activated something else at the same time, because after the faintest rumble the water began to bubble and churn.

I'll be like an onion boiling in a stew, Nicky thought.

He looked very good with his clothes off – all tanned flesh and firm muscles. She felt white and flabby next to him, but he kissed her all over and told her she was beautiful before completely ignoring the jacuzzi and leading her across the deep soft carpet to make love on the bed.

With his breath coming hard in her ears she couldn't hear the sound of the jacuzzi anymore. He was firm and strong, taking complete control and fulfilling her optimistic expectations that sex – after such a long time without it – might be just what she needed.

Afterwards they had a long soak in the jacuzzi and he opened a second bottle of wine.

'I shall have to get a taxi home,' she said, smiling across at him as he refilled her glass.

'Don't go home,' he said. 'Stay here.'

'I have to go to work in the morning.'

'Phone in and tell them you're sick.'

'I can't do that.' She was shocked yet at the same time secretly delighted that he wanted her to stay.

'What a conscientious little creature you are. Very well then stay here tonight and I'll set the alarm so that we get up early enough for you to pick up some clean clothes from Rebecca's and make it into work on time.'

'Don't you have to go to work?'

'Only if I feel like it. I've got things set up so that they can tick along very nicely without me for whole days at a time.'

The Chinese food appeared as he had promised but they only picked at it before returning to the bedroom with yet another bottle of red. Nicky's glass appeared to be full whenever she looked at it and it seemed somehow incumbent on her to make the level in the glass go down. After another session in the jacuzzi they returned to the bed, where Nicky consented to having her wrists secured to the two posts at either side of the head board with a pair of black silk scarves. She had never entertained such an idea before and was startled to discover just how much she liked it.

Next morning he delivered her safely to work on time as promised.

Chapter Twenty-One

1969

Room 3 was swamped beneath the canopy of drowsy summer heat. The windows had all been thrown open in a vain attempt at freshening the air, but nothing was coming inside except the distant intimations of an unseen rounders match. Whilst Mrs Rollins endeavoured to keep the collective interest of IH focussed on the poetry in 'Alice's Adventures in Wonderland', she had observed that Paula Morrison's head had been bent over her desk for some time. For a moment she half wondered if the girl was nodding off to sleep, but then Joanne Embury – who was sitting immediately in front of Paula – had shifted slightly to the left and Mrs Rollins realised that Paula was writing something.

'So,' said Mrs Rollins, gliding away from the blackboard as she continued to address the class. 'What did you first think of when you heard the word bandersnatch – what does it conjure up for you, Veronica?'

Ronnie, who had been listening attentively said, 'It

made me think of a blunderbuss. But it's obviously some sort of creature, so perhaps a cross between an animal and a blunderbuss?'

As Ronnie was speaking Mrs Rollins had been advancing silently down the aisle between the desks which stood nearest the windows. The others saw the impending danger but were helpless to warn Paula, who was completely engrossed in whatever it was that she was doing, head bent, daisy garland falling down in the direction of one ear. Only as Mrs Rollins arrived alongside her desk did the immediate presence of a teacher intrude into Paula's consciousness. She attempted to conceal what she had been writing by thrusting it under her pencil case but it was far too late.

'Give that to me please.' Mrs Rollins held out her hand.

Paula handed over the sheet of paper without daring to make eye contact.

'See me at the end of the lesson.' To the class, whose inquisitive faces were now universally turned towards that corner of the room, Mrs Rollins said briskly, 'Face the front, please. That's very interesting Veronica. Let's try you Colleen. What did you see in your head when you heard the word bandersnatch?'

'Nothing miss,' mumbled Colleen, whose stolid lack of imagination was well known.

'Well what did you *think* then when you heard the words Adele has just read out for us? You must have thought of something.'

'I thought they didn't make sense, miss.'

A suppressed titter came from somewhere at the back.

Mrs Rollins emitted a deep sigh. 'On one level Colleen, of course they don't make sense. Indeed some people might describe this as a nonsense rhyme. But on another level Lewis Carroll is trying to paint a picture for us using these words. It is for us – the readers – to see what we can make of it.'

Sensing a mild rebuke, Colleen blushed under a suntan acquired after spending her lunch hours lying in the middle of the athletics field and tried but failed to affect an expression of comprehension.

'Read it out for us again please Adele,' said Mrs Rollins. 'Listen carefully to the words everyone.'

While Adele worked her way through the slithy toves and tulgey wood for a second time, Mrs Rollins took a moment to scan the contents of the confiscated paper, which she had by now placed face upwards on her desk. It was not, as she had first suspected it to be, a note to one of Paula's friends. In fact it appeared to be a poem.

You are old, Miss Forster, the young girl said,
And your legs are exceedingly thin.
Is that why you make such a fuss about people's shoes
And think running in the corridor's a sin?

In my youth, Miss Forster replied to this chit,
Girls knew their place in my schools,
Whereas now they mistake idle chatter as wit
And go round ignoring my rules.

Mrs Rollins lips crept into a smile which she quickly suppressed. Meanwhile at the back of the room Paula sat quaking. Becky flashed her a look of sympathy from the adjacent desk. Paula knew that Nicky and Jo would be feeling for her too, but they were sitting in front of her and couldn't do anything without turning their heads, which would only attract Mrs Rollins's attention and make things much worse.

Not that they could be much worse, Paula thought. Mrs Rollins would be'sure to put her in detention at the very least and that would mean taking a detention slip home for Mum and Dad to sign. A nightmare scenario. Her mother had gone through seven years at Eleanor Vaux without getting a single detention and Paula experienced a sense of hopelessness whenever she remembered the expectation laid upon her to emulate this unblemished record. She already had two order marks from Miss Mislet, incurred by forgetting to bring the right books to lessons. A third order mark equalled automatic detention. If she could manage to stay in Miss Mislet's good graces until the end of term the order marks would be wiped out and she would start with a clean slate in September, but although the end of term was drawing ever nearer, she still approached each maths lesson with trepidation. And now she had really blown it. Mrs Rollins was going to give her detention and her parents would be furious, not least because she had tarnished her record quite needlessly, by sitting in class writing silly verses for the amusement of her friends when she ought to have been paying attention to the lesson.

At the end of class Paula packed her books away so slowly that the room had almost entirely emptied out before she approached Mrs Rollins, who was seated at her desk apparently engrossed in one of her text books and not interested in Paula at all. Like all the teacher's desks at Eleanor Vaux it was a raised Dickensian affair, which looked like the sort of furnishing which might have been provided for Bob Cratchit at the offices of Scrooge and Marley. As the last of the class clattered and shuffled their way out of the room Paula knew that her friends would be waiting for her out in the corridor, which meant that at least if Mrs Rollins made her late for next lesson she wouldn't have to walk into it alone. As she stood waiting for the teacher to look up it belatedly occurred to her that it might be a good idea to take the daisy chain off her head. It wasn't an opportune moment to strike a blow for the Daisy Chain League, or D.C.L. as it was now known, even if Mrs Rollins didn't seem to bother about the daisy chains… unlike Mrs Venables in whom they inspired a very satisfactory level of irritation.

Mrs Rollins finally shut her book and then packed all her things steadily into her briefcase, as if she had nothing on her mind except keeping her appointment with IIL in Room 16. Eventually after what seemed like an eternity she turned to Paula and said, 'I expect you to pay full attention in my lessons Paula. If you wish to develop the poetry we have been working on then that is very commendable, but it is something you must do in your own time.'

Paula concluded that a reply was expected. 'Yes miss,' she said, in a voice so low that if there had been anyone left sitting in the front desks they would scarcely have been able to catch it.

'A humorous poem about a member of staff is not the sort of thing you should be caught writing in school.'

Paula wondered if she had imagined the faintest hint of emphasis placed on the word caught.

She realised that Mrs Rollins was holding out the

confiscated sheet to her. 'Your work is quite promising,' she said with just a suggestion of a smile. 'But my advice is take it home this evening and don't bring it back. And I think you need to look at that third and fourth line. They don't quite scan.'

The others were waiting for her out in the corridor. The thunder of a school on the move was dying to a murmur, but fortunately their next lesson was only a few doors down the corridor.

'What happened?' asked Jo. 'Did she give you a detention?'

'No.' Paula's voice held all the incredulity and delight of a condemned man reprieved. 'She said not to mess around in her lessons and then she sort of said she thought my poem was quite good.'

'Oh frabjous day!' exclaimed Becky, using the phrase they had adopted as their own, ever since Mrs Rollins had introduced them to 'Jaberwocky'.

*

Becky's jubilation was not destined to last. When her mother arrived home from work that afternoon she was in a particularly dispirited mood, snapping at the least little thing and keeping Becky on the hop with a series of tasks which culminated in running an errand to the outdoor. Becky did not like going into the outdoor to buy Mum's sherry. Mr Hyde never actually refused to sell it to her – although according to the notice pinned up inside the shop he should have done – but all the same an air of unease lingered over the transaction. The sherry came out of a big barrel. A steady stream of dark, sweet smelling liquid flowing from the tap into his measuring jug, its distinctive heady aroma reaching Becky on the far side of the counter. After taking care to close the tap tightly he would take her empty QC bottle, put his plastic funnel in the neck of it and transfer the contents from his jug into the bottle without losing a single drop. Finally he would screw on the cap and hand it back to her which was always the moment when he gave her the look: a funny sort of look, neither entirely disapproving nor entirely sympathetic, but somewhere in between the two. It always made her feel very uncomfortable. It was different with the cigarettes. Mr Hyde thought nothing about that. He knew they were for her mum and that people might go through any amount of cigarettes in a week, so he never gave her the funny look if she asked for cigarettes, even if it was the third or fourth time in a week.

She knew that drink was supposed to have a bad effect on people if they had too much of it, although things like beer and sherry which ordinary people drank all the time probably didn't count. It was something called spirits that people meant when they cautioned about the dangers of having too much to drink. Certainly the sherry made no discernable difference to Mum. She still moped about and cried and forgot to go to bed at night, whether she'd had any sherry or not. She still burned things or some days didn't get round to cooking anything at all.

Becky dawdled on her way back from the outdoor. It was far nicer being out in the evening sunshine than cooped up in the flat, which had got thick with dust lately and developed a queer musty smell. About a hundred yards from their front door, Becky noticed a youngish woman sitting out on a front step with a transistor radio next to her. It was playing a song she hadn't heard before. The woman smiled and Becky smiled back. The radio was probably tuned to Luxemburg which would account for the queer fading in and out effects of the music.

Becky was currently poised on the horns of a dilemma, musically speaking. She liked acquiring new records, not least because it was such a grown-up thing to do. Older girls and boys were always talking about pop music while they waited for the bus after school and by listening while pretending not to, Becky picked up a lot of tips on what was going out and what was coming in. She was currently saving her pocket money to buy 'Baby Make it Soon' by The Marmalade. The trouble was that the others all wanted to go and see 'The Love Bug' on Saturday at The Kingsway. There were hardly ever any films showing at the cinema which didn't have an X certificate, so it represented a rare opportunity to go to the pictures together, but going would mean sacrificing the record because she didn't have enough money to pay for both.

She recalled rather sadly that if Frank had still been around, dropping the appropriate hint might have led to being given enough money so that she could go to the pictures *and* have the record. She always felt awful now, when she remembered how generous he had been and the way she had shied away from kissing him to say thank you for things. She could have been so much nicer to him… would have been… if she had only known it was going to be for such a little while.

'You took your time,' her mother said, when she got

back to the flat. 'I've ironed your blouse for tomorrow.'

'Thank you,' Becky said.

She noticed that Mum's face had got that queer, white look again. As though she was angry but without being in a bad temper.

Becky took the freshly ironed shirt into her bedroom. After nearly ten months of intensive use all the stiffness had gone out of the collar and the cuffs were starting to show visible signs of wear, but at least the uniform (bought to allow for growth) all fitted her better now than it had at the start of the school year. There was no P.E. tomorrow so she could get away with ordinary white cotton pants which she added to the pile on the chair: clothes placed so they would be in the right order for putting them on: jumper and tie on the bottom, skirt, shirt then undies. She added a clean white Miss Berlei bra to complete the pile.

Her bras looked like children's playthings next to Mum's heavy duty, long-line, versions. Never mind... it didn't matter if you weren't very big. Who wanted great big boobs like Kay Fenton's anyway? So long as you were big enough to actually qualify for a bra that was all that mattered. Annette Maudesley's bra didn't count as the proper thing because everyone knew that she stuffed it with tissues. Poor old Paula was still as flat as a pancake which made her really miserable.

'Save up and buy a padded bra,' Jo had suggested. But Paula said her mum would never let her wear it and that anyway everyone would know it was padded and talk about her – which was true.

When she had collected all her other things together Becky went in search of her dinner money. Miss Forster had introduced an experimental scheme at Easter which required dinner money to be paid in advance on Fridays, in order to alleviate the usual Monday morning pre-assembly rush. Mum had inevitably grumbled about this, acidly noting that Miss Forster obviously didn't know what it was like to be 'short of a Thursday evening'.

Becky found her mother lying on the settee with a glass of sherry in her hand and the QC bottle on the table next to her. In the shaft of sunlight from the window Becky could see a band of dust dancing in the smoke which was rising from a cigarette balanced on the edge of the half filled ash tray. The television was on with the sound turned right down so that the figures moving across the screen went about their business dumbly, the meaning of their actions lost without the words.

If we opened the windows, Becky thought, we'd be able to hear the birds saying goodnight and maybe some fresh air would alleviate the stale smell which hung more strongly in the sitting room than anywhere else. 'Shall I open the window?' she asked.

'What do you want to do that for? You'll make a draught.'

It didn't seem worth arguing about. 'I need my dinner money,' she said.

'Please,' said her mother. 'I need my dinner money *please*.'

'Sorry.'

'Get it out of my purse.'

As Becky turned away her mother began to cry. She often began to cry for no apparent reason and Becky took no notice. It was hopeless trying to cheer Mum up. Nothing worked. The only thing that would make her feel better was the one thing she couldn't have. It's been six weeks now, Becky thought. She's got to get over it soon.

Her mother's purse was on the table in the kitchenette, where her mother had put it after extracting the money for Becky to go and buy the sherry: an errand from which there had been no change. She checked the main body of the purse first. There were some coppers and a sixpence which when counted out onto the table only totalled one shilling and tuppence. Dinner money was five shillings a week. She tried the zip pocket where Mum kept notes next, vainly probing into the corners in the hope of encountering any ten shilling notes which might have got crushed into the bottom.

With increasing panic Becky reached down the old tea caddy which stood on the mustard painted larder shelves alongside the genuine food receptacles. Her mother entertained the theory that concealing cash like that would fool burglars, though Becky privately thought that any burglar would have to be pretty desperate to bother with them.

The tea caddy was empty.

Failing to remember your dinner money was a serious offence. With a heavy heart, Becky returned to her bedroom and silently bidding farewell to 'Baby Make it Soon' and 'The Love Bug', extracted her precious savings from the little musical box she used as a safe. She knew that there wasn't any more money in the flat and it was no use thinking that she would be able to get it back after Mum was paid tomorrow, because a covert attempt would surely be detected while a direct approach entailed pointing up her mother's failure to lay the money aside and at this Mum would only start wailing and go into her latest routine: the one where she declared herself to be a hopeless mother and said 'they' – whoever 'they' were – would come and take Becky away from her. 'Then I'll have no one left in the world,' she would say: another phrase which was always a prelude to hysterical weeping.

It was much easier Becky thought, to just say nothing at all.

*

Quite suddenly it was the end of term.

The four friends walked down the lower drive in brilliant sunshine, knowing that on their return in September they would be second years with a new form room and a new form teacher. Today was the last possible day when any older girl might disparage them as mere fuzzers.

It had been an eventful last few weeks. Gail Foster and Debbie Reed had stopped speaking to one another for three whole days after a huge argument over a borrowed comb. An American called Neil Armstrong had landed on the moon, which had not generated nearly such a high level of interest and excitement among them as the news that a woman who had once gone to school in Birmingham had won the Wimbledon Ladies Singles. After all you could bag a court at lunch time and practice your tennis in the hope of emulating Ann Jones, whereas the opportunities to prepare for space exploration were pretty much non-existent.

One unfortunate consequence of the moon landing was that Paula had got into a big argument with her father about what a waste of money it was sending men to the moon, when people were starving to death in places like Biafra. This had escalated to the point where Paula was sent to her room for being cheeky, which they all knew was really just a parent's way of ending any argument which they were in danger of losing.

The summer exams had been conducted in silent stuffy classrooms and Joanne, who now sported a pair of owlish glasses, achieved improvements in every subject and was also awarded the first year prize for art. Alas Becky's end of year report was littered with phrases such as *Can do better* and *A disappointing examination result*. Miss Harrison's form teacher's comment said: *Rebecca made a good start to the year but has done less well latterly. She needs to concentrate more fully on her work*. Becky's mother had signed the proffered report as required, but whether or not she actually read or understood the comments, she said nothing about it to her daughter.

Lessons had been suspended altogether on the final afternoon of term while the upper sixth put on a show they had written themselves. It included versions of popular songs with the words changed to incorporate polite jokes about the school and those members of staff deemed to have a sense of humour. After the final curtain call, Linda Whitstable, the outgoing head girl had called the members of staff who were leaving onto the stage and presented them with gifts. Mrs Rollins was among those departing. 'English will never be the same without her,' whispered Nicky.

At the end of the last day as they walked past the windows of the sixth form common room on their way down the drive, they could see members of the upper sixth, some of them still in their costumes from the show, hugging each other and crying.

'It's the *very* last day for them,' said Nicky. 'They won't ever be coming back. Do you think we'll cry when it's our turn to go?'

'I won't,' Joanne said with conviction.

Paula shook her head, not because she agreed or disagreed with Jo but because it all seemed so very, very far away.

Chapter Twenty-Two

1984

Proximity to take-aways had made them lazy in London, Jo thought. Living in a Cornish village with the nearest chippy ten miles away meant proper cooking every night and since they often did not eat until quite late, there was a tendency to leave the washing up until the following morning. They always intended to do it after supper but then Jo would remember something she wanted to show Ant in 'The Guardian', or else Ant would have an idea about the gallery and they would both get so engrossed that they forget all about the stack of pans and dishes until they were too tired to tackle them and there seemed to be no question of doing anything at all apart from falling into bed.

Washing up had therefore become a morning job and Jo was just finishing the final bits and pieces from their meal the night before when she heard the letterbox snap. The kitchen window faced a bank of shale at the rear of the cottage and therefore gave no clue about anything which might be happening elsewhere. It was far too early for the postman. She dried her hands and went into the sitting room with a sinking heart.

There were only three rooms downstairs: the small kitchen at the back, the double fronted gallery which faced onto the village street and a sitting room which formed the hub, with an open plan staircase leading up to the first floor, doors to the kitchen, the gallery and the half glazed private entrance at the side of the cottage which had a letterbox in its lower half. The sitting room was clean and bright, notwithstanding its clutter of books, half burned candles and cheerful detritus of everyday living. An armchair stood between Joanne and the outside door but as soon as she got level with it she could see the knotted plastic bag, lying where it had fallen on the mat just inside the door. The mat had been placed there after one of these offerings had split on impact, scattering dog turds across the carpet. This morning's bag had fortunately stayed intact.

She unlocked the door and stepped outside to drop the thing into the dustbin. She knew it would be useless to walk down the side of the building and see who was in the street. Vile bastards, she wouldn't give them the satisfaction of going out to look.

With a sigh she bent and picked up the milk bottle from the step. They supported the local dairy's doorstep delivery and shopped in the village store. 'What do they want from us?' she asked the room in general as she went back inside. She already knew the answer.

Darling Ant was so much braver and more determined than she was. 'We won't let them drive us out,' that's what Ant said. 'When they see that it isn't getting us down they'll lose interest and gradually we'll be accepted.'

Jo was about to put the milk bottle into the fridge when she noticed that the top had been punctured. She held the bottle out in front of her and viewed it suspiciously from all angles, eventually carrying it across to the sink in order to observe it in a better light. Here she carefully worked the foil lid off and looked into the bottle. The cream on the top had clearly been adulterated with the addition of some brown liquid. With a sob born half of anger and half of fear she upended the contents into the sink.

'What's up with the milk?'

She turned to see that Antonia had come silently downstairs. Her cloud of dark corkscrew curls was marginally more dishevelled than usual and she was wearing her red silk dressing gown with nothing underneath. Ant was not a morning person.

'It's been tampered with,' Joanne said. 'Possibly by the same person who put dog shit through the letterbox again this morning.' She glanced down at the hand holding the bottle and realised that it was shaking.

Antonia crossed the room and hugged her. Neither of them said anything for a moment or two.

'Shall we have some real coffee? I'll make it,' Ant offered.

'I think it's getting worse,' said Joanne, taking a mug from the draining board and wiping it dry while Ant opened the cupboard where they kept the coffee grinder. 'We'll have to cancel the milk delivery and get it at the shop.'

'We've still got some milk left from yesterday, haven't we?' Ant put the grinder on the work surface and headed for the fridge.

'I never thought it would be like this,' said Joanne.

'I know Cornwall's not London but I never expected it. Everything seemed to be going all right at first. Everyone was really nice.'

'I put it down to our friend the electrician,' said Ant. This was not an original line of thought. They had been having variations on this same conversation for days. 'It all started after he came to sort out the wiring and saw that there was just the one double bed. Up until then I suppose they didn't realise we used the big bedroom as a studio and slept in the other one. They had us down as partners in the business sense only.'

'But surely,' Joanne began, as if they had not covered this ground a dozen times before. 'They must have realised… I mean in this day and age..?'

'Evidently not,' said Ant, combing the fingers of one hand through her hair without any visible effect. 'It was always assumed that women lived together for economic reasons. Compared with gay men we had it easy in the toleration stakes. So much for creating a thriving business and helping the local economy,' she concluded bitterly.

'Have we just been really unlucky? Do you think it's being in a village?' Joanne asked. 'Would it be different if we had set up in one of the bigger places down here?'

'I don't know,' said Antonia.

They had sunk everything into the gallery. So far there had been little to show by way of return but it was early days yet, with the main summer season still to come. They had expected a slow start and allowed for it in their calculations. During these first few off-season months they operated to restricted opening hours, supposedly to enable them to paint and explore before the tourists arrived in force. The trouble was that lately Joanne found she could not paint – not properly – because all the time she was trying to work upstairs, her mind was straying to the horrid possibilities which might be awaiting her on the doormat when she came back down again. You couldn't hear the letterbox when you were up in the studio.

'Let's go out for the day,' said Ant abruptly. 'Let's do lunch somewhere nice – the piggy bank will stand it – then drive up to the north coast.'

Their original plans were thwarted because as so often happened, the weather was different on the other side of the peninsula. Grey, forbidding fog hung across the lanes and drove them back to seek some sunshine in Mevagissey, where the streets and harbour were noisy with seagulls but virtually deserted of people. They got out their sketch books but Jo only messed around and although Ant covered several pages with roof tops and chimneys none of it pleased her. 'Too chocolate boxey for words,' she said, tossing her work bag onto the back seat of the car in disgust.

The drive home seemed to refresh their spirits. Viewed from within the heated car the brilliant blue sky could have fooled anyone into thinking that it was already high summer. Only bare branches and banks golden with daffs spoiled the illusion. Beethoven poured from the speakers daring them to be miserable. Joanne's heart rose. I must not allow these small minded bigots to get at me, she thought. Ant's right. We mustn't let prejudice drive us away. When the car reached the edge of the village she adopted a broad grin, just in case any of their tormentors was watching for signs of distress or capitulation.

As Ant steered the car into the small cobbled

parking area at the side of their cottage they both let out simultaneous cries, neither long nor loud, but enough to send a shockwave of distress pummelling its way around the car. Across the lower half of the cottage door, which Joanne had repainted white during the improvements they had undertaken on moving in, someone had painted three words in bright red gloss. In trying to make a joke of it later, Antonia commented that the worst offence in her opinion was the perpetrator's inability to render each of the letters the same size, space them adequately or even apply the paint without numerous drips and runs. Whoever had painted the words *FILTHY LEZZIES OUT*, she said, it was certainly not an artist.

It took several coats and the best part of a day to completely obscure the graffiti on the cottage door, but making it vanish beneath the smooth white gloss did not stop Jo from feeling that it was still there. It was a bit like hiding something under the bed. The fact that you couldn't see it didn't prevent your knowing that it was still lurking out of sight whenever you went into the room. In her darker moments she wondered just how far these people might go. 'People' she called them, these stealthy purveyors of hatred. People in the plural and yet maybe there weren't so many of them. Maybe hardly any at all. But it only took one extremist, one obsessive madman, who thought everyone should conform to his own sexual proclivities, or one old woman perhaps... her mind a closed book of religious fundamentalism. One person to post a lighted, petrol soaked rag through their letter box... that was all it would take.

Ant did not dismiss such fears as far fetched. She only

said it had not reached that level yet and probably never would, to which Jo responded grimly: 'Once would be enough.'

Jo took to covertly checking that the smoke alarm was working on an almost daily basis. They had discussed the possibility of notifying the police but only in a desultory sort of way. The police weren't exactly noted for their toleration of alternative sexual orientations. Besides which if the police started making enquiries in the village, that would very likely stir moderate opinion (assuming there was some) against them, thereby fostering even more local resentment. It might even leak into the local press, generating all the wrong sort of publicity for the gallery and perhaps attracting the interest of other potential persecutors for miles around.

'We have to meet prejudice and fight it,' said Ant.

They had just finished eating a rather good risotto and were sitting together on the sofa, sipping mugs of coffee. The washing up was still awaiting attention alongside the kitchen sink, surrounded by an invisible cloud of good intentions.

'Why?' asked Jo. 'Why do we have to fight?'

'Because we can't just sit back and let the bullies win,' said Antonia. 'If no one had ever stood up for what they believed in women still wouldn't have the vote. The toleration we get in society has been won for us by others who've gone before.'

Joanne acknowledged this speech with a reluctant gesture of her coffee mug.

'Women like us must have lived around here before,' Ant went on. 'But they would have had to hide behind a facade.

Hidden their true feelings and maybe lived a completely different life to the one they really wanted. We're like...' she hesitated for a word, '...like pioneers. Ambassadors for a cause.' She gave a short laugh and Joanne joined in.

There was a short silence. When Joanne finally broke it all the laughter had gone from her voice. 'I'm not like you,' she said. 'You almost relish a fight. You want to stand up for your rights and go on a crusade and break down barriers for the people who're going to come after. I don't want to live my life like that, Ant. I just want to be somewhere where I'm accepted. A place where walking down the street isn't an act of defiance. I'm not...' she grinned. 'I'm not some sort of missionary sister of the worldwide crusade for lesbians and gays. Maybe you're right and I do owe someone something for any acceptance that comes my way, but you have to remember that I've been fighting all my life... and now I'm tired of it.' Her eyes met her partner's in mute appeal. 'Your experiences were very different to mine. You grew up in a family where no one ever went short of anything and went to a boarding school where everyone came from the same sort of background. Some of the girls *felt* the way you did. It was acknowledged. There were people who understood. I went to a grammar school with posh ideas about itself, where I always felt out of place. I couldn't begin to tell even my best friends the way I felt about things. They were great girls and I loved them to pieces but as far as I knew there *were* no other girls like me – not at school – maybe not anywhere in the world. I used to feel that I had to pretend to fancy boys just to be normal. Otherwise I thought they would think I was a freak.'

Ant reached out a comforting hand.

‘I had to fight every step of the way,’ Joanne went on, her voice cracking unexpectedly. ‘I fought to be allowed to stay on at school, let alone to go to university. Then I had to fight at work against people called Penelope and Charles, who took one earful of my Brummie accent and automatically dismissed me as a moron. I’m really tired of fighting. Maybe you’ll think I’m a coward and a traitor to the cause and that I should just carry on fighting my whole life… but I don’t want to do it. Please don’t ask me to.’

Antonia had to brush away her own tears before replying. ‘We’ll see an agent and put the place on the market as soon as we can.’

Chapter Twenty-Three

1969-70

The sound of raised voices seeping up through the bedroom floor always made something inside Jo's stomach twist. Even tonight when the crescendos culminated in hearty laughter, she could not completely shake off the automatic nervous reaction. She knew only too well the ease with which merriment could topple over into something very different, though with the house full of visitors everything would probably be all right tonight. There had been a tense moment earlier when some sort of misunderstanding occurred over the cruet, but it had been defused by the timely arrival of the first guests, which had immediately transformed her father into affability itself, with all thoughts of blocked pepper pots completely expunged from his mind.

Babysitters were pretty much impossible to find on New Year's Eve, so half a dozen children had arrived with their parents and since children were surplus to requirements downstairs, where they might get in the way of the mysterious world of grown-up celebrations, these children had all been despatched upstairs to be entertained by Joanne.

'Our Joanne's very good with children,' she'd overheard her mother telling a woman she knew as Auntie Maureen. 'She'll keep them all quiet no trouble at all.'

During the initial stages of the evening the children had not in fact been particularly quiet while they played a series of games invented by Joanne, the most popular of which involved picking one of Brian's farm yard animals out of a box with your eyes closed, then having to be that animal for the next five minutes, which meant that you could only communicate using the appropriate sounds. The bedroom resounded with quacks and moos and clucks, but fortunately there was enough noise coming from the festivities down below to entirely blot out these noises from above.

It was the second year that the task of New Year's Eve Children's Entertainment Officer had fallen to Joanne. Previously it had always been Sonia's role, but it had been handed on automatically when Sonia left, just like the green winter coat and the tennis racket and the role of chief scapegoat when anything went wrong. It was pretty exhausting looking after a bunch of kids, most of whom were over-excited at being up late in unfamiliar surroundings, but eventually even the liveliest of them had dozed off, some curled up on Brian's bed and some on hers, all of them covered by a muddle of blankets and eiderdowns. By then the only bedding not trapped under or draped over a sleeping child was a grey candlewick bedspread which had been bundled up in a corner during an earlier game, so Joanne retrieved it and draped it around herself, sitting on the floor with her back to the bedroom wall, where she could keep all her sleeping charges in view. She had turned out the bedroom light, but the cotton curtains were no match for the street lamp outside and Jo could clearly see the little alarm clock with its green tipped hands which told her that it was only ten minutes to twelve. Another ten minutes and it would be 1970. It was quite exciting really. Every date she had ever written before was 1960 something. The sixties were almost over and the seventies were about to begin. She would become a teenager in 1970. In fact she would be a teenager for almost the whole of the seventies, which according to everything one read in magazines was the swingingest, grooviest thing in the world to be. Or just plain frabjous as Becka might say.

Of course her parents couldn't be expected to understand how close she was to being a grown-up. She thought about Sonia's copy of 'Je T'Aime' which was hidden in the bottom of her chest of drawers. Since the record was banned by the B.B.C. and therefore could not be played on 'Top of the Pops', the only way to hear it had been to borrow it from Sonia. Needless to say she could hardly listen to it on the radiogram in the living room, where there was always someone about, so she had taken it to Paula's house instead. Paula had recently acquired her parents' cast off record player, which still worked reasonably well and was built into such a stout carrying box that it doubled as a very useful extra seat when not being used to play records. The four of them had listened very carefully to the vocals of 'Je T'Aime' several times, turning it up as loudly as they dared to do without attracting the attention of Paula's mother.

'I don't see why it's banned,' Jo had said. 'It's not as if you can understand what they're saying.'

'If we'd done more French we might understand it,' said Nicky. 'If it's really dirty though, I don't suppose it's the sort of words we'd learn until sixth form.'

'It said in the paper *sexual overtones*,' said Becky. 'Do you think that means they were doing it when they were making the record?'

'What!' Paula squealed in shock and recoiled from the record that she had been about to remove from the turntable, while Nicky burst out giggling.

'Not really doing it,' suggested Paula. 'But maybe pretending to? You know… when she starts breathing all funny and sings in that really high voice.'

There was a short silence while they considered this possibility. The strange and mysterious world of sex seemed to be all around them. Records full of heavy breathing, X certificate films, XX films at The Jacey. That Adults Only shop with blacked out windows on the Stratford Road, weekly scandals in the 'News of the World' and 'The Sunday People'. All of it a closed book, happening behind doors which were barred to them or as in this particular case happening in a foreign language. It was very difficult to know where reliable information on the subject was to be had. Certainly not from the shamefaced session last term in the school hall, when a woman introduced as a 'special visitor' had shown them a model of a baby in a half assembled, rigid plastic womb, a colour diagram of some tadpoles swimming along a river and another one of a tadpole butting at a large football, but somehow never quite managing to explain how all these things came together to make a baby. Her cheerily pink cheeked invitation for anyone to ask questions ('Feel free to ask anything you want,') had elicited nothing more than some nervous shuffling and several people affecting great interest in their finger nails. Eventually Colleen Bell had bravely enquired whether there was any truth in the rumour that wearing tight elastic garters to hold up your school socks caused varicose veins. For non-garter wearers the session had produced no new information at all.

Nicky had summed up the 'Je T'Aime' question. 'I don't think it's a very good record. It's too slow and you can't understand what they're on about. I think it got to number one because buying it was the only way people could get to hear it and find out what all the fuss was about.'

Jo's thoughts were recalled to the present by the sound of the grown-ups' voices mounting to another crescendo. There was a lot of shouting and laughter and then from the street outside a cry of: 'Happy New Year'. The little clock was two minutes slow and thought it was still last year, which Joanne reasoned it easily could be up here in the bedroom where 1970 didn't feel any different to 1969.

The party began to break up soon afterwards. Mothers with flushed faces appeared at the bedroom door, looking to collect half waking children for the journey home. Julie, the child who belonged to Auntie Maureen, started to whimper because she couldn't find her doll but Joanne swiftly disentangled herself from her bedspread and recovered it from where it had fallen on the floor.

'Thank you, love,' said Auntie Maureen. She regarded the little girl standing before her through a haze induced by rather too many port and lemons. My goodness, but she's a plain little thing, she thought, taking in the ginger hair which straggled unevenly onto the girl's shoulders, the slightly pointed face covered in freckles and the bony white arms and legs which poked awkwardly from a garish pink and yellow striped nylon nightshirt (bought for Jo by her mother in a moment of madness at a Pippa Dee party). Thinking to say something kind, Auntie Maureen said, 'You've done really well looking after all this lot tonight. You'll make a smashing little wife and mother.'

Joanne attempted a smile before diving back under her bedspread, taut with the horror of it. Whatever happened she was determined never to be that.

*

Paula awoke early to the new decade. The first thing she saw was the Robert Redford poster facing her from the opposite wall. The poster had cost almost a whole week's pocket money but sitting up in bed with her chin on her knees, Paula felt that it was worth it. She had been in love with Robert Redford for three weeks now and having him on her bedroom wall was almost as good as having him in her bedroom in person. Actually, she thought it was probably better, because if he had really been there – in his guise as The Sundance Kid since she knew of him in no other – she wouldn't really have known what to say to him and obviously he would have found her pretty dull, got bored and left, whereas stuck on a poster he couldn't go anywhere. He had to stay in the bedroom with her whether he liked it or not.

They had managed to see 'Butch Cassidy and the

Sundance Kid' at The Kingsway, because Jo's sister Sonia had gone with them. Sometimes you could persuade strangers on their way into the cinema to pretend to be with you, so that the cashier would let you in to see an A certificate film, but having Sonia along had guaranteed them entry. They were unanimously of the opinion that it was the best film they had ever seen and phrases from it had been absorbed into their lexicon. 'Just keep thinking Butch, that's what you're good at,' they would say when congratulating each other on a bright idea. Even the theme song, although suspiciously akin to the sort of song their parents might like, had become part of the repertoire they sang in their corner of the form room while they were waiting for registration.

Paula's newly acquired poster of Robert Redford was so big that it dwarfed all the pictures of pop stars which she had cut out of her Jackie magazines. Her mother kept moaning about the holes that the drawing pins made in the wallpaper but then she was always moaning about something. Did her mother expect her to spend the next six years in a room decorated with a couple of framed Mabel Lucy Atwell prints and that sewn felt thing she had done in top juniors? Honestly!

Chapter Twenty-Four

1970

Claiming free school dinners was almost unknown at Eleanor Vaux, not because no one qualified, but because most girls would sooner die than be issued the green tickets printed with a large black F, which denoted that no money had changed hands in order to obtain them. At many schools the problem was discreetly alleviated by pupils bringing a packed lunch from home, but Miss Forster had never been in favour of such a scheme. At Eleanor Vaux girls either paid for a school lunch (which to her irritation they insisted on calling 'dinner') or produced a letter from their parents which confirmed that they would be going home for lunch (an option which was completely out of the question for the vast majority of pupils as they lived a bus ride away).

Miss Forster opposed sandwich lunches on a number of grounds. Firstly the prospect of girls bringing foodstuffs into school suggested to her the increased possibility of vermin. (The contradiction of allowing cookery ingredients onto the premises never crossed her mind.)

Secondly she considered the spectacle of girls eating sandwiches out of bread wrappers to be sloppy and not at all in keeping with the orderly queuing, proper cutlery and civilising presence of cruets and water jugs which prevailed in the dining hall. Finally she was convinced that the staple Eleanor Vaux fare of overcooked vegetables and soggy puddings was far more nutritious than the sort of rubbish girls might bring from home. However in the face of an unprecedented level of parental protest, Miss Forster for once decided to give way. A letter went home with every pupil, announcing that in future sandwich lunches could be brought from home, always providing that certain conditions were met.

Firstly a girl's parents had to write a letter to confirm that their daughter had permission to bring a sandwich lunch. Secondly all lunches must be transported to school in a rodent proof container and kept in the pupil's desk until lunch time. Thirdly any pupil discovered consuming part of her lunch before the appointed time would have the privilege of bringing a sandwich lunch withdrawn. Finally the girls having a sandwich lunch were to assemble in the covered cloister at the commencement of the lunch hour, where they would wait until they were conducted into the dining hall, where ... *space will be allocated for them to consume their lunch without causing disruption to the normal use of the dining room.*

Sensing the displeasure in every line and knowing that Miss Forster's displeasure was not something to be trifled with, a number of girls who had previously hailed sandwiches as a welcome escape from stringy lamb and Lancashire hot pot of dubious provenance, now decided to stick with school dinners after all.

Becky had easily persuaded her mother of the advantages, not least because she had promised to cut her own sandwiches every morning, but in spite of Paula's pleading Mrs Morrison saw things Miss Forster's way. A healthy cooked meal in the middle of the day was an essential part of the educational process so far as she was concerned and Mr Morrison agreed wholeheartedly. Joanne's mother opposed sandwiches on different grounds. 'I have enough to do in the mornings, getting our Brian out to school and they'll be stale if I make them up the night before. You stick with school dinners.' Meanwhile Mrs Christie agreed to give it a try, so on the day the new arrangements began there was a two way split with Becky and Nick heading for the sandwich line while Paula and Jo joined the dinner queue.

The covered cloister was an architectural oddity left over from the early days of the school. Originally built as a covered walkway which linked two classrooms on either side of a small quad, the construction of a new dining room in the nineteen fifties had rendered it redundant overnight – a corridor leading nowhere and open to the elements on one side. A pair of double doors led into the cloister from the adjacent dining room but these were not normally used because the area beyond the cloister had become the teachers' car park and was therefore out of bounds except in the event of an emergency evacuation.

The open side of the cloister faced north which made it a chilly place to linger even on a warm spring day and the girls congregating there on the first day of the new sandwich system were completely cut off from the dinner queue on the south side of the dining hall as they stood clutching their rodent proof lunch boxes (with here and there a less than rodent proof Nimble bag) watching through the dining room windows while the rest of the school went about their normal lunchtime routine.

Miss Forster's letter about bringing sandwiches had also mentioned *financial circumstances* and the intimation that anyone taking up the sandwich option would be deemed to have done so because they could not afford to meet the increased price of a school lunch, had been felt almost as keenly by many parents as the potential shame in applying for free dinners, all of which had discouraged take-up so that by the first day it was permitted to bring a sandwich lunch, fewer than forty girls gathered to wait in the covered cloister. Here they stood watching through the windows as lines of diners entered the hall, consumed their meals and left again, mostly oblivious to the hungry spectators outside. As time passed there was mounting speculation among the group that they might have been forgotten. The normal unspoken barriers between year groups broke down as a fourth year reassured a lonely first year that it was probably just a misunderstanding because it was the first day of the new system.

When the dining hall was emptying out a dinner lady carefully cleared the cruets and water jugs from a row of five tables alongside the windows before finally opening the doors to admit them. A third former who spotted some friends still finishing their pudding and attempted to join them was fetched back to sit in the appointed area. The instructions were absolutely clear. There was to be no fraternisation with other, more deserving users of the dining room. Even the use of school water jugs and cruets was out of the question. Any girl requiring a glass of water was to fetch it herself from the tap near the dirty tray hatch.

The same dinner lady then appeared with a broom and informed the occupants of the table nearest to the doors that when the whole group had finished eating, someone must stay behind and sweep around the tables where the sandwiches had been consumed. The occupants of the chosen table looked at each other. Time was ticking by and this was undoubtedly going to make someone late for afternoon lessons.

'It's not fair,' said the third year who had initially tried to break away. 'Other people were sitting here before us. We haven't made any mess at all. I didn't drop this chip,' she added, nudging at the item in question with the side of her shoe.

'People having school dinners aren't told to sweep up.' Another third year joined in.

'It's just spite,' said Charlie Young from IIC.

'I'll do it today,' said the fourth year who had previously been kind to one of the first years in the cloister. 'I suppose we'll have to take turns if it's got to be done every day.'

By the end of the first week it had become obvious that anyone who intended to stick with sandwich lunches was destined to forfeit the usual lunchtime gossip with their friends because 'sandwich girls' had to be lined up in the covered cloister until tables became available.

Gail Foster tried to buck the system by spending the first half of one lunch break on the school playing field with her friends, but in anticipation of this sort of initiative the dinner ladies started to take impromptu head counts to make sure all the 'sandwich girls' were where they should be, in a state of constant readiness to enter the dining room just in case tables mysteriously became available, although of course they never did until the very end of the lunch period. Any girl identified as missing from the cloister was reported to their form teachers who issued the absentee with a detention at afternoon registration on the same day. At the end of the second week Gail's parents wrote a letter saying that they had had a change of heart and Gail went back to purchasing dinner tickets.

Miss Forster noted the dwindling numbers in the covered cloister with satisfaction. She had been right to resist the introduction of something which was only wanted by a tiny minority. Eleanor Vaux had not become the school it undoubtedly was by pandering to the whims of tiny minorities.

Nicola and Becky stuck with the sandwich line into a third week which meant that on the day Joanne was scheduled to attend an optician's appointment Paula found herself alone at lunch time: a situation which she dreaded. Someone whose usual friends were absent could not just assume that she would be welcome to tag along with anyone else, so when Becka and Nicky departed for the covered cloister Paula wandered miserably along the lower drive hoping to meet Jo on her way back from the optician, because she certainly didn't want to go into dinner on her own if there was any chance at all of Jo going in with her. Half way along the lower drive she noticed her classmates, Colleen Bell and Penny Lynch, lurking near the bushes by the gates. Their body language suggested a secretive dimension to their activities and guessing that they wouldn't welcome her company, Paula turned and headed back towards the school buildings. She decided to make for the library which was one of the few indoor refuges legitimately available for the studious or the lonely to spend their lunch hour and provided a respite from wandering around outside, where she would continually pass groups of other girls who regarded her with pity or contempt, marked down as a person with whom no one else cared to associate.

Paula did not get as far as the library because she encountered their form mistress, Mrs James, outside Room 20.

'Ah… Paula. Would you do an errand for me please? I want Miss Forster to have this straight away.' So saying, Mrs James held out a manilla folder which Paula accepted as if she thought it might bite her.

Paula carried the file along the deserted corridor, reflecting that since Miss Forster's room was only a matter of yards away Mrs James could easily have taken the file herself and probably would have done, if a pupil hadn't happened to appear at just the right moment to save her the trouble. Paula had passed Miss Forster's office door many times but she never seen inside. She rapped nervously on one of the panels.

'Come in.' The headmistress's clear, ringing voice seemed to be a long way off.

Quaking with nerves, Paula turned the round brass door knob and opened the door onto Miss Forster's personal sanctuary. She had not realised that the room would be so big, extending from the corridor to the front of the building, the full width of a classroom. Miss Forster was sitting behind her desk, which stood at the furthest end of the room alongside the window. It was the biggest desk Paula had ever seen: the size of a double bed at least. Even more astonishingly the floor was carpeted and together with the arm chairs, glass fronted book cases, even a potted palm and occasional tables, this gave the impression of having stepped completely outside of school and into someone's sitting room. Confronted by the unexpected spectacle of Miss Forster in her private domain Paula hovered speechless in the doorway.

'Come in,' Miss Forster repeated, not unkindly. 'What can I do for you? Did you want to see me about something?'

The idea that any pupil might casually tap on the door and initiate a meeting between herself and Miss Forster had never occurred to Paula and it was as much as she could do to stumble across the room holding out the folder. Miss Forster held her hand out to receive it and Paula was forced to go alongside the gargantuan desk so that the headmistress could reach it.

'Mrs James sent me to give you this,' Paula managed to stammer out.

'Thank you. Is there a message to go back?'

Paula hesitated. Mrs James had not said there was but there might be. You were so often just expected to know these things. 'Mrs James didn't say,' she said, not daring to look straight at Miss Forster, focussing instead on the pattern of ivy leaves woven into the carpet. She had never been so close to Miss Forster before and noticed that she gave off a distinctive smell of peppermints and lavender.

'Then we must assume that there isn't,' said Miss Forster, a touch more briskly.

Paula lingered, unsure whether or not this could be taken as an indication to leave.

'Well go along then,' said the head a shade irritably. 'Unless there's something else?'

'No miss.' Paula made hurriedly for the door, where in her haste to effect an escape she fumbled hopelessly with the door knob for several seconds before finally managing to secure her release into the corridor. As she emerged from Miss Forster's room she almost walked into a pair of her classmates, Helen Staveley and Naomi Wiseman, who were cutting along the top corridor to get to choir practice.

'Joanne's looking for you,' Helen said. 'We saw her on her way to the dinner queue.'

'Thanks,' said Paula. Frabjous. That meant Jo was back from her appointment and she wouldn't have to go in to dinner on her own after all.

*

The moment Mrs James walked into registration that afternoon everyone knew that something was up. The normal practice was for the form captains to scan around the room, checking who was and was not present and marking the register accordingly, while the rest of the form sat chatting or singing or putting together the books they needed for afternoon lessons. Mrs James usually appeared just in time to collect the completed register and query any absentees before the first bell went to signal that lessons were imminent, so her unexpected arrival immediately saw people scrambling off their desktops, cease playing with the window cords or flicking bus tickets at their neighbours and for the general hubbub to diminish into silence as people slid into their seats. As Mrs James began to call the register: 'Abbott, Addison, Bell, Christie…' her tone provided abundant confirmation that she was on the rampage about something.

Mrs James was a short fat woman, who never attempted the undignified climb into the high chair belonging to the teacher's desk unless she intended to stay there for a sufficient length of time to make the effort worthwhile. She stood alongside the desk to call the register and then addressed the class. 'You all know the rules about staying on school premises at lunchtime.' Her eyes roved across their faces as she spoke. 'It has been brought to my attention that two girls from this form left school premises today without permission. I am offering those girls the opportunity to own up and give me an explanation.'

Joanne began to fumble for the pass she had been issued which allowed her to keep her optician's appointment. Red faced in spite of the pass in her possession, she raised her hand.

'Don't be silly Joanne,' Mrs James barked. 'Don't you listen at all? I said *without* permission. You had a letter from home and a pass.' She looked impatiently from face to face while Joanne, redder than ever, brought her hand down to rest on her desk. No one else moved.

'Very well,' said Mrs James, glaring around as if she suspected that the entire form might be in on the conspiracy. 'Colleen Bell and Penny Lynch, come with me to Miss Forster.'

A suppressed gasp ran around the room. Penny and Colleen stood up slowly and followed Mrs James to the form room door. The door had scarcely closed behind them before an excited babble of talk broke out.

'Maybe it's a case of mistaken identity, ' Nicky pondered.

'I don't think it is a mistake,' said Paula. 'I saw them down by the lower gates when they must have been sneaking out.'

'It *is* true,' Nicky turned to Adele, who she had just heard indulging in speculation similar to her own. 'Paula saw them going out of school.'

This tit bit of news swept across the form room like a prairie fire. Going off school premises without permission was serious. Who knew what might happen next? Penny and Colleen reappeared part way through history and at the end of the lesson the full horror of their punishment was revealed. Miss Forster was writing to both sets of parents and the girls themselves were to forfeit all remaining lunch hours until the end of term. Lunchtime detention placed them at the beck and call of Miss Harkness, the deputy head. It was considered much worse than normal Tuesday evening detentions in which detainees did work set by the member of staff who had placed them there, in the relative comfort of a desk in Room 12. For lunchtime detentions Miss Harkness was in the habit of issuing sandpaper with which to smooth specified chair legs, buckets to fill with stones collected from the flower beds along the drive, or on at least one memorable occasion, toothbrushes with which to clean the front entrance steps. All tasks had to be completed in silence and to her complete satisfaction: otherwise they had to be repeated the following day.

It seemed a high price to pay for a visit to the local shops to purchase Lemon Fizz Cubes.

Paula realised that people were talking about her

at registration next morning. She overheard her name whispered and was aware of sidelong glances. There was a palpable sense of tension in the form room. No one was singing or playing around near the blackboard. Not even Ronnie and Adele were laughing. Paula didn't know exactly what was going on but she guessed that it was all somehow connected with Colleen and Penny getting into trouble the day before.

'What's going on?' she asked Nicky, but Nicky was putting in some last minute revision for a science test and said she didn't know. Jo and Becky had gone to retrieve Becka's text book which had somehow got left in the cloakroom. By the time they got back everyone was lining up for assembly.

It was double science after assembly. Glancing to her right, Paula could see that Becky was getting in a mess with the test on valences. She guessed that Becky wouldn't have learnt the work properly because she was so erratic about homework lately. She had already been put into detention twice this term for not giving in work on time and her marks made it obvious that she was skimping. Becky pretended not to care when test marks were read out, but Paula could tell that deep down she did. They had all asked Becky what was wrong but she just shrugged and changed the subject.

Science had been another source of disappointment for Paula. So far as she could remember they had never done any science at primary school so the prospect of doing science at senior school had represented something new and exciting. At the beginning of first year she had pictured herself in the laboratories, a model Evie enveloped in a blue science overall, adding drops of acid to a test tube and watching the contents boil and send out clouds of purple smoke. Alas there had been very little opportunity to do experiments and absolutely no purple smoke. Mostly it was just listening to Mrs Venables and copying the diagrams she drew on the blackboard. The blackboards in the labs were different to the rigid ones built into the ordinary form room walls. The lab blackboards were continuous loops mounted in tall wooden frames, so when Mrs Venables ran out of space she just pushed the board up or pulled it down to get a clean section. The nearest they had ever come to seeing purple smoke was the time when Mrs Venables had pulled the board down to reveal a rude drawing, concealed there earlier by some mischievous fourth formers.

After science it was history with Miss Pentland with the hundred years war in full swing and by morning break Paula had half forgotten the funny looks and whispers during registration. She was strolling along the back terrace above the hockey pitches with the others, when they saw a large group of their form mates round the corner of the building. Debbie Reed was there and Gail Foster and also Alex and Norma who didn't usually hang around with that group. All told, the grim faced deputation included almost half of IIJ.

'What's up with them?' asked Nicky.

The two groups stopped walking and stood face to face.

Gail, who appeared to be the self appointed leader, addressed Paula. 'Why did you tell on Colleen and Penny?' she demanded.

'I didn't,' said Paula, turning scarlet in the face of such an unfair accusation.

'Yes you did. Everyone knows it was you.'

'I didn't,' repeated Paula. 'It wasn't me.'

'You admitted it. You told everyone that you'd seen them go out of school,' said Norma.

'Yes but…'

'Helen and Naomi saw you coming out of Miss Forster's room,' Alex said in a triumphant voice.

'Don't be stupid,' Nicky broke in. 'What would Paula have been doing in Miss Forster's room?'

Paula tried to get a word in but at this Gail angrily turned on Nicky and asked if she was suggesting that Helen and Naomi were liars.

'We have all the evidence we need,' said Alex. 'We have decided that you are a worthless snake in the grass and no one is speaking to you.'

'And if you stay friends with *her*,' Gail directed her words at Becky, Jo and Nicky while simultaneously jerking her head in Paula's direction, 'We won't speak to you either.'

'Well that'll be no loss,' Joanne shouted after them as the other group began to move away.

Paula could feel herself shaking with anger and misery. She must not cry. Whatever happened, she must not cry.

'They've all gone mad,' said Becky.

'Why on earth did Helen and Naomi say they'd seen you coming out of Miss Forster's room?' asked Jo.

'Because they did,' said Paula. 'But I hadn't gone in there to tell on Colleen and Penny. I'd been on a message for Mrs James.'

'You never told us that,' said Becky.

It was not an accusation but in her highly charged state Paula took it as one. 'Now even you don't trust me,' she blurted out. Full of self righteous indignation she turned on her heel and marched off in the direction of their form room. She had expected the others to come straight after her and say that they were sorry but they didn't. She stomped back to her desk in the furthest corner of the form room, running the gauntlet of staring faces and hostile murmurings on the way. When the others got back to the classroom she didn't look at them, thrusting her books for English and geography into her bag with such force that some pages caught on the zip of her pencil case and tore at the edges.

In English Mrs Rollins's replacement, Mrs Heslop, was dealing with adverbs. Paula concentrated hard, not looking at anyone except Mrs Heslop. She loitered at the end of the lesson, hoping that the others would automatically fall into step with her but they continued ignoring her as pointedly as the rest of the form. A line had been crossed and no one was going to back down. They think I did it too, Paula thought miserably.

All she could think about during geography was the approaching lunch hour. Mr Tresham gave out blank maps of Australia to be labelled for homework and in an unthinking moment she folded hers into four and put it into her pencil case. Oh God, now it would be all creased up before she even started *and* it had got a green mark across it where it had brushed against that leaky felt tip. She fished it out and tried to flatten it between the pages of her Atlas.

Her hopes that Joanne would be forced to make peace in order to avoid spending the lunch hour alone were dashed when she overheard Annette Maudsley asking Jo whether she would like to go into dinner with herself and Kay. Paula decided to get dinner over as quickly as possible before hiding in the library. She shuffled up the dinner queue trying not to look at anyone and sat down at a table where a bunch of first years were eating. You didn't have to ask fuzzers if it was O.K. to sit with them. Not that you would normally choose to sit with them because their childish chattering was beneath contempt, but at least there was no risk of them saying that they were saving the place for someone else and therefore that you couldn't sit there. Even so it was humiliating. She felt as if the entire school was staring at her and every mouthful of cheese flan, mashed potatoes and mixed veg tasted like cardboard. Even her favourite chocolate concrete turned to dust in her mouth.

While she pretended to be reading in the library, Paula formulated a plan to confront Gail at afternoon registration and insist on getting a fair hearing, but when she returned to the classroom and walked over to Gail's desk, the other girl merely turned her back, remarking to the room at large that there seemed to be a funny smell in the vicinity and though Paula stood there for a moment or two, she couldn't pluck up the courage to say anything and eventually returned to her desk to collect her books for afternoon lessons, while trying to bite back tears.

By the end of school she was desperate. How could her friends believe her capable of such a terrible thing? She had to follow Gail and Debbie's coterie down the drive and they obviously knew she was there, because they kept on talking loudly about what a horrible time Colleen and Penny had been subjected to at lunchtime and how none of it would have happened if it hadn't been for a *certain person*.

That evening Paula kept mostly to her bedroom. She made a mess of her map by labelling Adelaide and

Melbourne the wrong way round in ink, so that she had to cross them out and write the names in again. The scale of the map didn't allow for that sort of amendment and with Sydney and Canberra squashed down in the bottom right hand corner as well, Melbourne ended up looking as if it was in the sea. Bother the Australians. Why did they have to put so many cities all in one bit of their country when there were acres of space available in the top left?

The thought of going to school the next day made her feel sick. She tried to lose herself in her books, turning for comfort to Mallory Towers (books which she would never publicly admit to reading now that she was thirteen). It was not a happy choice. Even there the pupils seemed to be ganging up unkindly on one another. She lay awake until long after she had heard her parents come up to bed, taking small comfort in the thought that if she was suddenly struck down by some fatal mystery illness and died in her sleep they would all be very sorry for the way they had treated her.

Chapter Twenty-Five

1984

Nicky had grown up in a street full of houses inhabited by mums and dads and children. She had gone straight from her parents' home to marriage with Mark. She had never envisaged the possibility of living on her own. Everything had seemed safe and certain back then. It was always taken as read that she would get married. Even with her marriage over she had returned to her childhood home and then lodged with Becky. The thought of one day having to live on her own, quite aside from being financially untenable, was unappealing on a variety of other levels too. Since leaving Mark thoughts about the future gnawed at her, creeping up when she wasn't looking and refusing to go away

One of the differences between herself and Becky, she thought, was the way Becky was so self sufficient. Becka had moved into her own bedsit the moment she could afford to, gone from a bedsit to a flat and now she was buying her own house. Living alone seemed an entirely natural state for Becky. But I'm not like that, Nicky thought. Perhaps being an only child with her mother out at work all day, Becka had got used to being on her own, whereas in the Christie household there had always been someone around. Getting her own door key at the age of sixteen had been a mere formality because the kitchen door was hardly ever locked: even if Mum and Dad were out one or other of her brothers had invariably been at home. Becka didn't notice silence but it preyed on Nicky, who had been used to the Christies chattering their way through family life against a constant background of the radio and television: only being shushed into silence for the early evening news and the Saturday football results, when their father checked his coupon in the vain hope of riches beyond their wildest dreams. She had always filled their apartment in Pittsburgh with background noise, because silence had a scary sound all of its own. Now that she lived with Becky, she'd had to curb her instinctive tendency to blot out the silence by singing, humming, or turning on the radio, because she did not want to wear out her welcome by annoying her friend.

It was not noise however, which risked coming between them. She was well aware of the fact that Becky did not approve of her relationship with Clive. Not that it was anything to do with Becky. She was an adult and could see whoever she pleased... but it made things awkward.

She marked the length of her relationship with Clive by the changes in his garden. The snowdrops were long past, the daffodils had come and gone and now a carpet of bluebells hovered against the shady bank which rose beyond the bed where a salmon pink azalea was preparing to do its best.

Clive had a man come to do the garden and a cleaning

lady to take care of the house. His car was taken away for washing and valeting once a week. If something in the house went wrong he got on the phone to have someone come and fix it. At weekends he watched football from the comfort of an executive box at Villa Park. (Nicky – who didn't understand football – did not accompany him.) When he took her out to dinner it was always to an expensive restaurant, conveyed there in the comfort of a mini-cab from the up market firm he used. When he ordered wine the bottle price was in double figures. Sometimes he ordered champagne.

Mostly however he preferred to stay at home. He had an account with a newly opened video club who delivered the films he ordered over the phone. His state of the art sound system was capable of piping music into every room in the house. (Nicky privately thought it something of a misfortune that he was so addicted to Elvis Presley and The Shadows.) Since watching '10', he had joined Bo Derek in the opinion that 'Bolero' was good music to screw to. He was also a fan of 'Je T'Aime' and occasionally put it on repeat play when they adjourned, as they always did, to the four poster for what Clive sometimes called 'a little action'.

This side of their relationship had been a revelation to Nicky. After the bruising rejection of Mark's adultery she was enraptured to find herself the object of a handsome man's attentions. Clive not only fostered a pleasing sense of her own desirability but also a feeling that she was engaged in an advanced level of sexual relationship, in which they explored what was for her previously unknown territory and if she occasionally experienced doubts about the direction they were heading in, Clive's powers of persuasion soon overcame them. His inventiveness sometimes unnerved her but invariably aroused her as well.

Nothing embarrassed Clive and she knew that he would scorn her if she proved too timid to try new things. At his suggestion they had obtained a gymslip for her and a master's gown and 'Whacko' style cane for him. The results had been initially ecstatic, though her backside had tingled a bit afterwards and the mere recollection of these activities had made her blush like fury at work next day.

She spent a good many of her working hours wishing that she was with Clive. When she sat at her computer terminal, inputting invoice after dreary invoice, surrounded by colourless people the highlight of whose lives appeared to be the events of the previous night's 'Coronation Street', she revelled in the knowledge of her exciting secret life with Clive. He was like a brilliant flash of sunlight in an otherwise dull existence.

He made no secret of his opinion that her job was nothing more than an irritating distraction. 'Give it up,' he'd said on more than one occasion. 'Give it up. Come and live with me.'

The first few times he'd said it she'd assumed that he was joking, but eventually she had asked him if he was serious.

'Of course I am,' he said. 'I want you here with me all the time.'

The discussion had progressed no further because at that point he had kissed her and shoved his hand between her legs, making her wriggle and moan but subsequently she had begun to think seriously about the whole question of moving in. Suppose she kept on saying no? Wasn't there a danger that he might assume she wasn't interested and start looking for someone else? And what difference would moving in make? She spent nearly every night with him already and then he had to put himself out to get her into work on time. And he was right about the job. It was boring and only paid peanuts. He had enough coming in to keep them both. Even with occasional overtime she did not earn enough to be truly independent… and why should she feel squeamish about being kept by him? She had been kept by Mark after all and he was a first grade cheater. Clive didn't have anyone else on the go, she was absolutely confident about that. He wanted to settle down. He was forty three. Mark hadn't been ready to settle down with just one woman. They'd got married too young, that was half the trouble.

A voice at the back of her head said that Clive had not actually said anything about settling down… just moving in… but settling down together was what he meant and of course he could hardly raise the issue of marriage until her divorce came through.

One evening in mid-May she surprised Becky by producing and opening a bottle of wine as they sat down to eat. 'It's a thank you,' she said. 'For giving me a roof over my head all these months.'

'No problem… you're not thinking of leaving are you?'

'Well actually…' Nicky went for a very bright smile, 'Clive has asked me to move in with him.'

'But you're not going to are you?' asked Becky, putting her glass down so abruptly that a few drops of wine sloshed onto the pine table.

'Now look Becka, I know you don't really like him…'

'I wouldn't say that. What I would say is that I don't really trust him.'

'You don't know him the way I do,' Nicky began to protest.

'I don't want to know him the way you know him,' said Becky pointedly.

'My God Becka, sometimes you are just so bloody superior.' Little spots of red appeared in Nicky's cheeks. When she put down her fork it missed the edge of the plate and clattered against the table.

Becky decided to attempt an appeal to reason. 'You haven't known him very long Nick. Please give it a bit more time. He's got a terrible reputation. O.K... O.K.' She raised her hand to ward off Nicky's exclamation. 'Everyone may have him all wrong. It's only gossip and I agree that I don't know him very well. Perhaps people *have* got him all wrong. What I'm saying is give it a bit more time. Get to know him better before you commit yourself to moving in with him.'

'You're not my mother you know.' Nicky tried to sound a light hearted note. 'And I can't live here forever.'

'You can live here as long as you like.' Becky attempted to engage eye contact but Nicola wouldn't look at her. 'For goodness sake don't... well, jump in with Clive because you feel there's nothing better. You've got your whole life ahead of you. You can build up and get back on your feet...'

'It's all very well for you,' said Nicky. 'You've got your nice home, your job... your life's all sorted out. And anyway I think... well I think I'm in love with Clive.'

'You think? Look... Staying on here would give you time to sort your life out too.' Becky was almost pleading.

'You don't have to stay in the job you've got now. You could get a place at college. Train for something. Do a degree with the O.U...'

'I'm not you,' said Nicky coldly. 'And thank you for the pep talk but I can run my own life.'

'You're being a bloody fool,' said Becky.

'Well that's really none of your business is it?' Nicky pushed her plate away, stood up and made for the door.

'Just look me in the eye and tell me you're in love with him,' Becky demanded of her friend's retreating back, but Nicky left the room without another word.

Becky picked at her food for a while and when Nicky didn't return she scraped the remnants of her own meal into the kitchen bin, before she cling filmed her friend's almost untouched plate and put it into the fridge. Later she tried tapping on Nicky's bedroom door and calling her name through the panels, but the door remained closed and there was no reply. She did not attempt to pursue the matter any further, reasoning that there would be other opportunities to talk and perhaps get Nicky to see the sense in at least waiting a while longer before committing to move in with Clive, but when Becky arrived home the following evening she found a bunch of flowers in a vase on the table, with a card propped up against them and the set of door keys she had provided lying beside it. *Thanks for everything* she read. Upstairs Nicky's bed was neatly stripped and all her belongings had gone.

Becky was not sure how to read the card. It seemed abrupt and after their row the night before she suspected that it might be tinged with sarcasm. She had Clive's phone number and toyed with the idea of ringing Nick to acknowledge the flowers, but eventually decided to let sleeping dogs lie. Anyway if Nicky and Clive were in the middle of celebrating the start of this new phase in their relationship, they would not want to be interrupted by a phone call from her.

In the days that followed Becky wondered if she ought to call and apologise for trying to interfere. It was understandable that Nicky would resent advice from someone upon whom she had become financially dependent. It placed them on a slightly difficult footing. Maybe she should have been more tactful. And perhaps she was wrong about Clive. (She bit back the temptation to justify herself by recalling just how right she had been about Mark.) Worse still she began to question her own motives. Though Nicky had been spending more and more time at Clive's, Becky found the sudden emptiness of the house hard to deal with. About a week after her friend's abrupt departure Becky was cleaning the top shelves of the kitchen cupboards when she discovered Nicky's forgotten hoard of Walnut Whips. She promptly burst into tears. 'Sad bugger,' she chided herself. 'Is that why you were so keen not to let her go?'

Chapter Twenty-Six

1970

Becky lay in bed thinking over the events of the day while simultaneously trying not to think about the map of Australia. It was supposed to be completed and handed in for marking tomorrow morning and if she did not give hers in, Mr Tresham would probably give her a detention. She didn't much care about the detention. It was more common to get detentions in the second year. A girl called Mandy Hill in IIB got one nearly every week and only people like Alex and Norma, or people with parent's like Paula's who really cared one way or the other, made a big deal out of it. Her own mother just signed the detention slips without even asking what the detention was for.

She cared more about not registering a mark for the map in Mr Tresham's mark book, because she hated the thought of coming a long way down the class at the end of term. Deep down she knew that she was as clever as Alex and Norma if she could only be bothered to do the work and at the back of her mind an insistent voice reminded her that she was actually interested. She really cared that Australia was a vast country full of deserts and mountain ranges, where people lived out on farms miles and miles away from their nearest neighbours, with hundreds (or was it thousands?) of sheep and cattle to take care of. Before they moved on to Australia they had been learning about South America and Becky had been fascinated by all of that too. There was a world out there beyond Birmingham, a world full of gauchos and dingos and kangaroos… and one day she was going to see it all. They would all go and see it, herself and Nicky, Paula and Jo. Paula would write a bestseller to pay for it. Or if she didn't they could become air hostesses. She had once read a book from the school library called 'Air Hostess Ann' which made being an air hostess sound like pretty good fun. Much more fun than being a nurse anyway, with its dual drawbacks of too much blood and not enough travelling.

Obviously they would have to make things up with Paula first. She shouldn't have gone off in a huff like that and since she was the one who had stormed off, it was a point of honour that she should be the one to apologise.

Becky glanced at the little travelling alarm clock which she had picked up for threepence at a jumble sale. There was just enough light coming in from the landing to see that it was not long after eleven. Mum hadn't gone to bed yet. Perhaps it was going to be one of those nights when she didn't bother. Frank had been dead for more than a year now and Becky had accepted that life wasn't ever going to get back to the way it had been before.

She slid out of bed, propped the door open a little bit wider, got out her geography book and her map and spread them on the floor in the half light from the landing, ready to push them out of sight and hop back into bed if she heard her mother on the move. The cartridge in her pen had run out and since she did not have the money to buy another she would have to use pencil, then ink it over first thing tomorrow when she could dip her pen nib in the school ink for nothing. She reminded herself for the hundredth time that when she next bought a pen she would get one with a reservoir, so that she could keep filling it up at school. It had been stupid to buy a cartridge pen when her last one broke. She had only done it to be the same as everyone else, because cartridge pens were all the fashion.

The map didn't take very long so she decided that while she was at it she'd better do her maths as well. Miss Mislet would be pretty mad with anyone who failed to hand it in and since being demoted to middle set for maths, she'd been in trouble several times with Miss Mislet about homework. When Miss Mislet had asked her why she was not handing in her work she hadn't been able to think of an answer. It was something she couldn't explain, even to herself. She meant to do the work. She always started off *meaning* to do it, but if Mum was having one of her bad days Becky had to do the tea and clear up afterwards and after that she would sit down for five minutes and end up getting engrossed in something on the telly or distracted by a book and then she would suddenly realise that it was nine o'clock and get into a kind of panic, feeling as if she couldn't do the work now because it had got too late and there were her sandwiches to sort out for the morning and this would often coincide with Mum switching off the telly because she said the news was too depressing. Then Mum would start to go on about how hard up they were and how Frank had been taken from them and how there was no justice in the world, until Becky just felt that all she wanted to do was run and hide somewhere far, far away from Mum and the flat and Eleanor Vaux.

On nights like that she invariably ended up lying in bed, worrying about the consequences of the undone homework and yet still not being able to motivate herself to do it. But not tonight. By midnight it was all completed in pencil, ready to be inked in during registration.

Chapter Twenty-Seven

1984

It had been raining heavily for most of the evening and this always made for a quieter night at the Drop In Centre. By half past eight Becky had seen everyone who was waiting and was able to slip into the little kitchen and make herself a mug of tea. She had been volunteering at the centre for more than a year, giving free legal advice to anyone who came in search of it. Doling out leaflets and wisdom and sympathy from behind the desk whose chipped corners caught on her clothes if she did not remember to give them a wide berth. Though she came straight from work Becky tried to dress down a little bit on Thursday evenings, conscious that even a silk blouse and a well cut jacket could be intimidating. Clients dressed up when they came to see her at the office but no one dressed up to come here. People who came here in search of her help wore the same tired, market-bought apparel that they wore every day. Someone had once said that Labour voters didn't turn out in the rain, she thought, which might have had something to do with the fact that they were the people least likely to have a car or a waterproof coat at their disposal.

Some of the other volunteers, for example Pip who worked for the council by day and gave advice on housing and benefits two evenings a week, were highly political but that was not Becky's motivation. She'd first heard about the Drop In Centre from one of the social workers she met in court and when she heard that they were short on people with a legal background she got in touch. It was a way of putting something back. There but for the grace of God…

The centre existed almost entirely on charitable donations. The furniture was dilapidated, the flat roof leaked in two or three places when it rained and even the electric kettle was dodgy. The heating system was inadequate which probably accounted for the permanent smell of damp. After a few months the clients merged into a mass of familiar types, the women with prematurely aged faces, the young men whose abrasive exteriors masked inner doubts and fears. Disputes with landlords, neighbours, spouses, partners. Documents they did not understand (or sometimes could not read) summonses in respect of unpaid fines. The hopeless, the helpless, the scallywags, the saints, the illegal immigrant, the battered wife, the downright loony: she had learnt to read them so well that she often knew who they were and why they had come while they were still sitting themselves down on the other side of the desk. Occasionally there had been surprises. The smartly dressed business man who arrived bearing a bulky envelope. A thank you, he said, a donation to the centre because she had helped his son. He did not want to give his name. He had waited his turn to see her for more than forty minutes and once shown into her cubby hole, he did not even sit down, was in and out in a moment. She never knew which boy he was referring to. The envelope contained one thousand pounds in cash. One or two people bought cards, once there had been a box of Milk Tray and once some home-made samosas, but more often than not she never saw them again.

Often there was little or nothing she could offer in the way of help. It was not the most cheerful of ways to spend an evening but then the law was like that. If you wanted happy, she told herself, you should have been a party planner.

Chapter Twenty-Eight

1970

'What do you mean exactly,' Mrs Morrison asked. 'When you say you don't feel very well?'

'I don't know,' said Paula, leaning against the banisters to give a better impression of an ailing constitution. 'I feel sort of shaky and sick.' (Which to a significant degree was no more than the truth.)

Mrs Morrison reached up and put her hand on Paula's forehead. 'You haven't got a temperature,' she said. 'And you look all right. You only ate the same as we did last night. No sign of a tummy upset.'

How do you know? Paula thought. Why is it everyone is so damned interested in monitoring my bodily functions? Aloud she said: 'I feel a bit sick.'

'But you haven't *been* sick, have you?' said her mother. 'What lessons have you got today?'

Paula knew when to stop pushing it. Next thing she would be getting an interrogation about whether there was anything wrong at school and the dreaded phrase 'write a letter' would be wheeled out or even worse, 'I could pop in and have a word with Mrs James.'

'I expect I'll feel all right later,' said Paula.

She usually met the others when she got off the bus but there was no one waiting for her there. It did occur to her that she was probably the first one to arrive but as she could not bear the thought of waiting, only for them to walk straight past her, she walked to school alone, arriving in the form room early enough to get across to her desk without attracting any attention from the little knot of girls who had congregated to talk (probably about me, she thought) in the other back corner of the room. She gathered together everything she needed for the three periods between assembly and morning break and then sat at her desk, concentrating with all her might on an Hercule Poirot mystery. (She had just discovered Agatha Christie and was reading her novels one after another.)

When Becky arrived she sat straight down at her desk and started inking in the homework she had done the night before. Jo and Nicky were hunting for something in Jo's desk and did not look her way. Paula pretended not to notice that they were there and when the form lined up to march into assembly she took a long time over putting her bookmark into 'Death on the Nile' and ended up at the very back of the line.

In assembly they sang 'For All The Saints'. Paula loved the line about the sunset fading in the west. It made her think of summer holidays in Cornwall, where she had first been able to see the sun setting without row upon row of rooftops getting in the way. When I'm old enough, she thought, I'll go and live somewhere that I can properly see the sunset. Somewhere a long way away from here, where everyone isn't so horrible.

Their first lesson was P.E. The P.E. changing room had wooden benches running around the walls and coat pegs mounted on the walls above the benches. It would not have been easy to hang an entire school uniform onto a single coat peg in the best of circumstances and the changing rooms were so cramped that avoiding the elbows of one's neighbours as you divested yourself of your school sweater was just another hazard of P.E. lessons.

Paula hated getting changed for P.E. because although she had finally grown enough to justify getting a bra, she still felt like an ugly white stick insect alongside Kay Fenton with her Marilyn Monroe size boobs. Nor did her periods happen regularly which was something else that she assumed everyone in the class must be secretly laughing about, because it must be common knowledge that she hardly ever had a note to get out of showers. She wasn't a proper woman like the others. She would never be able to get married. No man would want her when people like Kay Fenton were available.

Once they were all outside Miss Leopold appointed Gail and Debbie as team captains and they took turns to select their teams for rounders, choosing one person at a time from the remaining members of the form. Miss Leopold always nominated the team captains from a select handful of favourites. Girls who suffered the humiliation of being the last to be chosen week after week, never got a turn to do the choosing and that morning Paula knew she would be left until the very end. Even Kay, who was not built for running and a liability to any team, got picked ahead of her.

'You can be backstop,' Gail told Paula as they walked towards the rounders pitch.

Paula knew that she had been put there out of spite. At least half the batters were guaranteed to miss and if she failed to catch the ball she would have to turn and race after it in a desperate bid to stop the other team scoring half a rounder, accompanied as like as not by Miss Leopold yelling what she imagined to be encouragement.

After the miserable endurance test of fielding, Paula's team went in to bat. Gail ran Paula out on purpose which actually suited Paula very well, because it meant that she could go and sit on the bank among the daisies. Everyone had pretty much forgotten about the D.C.L. this year. They were too grown up for that sort of thing now but she idly picked a few daisies and threaded them together for old time's sake.

She was soon joined by Annette Maudesley who tossed herself down on the bank saying, 'Thank goodness for that! I thought I was never going to be out.' Then in a different tone, 'Oh I forgot. We're not speaking to you.' She picked herself up again and pointedly moved to sit a few yards away.

For once Miss Leopold let them get back to the changing rooms in good time for next lesson. Paula grabbed one of the towels from the basket (a white cotton square which had clearly not been designed to cover the modesty or dry the body of a growing school girl) and threw off her clothes, hoping to get through the showers before Miss Leopold positioned herself alongside them to stare at everyone. As it happened Miss Leopold was still busy with her big book, noting down the names of those who had brought letters to say they were excused showers. For a second or two Paula thought she was well ahead of everyone, but then she realised that Renata McPharlane, one of Gail and Debbie's crowd, had entered the showers behind her. Paula was half way through the tiled tunnel – the water tepid today, more of a trickle than a deluge – when Gail Foster suddenly appeared at the exit. Nakedness didn't seem to bother Gail. The confidence which emanated from her naked body was unnerving in itself. Paula had been hurrying to get through but now she hesitated as Gail stood hands on hips, blocking the way.

Gail and Renata both hailed from the council estate at the back of the Hare and Hounds. It was an unspoken truth that some of the gentler girls were afraid of them and kept their distance. Gail had very dark eyes and when she looked straight at you, Paula thought, those eyes seemed to pin you to the wall.

'Can I get past please?' Paula was conscious of the tremor in her voice. She wanted to come across as tough and brave but she knew it wasn't working.

'Colleen and Penny had to spend all yesterday lunchtime scrubbing the greenhouse windows,' said Gail. 'Somebody's going to pay for that.'

'Gail!' For once Miss Leopold's bark was more than welcome. 'What are you doing going in that way? Come out and go through properly.'

Gail vanished the way she had come and Paula made for the exit, almost crying with relief, but as she grabbed her towel from the peg where she had left it, Renata's voice came close to her ear. 'We're gonna get you at break-time.'

As break approached Paula could not concentrate at all

as Miss Hardiker went round the class, asking people to describe their eye and hair colour in French – as if anyone was ever going to need to do *that* in real life. Paula began to wonder what would happen if she just got her coat and ran out of school. She would be missed at afternoon registration if not before. Mum and Dad would find out and of course they wouldn't just let her go to some other school, because Mum thought Eleanor Vaux was absolutely wonderful. No... what they would do would be to pester and pester, going on and on until they got the whole story out of her and then they would write to Miss Forster or come in and see Mrs James and that would get Gail and Renata into trouble, which would only make matters far, far worse.

It was a double period of art after break and since she did not need any books for that, Paula avoided the form room and headed instead for the cloakroom. Gail and her cronies might not know the dodge of hiding behind the coats. Now she was taller it was not so easy as it had been last year, but Paula thought she could probably still get away with it and anyway it was her best hope of seeing out break time.

She had forgotten that it was the summer term. Oh God... how could she have been so stupid? She cast around the cloakroom where blazers hung from nearly every peg, wondering if she had time to collect up the half dozen macs she could see and hang them all together. Surely no one would mind so long as she put them all back in their rightful places at the end of break? She was about to do this when she remembered that the trick relied on being camouflaged by a long row of macs. A single group with an obvious bulge under it would not achieve the same effect.

Then it was too late.

Someone must have followed her: watched then told the others where she had gone. The situation was much worse than she had anticipated. Gail and her friends were accompanied by a quartet of bigger girls from the third year. Rough girls, as Paula thought of them, with whom Gail and the others sometimes hung around. Paula waited at the furthest end of the cloakroom while they advanced. She could have tried running but they were well placed to cut her off from the doors and anyway her legs wouldn't respond.

'So this is the grasser is it?' said one of the older girls as the group closed in.

Paula did not bother to try and deny anything.

'We don't like people who grass,' one of the other big girls said, jabbing at Paula, who stepped back to avoid the finger making contact and came up against the last row of coat pegs.

'Leave her alone you cows!' Jo's voice, sounding scared but determined, rang across the room.

'Sod off Pipsqueak and mind your own business.' The third year who had first spoken barely bothered to look over her shoulder.

As if in a dream Paula saw Joanne move into view, white faced but determined. Becky and Nick were just behind her. To Paula's utter astonishment Joanne grabbed an old hockey stick which was had been lodged above some nearby coat pegs and brandished it in their direction.

'Don't you dare lay a hand on her. The first person who does gets a wallop with this,' said Jo. 'Now pack it in or Nicky'll go and fetch a teacher.'

'They're a right load of grassers in IIJ,' said one of the

bigger girls. Her tone was mocking, but Paula sensed that she was slightly disconcerted by this turn of events.

'Someone's asking for a good hiding.' The largest of the third formers took a step in Joanne's direction but although she flinched, Jo stood her ground.

'I can't be bothered with all this,' said another of the older girls, suddenly full of all the world weariness a fourteen year old girl can muster. 'Bloody second years. Let them sort out their own problems. I'm off to buy a bag of crisps.'

This seemed to signal a sea change among the third years, who all joined in with various degrees of contemptuous agreement. The group shambled off in the direction of the dining hall, leaving Gail, Renata and Debbie standing somewhat uncertainly in front of Paula.

'You're horrible Gail Foster,' Nicky burst out.

'*She* told on Colleen and Penny,' said Gail. 'You can't just let that go by.'

'Rubbish,' said Becky. 'Paula wouldn't do a thing like that. And what do you know about it anyway? You're always jumping on the bandwagon.'

Paula watched open mouthed. No one ever talked back to Gail Foster.

'We're going to get the whole form together at lunch time and sort this out,' said Nicky. 'It's just a stupid mistake, that's all.'

'Now get lost,' said Joanne, holding out her hand to signal Paula to join them, then dropping it as Paula stepped closer because girls who touched under any but very particular circumstances were branded as 'lesbie friends' and no one wanted to attract a label like that.

'I'm sorry we weren't your friend,' Nicky said, as soon as Gail and her cronies had gone.

'It was my fault,' said Paula. 'I shouldn't have walked off.'

'We're going to sort things out,' said Joanne. 'And if no one will listen, well they'll just have to send us to Coventry as well.'

'It doesn't matter what anyone else does so long as we stay friends,' said Becky.

Mr Morrison happened to finish work early that afternoon and when his wife mentioned that Paula might be feeling unwell, he took the unusual step of driving to Eleanor Vaux in order to pick his daughter up. He parked his car outside the bottom set of gates, from which position he could see the girls coming down the lower drive. Typical of Jean to worry over nothing, he thought. For there was Paula, arms linked with her three friends doing some sort of old style vaudeville dance routine, with their legs crossing over one another's as they walked. Through the open window he could hear them singing 'Raindrops Keep Falling on my Head' at the tops of their voices.

Chapter Twenty-Nine

1984

Days merged into weeks without any word from Nicky. Becky vaguely intended to get in touch with her and equally she half expected each message on the answering machine to be from her old friend, but then she discovered that Nick had been into the office to see Gerry about her divorce without bothering to so much as suggest that they got together for a coffee and smarting from this she allowed the silence to continue on through the summer and into the run up to Christmas.

Becky always dreaded Christmas with her mother but felt a responsibility to go through the required rituals every year. To avoid the awfulness of spending Christmas Day at her mother's house Becky had booked the two of them for Christmas lunch at a good restaurant. In truth she would far rather have spent Christmas holed up on her own, but she couldn't leave Mum on *her* own – not now that her despised step-father had fallen victim to the cancer which was the almost inevitable lot of a forty a day man.

Mum didn't really have anyone else. She had a few friends of course. Mainly women friends these days: widows like herself, but there was no other family to speak of. Which is why I haven't got any family either, Becky thought. Nor even many friends... certainly none close enough to spend Christmas with.

Shopping in her lunch hour she found the tinsel, the crowds and the festive muzak weighed on her like a haversack full of lead. It would be nice to do something thoroughly selfish and indulgent over Christmas. She thought wistfully of a weekend she had once spent with Sean at a country pub: the log fires and deep armchairs, the ambrosial dinner eaten by candlelight. You had to be part of a couple to do that sort of thing. Romantic breaks were not romantic when you were on your own.

Her thoughts turned inevitably to Nicky. Nicky who was so close at hand now, not like when she had been living on the other side of the world. Nicky who had not been in touch since she moved out... It was all my fault really, Becky thought. I wanted to be a good friend but I suppose I was just interfering. And that was only underlined by the fact that six months down the line Nicky was still with Clive, which much as it galled her to admit it, probably meant that she had been wrong about him after all. She couldn't exactly recall what she had said about him but it was obviously up to her to make the first move. Her initial idea had been to put a note in Nick's Christmas card, suggesting they were overdue a get together... something cheery and normal as if there was really nothing wrong, but part of her said that was ridiculous when they had not spoken for so long. Eventually she decided to ring and ask

Nicky to meet her: if necessary apologising and saying that she had been in the wrong.

She worked herself up to calling one evening in mid-December, but after three rings the answering machine cut in and Clive's voice, smug and self satisfied, informed callers that Clive and Nicky were skiing in Austria, burglars should note that the alarm system was directly linked to the local cop shop and friends should leave a message after the bleep.

Clive's voice conjured up an annoying mental image of him living it up in Austria, just at the precise moment when the television screen switched to pictures of the famine in Ethiopia. Becky put the phone down without leaving a message. Even the people who came to use the free legal advice service at the Drop In Centre had been collecting money for the famine victims. She pulled herself up short. She must not be judgemental. For all she knew, Clive might give a mint of money to charity on a regular basis. In fact now she stopped to think about it, hadn't it been a charity dinner where Nicky had first met him? That had been all her fault too. She wished now that she had never persuaded Nick to go along to the wretched event with her. If it hadn't been for that she might never have met the man. Another wave of guilt engulfed her when she remembered that meeting Clive had obviously made Nicky very happy. You're just jealous, she chided herself, that's your problem.

Chapter Thirty

1970

The first assembly of the new school year always took place on the second morning of term. Back in her white lab coat after a walking holiday in the Lake District, Mrs Venables sang 'Guide Me O Thou Great Redeemer' from memory, while her eyes scanned the ranks of girls standing nearest to her as she tried to locate those persistent voices singing 'Aston Villa, Aston Villa, we'll support you ever more'. The workings of the school girl mind frequently defeated her. It seemed as if any act of pointless rebellion was enthusiastically embraced by some girl or another in the school. 'Morning has broken, stick it with Bostik' – what was the point of marring an otherwise delightful hymn with silliness like that? Was it supposed to be funny?

The school timetable had bowled her a googly yesterday with IIIS coming to her for general science. Although she had not seen it happen, she was convinced that Veronica Nicholls could not have set fire to that sheet of paper by accident. Nor did she believe Joanne Embury's explanation about the mice. The cage simply could not have come undone by itself. Neither did she find it credible that so many girls were sufficiently afraid of mice that they had to clamber onto their stools and even onto the lab benches to escape from the poor terrified little creatures.

The lesson had been in complete disarray for a full fifteen minutes while the mice were caught. (The burning paper had been easily extinguished in the sink.) Well IIIS would find themselves in form detention if there was any repetition of that sort of behaviour. She would have spoken with their form teacher, but Mr Sinton was so lax that he could not be relied upon to do anything about it.

Mrs Venables had never liked third year classes. Third year was a dangerous age, the girls no longer eager and biddable as they had been further down the school. She preferred the specialisation of 'O' levels. The girls who chose chemistry and physics were always a pleasure to teach. The silly ones who affected not to understand the difference between elements and molecules always chose biology, because that was thought to be the easier option. Mrs Venable never taught 'O' level biology, a happy thought which brought an unconscious smile to her lips.

Miss Forster had taken the school's forthcoming golden jubilee as the theme for assembly. Technically the golden jubilee did not occur until 1971 but these things did not come together overnight and some preparations were already underway because Miss Forster had made her expectations known to the staff before the summer break. Every department was expected to participate in the celebrations and most of them had come up with a plan. The music department were going to hold a classical concert and in addition were joining with the English department to produce 'West Side Story'. (If it had to be something so lightweight, Miss Forster's own choice would have been 'The Sound of Music'.) The production was being jointly undertaken with the nearby boys' grammar school – Saint Luke's – an announcement which had created a visible ripple of interest among the pupils gathered in the hall.

As well as stand alone events of this nature, a gala day was scheduled for the end of the spring term and Miss Forster had invited every department to submit ideas. P.E.were going to put on a display of gymnastics. History were talking of a pageant of some kind and domestic science were offering a celebratory cake. Miss Mislet, a veteran of the school's silver jubilee in 1946, was very keen to repeat one of those marching displays in which girls made a series of moving shapes which eventually finished by forming the letters **EV**, all done in time to music out on the playing field whilst an assembled audience of dignitaries watched from the terrace above. Miss Forster was not sure that the modern school girl would find that sort of exercise very inspiring. It was a rather old fashioned idea and Miss Forster preferred to think that inasmuch as they needed to, Eleanor Vaux moved with the times. Miss Mislet however was very keen.

The question of the invited dignitaries would have to be considered in due course. The Lord and Lady Mayoress would be a bit of a coup. All the school governors of course and the local M.P. liked to be seen to take an interest in education. Mrs Venables had chipped in to suggest that prominent people who had a past connection with the school ought to be invited, for example ex-headmistresses and famous old girls, which was all very well but Miss Forster was only the fourth incumbent of the headmistress's office. Her immediate predecessor Miss Cresswall had died a couple of years ago at the age of eighty six and *her* predecessor Miss Butterworth had died in harness during the war years. The very first headmistress, a Miss Katherine Barr, had departed to take up the headship of a school somewhere in the north back in 1927 and had probably not been in the first flush of youth even then.

As for famous pupils… well Evies was not the sort of school which encouraged showing off. Solid effort and team work were the order of the day. There were only three names on the Roll of Honour which hung in the front entrance hall. One of these was a pupil whose claim to fame was a distinguished academic career at Cambridge. She had published a number of well received papers on Ancient Greece but she was hardly a household name. The other two were a girl who had been killed serving in the Wrens and one who had achieved notice by saving a fellow pupil from drowning after she got into difficulties on a school trip – which was all very commendable of course – but who knew where on earth she might be now? Never mind. The jubilee would be an inspiring affair with or without famous old girls. It would bring the school together, Miss Forster thought, fostering in them that spirit of tradition and continuity which made Eleanor Vaux what it was. At the commencement of this historic year she knew it was important to strike an appropriate note of enthusiasm. Unfortunately enthusiasm was not a keynote among young people these days. From what she heard of their out of school behaviour, they preferred to lie about in semi darkened rooms and mumble about giving peace a chance. Only this morning she had confiscated a badge which a fourth year had been sporting quite openly on her school sweater, which said *Make Love Not War.* A lot of good that sort of nonsense would have been when Hitler and his bully boys were poised just across the Channel. Was it for this that she had lost a brother at Dunkirk?

Chapter Thirty-One

1985

'It's a shame that Nick couldn't come over,' said Joanne. 'We don't often have a chance to get together.'

'I'm afraid it's all my fault,' Becky said with a sigh. 'She took umbrage when I advised her not to move in with Clive. I should've minded my own business.'

'Rubbish,' said Jo. 'Nick won't have taken offence. She's never borne a grudge in her life. She had something else on. It's just bad luck that's all.'

Becky didn't agree but she didn't feel like arguing. She had finally phoned Nicky the week before to tell her that Jo was coming up to Birmingham and would be staying overnight, but though Nicky had been ostensibly pleased to hear from her, their conversation had been unmistakably stilted and Nicky's excuse for not joining them had sounded thin: she said she and Clive already had something on, without specifying what.

'Where's that photograph?' Joanne asked, changing

the subject. 'The one you said you'd found of your Mum's wedding.'

Becky produced the photograph from on top of a pile of books on a nearby shelf and handed it over. Joanne took it and gave a huge guffaw of laughter.

'I know… I know,' Becky said. 'The girl who wore hot pants to her mother's wedding. Mind you,' she added. 'At the wedding before Mum's, the *bride* was actually wearing white satin hot pants! Can you imagine being stuck with that in your wedding album for the rest of your life?'

'She's probably divorced by now,' said Joanne, cheerfully. She considered the picture again. 'They don't look exactly overjoyed do they… your mum and Stan?'

'Joy wasn't a commodity Stan dealt in,' Becky said, moving to look over Jo's shoulder at the photograph, after topping up both their glasses. 'The only Joy he knew about was the one who sang with The Beverly Sisters.'

'I always thought it was a funny thing, the way he and your mum just suddenly got married. A proper whirlwind romance when you think about it.'

She handed the photograph back and Becky considered it briefly before saying, 'I don't think he ever saw it as romantic. If anything I think he saw it as convenient. His wife – the sainted Muriel – had died, he was on his own, so was Mum. They sort of knew each other, because he was the foreman where she worked…'

'And there was your mum as well… you always said she really loved Frank…'

'I think that was the key to it,' Becky said. 'You see by then she'd been mourning Frank for about a year and a half. If it hadn't been for Frank, I don't think she would ever have married Stan.' Seeing Joanne's uncomprehending look Becky continued: 'Frank had been sort of snatched away without Mum managing to have any kind of – well – ownership of him. She couldn't even go to his funeral because his wife and family organised it and she was The Other Woman so she didn't get any particular support or sympathy. She never had a chance to say goodbye. I suppose it's no wonder she just got folded up in her own grief and loneliness and then when Stan took an interest in her I think she was so terrified of losing another man that she scarcely stopped to consider how much she actually liked him… or maybe even whether she liked him all that much at all. She latched on to him and when he suggested getting married she didn't think twice. Next stop the register office. Classic marry in haste repent at leisure territory.'

'Sonia got married at the register office too,' Jo said. 'I remember thinking how awful it was, coming out into Broad Street with all the traffic whizzing by and having pictures taken over the road in front of the Hall of Remembrance. I know it's a nice building, but it *is* a war memorial. I mean it's not the brightest backdrop to start your married life against, is it?'

'It'll be a good thing if this new law comes in to let people marry in places other than churches and register offices,' said Becky.

Joanne nodded. 'There should be more choice. Sonia and Mick thought it was hypocritical to get married in church. Mind you the rest of the family went into a fit when they found out it was going to be the register office. Not that my dad ever set foot in a church if he could help it, but to hear him you would have thought he was the bloody

Archbishop of Canterbury. We even had "what will the neighbours think?" Crikey... as if our neighbours ever thought we were anything but common as muck.'

'Lots of people looked down on the register office as second best. It was where you got married if you were divorced or very young and trendy, both of which were perceived as socially suspicious in the seventies.' Becky laughed. 'Not that I told anyone except you guys that my mum was getting married. Admitting that she was divorced in the first place would have been even worse than admitting she was getting married in a register office.'

'Talking about weddings,' Jo said. 'Weren't you supposed to be getting married at one time? It all happened the year Ant and I went to Italy for the summer and it had fallen through again before I got home and had a chance to vet the guy. You never got round to telling me why you didn't go through with it... and I've always meant to ask... Of course you don't have to tell me if it's something too horrible.'

'I couldn't go through with it.' There was nothing in Becky's face or voice to suggest that she was upset to be asked. In response to her friend's questioning look she continued: 'It wasn't that I got cold feet or because I stopped loving him or he stopped loving me.'

'You still loved each other? Then why?'

'Because I found out something about Sean. Something that I hadn't realised when we were dating... I found out that he was Frank's son.'

'Frank's son?' Joanne almost choked on her drink. 'But how... what...?'

'I know.' Becky attempted a half smile. 'I ought to have

twigged on straight away I suppose. Sean McMahon. Worse Sean *Francis* McMahon. But it just didn't ring any bells. I mean when he first told me his name was McMahon I'd totally forgotten that Frank's name was McMahon. I never thought of him as Frank McMahon. He was just Frank.'

Jo nodded. He had been just Frank to all of them. In fact she had initially assumed he was Mr Addison. He had certainly never been Mr McMahon.

'Anyway even if I had remembered that it was Frank's name, I expect I would have just put it down to coincidence. I mean what are the odds of he and Sean being related?'

Joanne shook her head and raised her eyebrows in a form of mute agreement.

'I think Sean mentioned fairly early on that his father was dead. But lots of people's fathers are dead. It isn't that much of a rarity. You wouldn't immediately think... ' She looked across at Joanne and again received a gesture of concurrence. 'I think I asked him about his father once and he told me that it had been a road accident which happened while he was still at senior school. But I didn't know exactly how old he was when it happened and even if he'd told me, I probably wouldn't have done the sums and worked out that it was 1969 – the same year as Frank died.'

'So how did you find out?'

'We were round at Sean's mum's house one day and Win – that's his mum – got out some photographs of Sean and his brother when they were little. She showed me one of Sean with his father on a beach somewhere, building a sandcastle and I thought there was something familiar about his dad but I couldn't quite place it. Then she handed me another one which had been taken a few years later, with Sean standing next to his Dad. Win said something like, "That's a good one of Frank," and of course it *was*. I recognised him from that photo, even without the name, but the instant Win said his name I almost passed out from the shock.'

'Call me dense if you like,' Joanne said slowly. 'But I don't see why that would have stopped you from marrying Sean, if that was what you both wanted.'

Becky made an impatient gesture as if she was being bothered by an invisible fly. 'It just didn't feel right,' she said. 'It was almost… almost incestuous somehow.'

'Didn't you talk about it?'

'Of course we talked about it. We talked about it for hours. He told me that his mum had known there was someone else, but even so she never really believed that Frank would leave her. Sean said it nearly killed her when his father died. She adored Frank apparently, for all that he had been unfaithful and she would never willingly have given him a divorce. She always thought he would come to his senses and stop seeing this other woman. Can you imagine how she'd have felt, if she'd ever found out that I was the other woman's daughter?'

'She needn't have known,' began Joanne.

'It would have come out,' Becky said. 'It wouldn't have taken much. Don't forget that Mum knew a lot more about Frank and his wife than I ever did. I didn't even know he had a wife until after he was dead, but I reckon my mum knew all about Win and the boys and Win probably knew stuff about us as well. If we'd tried to conceal the truth it would probably have made matters worse. They might even have worked it out at the wedding. Can you imagine it? Two lonely widows, one on each side of the bride and groom, both still carrying a torch for the same man.'

'I still don't see why you couldn't have gone ahead,' said Joanne. 'The two mothers wouldn't have had to spend much time together and you can't let yourself be ruled by something that happened years and years ago. Whatever went on between your mum and Sean's dad it's all in the past now.'

Becky shook her head. 'It wasn't just them. It was about me too. It didn't feel right. It didn't feel... lucky.'

'But it was all in the past,' Joanne repeated. 'You can't keep worrying about the past.'

'You can't defeat the past either,' Becky said. 'It's always there and you can't change it.'

Chapter Thirty-Two

1970

No one seemed to know exactly where the rumour had come from. The story seemed both preposterous and yet not the sort of thing anyone would dare to make up. When Mr Sinton came into the form room at the very end of registration and simply told them to line up for assembly, no one felt that it was the sort of thing they could just come out and ask him about.

A sense of expectancy hung over the hall as line after line of blue clad girls filed in. On this December morning the big lights were all on, making the patches of sky which could be seen through the tall windows seem even darker. Unusually there were no hymn numbers displayed on the boards adjacent to the stage. People noticed this and caught each other's eye: it was another sure sign that something was up.

There was no audible sound but a collective frisson ran through the ranks as if everyone had seen – all in the same instant – Miss Harkness's brown perm appear as she mounted the back steps which led onto the stage. It was not unusual for someone other than Miss Forster to take assembly, but the point was that Miss Forster had not appeared to take a seat elsewhere in the hall either. Miss Harkness moved across to stand behind the table in the centre of the stage, where she gripped either side of the pine lectern which always stood on top of it and looked down across the sea of expectant faces, six hundred of them all told, to say nothing of the teaching staff who stood in front of the rows of chairs to either side of the room. 'Please sit down everyone,' she said.

Assembly invariably started with a hymn. Pupils exchanged looks as they lowered themselves to the floor. Several people noticed simultaneously that Miss Mislet was applying her hankie to her eyes.

'I have some very sad news to tell you.' Miss Harkness's voice was different this morning. It had lost its confident ring. 'Miss Forster was involved in an accident yesterday evening. She was knocked down and killed...'

There were gasps from all over the hall and a single low cry from somewhere among the first years, noises instantly hushed by the raising of Miss Harkness's right hand.

'We should all take comfort from the fact that Miss Forster died very quickly. She did not suffer.' Miss Harkness's voice faltered. She gathered herself with difficulty. For the first time, several pupils woke up to the fact that underneath the facade, Miss Harkness might actually be a human being. 'I know that you will all feel very upset. I also know that what Miss Forster would ask of you all is to carry on in the best way you can: to do everything in your power to make the job of the staff and myself as trouble free as possible. It is only a few days until the end of term and the Christmas holidays and I know that Miss Forster would wish all the usual traditions of the Christmas season to go ahead.' Miss Harkness paused again. 'There has been no time to prepare an assembly this morning, so I am going to ask you to observe a minute's silence for Miss Forster and then return to your form rooms.' She bowed her head and the entire school followed suit in a single movement. As Paula said later, she had never realised before that you could actually *hear* silence.

Miss Harkness broke the spell by clearing her throat. 'School dismiss,' she said.

They always left assembly via the back doors of the hall. The sixth form, who were allowed the luxury of sitting on long wooden benches at the very back, stood up first and the rest of school followed suit. Afterwards no one could ever say who began it but as the sixth form filed out a lone voice, almost immediately joined by another, began to sing 'Adeste Fidelis'. By the second line girls were joining in from all over the hall and by the time they reached the first Venite adoremus, Mr Sinton's fine baritone was all but lost among the multitude as every member of staff and school took up the carol, bearing it out of the hall and along the corridors, the sound resonating from every stone in the building and binding them together as one.

Chapter Thirty-Three

1985

Nicky was surprised to find Dennis on the doorstep of Cliveden at eleven o'clock on a weekday morning.

'Hi,' she said. 'What's up?'

'Nothing much. I was just passing so I thought I'd stop by for a cuppa.'

He followed her into the kitchen where she switched on the kettle and reached down mugs and tea bags. Dennis never drank coffee. 'Actually,' he said, watching as she poured boiling water into the mugs, 'I've come to tell you that I'm going to Australia.'

'Australia?' Nicky replaced the kettle and turned to face him. 'What for? When?'

'On Thursday,' he said.

'*This* Thursday?'

'Yeah,' said Dennis, carefully casual. 'For a while. I wondered if you could let Dad know. Only he and Vi are away at the moment.'

'*Den-nis* what do you mean, you're going to Australia

"for a while" on Thursday. People don't just go to Australia "for a while" at the drop of a hat. Are you in some sort of trouble?'

Dennis looked momentarily shifty. 'Two sugars for me,' he said. 'No, not in any trouble. Not as such.'

Nicky stirred the tea ferociously before asking, 'Why are you going to Australia, then?'

Dennis took the mug she handed him and followed her into the conservatory, which was comfortably warm thanks to the January sunshine augmented by sub tropical central heating.

'I owed a friend a favour,' he said. 'Only sorting that out, I got into a bit of bother with someone else. So this other friend has sorted me out with some papers…'

'What papers? What sort of papers?'

'Oh… passport, visa,' Dennis waved his free hand airily.

'Passport? You've already got a passport. You don't get passports from friends Den. Are you telling me these papers are illegal?'

'Nahh.' Dennis gave her a huge smile. 'Not illegal. Not technically.' He had adopted an expression she recognised at once. It was the one he had perfected at about three years old, which had never failed with Mum. 'Maybe a little bit illegal, yeah. But nothing serious.'

'Dennis,' she tried to sound serious and angry but something in his face gave her an irresistible desire to laugh. 'Are you in very bad trouble?'

'Not if I go to Australia, no.'

'But you don't know anyone in Australia. You've got no job. You've got nowhere to live there.'

'All taken care of,' Dennis said, in what was clearly

intended to be a reassuring tone. 'Friends of friends. Not a problem.'

'I wish Mum was still alive,' said Nicky.

'So do I,' said Dennis, smoothly.

'She'd talk some sense into you,' said Nicky without conviction.

'It's summer in Australia,' Dennis said. 'Great beaches so I've heard.'

'Take me with you,' said Nicky, suddenly.

'Can't do that.' Dennis grinned as if they were sharing a huge joke. 'Only got one set of papers.'

Nicky found that she was crying. 'When will you be able to come back?' she asked.

'Don't cry Sis.' Dennis stood up and put his arm around her somewhat awkwardly. They had never been a family who went in for physical displays of affection. 'I'll be all right. I'll send you a postcard as soon as I get there.'

Nicky mumbled something that he failed to catch.

'You'll be all right here,' he went on. 'You've got Clive haven't you? Top bloke Clive. You're well set up here aren't you?'

It was a statement not a question.

'Do you really have to go?' Nicky looked up at him. He was nearly twenty five but he still had the fresh faced looks of a primary school boy. He could still have walked away with the part of the Angel Gabriel in the school nativity play.

'It's that or get my head kicked in,' he said matter of factly.

'Oh Dennis,' she said. Then after a pause, 'I shall miss you.'

'I'll miss you too,' he said.

It was not that they saw each other very often, she thought. It wouldn't even be the first time that they had lived on opposite sides of the world. Perhaps it had upset her because it was such a shock: him just arriving out of the blue to say that he was going away and the more so because she knew in her heart of hearts that all this talk of friends and friends of friends, referred to the sort of people who no one in their right mind would ever want to have for friends.

He interrupted her reverie by saying, 'You couldn't lend me a few bob could you?'

She stared at him, incredulous. 'You can't be thinking of going to Australia without any money?'

'No, no,' Dennis reassured her. 'That's all sorted out, see? There'll be money waiting for me at the airport and there's a bank account set up ready and waiting for me in Australia. I've even got my train ticket down to Heathrow paid for. I'm being well looked after. It's just that I'm a bit short of ready cash for the next couple of days. I could just do with a bit to tide me over today and tomorrow.'

'I'll see what I've got,' said Nicky.

She found him a ten pound note and then wrote him a cheque for fifty pounds which was as much as her personal account would stand.

'Cheers,' he said. 'I'll pay you back.'

'Don't bother,' she said. 'Think of it as a going away present.'

He left soon afterwards. Had to see a chap about some business, he said.

After he was gone she sat in the conservatory, every so often glancing at the empty mug he had left on the glass topped table, the only tangible confirmation that he had really been there at all.

'Take me with you,' she had said and he had thought she was joking.

Had she been joking? What would she have done if he had suddenly said, 'O.K.'? By now she might have been speeding away with him, her suitcase in the back of his car on her way to start a new life in Australia. Not really. Nothing was ever that simple.

'Tell Dad,' he had said, but not 'tell Michael.' He hadn't mentioned Michael at all now she came to think about it and neither had she. Michael was almost like a stranger these days. A casual acquaintance from the past, someone that you might bump into and not know what to say, the acquaintance having been so slight that there was nothing in common. She seldom heard from him. He was wrapped up in his important new life in London with his important new friends. He's ashamed of us, Nicky thought. He doesn't want his posh London friends to meet us or risk them finding out how ordinary and common his family is. Not, she reflected, that they really were a family anymore.

She remembered very clearly how on the day that she and Mark got married, more than one of the guests had made fatuous comments about the patter of tiny feet. That's what everyone had expected then: that she and Mark would start to produce grandchildren for her parents. According to the script Mum and Dad would have been grandparents by now and Dennis would have been on the point of settling down with some nice girl too. All neat pieces fitting into the jigsaw. Only that was not how it was going to be. Ugly misshapen holes had appeared where pieces were missing.

It was all so unfair. Everything would have been different if she hadn't miscarried that baby. It would have bound herself and Mark together and a new generation might have given Mum something to live for. In moments like this she tended to forget that Mark was a serial adulterer.

'You'll be all right,' Dennis had said. 'You've got Clive.' The statement echoed and re-echoed in her head, filling her with gut wrenching self loathing and guilt.

She knew the precise moment when the excitement of her relationship with Clive had died. In the extremes of passion he had called her 'baby doll' and although she had not outwardly reacted, from that moment onwards the transaction had become no more than a mechanical operation on her part. The use of an expression innocently intended as a term of endearment had deflated her fervour as fast as a pin applied to a balloon and made her feel merely ridiculous as she looked in the mirror and saw a plump, twenty seven year old blonde, sleazily clad in fishnets and suspenders.

When she thought about it now it seemed to Nicky that her passion for Clive had burned dazzlingly hot and bright, like a match set to a scrap of paper which flared and sparked until without warning the paper was completely consumed and the flames abruptly gone, leaving only blackened ash behind. The flame had died just before Christmas and Nicky had been tasting ashes ever since. So far she had managed to conceal this change in her feelings from Clive. It wasn't just that she didn't want to hurt him. At least that would have been a noble motive. No, it was far worse, far worthier of contempt that that.

In fact it was a hideous mess. She was horribly conscious

of her total dependency upon Clive. He had persuaded her to give up work because he said he preferred her to stay at home, where he was willing to provide her with every material thing she could possibly need. In fact he positively encouraged her to buy whatever she wanted, accompanying her on shopping trips so that he could pick up the bills himself. All of which made her feel thoroughly disloyal and dishonest for faking and in constant dread that he would realise his feelings for her were no longer reciprocated.

The trouble was she didn't know what to do. She knew she couldn't turn to her father and Vi, who would probably take the view that having made her bed she should lie on it. (Which in this particular case she thought, had connotations they could not even dream of.) Her pride would not let her turn to Becky. Becky had rung only a few days previously, inviting her over because Joanne was coming to stay, but she had invented a prior engagement because she thought that Becka would only have to look into her face to know the truth… and also because Clive made no secret of the fact that he did not particularly like Becky.

To make matters worse, Clive had become more controlling. He liked to know where she was all the time. He had been in the room when she took the call from Becky and she noticed that he seemed pleased when she turned down Becky's invitation. Yet another concern lay in the nature of the diversions Clive enjoyed. These activities, however playful, seemed to be moving ever further in directions which made Nicky uncomfortable. She tried to tell herself that it was only because Clive no longer excited her, that the games in the bedroom had developed a frightening edge. She might have put up more objections but she had a variety of reasons for not saying 'no': not least that she was often so disgusted with herself that she could not help thinking she deserved whatever punishments and humiliations came her way.

Chapter Thirty-Four

1971

One winter term in the covered cloister had been enough to dampen all but the most diehard sandwich enthusiasts and even Becky had reverted to buying school dinners. In the meantime it had become more and more difficult to avoid eviction from the cloakroom, now that they were too big to hide behind the coats, but in their efforts to avoid being forced outdoors the four friends had come up with the ruse of sitting at the top of the stone steps which led up into the back of the assembly hall, where patrolling prefects often left them alone on the mistaken assumption that they had something to do with the 'West Side Story' rehearsals which were taking place inside on an almost daily basis.

Although the steps were a particularly chilly spot, they did have the advantage of being reasonably private, enabling conversations which one might not have undertaken in the more public arena of the form room and it was here during one lunch hour that Paula asked the other three: 'Does anyone know what preppy means?'

Paula had been reading 'Love Story' during R.E. with the paperback propped up behind her 'New English Bible'. The film hadn't reached Birmingham yet but Paula had bought a copy of the book and was going to lend it round as soon as she had finished it. She had saved her question until now because it never did to admit ignorance on any subject in the presence of Insufferable Alex or Know All Norma, who were all but guaranteed to exclaim: 'Fancy you not knowing that'.

'What?' asked Jo.

'Preppy,' said Paula. 'That's what the girl keeps calling him all through the book.'

'Is it a sort of nickname?' asked Becky.

'I don't think so. His name's Oliver Barrett.'

'Is there any you-know-what in it?' asked Nicky.

'Hardly any,' said Paula. 'But it's a very good book just the same.'

'Bagsy I have it next,' said Nicky.

'Did you see that programme about Hampton Court, last night?' asked Paula.

'My dad wouldn't have it on,' said Joanne.

'Didn't you tell him that Miss Pentland said to watch it because we're doing the Tudors?' asked Paula, to whose parents any suggestion from school that a television programme might have educational relevance was almost akin to a direct edict from the Almighty.

'Yes,' said Jo. ' And he said,' here she adopted a gruff, grumpy voice: '"When Miss Pentland pays our bleedin' T.V. licence then she can say what we have on." He's always the same,' she continued, reverting to her usual voice. 'If me or Bri wants to watch a programme the best thing is not to say anything and that way there's a one in three chance he'll have it on. But if he knows there's something on that we want to watch, he always pretends there's something he'd rather see on the other channel.'

'Not really?' asked Nicky.

'He does it with Mum, too. Last week there was this thing she wanted to watch on B.B.C.1. He couldn't pretend to want to watch ITV because it was Benny Hill and he can't stand Benny Hill so he had to put B.B.C. Two on. It was this programme about Ancient Egypt and he was bored to tears, but he had to watch it.' Joanne chuckled at the recollection.

'My dad's not like that,' said Nicky. 'Although if there's football on he won't let us watch anything else. And he keeps talking through 'Top of the Pops' and saying they're all a load of poufs.'

'It's a shame someone hasn't invented something where you can record programmes off the television,' said Paula. 'Then I could have recorded it for you. Did you see it Becka?'

'No,' said Becky. 'I was upstairs.'

She did not add that she would not have asked Stan if she could watch it under any circumstances, because although he would probably have agreed, he would also have made it sound like a huge favour and then brought it up at regular intervals when he chitted her for not helping more in the house.

'I saw it,' said Nicky. 'It was quite interesting although they didn't say anything about Catherine Howard's ghost.'

'I heard some first years saying that someone had seen Miss Forster again,' Jo broke in.

'You can't rely on first years,' said Becky.

'No one in our form has seen her yet,' said Nicky. 'I tell

you what though… Have you noticed that Miss Harkness doesn't use Miss Forster's old room? I bet it's because she doesn't want to be in there on her own.'

'More likely because she's not the proper headmistress,' said Paula. 'She's probably not allowed to use it.'

'According to these first years someone saw Miss Forster sitting at her desk, when they were walking past the window,' said Jo.

'I don't believe that,' said Becky. 'For a start no one's allowed on that bit of the top drive so how could they have seen through the window?'

'Well I wouldn't like to be the new headmistress,' said Nicky. 'Having to sit all by myself in that room.' She gave a visible shiver, induced not just by the cold stone floor they were sitting on but also by pleasurable speculations on the supernatural.

'I wonder what it's like to live in a real haunted house,' said Paula. 'I think I might write a ghost story next.'

'Our house might as well be haunted,' said Becky grimly. 'The spirit of Marvellous Muriel is everywhere you look.'

'How do you mean?' asked Jo.

'Me and Mum aren't allowed to change anything. Mum wanted to move this really horrible china cupid thing but Stan said it had been a present from Muriel's sister and he wanted it left where it was. He even likes the cups and saucers put in the cupboard a certain way because he says that's the way *we* have them, when what he means is, that's the way he and Muriel always had them. There's even this picture of Muriel on the living room wall. It's not right. Mum's his wife now and there isn't a picture of her up anywhere. I hate that picture. The eyes follow you everywhere.' From within the hall, they heard the piano strike up and a voice began to sing, 'I like to be in America'.

'I just hate fat faced old Muriel,' Becky sang along, struggling to fit her own words to the tune.

'What are you four doing here?'

None of them had registered the approach of the sixth former.

'We're just going into rehearsals,' Joanne lied.

'Come on then.' The older girl stepped round them and called their bluff by opening the door to reveal an unhappy looking Mr Sinton, who had just signalled to cut off his vocalist mid-bar.

Mr Sinton was not having a good day. Miss Mislet had been making difficulties about his having the hall again, demanding that she have the use of it at least once a week, to practice the girls who had volunteered for that silly marching about business that she had insisted on organising for the gala day. The actual display was scheduled to take place on the playing field, but it was currently impossible to practice out there because the ground was too muddy. (His suggestion that the participants all wear their hockey boots had been dismissed as facetious.) When he had offered her the use of the hall on Thursdays – the day which best suited himself and the others involved in 'West Side Story' – she had dismissed it out of hand because Thursday lunchtimes was when maths club took place. Until that moment Mr Sinton had had no idea that there *was* such a thing as maths club. Then he'd suggested she use the gym, but Miss Leopold had refused to make the gym available to either party in case her equipment was interfered with.

Though he had eventually won the battle for possession

of the hall, things were still not going well. The music and drama departments of Eleanor Vaux and Saint Luke's had chosen 'West Side Story' on the grounds that each institution had pupils at their disposal with strong enough voices to carry the respective male and female leads… but voices were not everything. The chief musical star from Saint Luke's was a boy called Dean Chatterton and while there was no doubt that he could sing, he was not a natural Tony, being a short, thickset youth, whose acting abilities seemed next to non-existent. To make matters worse Dean appeared to be completely in awe of the opposite sex and approached Eleanor Vaux's Maria, a fourth former called Lynda Jackson, much as a newly appointed zoo keeper might approach a dangerous snake. The situation was not improved by Lynda Jackson's habit of unexpectedly being consumed by giggles for no apparent reason.

Preoccupied with his problems, Mr Sinton did not even notice the back door of the hall opening. 'Again, again,' he said, rapping his pencil impatiently against his music. 'I like the city of San Juan… come on… Oh what on earth is it now?'

'I think someone wants you, sir.' One of the Saint Luke's boys piped up from where he and the other Sharks and Jets were lurking at one side of the hall.

Mr Sinton turned to find that a prefect had appeared behind him with four members of his form in tow. 'What is it?' The music teacher's tone was uncharacteristically sharp.

'I found these girls outside the hall, sir,' the girl said, taken aback by her reception. 'They said they were allowed to be there because they're something to do with the show.'

Mr Sinton stared at the prefect, only half listening and not grasping the point of this latest interruption. There weren't any third formers in 'West Side Story' because none of the younger girls had passed the auditions. Why then had she brought these girls into rehearsal? 'Very well,' he said. 'Yes, thank you.' He turned away and gave a tap on the music.

The prefect decided that she had been dismissed and left the way she had come, leaving the four members of IIIS standing at the back of the hall, uncertain what to do next.

Thoroughly ruffled by the incident, Mr Sinton felt for his pocket and found that it wasn't there. 'Damn,' he said. 'I've left my coat in the music room.'

'Shall I fetch it for you, sir?' Joanne Embury appeared alongside him like a small, eager guardian angel. It felt like the first helpful suggestion anyone had made all day and when he nodded she set off smartly, returning with the coat in no time at all.

At the end of the rehearsal he noticed the way Joanne and her friends stayed behind to put all the chairs back in their rightful places without being asked. He couldn't for the life of him remember what they were doing there, but it was very nice of them to be so helpful and when they appeared in the hall at each lunchtime rehearsal thereafter he simply accepted their presence without question. The four girls were very quiet and well behaved and always kept well out of the way unless there was an errand to run. Mr Sinton was never quite sure how they came to be involved, but concluded that it had been a good initiative on somebody's part because a spare body or two to run errands did not come amiss at all.

Chapter Thirty-Five

1985

'I've been wondering whether I ought to ring Nicky,' Joanne mused. 'You know… maybe try to get some sort of reconciliation going between her and Becky.'

'It'll probably blow over. It's only a spat over some bloke. If you ask me, I think you'd be better keeping out of it.' Ant was reading through some papers which had arrived about the sale of the gallery and was clearly not willing to give the matter her full attention.

'That may be how it started but it's been going on for months now. It's made things feel really awkward. After Nicky made an excuse not to meet up I sort of feel like I can't ring her either.'

'So what? You often go for quite a long time without being in touch with either of them. It's kind of inevitable you know? People grow up, move on, move away.'

Joanne was about to say that could never happen when she remembered that Ant did not really like her going on about her old school friends. Instead she asked: 'So this is definitely it? We sign next Tuesday and book the removal men?'

'Yup. Goodbye Cornwall.'

'I just hope we're not heading out of the frying pan and into the fire.'

'Jeez – you are *so* Glass Half Full Girl lately.'

'It's another rural area and it's way up north.'

'But you loved it when we went up there. You were inspired. Don't tell me you're getting cold feet now?'

'Maybe it isn't the place. Maybe it's the time. We're getting a lot of really bad press just now.'

'You and me? I didn't even know we'd been in the press.'

'You know what I mean.'

'We can't hide away in a London lesbian ghetto for the rest of our lives. We've got our dreams and we're the only people who can achieve them. Everywhere won't be like this.'

'Suppose...' Joanne stopped. She had been about to ask, suppose it is? But she knew they had been through the whys and wherefores many times before and ultimately agreed that if this second attempt did not make good then a return to what Ant jokingly described as their London lesbian ghetto might well be the only option left on the table. She stood up and started to tidy away the pile of magazines and newspaper which was spilling all over the table, unconsciously humming to herself – an old favourite from 'West Side Story'.

Ant put her papers aside and held out her arms. 'There *is* a place for us,' she said. 'And we will find it. In fact, let's hope we're on our way there now.'

Chapter Thirty-Six

1971

'Mrs Carpigo,' said Paula. 'Car-peeg-oh. It's Italian.'

'My word that's a new departure,' said her mother.

'Mr Sinton said it's because her husband is of Italian descent. It's probably not that unusual in Italy.'

'I wasn't referring to her name,' Mrs Morrison said. 'I meant that it's unusual to have a Mrs. There's never been a *married* head at Evies. It was dear old Miss Butterworth when I started. She was only the second person to be headmistress and I'm sure the first one wasn't married. Then of course Miss Butterworth died when I was doing school certificate and Miss Cresswall came. Isn't it funny the way the same thing has happened to you?'

The way she smiled, Paula thought, anyone might think that this unfortunate business of headmistresses dropping dead made for some jolly point of commonality between them. Ignoring the smile she said: 'I've got to go into school on Saturday for rehearsals.'

'Oh dear.' Her mother's smile vanished. 'I do hope that

while you're spending so much time on this school play you're not neglecting other, more important things.'

'Such as?' Paula enquired in a tone she knew her mother considered borderline rude.

'Well your maths marks are nothing to write home about.'

'I wouldn't be doing maths on a Saturday.'

'Well perhaps you should be. You know Daddy would gladly sit down with you for an hour or so on a Saturday to give you some extra help. Or you might be playing tennis. Just think, this year if you practiced a bit more…'

'Alex and Norma are automatic selection for the team,' Paula cut in. 'They're really good Mum, so it doesn't matter how much I practice…'

'Well I don't want to push you,' her mother said doubtfully. 'But we could always pay for some coaching.'

'It wouldn't do any good,' Paula said.

This was absolutely true because she had still managed to avoid letting Miss Leopold know that she could serve overarm and she had no intention of doing anything differently in the future.

'I don't see why you need to be at all these rehearsals,' Mrs Morrison began. 'It's not as if you're actually *in* the play.'

'We're in charge of the props table!' Paula exclaimed. 'Of course we have to be there. It's vital to have the right things handed to the cast at the right times. I have to give Chino his gun when he makes his final entrance.' How typical of her mother, she thought, to belittle what she was doing as if it was some unseen, hole in the corner aspect of the production, instead of appreciating the serious implications of having everything in the right place at the right time.

'West Side Story' had become the single most important thing around which their lives revolved. From the status of accidental spectators at rehearsals, they had graduated to the point of knowing every word by heart (which was more than could be said for some of the cast). As the youngest pupils present, they had initially been regarded with amused tolerance by their elders, which did not matter at all... just being allowed to watch from a distance had been enough in the beginning, because mere third years could not expect to mix with the cast, but then Mrs Heslop had put them in charge of the growing number of small props, together with a script highlighted in red biro to indicate precisely when props were needed. It gave you real status, Paula thought, having a script of your own.

Fortunately they had managed to see 'Love Story' the weekend before Saturday rehearsals began. Nicky went through a whole packet of Handy Andys and was still sniffing when they went round the Pick n'Mix in Woollies afterwards. 'Wasn't it awful when you knew she was going to die?' she said.

'We knew she was going to die before it started,' said Joanne. 'We'd all read the book. Did you notice how skinny Ali McGraw's legs are?'

Paula felt that Joanne wasn't on the same wavelength as herself when it came to grasping the great tragedy of love. Clearly all great love stories ended in tragedy. Really romantic lovers didn't finish up boringly married and living for twenty years in the suburbs of Birmingham, the way her parents had done. 'If you're going to die for love,' she mused, transferring the toffee she was eating to one side of her mouth to better facilitate talking. 'Then I should think leukaemia is a better way to go than being shot like Tony or drinking poison like Romeo.'

'The poison was pretty quick,' said Becky.

'I expect it tasted pretty horrible,' said Nicky.

'Anything would be better than stabbing yourself like Juliet did,' said Becky. 'That must be really awful.'

'Or hanging yourself,' said Nicky.

'Who hung themselves?' asked Paula.

'No one in particular. I was just saying.'

'Do you think you could stab yourself?' asked Jo.

'I couldn't,' said Becky. 'I'd have to take tablets.'

'No, I don't mean could *you* do it. I mean would it work? If you stabbed yourself just once, would that be enough to kill you?'

'You'd have to do it just right,' Paula speculated. 'If you didn't hit the heart, I don't think it would work. You do hear of people surviving stab wounds.'

'Well Juliet only stabbed herself once,' said Nicky. 'And it did the trick for her.'

'Yes but that's Shakespeare,' Jo said. 'And he could get away with anything. Look at that bit in 'Julius Caesar' where he has somebody telling the other characters to take off their hats, when everyone knows that they wouldn't have been wearing any because it was Ancient Rome. We'd never get away with writing anything like that. Mrs Heslop would put a line through it and tell you off for not doing your research properly.'

*

For Saturday rehearsals everyone had permission to wear their ordinary clothes, so after much consultation the four youngest members of the backstage team had all decided to wear pink cord flares, which proved a happy choice because almost every pupil turned up in a similar pair of trousers. It felt strange to be in school on a Saturday. The empty corridors echoed and the building had a different air, as though it was enjoying the sense of being relaxed and off duty as much as they were.

As soon as they arrived Mrs Heslop introduced them to Stu Redbridge, a boy from Saint Luke's lower sixth, who had worked on past school productions as the stage manager and was so trusted by the staff that he was to be left in overall charge of everything behind the scenes. They took to Stu at once. He talked to them in a thoroughly business-like, unpatronising way. ('Perhaps,' said Becky, 'he doesn't realise that we're only third years.') While the cast were engaged elsewhere, Stu ran through the various scene changes that would need to be accomplished. All went well until his team of scene shifters tried carrying on the tables and dummies which were used in the dress shop scene and the table intended to represent a counter got tilted on the stairs so that some of its contents rolled off.

'Fuck,' said Stu, whose vocabulary had become more colourful in the absence of any teachers.

'Excuse me,' said Becky. 'But if we followed the… the others onto the stage carrying those things on trays, it wouldn't take any longer than a few seconds for us to put them where they have to go.'

'Good idea,' said Stu and Becky blushed deep crimson, secretly wishing that the rest of IIIS could see her hobnobbing with these lower sixth boys. 'Let's try it that way. Where can we get some trays?'

'I'll get some from the dining hall.' Joanne bolted away at top speed. After all there were no prefects around to order her to stop running.

By the time the cast attempted their first full run through, the back stage team was working like a well oiled machine. 'When we have the dress rehearsal next Saturday,' Stu told them. 'We've got to keep these wings clear of any non-essential people. There's going to be a whole lot of girls from your school involved with wardrobe and make-up and we can't have them sneaking in here for a look, so if any of them show up – and they will – I remember how it was when we did 'HMS Pinafore' – just tell them to clear off.'

'What if they won't go?' asked Jo. 'Some of them might be older than us,' she added by way of an explanation.

'Doesn't matter how old they are,' said Stu. 'You're in charge here. If you have any trouble,' he added, 'just fetch me.'

'Isn't he dreamy,' Nicky asked the others on their way home. 'I love his hair. It's a bit like Marc Bolan's only blonde.'

'I like the one called Andy better,' said Becky. 'He's sort of shy.'

'Is that the tall thin one who does the lights?'

'No, not him. He's a complete wombat. The one with the Black Sabbath tee shirt.'

Paula had privately taken a liking to a boy with glasses and bad acne, because he was so cheerful and had something funny to say about everything, but she did not say so. Apart from anything else she didn't want to describe him to the others in those terms. However it wasn't easy to discover what his name was. The teachers from St Luke's all called the boys by their surnames, while the boys themselves mostly called each other names like Wagger and Muzzo. She'd overheard one teacher calling the boy with the sense of humour Neary, but she couldn't call him that. It would be really frabjous if he had noticed her too. It didn't really matter about his spots because it wasn't as if he was likely to want to kiss her or anything like that. It would be enough if he would just talk to her for a bit.

To cater for the demand from both schools 'West Side Story' was playing for five consecutive nights, starting on a Tuesday and running through until Saturday. Seven months of effort and it would all be over in less than a week.

The dress rehearsal did not go well. Dean Chatterton's dying scene had been marred by a particularly hysterical fit of giggles from his leading lady. The girl playing Anita had been simply wonderful until her black wig fell over her eyes, and soon after that two Jets had collided during a dance routine and ended up in an undignified heap on the floor. At the end of it all Mr Sinton went home to get drunk, vowing as he always did on the eve of school productions that he would never agree to do another.

By the opening night Mr Sinton was stalking the corridors looking like a condemned man. Most of the cast and crew lived too far away to make it worth their while travelling home after school, so instead they changed out of their uniforms within seconds of the final bell, or in some cases merely removed ties and undid top buttons, because they would be getting into costumes later. Wherever he went Mr Sinton all but fell over groups playing cards or eating sandwiches (if the shade of Miss Forster truly haunted the school, she must have been pale with horror at the sight of so many crumbs and rodent enticing goodies being consumed all over the building). Cutting through the wings he found Rebecca Addison standing guard over the props table. She had improvised a clipboard out of a piece of thick card and a bulldog clip and looked formidably efficient. The other three musketeers were missing, but he met them a few minutes later coming along the top corridor.

'Good luck sir,' Nicola Christie said brightly.

'Crumbs,' said Paula, when they reached the wings. 'Mr Sinton looks as nervous as if he'd got to go on himself.'

'You should see what they've done to Room 12,' Paula said to Becky. 'They've moved all the desks back except for one row at the front where they've put mirrors. They're going to use it for make-up. There's towels and plastic capes laid out on each chair and the biggest jar of Nivea cream you've ever seen in your life.'

Becky had something of her own to show them. It was the programme, hot off the school duplicator.

'Wow,' said Jo. 'I love the drawing on the front.'

'A sixth former did it,' said Becky. 'But never mind that. Look inside... there... down at the bottom of the second page.'

The proffered page drew gasps of delight and amazement.

Stage Manager: Stuart Redbridge

Stage Crew: Andrew Bleasdale, John Matthews, Jonathan Neary, Christian Shaw, Rebecca Addison, Nicola Christie, Joanne Embury & Paula Morrison.

'Oh my God,' squealed Nicky. 'We're in the programme.

How can I get one? I've got to take one home to show Mum and Dad.'

'Just ask the people on the door,' said Becky. 'They've got hundreds. Stu came round with some but he says there are loads more.'

Nicola dashed away to obtain another programme while Becky went off to poke her head into make-up and wardrobe.

'I'm dying for the loo,' said Jo. 'Will you stand guard for a few minutes?'

'Of course,' said Paula. 'I'll be fine.'

When she lay in bed at night Paula had sometimes pictured the props table, challenging herself to remember everything on it. She knew every single thing on it, every single cue… They had never put a foot wrong at rehearsals but suppose it all went wrong tonight? She pulled herself together. Nothing was going to go wrong. She didn't need to know things from memory because they had marked scripts and a master list compiled by Becky, which had been written and re-written until it was perfect. Thank goodness I'm backstage, she thought. I'd be beside myself now if I actually had to go on.

At that moment two of her fellow stage crew appeared, one of whom she now knew was called Jonathan Neary. 'Hello,' he said. 'All on your own?'

It was the first time he had ever spoken to her directly. She was struck dumb with the weightiness of the moment. 'Yeah,' was all she managed to say.

The two boys wandered out again, leaving Paula to wonder whether she was really the most stupid person in the whole world.

At half past five the girls decided that it was time to eat their tea, swapping their cakes and sandwiches between them. Nicky's Mum had provided a whole box of Mr Kipling's Jam Tarts, which they readily agreed were superior in every way to the strange cardboard and glue versions which they had manufactured in domestic science the day before. They had already drawn all the heavy, black lined curtains at the hall windows. The torches they used in the wings had been checked and Stu had put spare batteries at the ready – just in case. At 6.30 the first members of the audience began to appear, their route to the hall carefully segregated from the parts of the school now officially designated 'backstage'.

The fourth year girl who was playing Consuela appeared in the wings and was about to ascend the steps onto the stage when Stu stopped her. 'What are you doing?' he asked.

'I was just going to peep through the curtains to see if my parents are here yet.'

'Well don't,' he said. 'You wouldn't see a professional actress peeping through the curtains would you?'

Thoroughly abashed, the girl withdrew at once. The props assistants exchanged knowing looks. You wouldn't catch them doing anything so unprofessional, whether their parents were out front or not. Nicola's Mum had bought a ticket for Thursday evening, saying: 'Although I won't be able to see you, love, I know you'll be doing your bit at the back of the stage.'

Joanne's parents had taken a different line. 'It's not as though you're in it,' her father said. 'Anyway it's only a bunch of kids. If I want to see something half decent I'll stay here and watch the telly.'

Becky hadn't bothered to ask her mother if she wanted any tickets. Paula's parents had come 'to support the school'.

With ten minutes to curtain up Paula suddenly remembered that she had left her school uniform and bag in their form room.

'You'd better go and fetch it now,' said Nicky. 'If the room isn't already locked up.'

Paula sprinted along the top corridor, avoiding a posse of Sharks, Jets and make-up girls who were watching Anita shaking her head violently in order to demonstrate that her wig was well and truly anchored to her head. The form room was in darkness, but to Paula's immense relief it was not locked and even without switching on the lights there was enough light coming in through the windows on the corridor side to see that the shadowy lump of her school uniform was still lying where she had dumped it on top of her desk and on the chair beside it stood the plastic carrier bag which she now used for school, because everyone in the third year knew that satchels and brief cases simply weren't cool.

She was already half way across the room to retrieve her things when she realised that she was not alone. Dean Chatterton had been standing by the outside windows in the dark, apparently watching the latecomers filtering in along the top drive.

'Ooh, sorry,' exclaimed Paula. 'I didn't know there was anyone in here. I've just come to collect my stuff.'

She was afraid that she had startled him. He was all ready to go on, his hair tamed with Brylcream, his face tanned pale orange by an unskilled but enthusiastic make-up artiste and he was wearing the leather jacket (which looked really good from a distance) made by Mrs Badham, the needlework teacher, out of a job lot of black P.V.C.

'It's all right,' he said.

Paula had never spoken to or been addressed by Dean before, but something in his voice and demeanour made her brave. 'Are you O.K?' she asked. 'Is there anything I can get for you?'

'I doubt it,' he said. 'Not unless you can get me out of here.' He gave a weak laugh.

Oh no, she thought. He's got stage fright. He's not going to go on. She took a deep breath. 'You must be very nervous,' she said. 'I'm nervous and I've only got to carry a few things on and off the stage. I do the props. It's me who hands Chino the gun he uses to shoot you.' She gathered up her clothes and bag of books, clutching them to her chest while she was speaking.

'I know,' he said.

There was an awkward silence.

'It'll fine once we get going,' Paula said. 'It's just this last bit of waiting that's really hard.'

He did not reply.

Paula had reached the classroom door but she couldn't manage to open it with both hands full, so she had to stop and temporarily dump some of her load on the nearest desk. 'Where we stand we can hear you beautifully,' she said shyly, not looking at him while she crumpled her school skirt into a ball and tried to force it into the top of her bag. 'When you sing 'Maria' it sends shivers up my spine.'

'No kidding?'

She did not mind him laughing at her if she had

managed to cheer him up a bit. 'Are you going to be a professional singer?' she asked. 'When you grow… I mean leave school?'

'No,' he said. 'I'm going to be an engineer.'

It was a total conversation stopper. Paula was not at all clear what an engineer did. She thought it might have something to do with railway trains.

'Here,' he crossed the room and opened the door. 'Let me hold it for you.'

'Thanks,' she said. 'Good Luck. For tonight I mean. Not that you need it. You're really good.' She blushed. It was the longest conversation she had had with one of the Saint Luke's boys but if it made him feel more confident then it was worth the effort.

Nerves or not, Dean Chatterton sang wonderfully that night and in each of the succeeding performances. On the last night the entire cast took several curtain calls and a protesting Mr Sinton was dragged centre stage amid shouts of 'Producer!'

In spite of this rapturous reaction from the majority of the audience, the production did not generate universal approval. Although not due to take up her post until after Easter, Mrs Carpigo had deemed it appropriate to put in an appearance at the final performance. She had been rather surprised to learn that the school was doing 'West Side Story', which she considered a questionable choice with its knife fights and dialogue which hinted at the existence of prostitution. During the first half of the show she sat stone faced in the front row, confirmed in her opinion that this was completely unsuitable material for school children. And some of the costumes! The girl playing the female lead made her initial appearance in what amounted to no more than a petticoat.

During the interval while she was taking a cup of tea in the dining hall, she almost collided with Mr Sinton, whom she suspected of bearing a substantial degree of responsibility for the choice and execution of the material. He was, she thought, a singularly untidy little man and the way he kept mopping his brow with a ridiculously large handkerchief irritated her profoundly.

'It must have taken a great many hours to put all this together,' she said, thinking of all the unsuitably late nights and skimped homeworks which must necessarily have been involved.

'Oh yes indeed. But well worth it.' Mr Sinton was so pleased with the way everything was going and so relieved to have almost got through the school production for another year, that his ebullience was undiminished, in spite of not spotting this cold fish until it was too late to take evasive action. 'The pupils have worked really hard,' he said. 'But they've had tremendous fun too.'

Mrs Carpigo's left eyebrow twitched upward. She always viewed the F word with suspicion. Fortunately a school governor chose that moment to home in on the new headmistress and Mr Sinton was able to make his escape.

At the end of the performance Mrs Carpigo did no more than go through the motions of applauding politely, although she observed that some of the women in the audience had actually applied tissues to their eyes when Tony and Maria sang 'There's A Place For Us'. A certain class of person was always easily entertained.

Eleanor Vaux was Mrs Carpigo's first headship and she

had no intention of underestimating the challenges which lay ahead. A school like Eleanor Vaux could not afford to let standards slip, she thought. In her scheme of things there would be very little leeway for wasting excessive amounts of time on art and drama. Nor would the false pretensions of faded academics be allowed to dictate the agenda. Latin, Greek and classical studies would need to be discreetly faded out because with Britain soon to join the Common Market, modern languages were the way forward, together with an emphasis on the important things, maths, English and 'O' level science: the sort of subjects which got girls into good solid careers in teaching, nursing and banking. And if standards were not to fall, discipline was the key.

As she walked down the drive to reach her parked car, Mrs Carpigo glanced across at the school building. Beyond the darkened classrooms, sections of the brightly lit top corridor could be seen through the internal windows and she was not amused to glimpse a conga line weaving its way along. Although her view was impeded by the internal classroom walls, she was fairly sure that it was being led by Mr Sinton.

Chapter Thirty-Seven

1985

By mutual consent Ant had gone into Keswick to shop for food while Jo continued to tackle the unpacking. Their main priority had been to get the gallery side of the premises up and running, which meant that after a week's residence they had barely scratched the surface when it came to sorting out their domestic possessions. Jo was at a point where she felt she would make faster progress on her own and as Ant could not always be relied upon to stay on task, it was no surprise when she returned from Keswick bearing not only groceries, but three second hand paperbacks and the new recording of 'West Side Story', featuring Kiri Te Kanawa and Jose Carreras.

'We did 'West Side Story' at school one year,' said Jo.

'As a school production? That was a bit ambitious wasn't it?'

'I know… but there happened to be quite a few people at the school who were really good singers.'

'Were you in it?'

'With my voice? No chance.' Joanne laughed. 'I was helping out backstage. It was before I got involved with painting the scenery. For 'West Side Story' I was just working with the props and doing a bit of scenery shifting. It was great fun. I loved every minute of it.' She continued to unpack things from the tea chest while she was talking.

'I'll put all the stuff from the supermarket away and then I'll make some proper coffee,' Ant said. 'And after that I'll get started on another box. Seeing you makes me feel quite guilty. You should have come into Keswick with me and given yourself a break.'

'I'm all right. Anyway it was a good job someone stayed. That woman came to pick up her framing while you were out. She seemed really pleased with it. Pretty good going, getting some work right off like that when we've not even opened full time.'

'Definitely a case of so far so good,' said Antonia. 'The natives really do seem friendly. The man at Holme Lea was out in his garden again and he made a point of speaking to me as I got out of the car.'

'Oh look,' exclaimed Joanne. 'Isn't that funny? We were just talking about 'West Side Story' and now I've come across the photos.' She held out some paper photograph wallets, the first of which she had opened. Forgetting her urgent need for caffeine Ant came over to look.

'These were taken on the last night I think,' said Joanne. 'Everyone's on there… even the backstage people and the make-up girls. Here's me…' Her finger hovered over a girl with long auburn hair whose face was mostly obscured behind owlish glasses.

'You'd still got your specs,' Antonia commented.

'I didn't get contacts until ages after I left school. Oh look… there's Gill Rogers. She played Anybodies. I had a huge crush on her. She had the most wonderful bone structure and I used to cover sheets and sheets of paper at home, trying to draw her from memory.'

'Was it reciprocated?'

'I shouldn't think so. She was three years ahead of me. And she was probably straight.'

'Is this Becky?'

'Yes. And here's Paula and here's Nick. Goodness how young we all looked. And this is Mr Sinton. He was our form teacher that year as well as being in charge of the play. That might have been how we got involved… I can't remember how it happened now. That guy there, the one with the blonde frizzy hair, was called Stu. He was the stage manager. He was really nice. Oh and this girl here – the one in the scary black wig – is Julie Shaw who played Anita. She actually went on to become a real actress on T.V. although nothing much was ever made of it. It wasn't an Evie sort of thing… becoming an actress. It was seen as a bit racy and not quite respectable.'

Antonia grinned. 'Not at all like becoming a lesbian painter then?'

'Put it like this, I don't think either of us are going to get invited back to present the prizes on speech day any time soon.'

They worked on through the remainder of the afternoon and into the evening, breaking off only for the pizza and a ready prepared salad which Ant had purchased earlier in the day.

'This moving business is absolutely knackering,' Jo

moaned as they settled into bed. 'It's only just after ten and I'm exhausted.'

Before Ant could reply they both heard the distinct snap of the letterbox springing shut. Joanne sat bolt upright.

'Bit late for the postman,' said Ant, in a carefully light hearted tone. 'Let's leave it for tonight whatever it is.'

'I'll have to go down and have a look,' said Jo.

'Leave it for now. '

'I'll never sleep otherwise.'

Antonia sighed. 'Let me go,' she said, but Jo's feet were already over the side of the bed.

'Shall I come down with you?'

'Of course not.'

Jo moved with a very light step but even so the elderly stairs creaked in protest, registering both her cautious descent and then a moment or two later her somewhat speedier return. When she re-entered the room Ant was relieved to see that she was holding an innocuous looking envelope in one hand and the card she had obviously extracted from it in the other.

'It's from Hugh and Mary at Holme Lea,' said Jo. 'Asking if we'd like to go round for supper on Thursday evening.'

Antonia's face broke into a grin. She held out her arms to Jo and they hugged one another silently for a moment before Jo whispered, 'I think it's going to be O.K.'

Chapter Thirty-Eight

1971

It was almost the end of the summer term when Miss Barr came to address the school in a special assembly. Unbeknown to the pupils Miss Barr had virtually invited herself, writing to Mrs Carpigo in a clear, copperplate hand, saying that she noted it was the year of the school's golden jubilee and that having addressed the school on the occasion of the silver jubilee in 1946, she wondered if it might be possible to repeat the exercise in 1971. She had even suggested a convenient date.

Having checked a copy of the school history and established that Miss Barr was the only surviving incumbent of the headship apart from herself, Mrs Carpigo had written back, cautiously accepting Miss Barr's suggestion, while inwardly wondering what special arrangements they might need to make in order to accommodate this presumably frail octogenarian. In the event Miss Barr had paid off her taxi driver, mounted the front steps (with considerably more agility or enthusiasm than Miss Mislet had managed for some years) and engaged two passing pupils in conversation before Mrs Carpigo – who had been watching for the arrival of their guest from her nearby office window – was able to get out into the entrance hall to greet her.

Miss Barr had no difficulty in mounting the platform in the hall and sang the first hymn ('He Who Would Valiant Be') in a fine contralto, without need to refer to the hymn book in her hand. When Mrs Carpigo introduced her, Miss Barr stood up and moved as delicately as a dancer to the centre of the platform, where she stood for some time with her face tilted slightly upward and her eyes apparently focussed on a point somewhere near the ceiling. She appeared to be inhaling deeply. There was a prolonged pause.

Mrs Carpigo had just decided that her guest was senile after all and was about to exchange a despairing look with Miss Harkness when Miss Barr said: 'Yes… it still smells the same.'

After a fraction's hesitation while they judged her mood, the entire school burst into gales of laughter. Judging her moment like a seasoned entertainer, Miss Barr waited just long enough for them to settle before she continued, 'It's good to be back.'

All over the hall girls surreptitiously eased themselves into more comfortable positions. She had their attention now.

'I only spent seven years at Eleanor Vaux,' she said. 'But that is the longest time any of you will be here too so that gives us a common link if you like. I was much younger then. In fact I was not so very far away from my own school days. I still felt that I had much to achieve in life and I shared the hopes and dreams of my girls. For education is all about hopes and dreams and how to attain them. I grew up in an age when it was not the norm to offer women a good education, but I have always believed in the cause of education for women. I was the daughter of enlightened parents who sent me to school and then encouraged me to go on to university at a time when many girls were educated at home: a time when women were not welcomed into universities as they are now. It was a time when young women from working class homes were denied all but the most basic education before being sent to work in factories.

'Those girls had hopes and dreams too. Do not think that all those young women in the textile mills in Lancashire or the Birmingham wire works did not have hope and dreams: but so very many were denied the chance to achieve them. So much talent and intelligence went to waste.

'Schools like this one became a place where hopes could be nurtured and dreams transformed into reality. Every week I used to have a different group of girls into my study for tea after last lesson on Wednesday afternoons. I hope that tradition still continues,' she turned momentarily to Mrs Carpigo, but fortunately did not wait for an answer. 'We talked together about their ambitions and what the school could do to help achieve them. When each girl left I charged her to write to me every year and tell me what she was doing with her life. Many of them are writing to me still.

'I am a very fortunate woman. I have never forgotten that of all the gifts I have received in my life, education was the greatest gift of all.'

She continued to speak for a further twenty minutes, never once referring to any notes, neither hesitating nor repeating herself, her slight frame betraying no sign that she was tiring, her light, musical voice, holding the audience in the palm of her hand.

'I wish she was still the head here,' said Paula afterwards. 'Instead of Cow-Pig-O.'

Chapter Thirty-Nine

1985

Becky did not recognise the writing on the card – but of course anyone who wanted to avoid giving away their identity could get the florist to write the card for them.

Be my Valentine.

Meet me at 6pm by Victoria's statue.

'Red roses,' exclaimed Sadie, who had brought the bouquet up to Becky's office from reception, where it had been delivered. 'Someone's got a secret admirer. Shall I put them in some water for you? Your next client's already waiting downstairs.'

'Thanks. You are a sweet,' Becky responded. 'I've absolutely got to make a call, but once I'm done with that you can show him in.'

'No problem. Shall you go?'

'Go where?'

'To meet this guy, tonight?'

'Of course not,' said Becky. 'I don't know who it is. It

might be the Mad Axe Man of Great Barr for all we know. Or more likely it's a hoax.'

'Pretty expensive hoax,' said Sadie, turning the bouquet admiringly in her hands. 'It won't be a hoax. Do you know how much it costs to get even a single red rose delivered on Valentine's Day? There's…' she paused to double check. 'Nine here. Nine's a funny sort of number to send. I mean, people usually go for a single one or a dozen or a half dozen… or maybe even a round ten…'

'Yes, yes,' Becky laughed. 'I get the picture. We've got a nutter with a fixation for the number nine or an innumerate florist who can't count up to ten. Sadie, I *must* make this call.'

She pressed zero for an outside line and began to dial as Sadie departed, still gazing enviously at the flowers. While the phone at the other end rang out Becky considered the significance of the number nine. Three times three: a configuration that might appear specially significant to someone who believed that their lucky number was three. This ran through her mind in the milliseconds that it took for the phone to be answered at the other end. She asked for her client but was informed that he was on another line. Damn. No… she didn't want to speak with his secretary. (He had particularly instructed her not to discuss anything with his secretary.) Now he would be sure to call back when she was engaged with someone else. After leaving word that she had called, she buzzed reception to say they could show Mr Leverman up, but when her office door opened it was not Mr Leverman but Sadie, returning with the roses which had now been neatly arranged in an old fashioned glass vase.

‘I’ve saved the cellophane,’ she said. ‘So you can use it to take them home. Are you going to leave them here overnight while you go on your date?’

‘I’m not going on a date,’ said Becky firmly.

‘You’ve got no idea who sent them?’ Sadie sounded incredulous.

‘None at all,’ said Becky.

Having a suspicion was not the same as knowing. In any case she had no intention of letting the whole building in on her private affairs. Not that she had any private affairs to let them in on. If the flowers had come from the source she suspected then it wasn’t a live, ongoing affair. It was just something from the past. Something she had put in a box and closed the lid on. Something she wasn’t going to reopen or even think about, because that would hurt too much.

Sadie had plonked the vase down right in the centre of Becky’s desk, where not only would the roses sit directly between her and her clients, they were also in a sure fire position to get knocked over. She now regretted agreeing to Sadie’s putting them in a vase at all. They were so ostentatious and showy. It would have been much better to fill a sink in the ladies loo and keep them there, relatively out of sight and more easily out of mind, until she could take them home.

She carried the vase across to the window ledge, where she had to re-arrange a few files in order to make room for them. Even when relegated to the window sill, they were still very noticeable. For the remainder of the day, whether she was talking on the phone or working at her desk, the flowers contrived to sidle into view. Every time she wanted a file it happened to be located in a part of the room which allowed the flowers to loom up at her. There was simply no ignoring them.

She did not really have any doubts about where the flowers had come from. There hadn't been anyone else in her life since Sean. Nor ever would be, a little voice in her head chimed in unbidden. For some reason a picture of Miss Mislet loomed up in her mind. Miss Mislet had been an archetypal, middle aged spinster. There had been a whole posse of them at Eleanor Vaux. Spinsters of all shapes and sizes who were totally wrapped up in their work at Evies, just as she was now wrapped up in her own career. It was rumoured that Miss Mislet had once been involved in a tragic romance. Some people said that her fiancé had been killed in the war and this had rendered Miss Mislet an object of sympathetic pity. Not that it had been easy to imagine her as a participant in a doomed love affair, with her short, mousy hair and steel rimmed specs, but they had supposed that she must once have been young…

She was probably in her fifties when we knew her, Becky thought. A confirmed spinster devoted to her three cats. How was it that they knew Miss Mislet had had cats? But once upon a time Miss Mislet would only have been twenty eight. Was the tragic romance over and done with by then? Had Miss Mislet already consigned herself to the ranks of singletons forever? Or had she still hoped at twenty eight that maybe one day… getting on a train or standing in the grocer's buying food for her cats, she would somehow bump into Mr Right?

It was dark by half past four. A thin, slanting rain had begun to fall, leaving pale wet streaks across the dirty panes of her office window, and individual diamond droplets which glittered when they were caught by the lights on the upper decks of passing buses. Becky tried not to picture Sean as he vainly waited in the rain at the foot of the statue. Queen Victoria's statue had been on an island encircled by traffic when she was a child, but the area was pedestrianised now. It was very exposed there unless he sought shelter alongside the Town Hall. Of course it might have stopped raining by six o'clock.

Could she really leave him standing there? Was she that heartless? They had parted on good terms. Surely the least she could do would be to respond to his invitation by turning up to tell him yet again that it was no use? She would not agree to go for a drink with him, because she couldn't bear that, but perhaps she ought to at least walk down to Victoria Square and meet him. It was not even ten minutes out of her way. Standing him up was a cruel, horrible rejection, which he did not deserve. Then again if he saw her coming along New Street, it would send the wrong signal before she got a chance to explain. That too was a certain route to hurt and disappointment.

It had been one of those days when every appointment over ran. Her 4.45 was a garrulous woman whom she did not manage to usher from the premises until twenty minutes to six. Becky had to show the client downstairs herself because the girls in reception finished at 5.00 and the front door was locked once reception was unattended. All the partners and the cleaners had their own sets of keys, not least because the building was such a rabbit warren that it was difficult to be sure whether you were the last one in or not. On this particular evening Becky knew that she was not alone in the building, because she had overheard Gerry's voice speaking slowly and carefully into his Dictaphone when she passed his door on her way downstairs. As she returned to her office she all but collided with him on the first floor landing.

'Becky.' He hailed her as might a shipwrecked sailor confronted by the welcome sight of the lifeboat crew. 'I need to copy a document and the copier's playing up. Can you help?'

Gerry was notoriously bad at machines. He could manage his telephone and his Dictaphone but he refused to have anything to do with computers at all. 'I don't need to learn,' he insisted. 'I've only got a couple of years to go until I retire. I won't need a computer to sail my little boat.'

If it had been anyone else Becky would have been irritated. She tended to be prickly about her status as a general rule because the fact that she had worked her way up through the clerical route did not entitle people to bother her with pettifogging queries about photocopiers. This was Gerry however and she knew that with Gerry it was not just because it was her. He would have seized on Tony or Julian or Mel just as eagerly, if they had happened to be around.

'It's out of toner,' she said a couple of minutes later. 'All it needs is a new toner cartridge.'

Gerry regarded her helplessly.

'I'll sort it out… but you ought to watch me so that you'll know how to do it next time.'

She knew it was hopeless of course. Gerry would politely observe the operation and then the next time he pressed the copy button and the copy failed to magically appear in the plastic tray, he would still buttonhole the first person who was passing for help.

There was no more toner in the cupboard under the copier.

'Bum,' she said. 'I can't believe we've run out. I suppose it's been put away in the stationery store. Do you need this copying tonight?'

'I do.' Gerry looked apologetic. 'I've got to fax it through tonight and I can't send the original because there's a whole paragraph to be blocked out.'

'I'll have to go and get the keys out of Sadie's desk,' said Becky.

The stationery store was a little room on the top floor and Sadie's desk was in the ground floor reception, separated from it by four flights of stairs. Becky normally loved the quirky Victorian building but at moments like this she longed for the efficiency of a single level of concrete and glass or better still a building with a lift.

There were half a dozen boxed toner cartridges in the stationery store. She carried the whole lot downstairs because it was utterly pointless to keep them anywhere except with the photocopier. Only when Gerry was happily in possession of his photocopy did she return to her own office, lift her briefcase onto the desk and check her wrist watch in the same movement. It was three minutes to six. Victoria Square was six or seven minutes walk away and she still had to gather her things together. She told herself that she had never honestly intended to keep the rendezvous and now the choice had been made for her, because she could not possibly get there in time. It was like a sign. A clear sign that it was not meant to be.

Chapter Forty

1971

'I just can't believe it,' Nicky exclaimed. 'Why didn't anyone ever tell us that science was compulsory right up to 'O' level. I might have paid more attention if I'd known.'

'Every subject in group one is science,' Jo agreed gloomily. 'Physics, chemistry or biology. What a choice!'

'It's not a choice at all,' said Paula. 'It's science, science, or science.'

They were sitting on their desks during morning break, pondering the sheets Mr Sinton had given out at morning registration which explained how they should go about choosing the subjects they would be studying for the next two years.

'So it's English language, English lit., maths and French plus one subject from each of the four groups,' said Becky. 'And the first group is all sciences. That means we only get to choose three subjects we actually *want* to do.'

'*And* we still have to do compulsory P.E.,' groaned Paula.

'I can't see how this is going to work out.' Nicky was frowning. 'I want to do art, domestic science and history, but D.S. is only in group four so if I choose it that means I *have* to do history out of group two, but then I can't do art because art isn't included in group three – only in two and four.'

'Can't you do history in group three?'

'No. It's only in two and four. If I want to do D.S. then I'll have to do geography or R.E. instead of history. I'm not doing Latin!'

'My parents want me to do Latin,' said Paula. 'My Latin marks aren't too bad and they think it's a respected subject at university.'

'My mum said I ought to take cookery,' said Nicky. 'Because all girls should be able to cook. I suppose I don't mind doing it because it's not very hard.'

'I hope I'll be allowed to do geography,' said Jo. 'My mark in the exam was only half way up the class.'

'My French was so bad that I'm being put down a set,' said Becky. 'Which won't stop me from having to do it worst luck.'

By the end of break they had sorted out their subject choices for the following year.

'I'm not going to be with you guys for anything,' wailed Nicky. 'I'm on my own for art, geography and D.S. And now I'm the only one of us in bottom set for French *and* maths. I shall only see you in English and biology.'

'Don't worry,' said Jo. 'I'll probably be coming back down to your French set after Christmas. And I'll be on my own in the group four art class.'

Nicky was not to be mollified. 'Suppose all the horrible

people choose the same subjects as me. I might have to sit with Gail Foster or share a table with her in cookery.'

'You won't,' Paula said. 'She's not taking cookery. She's going for 'O' level bitchery in group four. Then she's taking tartiness in group three and being common in group two. '

'Mrs Carpigo caught her wearing a ring the other day and confiscated it,' said Nicky. 'I heard her telling Renata about it when we were getting changed for P.E.'

'Didn't Mrs Carpigo say anything about her hair?' asked Paula.

'I don't think so.'

Gail's hair had recently been transformed into a fashionable feather cut complete with silvery blonde streaks and her dark eyes were even more noticeable, since she had started outlining them with black eyeliner pencil. She had also taken to going about the school with the sleeves of her shirt rolled up to the elbow, in the closest approximation school uniform would allow to the skinhead style fashions which she wore outside.

Even as she spoke, Paula thought that while it was easy to score cheap points against Gail between themselves, it didn't stop Gail from despising them because they didn't have boyfriends or go to weekend discos, or basically because she just thought they were absolutely pathetic. Her feelings towards Gail were a confusion of loathing and envy. On the one hand she did not really want to be like Gail but on the other she wished she could be. Gail always appeared to be having fun and never seemed to worry about anything. She didn't seem to care very much if she got into trouble at school and she certainly didn't care what anyone else thought of her.

Chapter Forty-One

1985

Sean got stuck behind a line of cars going into the multi-storey. Why, why were people so stupid about wanting to grab the first empty space they saw? If only everyone would just keep going up to the higher floors, they could drive straight into entire blocks of empty spaces on the fourth and fifth floors instead of holding up a whole line of traffic while they waited for someone else to reverse out of a space and then took an age to manoeuvre into it.

If only he had said 6.30 instead of 6.00... because it was going to be a struggle to make it in time. By almost running up Pinfold Street (why were you always confronted with an uphill slope when you were in a hurry?) he was within sight of the statue of Queen Victoria by a minute to six. He tilted his umbrella to get a better look at the area around the base of the statue, just in case she was already there, but this achieved nothing apart from a cascade of water down the backs of his trouser legs. There was no one standing there – but maybe she was late – or perhaps sheltering among the Doric columns alongside the Town Hall. He scanned every possible location but he could not see her anywhere. Although he had tried to steel himself against it, he had not managed to extinguish the hope that he would arrive and find her waiting for him.

He took up his post beside the statue, umbrella tilted against the rain, alert to every approaching female figure. Each one proved to be a false hope. An occasional gust of wind sent sprays of raindrops bouncing across the square and he became conscious of a damp sock. Evidently his shoes let in.

'Forget me,' she had said. 'You'll find someone else.'

Well he had tried and failed on both counts.

'I don't want anyone else,' he'd said. 'I only want you.'

It was as true now as it had been three years ago. She had been so convinced that they could not make a go of it: that history and circumstances were against them. Well she was wrong. They were meant for each other. He knew it and he still believed that deep down she knew it too.

Quarter past six and no sign of her. He continued to stare out from under the umbrella, every so often pivoting slowly to take in every possible approach and the open space leading into Chamberlain Square which was backed by the concrete pile of the Central Library. In spite of attracting a few curious glances from passers by (though most people were hunched against the rain and completely ignored him) he continued to stand there as the rain became torrential, bouncing up from the pavement as fiercely as hailstones. He was afraid that if he sought shelter in the shadows of the Town Hall she might fail to see him and turn back before she reached the statue, supposing him already gone.

The wind drove the rain in under his umbrella, covering his dark overcoat in a mist of jewels.

Perhaps she had taken her own advice and found someone else? It was two years since he had seen her last. She was an attractive woman. Who would not want her? The wind drove a spot of rain directly into the corner of his eye and he had to brush it away. It was only a raindrop... nothing more.

At 6.30 he gave it up and walked slowly back to his car. It was clear that she was not coming. The little box containing the engagement ring she had punctiliously returned to him sat like a millstone in the pocket next to his heart.

Chapter Forty-Two

1971

Starting 'O' levels was like starting school all over – or at least that was how it felt for the first couple of days. It was as though the first three years had been a rehearsal for the real start of school. There was an air of purpose and direction, talk of syllabuses to be covered and the commitment required to achieve a pass. Pretty soon however everyone settled back into the old routines.

Ronnie, the class clown, had developed a talent for making a strange creaking noise like a badly oiled door which was being opened very slowly. Something in the timbre of the sound made it impossible for staff to pinpoint just where it was coming from but this amusing diversion came to an end when Ronnie tried it in humourless Miss Bagshaw's French lesson and Miss Bagshaw announced that unless the culprit owned up she would put the whole group in detention. At this Ronnie immediately stood up and admitted responsibility, but Miss Bagshaw decided to put the whole group into detention anyway for laughing.

'Imagine giving out detentions for laughing,' grumbled Nicky. 'They'll be giving out detentions for breathing next.'

'It's getting more like Stalag 47 here every day,' agreed Adele, who happened to be sitting with them. 'If Herr Commandant Cow-Pig-O introduces any more new rules we'll never be able to remember them all.'

The latest decree to be announced in morning assembly was a prohibition on talking when they walked along the top corridor between lessons, because Mrs Carpigo claimed that when she was on the telephone or entertaining a visitor in her room, the noise level from passing chatter was intolerable.

'It never worried Miss Forster,' was inevitably the phrase on everyone's lips.

Miss Forster, an unlikely candidate for canonisation by school girls, was fast being elevated to a status approaching sainthood. Past injuries – real or imagined – which had been suffered at her behest were entirely erased from the collective memory after a term and a half of Mrs Carpigo's rule.

Mrs Heslop had revealed to them during a drama lesson that although Saint Luke's were keen to mount another joint production, Mrs Carpigo favoured Evie's going it alone with a play written by an ex-colleague of hers based on 'The Pied Piper of Hamelin'. Mrs Heslop had already solicited the help of her backstage team from 'West Side Story' and they had readily agreed to make themselves available, while privately giving full reign to their disgust with the material foisted upon them.

'She's treating us as if we were a bunch of complete amateurs,' said Nicky.

'It's just not fair', agreed Becky.

This discussion took place in their new form room, where they had contrived to take possession of their usual quartet of desks in the back corner beside the window. On one of the lower panes of the window Paula had Sellotaped a note which said: *Please DO NOT open this window as doing so will destroy Webster's home.* From time to time Webster the spider dangled outside waving a leg in gratitude for this consideration.

A rainy spell had led to the form rooms being regularly left open during lunch time. Gail and Renata had smuggled a transistor radio into school and when songs like 'Double Barrel' came on, Gail and her friends formed up in lines across the front of the room and did perfectly synchronised dances, stepping and turning as one in time to the music. Only the confident, fashionable girls joined in. In between these foot stomping extravaganzas, Gail and her entourage gossiped and lent each other pocket size mirrors to aid the plucking of eyebrows, or to effect minor changes to their hair and make-up.

Their form mistress for the year, Miss Prior, was already familiar to some of them from top set maths. She was a short, rather dumpy woman, a fact accentuated by the thick, tweedy suits she habitually wore. Her hair was an unnatural reddish colour and stood off her forehead in a stiff permanent wave and she wore so much loose face powder that she was said to leave a dusting of it on the front desks of every form room she taught in. Her particular method of calling the class to order was to lift the lid of the teacher's desk by a couple of inches and bring it down several times in quick succession. Arriving early for afternoon registration one day in November she did just that.

Everyone clambered into their seats while registering a greater or lesser degree of resentment. With first bell yet to ring, the summons seemed an unreasonable infringement on their own time. When everyone had settled, Miss Prior, not looking entirely comfortable, announced that Mrs Carpigo had decided a spot check was to be undertaken. Two prefects would be arriving shortly to assist her in a search of bags and desks.

'Spot check,' said Jo out of the side of her mouth. 'Since when did we have spot checks? We don't have our belongings searched unless something's been reported stolen.'

The prefects arrived and began to search alongside Miss Prior. Everyone knew that Gail had the forbidden radio either in her bag or in her desk. It had been belting out 'Coz I Luv You' right up until the moment Miss Prior walked in, when it had been hastily switched off. At least twenty pairs of eyes were covertly focussed on Diane Whitely, the prefect searching through Gail's property and as many faces registered bafflement when, having checked Gail's bag, she moved on to the next person down the aisle without making any comment at all. Not more than half a minute later Miss Prior, who was searching Renata's bag, pulled out a half smoked pack of ten Players No. 6 and a box of England's Glory matches.

'Are these yours?' she asked.

If it had been an unopened packet there might have been some mileage in trying to pretend that they had been bought for someone else.

'Yes miss.'

'Go and stand at the front,' said Miss Prior.

Renata did as she was told.

As the search continued Renata's friends took care to engage her with sympathetic looks, while the remainder of the form did their best to avoid looking her way at all because staring at Renata could easily lead to being duffed up in the cloakroom later.

When Miss Prior and her assistants had completed their search without discovering any further contraband Miss Prior escorted Renata, complete with her cigarettes, to see Mrs Carpigo.

Jo was among the first to learn the outcome in her art class and was able to pass it on to the others as they collected their coats at home-time. Word was that Renata had been sent home, suspended from school for a week. Gail, whose coat hung very near Joanne's, overheard and joined in their conversation, indignation forging a rare bond between them. 'Fancy being suspended over a packet of ciggies. It's a bleedin' disgrace.'

'How come they didn't spot your radio?' asked Nicky.

'She must have seen it,' said Gail. 'I'm sure she did, but that Diane Whitely's all right. She just pushed my atlas across in front of it and pretended not to notice.'

'They've got no right to search us like that,' said Becky. 'Charlie Young from IVT sits by me in history and she said Mr Tresham was searching their bags. It's not right, a man teacher poking about through your stuff. People have got Tampax and all sorts in their bags.'

'Do you think Renata's parents will be very mad?' Paula took advantage of the temporary amnesty to ask Gail.

'Her mum'll be all right about it,' said Gail. 'But her dad's a bit of a bastard.'

Though sentenced to only a week's suspension, Renata vanished entirely from their lives. She had just passed her fifteenth birthday and was therefore eligible to leave and get a job. Gail said it was what she wanted. Anything to get away from *this* place, she said. But secretly Paula wondered… She remembered an essay Renata had written just before the last summer holidays, which Mrs Heslop had read aloud as an example of what a good essay should be. In the essay, 'My Life's Ambition', Renata had written about her desire to become a journalist. Now according to information received from Gail, she was working on a till in British Home Stores.

Chapter Forty-Three

1985

Becky opened the front door, stepped inside, shook out her umbrella and wiped her feet. There was no post on the mat. She removed her shoes and coat, tossed her briefcase onto a handy chair and went into the sitting room where she flopped wearily onto the sofa. In a minute she would have to make herself a coffee and look in the fridge to see what there was to eat. She could not even be bothered to reach for the remote. These days there was never anything on T.V. that she wanted to watch.

She had fallen out of the television habit after her mother married Stan and had never entirely regained it. As Stan and the television had both occupied the living room, Becky had spent most of her time at home upstairs in her bedroom, where her idea of a good night in had been to fill a dinner plate with Ritz crackers, each adorned with a squirt of Primula cheese spread and to eat the lot while reading 'Lord of the Rings' or after it was adapted for T.V. and came out in a double paperback set, 'War and Peace'.

The memory made her smile which somehow pulled all her facial muscles the wrong way because next minute tears were rolling down her cheeks.

She had been a fool. How many people get a second chance at anything in life? She had made a terrible mistake in not going to meet him. Well O.K… you're supposed to be smart. You've made a mistake. How do you put it right? He won't still be there. It's past 7.00 now and he wouldn't have waited an hour… you still know his phone number. (By heart.)

It's a big step.

No it isn't. It's the only thing to do. He's the love of your life. Stop being a bloody fool and pick up the phone.

Partly to be doubly sure of the number and partly to play for time, she checked in the little address book that she kept beside the phone before dialling. She got the tone which signalled that the number was unobtainable. She tried again just in case she had hit a wrong button at the first attempt but the result was the same. She tried the regular phone book but he wasn't listed.

He must have changed his number and gone ex-directory. Or maybe he had moved.

A pair of tears welled simultaneously over each bottom lid leaving wet parallel lines down the centre of each of her cheeks. She examined them in the mirror above the phone, tracing one with a finger tip.

At that moment the doorbell rang. It would be the flaming Jehovah's Witnesses again. She knew that if she opened the sitting room door it would throw a shaft of brighter light into the hall and then they would be able to see her silhouette through the frosted glass in the front door and persist, knowing that there was someone at home, whereas if she stayed put they would probably assume that there was no one in and go away.

*

Out on the doorstep Sean wriggled his feet uneasily inside his shoes. They definitely let in, which was aggravating when he hadn't had them very long and had paid quite a lot for them. He knew that Becky was at home because there was a car parked outside and through the glass panels of the front door he could see a line of light which marked the bottom of the sitting room door. He watched for that door to open and the hall light to be turned on but nothing happened except that the rain began to beat down a little harder.

Perhaps she wasn't alone. There was no second car to indicate that she had company but that need not mean anything. It was Valentine's Day after all and perhaps there was a romantic supper in progress. It wasn't a big house. It didn't take long to answer the door. Was it possible that she had somehow peeked through the curtains without him noticing? Maybe looked out of one of the darkened windows upstairs and seen that it was him. She had left him standing in Victoria Square and now she would not answer the door to him. Message received and understood. He had tried to win her back but it was too late… far too late.

The rain began to pelt him with increased ferocity. He turned up his coat collar and thrust his hands deep into his pockets. He'd left his umbrella in the car and under normal circumstances he would have made a run for it but he was so wet now that it did not seem to matter. He turned slowly back towards the car. What was the point in hurrying? He hadn't got anywhere in particular to go.

The rain was thrashing down so hard that he did not hear the front door open.

'Sean?' There was a tremor of disbelief in her voice.

When he turned she was standing against the lighted hall so he could not see the expression on her face. For the briefest of moments they were both silent, she a dark silhouette on the doorstep, him hesitant and bedraggled in the shining rain. Then he reached into his inside pocket, fumbling only slightly with the ring box before he dropped down on one knee regardless of the pouring rain.

Chapter Forty-Four

1971

Paula stood at the bedroom mirror, appraising her reflection. She had been allowed to buy a new outfit for her cousin's wedding and given carte blanche in choosing it. The burgundy midi-skirt looked great, she thought and the black boots completely hid her legs, which she considered to be among the worst of her many unattractive features. The cream coloured blouse with its frilled neckline was more of a worry. It had received unanimous approval from Becky, Jo and Nick, when she tried it on in the changing rooms of Chelsea Girl but she was not so sure about it now. It was cut quite low and the expanse of white skin it revealed only seemed to emphasise her lack of cleavage. She had tried stuffing her bra with tissues but that gave her breasts a knobbly appearance so she'd immediately dragged them out again.

'Come on Paula,' her mother called. 'Are you nearly ready? Daddy wants to set off in five minutes.'

'Coming.'

Since this was Paula's stock response irrespective of whether she was ready or not, her mother, wearing a lemon two piece and matching hat, came barging in to check: a regular intrusion which Paula hated even when she was fully dressed.

'Oh dear,' her mother sighed. 'You're not going to put on a lot of make-up are you? It doesn't look nice on a young girl you know.'

'I'm nearly fifteen.' Paula's response was muffled, emerging from rigid lips as she tried to keep her face absolutely still while applying bright blue eye shadow.

Her mother emitted a disapproving cluck while continuing to gaze around the bedroom as if she was looking for something. Nervous at being watched, Paula blobbed her mascara and had to take emergency action with a tissue.

'Are you ready?' It was her father's voice now. 'What on earth are you both doing up there?'

'We're on our way dear… Come *along* Paula. I've picked up the black cat for you to give to Louise.'

'You can give it to her,' said Paula. 'I'll feel silly.'

'Why on earth…?'

'Because it will look so babyish.'

'Of course it won't,' said her Mother. 'I'll keep it in my bag for now. Yours isn't big enough.'

Paula thought the ceremony disappointingly unromantic. The hymn singing was uncertain, the bride and groom's responses inaudible and the sermon largely drowned out by a toddler shouting at the back. When everyone got outside the church the photographer marched them all across the damp grass to stand in front of some laurel bushes for the photographs. After half an hour of being marshalled with shouts of 'Bride's family' and 'Groom's family', everyone drove to the reception which was being held in the hall of the nearby primary school. Here the photographer took one final shot of the bride and groom poised to cut the three tier cake, before the guests were free to descend on the buffet.

Paula sat with her parents at a large table surrounded by a crowd of other relations, none of whom were her own age. While she tried to eat her prawn vol-au-vent, ham sandwiches and pickled onions, well meaning aunties kept leaning across and asking how she was getting on at school. There was no easy answer to this. Paula wasn't even sure what the question really meant and wished that they would just leave her alone, but of course she had to be polite and pretend to be interested in any aspects of school that they asked her about and then pretend to find Uncle Reg's remarks about modern music amusing, instead of merely tedious.

'You can't hear what they're singing about half the time can you?' he said. 'Must be muffled by all that long hair they've got.' He gave a beery laugh.

They were all looking at her so Paula forced a smile, although she did not suppose that Uncle Reg would be expected to find it funny if she kept making silly remarks and belittling the sort of music he liked.

'Haven't you got anything to drink?' her mother asked. 'Pop to the bar and get yourself something.'

'I haven't got any money,' said Paula.

'You don't need any,' her mother said. 'It's a wedding. The bar's free.'

Glad to escape Uncle Reg but nervous about approaching

a bar, Paula walked slowly towards the far end of the hall, where three men in their shirt sleeves and a couple of women who had put on aprons over their best clothes, were serving drinks from behind trestle tables on which an improvised bar had been set up. Bitter and mild was being dispensed out of bumper size tins and Paula could see that on the floor behind the bar tenders there were crates filled with bottles of Babycham and Pony with their pretty sapphire and ruby paper tops. She had to stand and wait her turn for some time, which she spent wondering whether she dared to ask for something alcoholic. Finally one of the men spotted her and said, 'What would you like, love? We've got orange squash, lemonade or lime cordial.' Paula settled for a glass of lemonade which she carried back to her seat.

Uncle Reg had moved from pop music to football. 'Look at that Chico Hamilton who plays for the Villa,' he said. 'He's got hair like a girl's. I bet he puts it in rollers at night.'

This generated a ripple of merriment among the other men.

'What do you think about it Paula?' Reg turned to her. 'You wouldn't be seen out with one of these Nancy boys, would you?'

Paula looked around helplessly but Uncle Reg did not appear to require a reply. He finished another mouthful of scotch egg before saying, 'Chico Hamilton, Rod Stewart, that one in T.Rex. They're all the same. Look at that lot in The Slade. They're from Wolverhampton. They ought to know better.'

Paula chewed her way through her last few crisps. She

tried to make them last as long as possible but there was no escape.

'You surely don't like these long haired yobbos do you?' asked Reg.

He was using the teasing, patronising tone that always made her angry. It was not a voice an adult would ever use to address another adult. It was specially perfected to bait young people whose good manners precluded them from answering back.

'I don't mind.' It was the most non-committal, non-specific response she could come up with. She did not want to engage in an outright disagreement because that was cheeky, but nor did she want to deny her generation their music and their tastes.

Uncle Reg could not leave it. 'Surely you wouldn't go out with a long haired lout?'

Chance would be a fine thing, thought Paula.

'They all look like a load of poufs. Do you think they bring their handbags out on dates?' Reg affected a mincing walk without leaving his seat. 'You surely wouldn't want to be seen walking down the street with a chap like that?'

'Well I'd rather be seen out with someone who had long hair than with someone who was bald,' said Paula steadily.

There was an almost universal guffaw around the table. Reg – who had a Bobby Charlton style comb-over – went bright red.

'Paula! What's got into you?' exclaimed her mother. 'That was very rude. Apologise at once.'

'Sorry,' said Paula, not entirely as though she meant it.

'That's all right. No offence taken,' said Reg, not entirely as though he meant it either.

He left her alone after that, which made her feel that being told off in public worth it. She angled her chair slightly away from the table so that she could watch the guys from the mobile disco carrying in their kit. It was some time before the music actually started. First there was a lot of equipment testing, coupled with prolonged electronic pings and wails from the speakers, but finally the rows of coloured light bulbs mounted on a big black box which had *Jed's Sounds* painted on the front of it, began to flash in sequence and Jed opened up proceedings by getting the bride and groom into the middle of the dance floor while he put on a waltz and the newly-weds, looking far from comfortable, made a few crabwise shuffles to applause from everyone else, before they were joined on the floor by all the middle aged relations who actually knew how to waltz.

It was at this point that Paula noticed there was someone else in the room of roughly her own age. He was sitting on the other side of the hall among a group of older people and she caught him glancing across at her between the couples moving around the dance floor, at which point they both looked away quickly, but not before she had taken in the shoulder length blonde hair, chocolate brown suit with wonderfully wide flared trousers, cream shirt and fashionable kipper tie.

When the waltz ended Jed put on some disco music and the floor emptied at once.

'Isn't this your sort of thing Paula?' said one of her aunties. 'Why don't you get up and show us what you can do?'

Paula shook her head. The dance floor loomed vast and

empty alongside her chair. She could do a couple of dances she had practiced with her friends, but they all involved a group of people dancing in a line. It looked stupid doing those sort of dances on your own.

'I'll get up with you,' her mother offered. 'If you don't want to dance on your own.'

'No thank you,' said Paula firmly. 'I don't want to.'

Dancing with her mother would look unspeakably babyish.

After a while the disco changed to old favourites like 'The Twist' and 'Rock Around the Clock' so all the aunties were in their element again and one or two of the braver uncles were persuaded to join in. At a table laden with presents the bride and groom were steadily working their way through a mountain of parcels and had just unwrapped their third stainless steel butter dish.

Paula adjusted the angle of her chair slightly so that she could look at the boy across the room without being too obvious about it. He kept looking over at her and once she thought he smiled at her but she couldn't be sure because someone moved between them before she could return the compliment. Jed reverted to disco music again and this time a group of the bride's girlfriends made their way into the centre of the room. If only the blonde boy would come over and ask if she wanted to dance. Of course she would have to say no, because in spite of religiously watching 'Top of the Pops' and practicing in front of the bedroom mirror, she still wasn't confident that she could pull it off… but it would be so nice if he would just come across and ask. Deciding that he might be put off from making an approach while she was sitting among a great gang of relations, she made her way across to the buffet where a few curled up sandwiches and soggy vol-au-vents were still available. She ate another pickled onion in a desultory sort of way and hung about there for a minute or two but the boy did not come over to join her. After that she tried returning to the bar for a lemonade refill, where she was served by the same man as before, although he looked much redder in the face this time.

When she turned back towards the room she saw that she had been the victim of bad timing. The boy was approaching with an empty glass in his hand, but she couldn't just stand there – it would be too obvious and anyway there were people waiting – so she walked back to her seat, wondering if maybe… just maybe… he had come to the bar in the hope of bumping into her.

She needed to think of some other way of setting up a possible encounter. (It said in 'Jackie' that girls should not be shy about taking the initiative because we are all liberated women now.) After a few minutes she said to her mother, 'I feel a bit hot in here. I'm just going to stand outside and cool down a bit.'

'Not right outside,' protested her mother. 'It's freezing out there and it's dark too.'

'No,' said Paula. 'I'll just go out into the corridor.'

She walked to the door as slowly as she reasonably could in order to give him the best possible chance of seeing her leave the room. She didn't dare look over her shoulder to see if he was watching.

The area outside the hall doors was just a large entrance vestibule with doors going into the ladies and gents toilets and a pair of double doors which led to the outside world.

Paula would have liked to check that her make-up wasn't smudged, but she was afraid that if she went into the ladies and the boy did come out of the hall she would miss him. A minute or two passed. A man came through to the gents, quickly followed by another. Then a half familiar female relation passed on her way to the ladies. Paula felt stupidly conspicuous. There was nothing to detain her there and any minute some busybody was sure to ask her what she was doing. She began to read the school notice board, just to avoid eye contact with every passing grown-up on their way to the loo. Notices had been pinned up announcing the results of the football and skittle ball teams and there was a bigger notice to say that the green team had won the weekly house cup.

'Anything interesting?'

She jumped and felt herself blushing. He was really tall close up. He had taken off the jacket and the kipper tie and undone the top button of his shirt.

'No,' she stammered. 'Nothing at all.'

'Better than sitting in there though isn't it?' He gave her a conspiratorial smile.

He was really nice looking. Really, really nice.

'I was dead bored,' he said.

'So was I.'

'They never play any decent music at weddings,' he said.

'What sort of music do you like?' she asked.

'Deep Purple's my favourite,' he said. 'Do you like 'Fireball'?'

'I love it,' she said. She had heard it at least once.

'I'm going to get the album,' he said.

Paula tried to look interested and intelligent. Album – he was obviously a musical sophisticate – not like her parents who still said L.P.

'What's your name?' he asked.

'Paula. I'm one of the groom's cousins.'

'Ralph,' he said. 'One of the bride's cousins. My little sister was one of the bridesmaids,' he added, as though this element of the arrangements had been a sore trial to him.

Next they established which schools they each attended, what they thought of the disco (rubbish) and what they liked to watch on television. After that the conversation petered out and they stood facing one another, no more than a couple of feet apart.

I wish he would kiss me, Paula thought. She wondered whether if she willed him to do it hard enough, he would. He'd followed her out there after all. He's thinking about it, she thought. I know he's thinking about it. Any minute now he's going to kiss me.

'Paula.' Her mother's voice startled her. 'We're going home now. Daddy is giving Auntie Mary a lift.'

'Coming,' Paula said over her shoulder.

Her mother stayed put in the doorway, refusing to take the hint. 'Say goodbye to your friend,' she said.

Oh God. She was such a humiliation. *Say goodbye to your friend*. As though she was being fetched home from a kiddies' tea party or something. Paula felt like crying with mortification.

'Bye Ralph,' she said.

'See you,' he said.

Paula fell into step with her mother who then added insult to injury by spending the next fifteen minutes trailing around the room, saying her farewells to all and sundry.

Stupid, stupid woman, thought Paula. She'll never know how she's just blighted my life.

Chapter Forty-Five

1985

Nicky took a last glance at the postcard of Sydney Opera House before putting it into the kitchen drawer, where such items were kept for a while before being consigned to the bin. Clive didn't like having postcards lying about. In fact he didn't like having anything lying about. Cliveden was kept in an immaculate state which approached the anonymity of a newly occupied holiday property. He permitted a slightly less tidy, if not exactly disordered state, in the garden. No weeds of course but at least there was some attempt at a natural look. The garden had become a source of focus in her otherwise barren life. Barren in every sense, she thought. Clive didn't want children. Everywhere she looked people were having babies. The Princess of Wales had two now. Everyone but me, Nicky thought.

She wondered if that was why she had developed such an interest in the garden. Growing things in the earth as a substitute for growing things in her womb. Clive did not understand her interest in the garden at all. He paid someone to come and see to it once a week and so long as it looked nice that was the beginning and end of it. He didn't mind her 'grubbing about out there' as he put it, but he did not want to be bored with it himself. It wasn't his scene.

The hired gardener came on Thursdays. His name was Rob and he had a limp. When Clive first told her that he had a gardener Nicky had expected an elderly Percy Thrower type, complete with flat cap and a pipe, but Rob did not look as old as she was herself.

She always took him a mug of tea. She was not entirely convinced that he welcomed this weekly offering, but it afforded her an opening to ask his advice about planting and pruning and also, if she was absolutely honest, it gave her the opportunity to converse with a fellow human being – albeit briefly – in an otherwise empty day.

Today she wanted to sound him out about her idea of planting lavender down both sides of the path which ran between the patio and the lawn. While he drank his mug of tea they walked across to view the area together, she trying to avoid making it obvious that she had to slow down to allow for his strange dragging gait. She wondered if he had been born like that or had perhaps suffered some kind of dreadful accident. Gardening was fraught with scythes and chain saws when all was said and done.

'The soil's quite poor just here so you'll need to prepare the ground well,' he said. 'But it would look really effective once it was established. And when it's grown up a bit and overhangs the edge of the path you'll get a lovely scent of lavender every time your skirt brushes the plants as you walk along here.'

'Thanks,' said Nicky. 'I'm sorry to keep on asking you

so many questions. I expect you think I'm a bit of an idiot. I don't know anything about gardening. I'm a complete beginner.'

'You've got an eye for planting,' he said. 'And that's a good start. Lovely idea that – planting lavender alongside this path.'

It was the nearest he had ever come to paying her a compliment. In general he did not make any sort of unsolicited remarks at all and now, almost as if he was embarrassed, he limped hurriedly back to where he had been working, his body language making it abundantly clear that he did not expect her to follow him.

The truth was that Rob Grafton was instinctively wary of women in big houses with time on their hands. Some of them were just a pain, wanting to stand over him all the time to see that they got their money's worth. Others wanted him to embark on schemes of toe curling hideousness, involving marigolds and tulips in orderly rows, while a third category of clients were more terrifying still… these were the Lady Chatterley wannabes, who thought that a gardener with a gammy leg was probably desperate enough to overlook a thirty year age discrepancy.

Not that she was like any of that sort, this woman at Cliveden. She seemed genuinely interested in the garden… spent a lot of time out there in fact. She was getting so keen that they wouldn't need him soon except for the mowing. Not that this would matter much one way or the other providing his plans for starting the nursery came to fruition.

She appeared outside again about half an hour later, this time to collect his mug. There was no need because he never forgot to return it to the kitchen doorstep when he finished work, but then it turned out that she had thought of something else she wanted to ask him – this time about the astilbes. However he barely had time to finish his answer before she turned her head in the direction of the house and said, 'Here's Clive.'

She must have phenomenal hearing, he thought, because there was nothing wrong with his own and he hadn't heard the faint sound of car tyres scrunching on the gravel at the front of the house until after she'd spoken. He noticed something else too. The way a new expression came into her eyes the moment she registered the sound of that approaching car.

'I'd better go in,' she said. 'Thanks very much for all your help again.'

Clive appeared around the side of the house and Nicky met him as she reached the kitchen door.

'Hello,' he said, planting a kiss on her forehead. 'What have you been up to?'

'I was just asking Rob about my ideas for the garden.'

'Don't ask him,' said Clive, with a good humoured smile. 'Tell him what you want and he'll do it. That's what he's paid for.'

'I didn't mean ask him like that,' Nicky began, but Clive had preceded her into the kitchen and wasn't really listening.

'Hey,' he said. 'How come there's no beer in the fridge?'

'We're out of it,' Nicky said. 'I meant to go and get some more…'

'But you've been too busy chatting about the garden with Peg Leg Pete.' He wasn't annoyed. His voice was perfectly affable.

'I didn't realise you were going to come home early. If I'd known I would have gone out for some this morning. And I wish you wouldn't call him that. He'll hear you one of these days.'

'So what if he does? He knows what he can do if he doesn't like it. Gardeners are ten a penny.'

'I'll go and buy some beer now,' said Nicky, hurriedly opening the drawer where she kept her purse.

'Don't be silly,' said Clive. 'I don't need a beer. What I need is you.'

He caught hold of her wrist. She fought and conquered the instinct to pull away.

'I haven't got long,' he said. 'I've got an appointment back in the office at two.'

Oh God, she thought. He's come home to have sex in his lunch hour, the way he might make time for a session with a prostitute. Stop it, stop it. She must not think of it like that. She must not think of herself like that.

Out in the garden Rob Grafton was approaching the end of his scheduled time at Cliveden. His next appointment was a few miles away with Mrs Redvers who hired him on an occasional basis, when she needed any heavy work doing. She had finally decided that he should remove that tree stump from the bed near her pond. He rather hoped that she would be out when he got there so that he could just get on with the job. Mrs Redvers was one of those women who always thought they knew better than he did how any job should be done.

At least Mrs Cliveden wasn't like that, he thought, as he methodically replaced his tools in the back of the truck. He thought of her as Mrs Cliveden because he didn't know her real name. He knew she wasn't married to Mr Aston, because right from when she first appeared on the scene he'd noticed that she wasn't wearing a wedding ring. She was obviously the latest live-in girlfriend. Funny, he mused, the way the live-in girlfriends at these sorts of houses were invariably blondes. He was pretty sure that Mrs Cliveden was a natural blonde. She was quite attractive in a sort of un-messed about way. She didn't dye her hair and she hadn't got that peculiar artificial tan which so many of these women acquired from lying for hours on a sun bed. Nor did she feel she had to plaster herself with make-up before she could come out into the garden.

As he climbed into the cab he suddenly remembered the way she'd looked when she heard the Lord and Master's car arrive and he realised what it reminded him of. It was the same look the dogs sometimes had in the kennels at the Animal Rescue Shelter where his sister worked.

Chapter Forty-Six

1971

The Christies' home-made candles were not a success. Not only was the light they gave off pitifully short lived, but the ghastly smell of melting lard outlasted the life of the string wicks by several hours. Dennis, whose invention they had been, was extremely disappointed. They faltered out while Nicky was still writing up her biology experiment and she realised that she would have to leave the diagram until she got to school, because it was impossible to see pencil lines drawn by the light of the single remaining candle and besides which everyone wanted her off the table so that they could play cards. That was the one consolation of the power cuts – the whole family did things together. The boys thought it was great. Dennis was allegedly excused homework on power cut nights and Michael still wasn't old enough to have any homework, so once the table was clear they all settled down to play Whist or Newmarket or a new game Nicky had learned from Jo, called Crazy Eights.

At Dennis's school the boys were being given extra

time to get homework done, but at Eleanor Vaux it was business as usual. Miss Bagshaw summed up the situation. 'The Joint Matriculation Board won't be interested in excuses about power cuts,' she said. 'So the work has got to be done.' There had been some desultory rumblings in IVP about mass disobedience, but the majority of the form wouldn't contemplate it and besides which not everyone was experiencing the same level of problems. The city had been divided up into different areas, supposedly in order to share the power cuts around as fairly as possible and Eleanor Vaux drew its pupils from all over south Birmingham, so different pupils were without electricity at different times and with stocks of candles and batteries sold out everywhere, even among families who lost power for the same periods each day, some were significantly worse off than others depending on what means of light they had available to them.

Joanne's father had managed to buy a box of candles from a man in a pub, while Paula's parents, who were habitually careful enough to keep a good stock of plain white candles against the possibility of a power cut, also had a dozen twisty pink candles, purchased in anticipation of the rare occasions when they had visitors to dinner. The Christies were in a much worse predicament. Mrs Christie haunted the local shops against the rumour of candles, decorative oil lamps, anything which could provide a source of light without needing to be plugged into a socket.

Some shopkeepers would only sell candles in accompaniment with other products – such as light bulbs whose sales had declined in direct proportion to the demand for non-electrical alternatives – and even then customers were restricted to no more than six light bulbs and six candles per person. 'They ought to bring in proper rationing,' Mrs Christie said. 'Like what we had in the war.'

Life took on a strange new complexion, Nicky thought, without the electric lights they normally took for granted. She had never experienced the house in complete darkness before, because even with the interior lights switched off, the street lights had always shone in through the landing window and the gaps where the bedroom curtains did not always meet... but now there was not a light to be seen in the whole neighbourhood. Going upstairs to the loo by the light of Dennis's fading pocket torch was like walking through a dream house, a queer, shadowy place which looked like a version of their house, rather than the real thing. It was not so much scary as strange.

Coming home from school felt different too. Each successive power cut had put the timers on the street lights a little further out of kilter, so that the streets were as likely to be lit up in broad daylight as they were during the hours of darkness, much to the fury of the local residents who were being starved of power at night in order to save electricity. The 'Evening Mail' was full of readers' letter protesting about the situation and making dire predictions of an increase in the numbers of people likely to be run over.

'It's only like the black out,' Nicky's father said. 'Mind you, at least we had enough torches then. I blame this Conservative government. That Ted Heath! He wants to fall off his boat and drown himself.'

One morning Helen Staveley fainted at morning registration. On questioning her Miss Prior established that because the Staveley's kitchen was all electric, Helen had set out for school that morning without so much as a warm drink. When Helen had been revived and escorted off to the Medical Room, Miss Prior asked those in the class whose homes relied on electricity for cooking purposes to raise their hands.

'I have a gas appliance,' said Miss Prior gravely.

Ronnie Nicholls hastily stifled a snigger.

'From tomorrow and for the duration of these disturbances to the electricity supply I shall be bringing a flask of hot soup each morning, to be shared among any girls who would like some. There is no compulsion of course but I invite any other members of the form who are able and wish to, to do the same.'

From the following morning flasks of tomato soup, tea, even hot blackcurrant squash started to appear and for a few short weeks morning registration became a sociable occasion, with steaming drinks passed from hand to hand.

'It's the Dunkirk spirit,' said Paula. 'I think my grandma is actually rather enjoying it. She and her cronies have got it all worked out, whose houses have got electricity each night and whose will be cut off and they're taking it in turns to visit and cook for each other. They've even worked out how not to miss anything they specially want to see on telly. Grandma's got this massive, elaborate timetable taped up on her kitchen wall. And she's writing to all the places she thinks are being irresponsible about not cutting down on the amount of power they're using. It's a sort of modern equivalent of handing out white feathers.'

'Does anyone know why we're having these power cuts?' asked Nicky. 'I mean really know?'

'It's so we don't run out of electricity altogether,' said Becky. 'Although I suppose if the miners stay on strike long enough we will. Stan keeps saying "Why don't they bring in the army?" but then he's a complete fascist so he would.'

'Can't we just buy coal from somewhere else?' asked Jo. 'I mean if the geography syllabus is to be believed, people are digging it out of the ground just about all over the place. If a question ever asks you to name a local industry I always stick coal mining down. It's an absolute banker – nearly always worth a mark.'

'I don't know,' said Paula. 'I'm just getting fed up with it. It was a laugh at first but it's starting to get on my nerves.'

'I know,' said Nicky. 'Our mum was dead mad last night when the power went off just as 'Family At War' was coming on. She's never missed an episode so far.'

'I can't get on with my book,' agreed Paula.

'Which? The one you're reading or the one you're writing?'

'Both.'

Paula's mother had refused to let her read by candlelight for fear that it would ruin her eyesight, although completing her homework was deemed essential and therefore not an unacceptable optical risk. The prohibition on reading was driving Paula to distraction. It had taken her almost a week to get beyond the fiftieth page of 'Master of Falconhurst'. At this rate she would never get it finished and back to Ronnie who had a whole list of people waiting to borrow it due to its racy reputation.

The Morrisons did not while away their candlelit evenings with cards and board games, preferring to stick with the entertainment provided by the wireless. The wireless in the big radiogram would not work during power cuts, but the battery operated transistor radio which was normally kept in the kitchen had been brought into the sitting room, where it sat importantly in the centre of the coffee table as if aware of its newly elevated place in the scheme of things. Paula would have much preferred to sit up in her bedroom, where she could have covertly continued with 'Master of Falconhurst' (which was not the sort of book her parents approved of). She had pleaded to be allowed her own candle on the grounds that she could listen to her choice of programme on her own transistor but her mother was strictly rationing the candles and would not hear of it.

'Besides,' she said. 'You might set fire to the curtains or something.'

'Why on earth would I do that?'

'Well you are awfully scatty Paula.'

'For goodness sake!' exclaimed Paula. 'Anyone would think I was a child the way you go on. Of course I'm not going to set fire to the curtains.'

'Be that as it may we cannot spare the candles to light two rooms. We don't have an inexhaustible supply and I don't know what we're going to do when the ones we have are all gone. That horrid little man at the mini-market would only let me buy two with this week's groceries. I shan't be taking my custom there much longer if that's his attitude.'

'We've still got quite a few,' said Paula. 'There's a whole pack of the pink ones not opened yet, as well as the loose ones you bought yesterday.'

'They won't last forever,' said her mother. 'Who knows

how long this will go on for? There's talk of having to ration the gas next, so your grandma was telling me. She and her gang are talking about digging a sort of pit in one of their gardens and roasting big joints of meat in it. Where they think they're going to get the wood from heaven only knows. These awful trade unionists are trying to bring the country to its knees.'

Chapter Forty-Seven

1985

Joanne hovered in the doorway which connected the gallery to the rest of the house while Antonia finished wrapping a limited edition print and then chatted with the customers about how long they were staying in the area, careful not to betray to them that she was keen to get them out of the shop.

The moment the door finally closed behind them, before even the little bell which hung above it had time to stop jangling, Joanne, grinning irrepressibly, burst out, 'You'll never guess what!'

'Won't have to,' Ant replied cheerfully. 'You're going to tell me anyway.'

'That was Becka on the phone, ringing to tell us that she got married last week. She and Sean went off to Scotland and did the deed in secret. They only got back home the day before yesterday.'

'Brilliant,' said Ant. 'A romantic elopement.'

'There's more,' said Jo. 'She's expecting a baby.'

'Whoa... now you're making it sound more like a shotgun wedding.'

'Don't be daft,' said Jo. 'Becka says it's deliberate. They don't want to waste any more time, she said. The old biological clock and all that. She'll be thirty next year.'

'Poor old thing,' said thirty four year old Ant, deadpan but with a twinkle. 'Ought we to send a present?'

'I'd like to,' said Jo. 'The difficulty is knowing what to send. They've probably got everything – twice. Tell you what. Let's get one of those companies that deliver champagne to send them a bottle.'

'Mmm – do you think she'll be drinking? Lots of women give it up completely when they're preggers. Why not a huge bunch of flowers and a card saying how supremely pleased we are for them?'

'That would be nice. And do you know what else? *We've* still got that bottle of champagne we never opened. The one we bought for ourselves as a moving in present then didn't drink for fear of tempting fate. Let's open it tonight and drink their health.'

'That,' said Ant, giving her a hug, 'Is a truly splendid idea.'

Nearly two hundred miles further south, Nicky had received the same news via the morning post. It was a friendly note, scribbled inside a card with a tasteful reproduction of a Scottish castle on the front. The very fact that it was a note rather than a phone call spoke volumes, Nicky thought. She knew that Beck had sent the news with the best of intentions and that her first reaction on receiving it should be to get on the phone, full of joyful congratulations, but the news that one of her dearest friends was now Mrs Rebecca McMahon and that there was a little McMahon already on the way only filled her with sick envy. Still holding the card she stumbled out into the garden where life sometimes seemed less oppressive, sat on the wooden bench facing the azaleas and burst into noisy tears.

It was here that Rob Grafton found her when he arrived for work shortly afterwards. She obviously hadn't heard him approaching and for a moment he considered slipping away, but after hesitating a moment he asked: 'Is there something wrong?'

Nicky jumped visibly, automatically raising her blotchy tear stained face. She had completely forgotten that it was Rob's day to come.

'It's none of my business of course…' he said, then hesitated again, glancing down at the card in her hand. 'Bad news is it? If there's anything you'd like me to do… not that there will be, I don't suppose, but… you know… or maybe you'd rather I just took myself off. I could easily come back another day. You know… just give it a miss… if you wanted to be on your own…' he trailed into awkward silence.

It was the longest speech Nicky had ever heard him make which didn't involve pruning or compost.

'No,' she said, quickly. 'Don't go. Honestly I'd really much rather you stayed. It's not even bad news. It's actually good news. Very good news. An old friend of mine has got married and she's having a baby.' Nicky's voice quivered dangerously on this last word. Pulling herself together she continued, 'I expect you think I'm mad. Crying like this over someone's good news.'

To her surprise he said quietly: 'Someone else's good news isn't always easy to share. Not if it brings home that they've got something you want.'

Nicky looked up at him gratefully. He understood. He wasn't judging her so harshly as she judged herself. With a sudden burst of candour she said: 'I badly want a baby you see. But Clive doesn't want to have any children.'

'Bit selfish of him isn't it?'

'It doesn't fit in with the sort of life he wants,' said Nicky. 'He doesn't want to have children or… or even to marry me.'

'Well he's daft then,' said Rob. 'Any right minded chap would be glad to marry you.'

There was an awkward silence. Each suddenly realising that they had said far more than they had intended to. Nicky got to her feet, carefully focussing on some vague point in the middle distance and said in the lightest tone she could muster, 'Thanks Rob. That was very sweet. You've cheered me up no end.'

'Right,' he said, his voice carefully neutral. 'I'll be getting started then.'

They walked away in opposite directions, she towards the house and he towards the tool shed, both taking care not to look back.

Nicky dithered for some time over whether or not she should take him his usual mid-morning mug of tea. On the one hand she felt that she ought to thank him again for being so supportive. It had helped to feel that there was someone who understood, neither condemning nor ridiculing her for her reaction to her friend's good news. At the same time there was embarrassment too, because she knew and he knew that they had crossed a line… indulged in an inappropriate conversation. So when she eventually took out the tea she handed it to him without attempting to linger, didn't stop to ask his advice about anything or comment on what he had been doing as she usually did. He just said, 'Thanks,' and took the mug without really looking at her. At the end of his shift when he left the cup at the kitchen door she called out a casual goodbye from the other side of the room. It had only been his natural kindness of course. There was nothing in it.

She knew that she ought to ring Becky. The longer she left it, the more awkward it was going to get, but she shied away from making the call on a whole series of levels. She wasn't sure if she could bear to talk about the coming baby. The whole question of babies and pregnancy was like a raw nerve. She didn't even know if she *could* have a baby. She had been pregnant before and miscarried. She might be one of those women who couldn't carry a baby to full term. It was all so hopeless whichever way she turned.

She decided that the obvious way out was to send Becky and Sean a card. She would find a really nice one. Coward, she said to herself. A card was cold and distant. They ought to meet up. Good grief! Becky only lived a few miles up the road. Or at the very least they should be able to talk on the phone the way real mates did.

She remembered how one of her old work colleagues had been forever complaining that her teenage daughter was never off the phone. 'I don't know what they find to talk about,' the woman had said. 'They've been together all day at school, then five minutes after they get home they're on the phone to one another again, yap, yap, yap.'

It hadn't been like that when she had been at school. When Becky and her mum had lived in their flat they didn't even have a phone. Paula and Nicky had phones in their homes but phones had been serious instruments in those days. A telephone was there to receive notification from relatives of illness and death, to ring the gas board on important, grown-up business or to summon the emergency services in the unlikely event of requiring them. As any parent worthy of the name had been forever pointing out, phone calls cost money and telephones were not installed in people's houses in order to facilitate frivolous chattering between schoolgirls.

The Christies' telephone had often stood silent for days at a time but all the same, on the rare occasions when one of her friends *had* called, her father had invariably said: 'Don't be long on that phone Nicola. Someone might be trying to get through.' But then, Nicky reflected, as the telephone was in the room where the rest of the family was sitting, no one would have wanted to stay on it for long, with parents and younger brothers hanging on every word. Multiple extensions had opened up a whole new world for teenagers, she thought.

Though these recollections briefly provoked a smile, none of this took her any further forward on the question of ringing Becky. She remembered with shame what a good friend Becky had been when she first got back from America. The fleeting thought of her return from America raised the old spectre of another failure. She had only had two significant relationships in her life and they had both turned out badly. No... she mustn't think that about Clive. He did care for her and just because he did not want the same things as her, that did not make him a bad person or even necessarily the wrong person for her.

She went into the garden to tidy the patio pots and hanging baskets. Rob never touched them. They were entirely her own private project and they had not turned out at all badly, considering that she was a complete beginner. She ran her fingers gently through the snaking strands of Indian Mint, so that its fragrance rose to meet her.

She had chosen the combination of plants really well. What a pity she hadn't been so good at choosing men. If she had been proactive in the matter at all… Wasn't it really the case that they had chosen her and she had let them? Clive had plucked her out of an office reception one day. Mark had sashayed up in a pub and introduced himself. She had been vaguely aware of both of them already. Clive from the charity event and Mark had been an acquaintance of an acquaintance. Both handsome and sought after, so that she had been flattered when they had taken an interest in her.

She had never thought of herself as especially pretty and she was certainly not slim or witty or clever. No wonder she had always been so chuffed, when a member of the opposite sex took any notice of her. She could still remember feeling slightly envious of what she had perceived as Jo's self confidence: the way she was never desperate enough to settle for any old chap who asked her out. At the time she'd attributed this to Jo's greater sense of personal self worth – the knowledge that she could afford to wait for someone better to come along – whereas she realised now that there had been completely different factors at work.

She had been ecstatically happy when Mark first asked her out. She'd caught him two timing her quite early on in their relationship, but she had been eager to forgive him and wanted to believe him when he said that it would never happen again. With Clive too, she thought, she had persuaded herself to see only what she wanted to see.

I've always been attracted to the wrong sort of man, she thought. I go for the flashy, obvious types, but the sort of man I ought to be with is a quiet, steady chap. Someone I feel easy and comfortable with.

Someone like Rob.

No. No. Didn't mean to think that. Absolutely mustn't start thinking silly things like that. He's probably got a wife and three kids anyway.

She pulled a sliver of grass out of the nearest bed of lobelia with unnecessary savagery.

Chapter Forty-Eight

1971

The fourth form disco had become pretty much the sole topic of conversation, not least because it was a source of amazement that Mrs Carpigo had consented to its taking place at all. True she kept referring to it as a dance and had laid down strict conditions about the numbers of tickets any girl might purchase and to whom they could be sold, to say nothing of issuing dire warnings about the consequences which would be faced by anyone attempting to introduce tobacco or alcohol onto the premises. In fact it had been Mrs Carpigo's intention to prevent any young man not personally known to a fourth form pupil from attending the disco, but a scheme to circumvent this was soon in operation. Girls who were not acquainted with any young men at all purchased their full quota of tickets which they passed on to girls who had brothers at local boys' schools, where a healthy black market trade in Evie disco tickets sprang up.

On the Saturday before the event half of the fourth year kept bumping into the other half as they trawled the city centre shops in search of suitable outfits to wear. Becky and Jo had no money to buy anything but were happy to accompany Paula and Nicky in an advisory capacity. And not having any money had never been a stop to joining in the fun of trying things on. Paula liked the changing rooms in Etam best because they were curtained cubicles, rather than the communal ones in Bus Stop and Chelsea Girl, where other people could stare at you. She and Jo were squashed into one of Etam's basement cubicles when Becky's head suddenly appeared above the partition.

'We need some help,' Becky stage whispered. 'Nick's got stuck in a smock top.'

'What?'

'Nick's stuck. She put this top on and now she can't get it off. It said size 14 on the hanger but I've just checked the label in the back and it's really a 10.'

'Bloody hell.'

'I know. Can one of you come round?'

'I'll come,' said Paula, who was already back in her own clothes. 'You keep looking over the top to make sure the coast's clear.'

The assistants in Etam generally stayed upstairs gossiping near the till, so there was no difficulty about Paula diving out of one cubicle and into the next. Joanne, who was still in her underwear, copied Becky's example and clambered onto the stool so that she could see over the hardboard partition into the adjacent cubicle, which was now extremely crowded with three bodies crammed into a space primarily designed for one. Nicky, very red in the face, was bulging beneath a black cotton smock top which was embroidered with flowers in purple, scarlet and crocus yellow. Though intended to be a loose fit, the smock appeared to be pretty much skin tight.

'How on earth did you get into it?' asked Paula.

'I was all right getting it on,' said Nicky. 'It seemed to go tight afterwards. I think it might be restricting my breathing.'

'Are there any fastenings you can undo?' asked Jo.

'No. You're supposed to get it on and off over your head.'

'Put your arms up,' instructed Becky. 'Me and Pau will try to get it off.'

'It's horrible anyway,' said Jo unhelpfully. 'What on earth made you try it on in the first place?'

Nicky ignored the question, concentrating on manoeuvring her arms above her head.

'Ow,' said Becky. 'That was my nose.'

'Sorry.'

'O.K... now if we both get hold of it... one each side...'

'Look out! Don't split it.'

'If you rip it you'll have to pay for it,' Joanne's voice came from above their heads.

'Thank you Joanne Embury, specialist subject Stating the Bleedin' Obvious,' said Becky.

'Look out,' said Nicky. 'You're suffocating me.'

'It won't go any further,' said Paula. 'How on earth did you get it over your boobs before?'

'It's not my fault,' came a voice muffled beneath a black cotton shroud. 'It was on the wrong hanger.'

'She'll just have to keep it on,' Paula said a few minutes later. 'We'll have to club together and pay for it and then cut her out of it when we get outside.'

'Surgical removal from a smock top,' murmured Jo.

'It won't go back down either,' said Becky. 'It's completely stuck on my side now. It's sort of rolled up into itself.'

'I can't stay like this,' said Nicky. 'My arms are getting tired.'

'We can't take her up to the till like that,' said Paula.

'We could say she's part of an enclosed order of nuns,' said Joanne. 'You know… decided to take the veil and can't show her face to the world.'

'And I suppose she has to keep her arms held above her head in constant supplication,' said Becky. They all began to giggle hopelessly.

'Has anyone got any nail scissors on them?' asked Paula. 'Perhaps we could unpick one of the seams, get Nick out and then sew it back up again. No one would be any the wiser.'

Becky shook her head. 'The nun idea was better than that,' she said.

'Someone's got to do something,' pleaded Nicky. 'My arms are killing me. This must be what wearing a straight jacket is like.'

'Come on,' said Becky. 'One last go. Try sort of rolling it up. There… that's moved it at least an inch further up on my side.'

'Ouch,' protested Nicky. 'You're taking my skin off.'

'A small price to pay,' said Becky firmly. 'If it's that or being a nun. Anyway if we can't get you out of this and you have to pay for it, you won't be able to go back to Chelsea Girl and get that skirt you want.'

'Do you know,' said Jo, as Nicky was finally liberated

from the rogue garment. 'That's the third time they've played 'Metal Guru', since we've been down here. I don't think I'll ever hear that song again without picturing Nick stuck with a smock over her head.'

Paula's mother had given permission for her friends to come over on the night of the disco and had even agreed that they could all stay the night afterwards. Getting ready at Paula's was their unanimous first choice because she had the biggest bedroom and although her parents tended to fuss, at least they were not given to making spiteful comments like Stan and nor did Paula have younger brothers like Dennis hanging around.

Paula had made her mother promise not to enter the bedroom while they were getting ready, which was just as well because ten minutes into the process the room was a shipwreck of discarded clothes littering every surface, with bags, school books, night clothes and all manner of toiletries scattered all over the floor. Further disarray resulted when a plan to spray glitter into their hair went horribly wrong. Paula's theory that one person stood still, while another sprinkled glitter onto her hair and a third frantically applied hairspray was evidently not the way the stars achieved the effect on 'Top of the Pops'. A good deal of glitter ended up on the floor, while the rest of it adhered to just about everything but the subject's hair.

'I look as though I've got sparkly dandruff,' Becky wailed, on examining her reflection in the mirror.

Nicky varnished her nails a lurid shade of purple to match her new skirt, then agonised over how satisfactory the effect could ever be on nails as badly bitten as hers. Paula spent ages debating between black or coloured tights, neither of which did much to make her legs look any less skinny in her new platform shoes. Jo helpfully painted tiny flowers at the outer corners of their eyes using blue and silver eye shadow.

When they were finally ready Mr Morrison gave them a lift to school, dropping them right outside the door which removed any possible excuse to linger outside. Becky handed in their four tickets and they walked into the hall, trying to look confident. The curtains had been closed and lighting reduced to an absolute minimum. Two sets of disco bulbs had been set up on the stage and they flashed out across an empty dance floor, while small groups of teenagers stood around the edges, many with their backs pointedly towards the rest of the room. Becky led the others to a vacant spot from which they could direct each other's attention to what everyone else was wearing and who they were standing with. There were several groups of uneasy looking youths scattered around the room, but no obvious signs that any of them were acquainted with any of the groups of girls or indeed that they ever intended to be. Occasionally there would be some half hearted nodding and foot tapping, as if to show that in different circumstances any one of them would be itching to dance… but not of course here and now.

After about half an hour of this, Gail Foster made her entrance in a big group of boys and girls. Within two minutes of arriving Gail was up on the stage in animated conversation with the man running the disco and as soon as the record he had been playing was finished, the immortal words 'I am the magnificent… ' rang out across the hall, at which Gail and all her female friends hurried into the centre of the floor and formed up a line for 'Double Barrel', while the boys they had brought with them continued to lurk at the side of the hall, keeping their Crombie overcoats on, as if uncertain whether or not they would be staying.

'Showoffs,' said Paula.

Show offs or not this broke the ice. Encouraged by Nicky the four friends eventually ventured a few feet from where they had been standing, formed a circle and danced to 'Get it On'.

Eventually boys began to emerge from their huddles and under the merciless gaze of their friends, approached girls to ask them for a dance. When the DJ played 'Psychedelic Shack' a boy with short dark hair who had been looking their way for some time, walked towards them.

'Look out,' hissed Nicky. 'He's going to ask one of us to dance with him.'

'Don't look, don't look,' said Becky. 'Pretend we haven't noticed.'

'His friend's coming as well,' whispered Joanne, who was best placed to see the boys' approach.

'Who's he looking at?' asked Paula.

'How do I know you idiot? He's looking at all of us.'

The first youth, looking extremely uncomfortable, was forced to tap Nicky on the shoulder, so resolutely was she pretending to be unaware of his approach. 'Do you want a dance?'

'O.K.' she said.

They took a few steps away from the others and began to jig uneasily, not quite in unison with each other or the beat.

The taller boy had come for Joanne.

Paula and Becky retired from the floor to stand against the wall and watch their friends. The first record ended and another began. Both couples stayed on the floor.

'We shouldn't just stand here watching,' said Paula. 'It'll make them nervous. Shall we go and get a drink or something?'

They walked along the top corridor to the dining hall, encountering various familiar faces coming the other way. Colleen Bell was holding hands with a boy they vaguely recognised from Saint Luke's. Helen Staveley was accompanied by Amira Patel's seriously handsome older brother.

'I'd sort of hoped Ralph would be here,' said Paula. 'I know someone was selling tickets at his school.'

Becky didn't answer. She thought it highly likely unlikely that Paula would ever actually see this Ralph boy she'd met at her cousin's wedding again, but she didn't like to say so. Paula had mooned on about him for ages after the wedding and the optimistic long shot that he might turn up at their school disco had set her off afresh. It was a hopeless case really, because although Paula knew his school, she didn't know his second name or where he lived, or anything at all in fact that might enable her to engineer a further meeting.

In the dining hall some volunteer prefects were dispensing orange squash into paper cups. Crisps and Wagon Wheels were also on sale. Mrs Venables, one of a large number of staff on the end of Mrs Carpigo's three line whip to police the event, had just waded in to stop three of the boys brought along by Gail Foster from throwing orange squash at one another. Together with Miss Bagshaw, she had decided to escort them from the premises. Gail and the rest of her group elected to leave with them.

'It's a bit boring anyway,' said Gail. She glanced around as she made the remark, as if pitying those who had nothing better to do than stay. Becky and Paula were acutely conscious that she had seen them standing in the refreshment queue, marked down as the social failures with whom no one wanted to dance.

As the witching hour of ten o'clock approached, everyone had gravitated back to the hall because they all knew that the disco would end with a slow number. Sure enough the DJ put on 'When a Man Loves a Woman' and every couple locked clumsily together and began to sway to the sultry crooning of Percy Sledge.

Miss Harkness, in her role as Mrs Carpigo's right hand woman, hastened up the steps and onto the stage where she could be seen remonstrating urgently with the disco man. 'When a Man Loves a Woman' came to an abrupt end in the middle of a note.

'Special request from the floor,' said the DJ, his sarcasm slightly lost amid crackles from the mic. 'Something really groovy to finish off with. Last track of the evening, 'Sugar Sugar' by The Archies.'

The dancers stood momentarily frozen. There was some limited booing: though not from Eleanor Vaux pupils, who were aware of Miss Harkness still on the stage, her beady eyes glaring out across the hall. No one attempted to dance. Instead there was a general move for the doors. Jo, catching sight of Becky and Paula, broke away from her partner with a quick word and came to join them as they headed towards the cloakroom. Nicky did not catch up with them until a few minutes later.

'I've given him my phone number,' she said, proudly.

'His name's Andy and he says he's going to ring me.'

Back in Paula's bedroom they sat up long after midnight, trying their best to keep their voices down.

'I couldn't believe it,' Nicky confided. 'After a couple of dances he just said, "Do you want to come outside for a snog?"'

'Very subtle,' said Becky. 'He's obviously got a real way with words.'

'Did you go outside with Thingummybob?' Paula asked Jo.

'Yes,' said Jo. 'Although I don't know why. He was horrible really. He tried to stick his tongue into my mouth. Dirty pig.'

'I can't believe what Miss Harkness did at the end,' said Nicky. 'Honestly! Eleanor Vaux will be the laughing stock of every school in the area.'

'She's become Cow-Pig-O's number one henchman,' said Paula.

'I hate that school,' said Jo. 'Sometimes I can't wait to get away.'

Chapter Forty-Nine

1985

Nicky had been watching 'Love Story' on video. She could still remember weeping buckets the first time she had seen it at the ABC in New Street. A decade later it seemed more than a bit silly. What self respecting man would have pursued Ali McGraw, the way she kept wise cracking and putting Ryan O'Neil down? It would never have got you anywhere with a lad in Birmingham but perhaps it had been different at Harvard. When she switched the video to rewind, the T.V. screen flicked to daytime television where they were talking about the terrible fire at the football ground in Bradford. There was never any good news. Nothing nice seemed to happen anymore.

It was about time she took Rob his mug of tea. She had not spoken to him yet to this morning, though she had observed him through the window as he worked his way steadily to and fro with the lawn mower. She felt reproached by his industry. Silly really. He didn't know that she had been whiling away the morning watching a video because she had nothing better to do with her life. It was not as if she needed to defend herself to him. She might have been in her den, running a high powered business or writing a best seller… or raising millions for charity from her well connected friends. Anyway it was none of his business. He was only the gardener for goodness sake.

She took his mug outside at the usual time. By now he was mowing the area furthest away from the house. She watched as he worked his way down the length of one green stripe while the noise of the petrol driven motor thrummed around him like a swarm of hyperactive bees. When he reached the edge of the lawn he made a neat about turn and started in the opposite direction. Nicky wondered if he was genuinely unaware of her presence or if after the awkwardness of the previous week, he was simply pretending not to see her, just in case she came over all emotional again. Perhaps he was hoping that she would just leave the tea on the path for him and go back inside. He wouldn't have been able to hear her approach because he had got ear protectors on, like a big pair of old fashioned headphones. When he used the scrimmer he wore a hard hat with a visor which came down over his eyes. It made him look a bit like a cyber man. She had once been tempted to greet him with the words, 'Your tea, O Cyber Leader,' but she wasn't sure if he would find it funny.

She stood watching as he limped away from her, the perspective of him changing. She could almost hear Miss Carling, telling her to look at how his size was altering while the distant oak tree she measured him against stayed just the same. 'Observe,' Miss Carling used to say. 'Only observe.' She had always enjoyed art at school, Nicky reflected. Perhaps she could take it up again. Maybe take a class. Give herself something to do.

Rob reached the end of the strip and turned himself and the mower in readiness to start the next. There was something deft and efficient about the execution of the turn which belied the assumed clumsiness she associated with his limp. Then he caught sight of her standing there and smiled in a friendly way which entirely banished any thoughts that he might have been ignoring her. He killed the noise of the mower, setting free the bird song which had been trapped within its racket and walked across to join her.

'I've brought your tea,' she said. A pointless remark, she thought, since he could see the mug in her hand. There was nothing defective about his eyesight.

'Thanks.' He received the mug from her and took a couple of sips.

'I'm sorry I'm a bit later than usual with it. I was doing something inside and I forgot the time.'

'It doesn't matter,' he said. 'Not obliged to make me a cup of tea at all are you?' He did not add that it was also entirely unnecessary as he had got a flask in his van.

She stopped herself just in time from saying that she liked to do it. I say such idiotic things sometimes, she thought. Next thing I'll be telling him I look forward to doing it or something daft like that.

'I wanted to see you actually,' he said. He had stopped smiling now. 'I need to give you and Mr Aston fair notice that I won't be coming here much longer.' Seeing her face he continued hastily, 'I'll come for another two or three weeks… to give you time to find a replacement.'

'Look Rob,' she said. 'I'm really sorry if I embarrassed you in any way last week. It won't happen again I promise you. Please don't stop coming because of that.'

'It's not because of that,' he said. 'I'm setting up my own nursery business so I'm cutting out all these gardening jobs. I won't have time for them any more.'

'Oh,' said Nicky, feeling very foolish.

'It's something I've been wanting to do for a long time. My compensation came through a while ago and once I'd got the capital I started looking for the right premises. I found somewhere a few weeks back and I exchange contracts tomorrow. It's not much of a place at the moment. Very run down. Loads of potential though and I'm not afraid of a bit of hard work.' Enthusiasm shone brightly in his voice.

Nicky listened dumbly. 'Compensation?' she said managed to say at last.

With his free hand he tapped his left thigh. 'For this. Got smashed up in a motorbike accident nearly four years ago. Bloke pulled out in front of me and I went straight into him. The case went to court and after a lot of argy bargy the guy's insurers finally paid up.'

Nicky was uncertain whether congratulations or commiserations were in order. 'So now you're going to start your own business,' she said.

'I'm already self employed,' he said with what she fancied was a touch of starchiness. 'But this is an opportunity to do something better. I've got real ambitions for the place.'

'It's a great opportunity for you then,' Nicky said. 'All's well that ends well.'

'So you'll let Mr Aston know for me?'

'Yes of course.'

'I'll miss some of my old clients,' he said. 'Their gardens I mean. Not being able to see how things develop. I shan't see how your lavender borders turn out… stuff like that.' He trailed off awkwardly.

A sudden breeze tossed a handful of pale pink azalea petals over them like confetti.

'I'd better go in,' she said.

'Yes,' he said. 'It's still cool out here if you haven't got enough layers on.'

She didn't move. Another gust carried the petals away, scattering them untidily across the half mown lawn.

'If Mr Aston is stuck for someone to replace me he could try Whitberrys. The number's in Yellow Pages. They're a reputable firm.'

'Thanks,' said Nicky. 'I'll tell him.'

He finished his tea, taking a long final draught which drained the mug. 'Thanks,' he said, handing it back to her.

There was no further reason to stand there. A cloud moved across the sun, sliding a shadow from left to right across the garden. Another gust sent a shower of petals scurrying across the lawn as if they were chasing the departing sunshine.

'Looks like that rain's on its way,' he said. 'I'd better get the grass finished before it starts.' He turned back to the mower, leaving her standing alone on the path. Another gust of wind made her shiver. She pulled herself together and walked slowly back to the house.

Chapter Fifty

1985

'I think I fancy being the electrician tonight,' said Clive.

He spoke as if he was choosing from a menu. In a different setting he might have been saying, 'I'll have the fish,' or 'I think I'll try the paella'.

Nicky looked up from the magazine she had been reading. She never refused him. Subservience was a price she felt she had to pay. It was a vicious circle because she loathed the parts he cast her in and despised herself for the playing them, but the punishment she had set herself was to endure with the pretence of enjoyment, those acts which would ultimately only make her view herself with more odium.

'I'll just go and check the wiring in the kitchen,' Clive said playfully.

Nicky knew that this was her cue to go upstairs, where the 'electrician' would find her in the process of getting changed, him appearing in the bedroom complete with his tool bag which contained such unlikely equipment as a length of rope and a pair of hand cuffs.

What am I doing here? she asked herself. Is this really my life?

When Clive arrived upstairs she was standing in her place in front of the full length mirror, but she had not removed any of her clothes. This caused him to register a look of mild surprise before he said, 'I've come to check the wiring.'

Oh God, he wasn't even inventive. It was the same stupid line every time.

'Shouldn't you have knocked?' she asked. 'Before you come barging into someone's bedroom?'

'Sorry,' he said. 'I didn't know there was anyone in here.'

He crossed the room and bent as if to do something with the electrical sockets on the far wall but instead started looking at her in the mirror. This was the signal for Nicky to ask him what he was looking at, but tonight she did not say anything. For a split second the thought crossed her mind that she did not have to do any of this. She could just walk out of the room, down the stairs, out of the front door, down the road to anywhere and everywhere. The thought came like someone lifting a curtain in a darkened room, revealing a glimpse of the lighted world beyond the window. But then the curtain dropped and the vision was gone. She had built up enough anger to leave Mark… but she had been angry with him… now she was just angry with herself.

'What are you looking at?' she said. 'Get on with your work.'

He moved anti-clockwise round the room to another set of sockets, where she could still see him reflected in the glass as he ogled her. In real life, she thought, any woman in her right mind would have been out of the room and on the phone to summon help by now.

'Will you stop looking at me,' she said. She was supposed to have added the words 'you impudent little man'. That was her line. It was all part of the game.

He moved around the room again so that he was at the nearest set of sockets, close enough to grab her which was what he was going to do next, saying his part about her being a stuck up little madam who needed to be taught a lesson.

She steeled herself for the move as she always did, but at the very last moment blind instinct took over and she darted out of reach just as he tried to grab her. Turning to face him she could see that he had interpreted this as an interesting new twist in the plot. She backed away. He advanced a step. She retreated again.

'Leave me alone,' she said, with more degree of conviction than she could normally manage to bring to her various bedroom roles. 'Don't touch me.'

A wide grin appeared on his face. She stood ready to take further evasive action, noting that he was perfectly positioned to block any attempt to escape via the bedroom door. His next move was too quick for her. She gave a little cry as his hand fastened on her arm. She tried to pull away, struggling even harder when she saw him drawing a long cord from his pocket with his free hand.

'Get off me you pervert,' she said.

It was all part of the game for her to put up a bit of a fight. He liked that. While she tried to prize his fingers off her arm, he attempted to loop the cord around the wrist that he held captive. She kicked at him but without shoes it was an ineffectual gesture and he laughed out loud. He gave up on the cord, making a grab in the general direction of her shoulder but only managing to connect with the neck of her shirt, which he used to tug her towards him, possibly with a view to forcing her to submit to a kiss. As she pulled hard the opposite way the shirt ripped audibly, shedding a button in the process, which lodged between her breasts. She bent forward and bit the hand that was still clamped on her arm.

This was definitely not in the script and he was sufficiently startled that he relaxed his hold enough for her to pull free. Their eyes met and she knew that whatever outward pretence either of them had adopted so far, from now on it was for real. She had nowhere to go except a further retreat in the direction of the arch which led into the bathroom. She took another step backwards while he examined his hand, rubbing the place where her teeth had connected. Any second now he would come at her again.

'Now you're really asking for it,' he said. His voice was still playful but his eyes were angry.

With him between her and the bedroom door the only possible refuge was the toilet which led off the bathroom and had a lockable door. She tried to make a dash for it but he was lean and fit with a longer stride. He was on her before she got past the jacuzzi, grabbing her from behind and looping one arm across her chest while he used his free hand to rip at her blouse, dragging it off while she did her best to fight free of him. This time he was too fey to leave any hands within reach of her teeth.

'Get…off…me,' she gasped.

He managed to pinion her arms behind her and wrestle the cord around them, twisting it a couple of times, then holding it in place while he propelled her roughly forward towards the shower cubicle, where he turned the water full on before thrusting her head and shoulders under it. The water gushed down onto the back of her head, rivulets finding their way around the sides of her face, into her ears, nose and mouth. She inhaled water, coughing and choking while fighting off the panic stricken idea that she could scarcely breathe and might even drown. She wanted to scream but she couldn't vocalise a sound and anyway, what was the point? There were no immediate neighbours.

After a frighteningly long time he dragged her out, bedraggled and half naked. She spat out water and struggled to free herself, but he responded by slapping her and thrusting her head and torso back into the torrent. When he dragged her out for a second time he forced her against the tiles while he secured the cord about her arms more tightly. He had her now and there was no escape.

Chapter Fifty-One

1972

Nicky sensed that something was up the minute she walked through the kitchen door after school. Her mother was pink and beaming, clearly over excited about something.

'Michael,' Mrs Christie called out as soon as she saw Nicky. 'Michael come and tell Nicky your news.'

Michael appeared in the sitting room doorway. 'I've passed for the High School,' he said.

'Oh wow. Congratulations.'

Nicky was genuinely impressed. King Edward's High was the crème de la crème of Birmingham grammar schools, so elite that entrance was based not on the eleven plus results, but on its own special examination for which only the brightest boys and girls in each year were entered. In Nicky's year only one girl from their primary school had tried for the High and she hadn't got in. The Christies did not know anyone else who went there.

'Just wait until your dad gets in from work,' said Mrs Christie. 'Won't he be pleased!'

Nicky decided that it was not a good moment to mention that she had got another detention. Luckily Baggy Bagshaw had to write out an individual detention slip for every single member of the class (serve her right too for issuing class detentions left right and centre) and she hadn't had time to get them all done before the end of school so Nicky hadn't got a slip for her parents to sign yet.

'They play rugby there – not football like they do at the tech.,' said Dennis.

'I'm not really interested in sports,' said Michael loftily. 'I'm going there for the academic side of things.'

He's my brother and I love him, Nicky thought, but I wish he wasn't quite such a precocious little brat. She drifted into the kitchen to see if she could scrounge a piece of cake or a jam sandwich but her mother shooed her out.

'You'll spoil your tea,' she said.

When their father came home he was predictably over the moon; saying that he hadn't been so excited since Villa won the cup final – and that was the year Nicky was born. 'I don't know where you get it from,' he said to Michael. 'Not me or your mother, that's for sure. You've always been the brightest of the bunch.'

Michael smirked.

'Seems as if every kid we've produced has managed to be a bit cleverer than the last. If we hadn't stopped at three we'd have produced Brain of Britain by now, eh Vera?'

Nicky could hardly fail to notice that this made her the dunce of the family. Something must have shown in her expression because her father reached across and rumpled her hair. 'Never mind love,' he said. 'Michael got the brains but you got all the looks.'

Nicky grinned back at him. She knew that he meant this consolation prize kindly. 'Have I got time to go up and get some homework done before tea?' she asked.

'You've got another half an hour yet,' replied her mother.

She was glad to get up to her bedroom where it was always cool even on a warm day. She lay full length on the bed, tracing her fingers along the lines in the orange candlewick bedspread. It was horrible of her to be jealous of Michael. It wasn't his fault that he was so clever. Actually she wasn't really jealous of him. Certainly not of his place at the High School, which was so prestigious as to be infinitely more terrifying than Eleanor Vaux had been. No, it was not that. It was the fact of him being a demonstrably special person. Whatever happened to him now, he could always say that he had passed for the High School. It singled him out as a member of the intellectual aristocracy of Birmingham school kids.

It was all very well her dad saying that she had got the looks. That didn't mean much in their family. She wasn't really pretty. She had that awful wavy hair when the fashion was for long and straight and a baby face and the Christie snub nose. If she had been really pretty boys would be falling over themselves to go out with her. She'd given that boy Andy her phone number at the school disco but he had never rung her. It was not as if she even shone at Eleanor Vaux never mind the flipping High School. She never came top in anything. She wasn't sporty – heaven forbid! She wasn't especially popular. I'm just ordinary, she thought. Dull, average and fairly worthless in the greater scheme of things.

About a mile and a half away, the Emburys were already

sitting down to their tea. They always ate early to fit in with Mr Embury's shift.

'Our Sonia says they're recruiting at Kendal Boxes,' Mr Embury remarked as he picked up his tea cup in readiness to wash down his final mouthful of faggots and peas. 'You want to get in quick Joanne. Get yourself an application form.'

Joanne stopped eating to stare at him. The observation had come completely out of the blue, apropos of nothing anyone had said earlier. Catching sight of his daughter's incredulous expression, Mr Embury added, 'Well better to start now. A lot of school leavers will wait until the end of term before they start looking for anything. Applying early shows a bit of initiative. Firms like that.'

'But I'm not a school leaver,' Joanne objected.

'I thought Joanne was going to stay and do her G.C.E.s,' said Mrs Embury, talking as if Joanne wasn't there. 'She's done the first year of them. It would be a waste not to finish them off for the sake of another year at school surely?'

Joanne looked from one to another while gathering up her last forkful of food. The proposition that she should leave school to work for the same company as her older sister had never been discussed before… not in her hearing at any rate. Yet her father was talking as if the whole issue was a foregone conclusion.

'She didn't have no choice but to do the first year of the G.C.E. course, did she?' Mr Embury also addressed his wife as if the subject of their conversation was not present. 'She can't leave until she's fifteen.'

'Well no,' agreed Mrs Embury. 'But if she gets her 'O' levels she might get a better job.'

'Our Sonia hasn't got any 'O' levels and she's done all right. Senior payroll clerk she is now. She could put in a good word for Joanne. Anyway now that Sonia's got married she's not likely to be there much longer, is she? 'O' levels or not, girls always leave to have a baby. If they can find someone to marry them that is.' The glance in Joanne's direction was clearly intended to convey that he did not necessarily think this could be taken as an absolute given in her case.

'I don't want to leave school.' Joanne found her voice, carefully laying her knife and fork onto her empty plate as she spoke. 'I don't want to work at Kendal Boxes either. I want to do something with art. Miss Carling says I could get a grade one 'O' level and go on to do art 'A' level.'

'Miss Carling!' her father exclaimed, much as if Joanne had quoted some ridiculous figure, such as Tommy Cooper or Norman Wisdom. 'What does she know? What good do you think an art 'A' level is going to do you? You don't see jobs for portrait painters advertised in the 'Mail', do you? The only thing an art 'A' level is any good for is teaching other people art. And that takes another two or three years in college and you needn't think I'm going to pay for that. It's about time you learned the value of money young lady and started looking to pay your way.'

Joanne struggled to keep herself in check. She did not want to let him see how much he had upset her, because he enjoyed that – it gave him the scent of victory – but on the other hand, she had to avoid displaying anything which could be construed as anger because that would just provoke him into a violent rage.

Moreover it was a very difficult argument to counter. Her knowledge of the career opportunities which might be opened up by further education was extremely limited. In her family people went into a factory when they left school or if they were luckier into an office. It was undeniably true that 'A' level art was no boost to securing either kind of employment. The only people she ran across who *had* gone on to study at college or university were indeed teachers at Eleanor Vaux and in truth she did not really see herself in that mould. Yet she knew instinctively that there was a world beyond Eleanor Vaux, her parents' house and Kendal Boxes. The world did not begin and end on the 11 bus route. She wanted to get out and see that world, hear it and taste it and drink it in… and ultimately escape from this one. None of which was easy to explain.

'If I stay on at school,' she said, trying hard to keep her voice absolutely casual and ordinary, so as not to invoke the accusations of cheekiness which were inevitably initiated by any attempt on her part to offer a contrary point of view to the one espoused by her father. 'If I stay on at school I'll get qualifications and in the end I'll get a better job. If I went on to university I'd get a better job still. Then I could pay you back. For my keep and for all the extra years you'd fed and clothed me.'

'Of course you could,' her father mocked her. 'That's if you hadn't got pregnant first and packed it all in.'

'I wouldn't,' said Joanne.

'Well you're not going to get the chance,' said her father. 'I'd sooner put my money on the gee-gees. Less of a gamble I'd say.'

'I'll find the money myself then,' said Joanne, with more than a hint of desperation. 'I'll get a job – a Saturday job – to help pay my way.'

'That's not going to feed you,' jeered her father. 'Nor keep you in these fancy clothes you like to wear.'

'I'll borrow money from somewhere,' said Joanne, pushing back her chair as she spoke and automatically starting to help her mother, who had already got up and begun to clear the table as if nothing very important was being discussed at all.

Her father gave a bellow of laughter. 'You kids live in a fantasy world. Who do you think is going to let you borrow money? They don't lend money to students, you silly girl. They'll only lend money to people with jobs, people who can pay it back. It's parents what pay for these kids who spend three years loafing about at universities and if the parents won't stump up the cash then that's it my girl.'

He stood up, throwing her an unmistakable look of triumph before marching upstairs to the lavatory. The discussion was clearly at an end.

'Come on Bri,' said Joanne. 'Hurry up and finish with that cup.'

She spoke calmly although she felt like hurling the crocks she'd already collected across the room. She knew that her father derived a perverse pleasure from wielding power. At work he was just one man among hundreds, doing a task like an automaton. He had no say in anything. At home he was a king. His word was law and he could dictate the lives of his subjects to suit his smallest whim. If it was his sworn opinion that further education was a waste of time and money then no one could gainsay him. Just as he liked to be sure they all understood that the television belonged to him and therefore absolute discretion regarding which programmes would be shown upon it was his to exercise, so too he enjoyed the knowledge that Joanne – whether she liked it or not – would have no alternative but to concede that he had authority over what she could and could not do.

When Joanne reported this conversation to her friends en route to school next morning it provoked instant outrage.

'You can't leave,' Nicky cried. 'We'll be split up. We haven't been split up since first year.'

'We'll have to be split up one day,' said Becky.

'Yes – but not yet.'

'You can't leave,' said Paula. 'You've got a right to your education. Remember what Miss Barr said in assembly when she came last year.'

'Try telling that to my dad,' said Joanne. 'He's still living in the Dark Ages.'

'You're brilliant at art,' said Becky. 'He can't just expect you to give all that up, just to go and work in some rat infested office.'

'Even in an office without rats' demurred Paula.

'Anyway,' said Becky. 'It's not in the script. Paula's going to be a famous novelist and you're going to be a famous artist. In fact you could illustrate Paula's books.'

'The sort of books I'm going to write don't have illustrations.'

'Well maybe not,' said Becky impatiently. 'But they'll have a picture on the cover. Someone's got to design that.'

'We can't all be famous if you go to work for Kendal Boxes,' said Nicky. 'Mind you, I still don't know what I'm going to do to be famous.'

'Anyway whatever happens, you can't leave at the end of this term,' said Paula.

Nothing further was said in the Embury household on the subject of Joanne's education until two days later when the family were at the tea table, this time eating steak and kidney pie with mashed potatoes and broad beans. Mr Embury, again speaking as though nothing of any great significance was under discussion announced: 'I was talking to a chap in the pub last night. Very sensible bloke, works at Cadbury's, and he said with them raising the school leaving age to sixteen from next year, there won't be anyone leaving school without taking some exams after this year. He reckoned that once everyone *has* to stay on an extra year and *has* to take some 'O' levels, employers are going to start expecting everyone to have some whether they mean anything or not. He reckons the time will come when employers think that anyone who hasn't got a couple of exams is a right thicko – so I've decided that our Joanne had better stay on the extra year at school after all.'

'Well yes,' Mrs Embury said. 'I think it would be for the best.'

Joanne knew better than to say anything at all.

Chapter Fifty-Two

1985

Nicky eventually fell asleep at around three in the morning and woke again a little after six. She ached from the brutal use of the night before but the pain in her heart was greater. She knew that Clive was due in London for a meeting later in the day and that he planned to catch an early train. He rose just before seven, showered, dressed, went downstairs and left the house without returning to the bedroom, apparently content to collude in the mutual pretence that Nicky was still asleep. Only when she heard the sound of his departing car did she give way to weeping, her whole body wracked and trembling beneath the bed covers.

It was a long time before she could gather herself sufficiently to climb out of bed and wrap her silk dressing gown loosely about her. She walked slowly through the archway into the bathroom, trying to avoid her reflection in the various mirrors while she ran water into the bath, glad of the way steam obscured the glass. The bath itself was unsatisfactory. Soaping her body gave her too much opportunity to notice bruises and there were some things that water could not clean away. Only as she climbed out of the bath did she remember that it was Rob's day for coming to work in the garden. She couldn't face taking him the accustomed cup of tea. She did not want to see him or anyone else. Then again she didn't want him to think that she was avoiding him by staying in the house. Her head seemed to throb with one confused idea after another, but the uppermost thought was that she ought to avoid being seen by the gardener. The most obvious alternative was to go out somewhere. That was it. If her car wasn't on the drive Rob would know that she wasn't there and wouldn't think badly of her for failing to provide any tea.

She dried herself and then attempted to drag a brush through her hair, which was tangled and matted from the previous night's wetting. She ought to have washed it but the thought of re-entering the shower made her feel sick. Each pull of the brush made her head throb a little more, but she knew that she would have to hurry up if she was going to get away before Rob arrived. He was invariably punctual. Without thinking she had put on her oldest jeans and a rather faded sweatshirt with a large pink elephant on the front of it. They were not the sort of clothes she would normally have gone out in and her hair refused to be tamed. A sideways glance in the full length mirror confirmed that she looked absolutely terrible. She was not dressed to go anywhere and anyway she had no idea where she should go. Dry panicky sobs began to force their way up from her chest again and she had to grab the bedpost to keep herself upright. Then she remembered what had taken place in that particular spot the night before and withdrew her hand as if it had been burned.

A new idea came to her. If she put her car – well Clive's second car really, but they called it her car – inside the garage, then she need not go anywhere. Rob would just note the absence of the car and draw his own conclusions. With the car hidden she could simply stay upstairs out of sight. Not in here, she thought with a shudder. In one of the spare bedrooms. The one she had done out with Laura Ashley fabrics. She could hide in there until he had gone. Her feet were still bare so she put her trainers on without any socks to save time. She noticed as she was tying the laces that her hands were still trembling.

When she got downstairs she could not find her car keys. She began to search more and more frantically, all but running from place to place before she spotted them on the hall floor where they had probably been knocked accidentally, from the little table where she must have put them down when she last came in at the front door. Stupid, stupid, how could she have missed seeing them there?

Her heart was beating ridiculously fast as she unlocked the front door and hurried across the wide block paved area at the front of the house to where the car was parked. When she reached the garage door she found that was locked too, which meant racing back into the house to get another set of keys. The brightness of the morning only served to remind her of how late it was getting and how soon Rob would be there.

In her haste she stalled the car before finally managing to engage reverse gear, swinging the car in a wide arc and then driving it forward into the garage. She took the keys from the ignition, scrambled out and slammed the driver's door which made a sound that re-echoed around the enclosed space and juddered her aching head. She had just got back outside and was reaching above her head to swing the up and over garage door closed when Rob's van turned in at the front gates. It came to her as she stood frozen like a rabbit in the glare of approaching headlights, that she need not have moved the car at all. If she had only stayed out of the way upstairs, Rob would have assumed that she was out somewhere with Clive in his car.

She might still have made it into the house – though of course he had seen her now, so the pretence of being out somewhere was already a lost cause – but this sudden cognisance of her own stupidity, the wholly unnecessary elaboration of a ludicrous plan involving the hiding of the car, made her hesitate. She stood in front of the garage door as the van drew up a few feet in front of her and he called a cheerful 'Good morning' out of the open window.

Clear blue sky and sunshine. In one sense it was a very good morning. She had not noticed. Unable to bear the thought of him looking at her, she focussed all her attention on closing the garage door, slowly turning the key and retrieving it from the lock, but when she turned she found that he had climbed out of the van and was looking straight at her.

He took in the swollen lower lip and reddened, haunted eyes. 'You're getting knocked about aren't you?' he said.

Nicky was too ashamed to face him. She stared down at her feet, mortified that she had been found out, but shocked too by his acknowledgement of things that should be kept secret. She had never expected him to say anything like that. Even if it was so obvious.

'You don't have to put up with it,' he said quietly. 'There's things you can do.'

Nicky shook her head. She tried to turn away towards the house but he laid his hand on her arm – very gently – not like Clive.

'Let someone help you,' he said. 'If there's no one else then let me help you.'

She raised her eyes and regarded him with disbelief.

'I don't mean to barge in,' he said. 'But if you're getting roughed up then something's got to be done about it.'

'I can't…' Nicky faltered.

'Have you got anyone you can go to?'

Nicky shook her head.

'No family? Friends?'

'My family wouldn't… anyway… I couldn't ask. No one knows you see. I've got a friend, but she's just got married, so I couldn't… and besides which she always warned me not to get mixed up with Clive in the first place.'

'Wise advice by the look of it.' He moved his hand from her arm and very gently lifted the hair at the side of her face, holding it up just long enough to reveal an emerging bruise. 'Did he do that to you?'

'I fell against the wall,' she said. 'And banged my head.'

Rob took a deep breath. 'Look Mrs Cliveden,' he said. 'It may be none of my business but it looks to me as though you need a way out of this. I've just moved into my own place so there's a spare room at my mum's. I know she'd put you up for a few days if I asked her to. She's good like that, my mum. Or if you'd rather you can stay at my cottage. But it's very basic… not what you're used to by a long chalk… And there'd be no one there but me, which might make you feel a bit uncomfortable. I don't suppose you're feeling too positive about men in general at the moment, so my mum's house would probably be best. It would buy you some time. *He* wouldn't be able to find you there either. Wouldn't know where to start looking.'

Nicky stared at him. 'Why are you doing this?' she asked.

'It's what any decent person would do.'

For a moment the curtain in the darkened room twitched upwards again but then it dropped back.

'I can't,' she said. 'I can't impose myself on other people. I haven't got any money you see, so I can't pay my way.'

'Garbage,' said Rob briskly. 'You can't stay here.'

She stood on the drive of Cliveden, teetering on the brink of the unknown. There was something in his voice which suggested that one of the reasons she could not stay any longer was that he just wouldn't allow it.

'Why don't you go and get your things together,' he suggested. 'I'll stand out here and if *he* comes back I'll sound the horn on the van to warn you, so that you can get back down here. I won't let him lay a finger on you, don't you worry about that.'

'He won't be back for hours,' she said. 'He's gone to London.'

'Well I'll be on guard just in case,' he said. 'You go and get your stuff.'

She entered the house in a trance like state. She could not find her suitcases and it took her a while to remember that they were somewhere in the loft. She hunted vainly for something else to pack a few things in. Only Clive's sports bag presented itself and she didn't want to take anything of Clive's. In desperation she got a couple of black dustbin liners from the roll kept in the utility room and began throwing things into them, taking only the clothes and shoes she had owned before she moved in with Clive – nothing bought with his money at all.

Her haste was dictated not by the fear of his imminent return – she knew he would not be back for many hours – but rather by the certainty that if she did not go quickly she would lose her nerve and stay. In the midst of this headlong dash, as she left drawers open and contents rifled, she was touched by the mental image of Rob standing guard, ready to protect her from the return of the abusive homeowner.

When she reappeared on the front doorstep a mere fifteen minutes later, struggling with the cumbersome dustbin liners, he did not look askance at her unorthodox luggage, but merely took one of them from her, smiled encouragingly and said: 'That was quick.'

He loaded the bin bags into the centre seat in the cab of his van. It was an open backed affair so there was not much provision for carrying personal luggage in the back.

'Now,' he said. 'Just make sure that the house is locked up and then post your keys back through the letterbox.'

'What about your job?' Nicky asked. 'You're supposed to be here to do some gardening. He won't pay you if you haven't done anything.'

'I was only coming for another couple of weeks in any case,' he said. 'Let the bastard cut his own lawn.'

Chapter Fifty-Three

1972

Ronnie had been unwise to play Top Banana in Miss Bagshaw's lesson. She would have done far better to have ignored the fact that Kay had used the word 'top' in a sentence but Ronnie wouldn't have been Ronnie if she had failed to take up the challenge. The rules of Top Banana were extremely simple. Every time someone said 'top' the next person to speak (not including teachers of course) had to include the word 'banana' in whatever she said. It was all very well playing a game like that in English, where there was scope for saying all sorts of inexplicable things and where even more crucially the class was being taken by Mrs Heslop who was not continually on the alert for any suspected subversion, but when Miss Bagshaw was picking on people at random to continue the French translation it was an entirely different scenario.

Whether Kay had thrown down the gauntlet on purpose or whether she had used the word 'top' entirely without thinking, when Miss Bagshaw singled out Ronnie as her next victim Ronnie could not resist translating *Robert a ravi* as 'Robert's got a banana'.

A ripple of delighted giggles swept across the room but Miss Bagshaw was not amused.

'I rather think that the staff have all had enough of this childish obsession the fourth year has with bananas,' she said. 'You have just earned a detention for the whole class Veronica.'

There were some audible groans.

'You will spend the detention writing out the word 'banana' – it might help some of you get over your fixation with the fruit. And if I hear any more of those moaning noises,' the class fell instantly silent, 'You will all find yourselves in detention the following week as well. Now Colleen can you please continue translating – since Veronica seems unable to manage it – at line twelve... *Robert a ravi.*'

'The staff must have been talking amongst themselves,' said Nicky indignantly, when the lesson was over. 'Otherwise Miss Bagshaw wouldn't have known anything about it. We've never done Top Banana in her lesson before.'

Not everyone accepted their fate so equitably. 'Why do you have to be such an idiot?' Helen Staveley snapped at Ronnie. 'You're always getting the rest of us into trouble.'

'You need to grow up Veronica Nicholls,' said Alex. Alex was in the top set for French and thus had not actually received a detention but of course she had heard all about it.

'I'd never had a single detention until you went and got the whole class one from Miss Bagshaw for making silly noises that time,' said Naomi Wiseman. 'And now you've gone and got me another one. It isn't fair.'

'There isn't a prize at the end you know. For never having a detention,' Ronnie said sarcastically. Ronnie was a veteran of Tuesday night detentions and could not really see what all the fuss was about. 'It's not my fault if Baggy Bagshaw is totally unfair. I didn't ask her to give everyone a detention.'

'But it was your childish behaviour that made her do it,' said Alex.

'Oh why don't you dry up?' Adele joined in on behalf of her friend. 'No one's given you a detention have they?'

'No.'

'Well shut up and mind your own business then.'

'It's all our business,' said Alex pompously. 'If one person keeps letting the whole form down.'

'Do me a favour,' exclaimed Adele. 'Who cares about that sort of rubbish?'

'Ronnie is fun,' said Nicky. 'I'd rather have the occasional detention because we've got people like Ronnie in the form than have no detentions and a form full of bitchy, boring old cows.'

It was fortunate that at this juncture the bell rang to signal the end of break. The group moved off in different directions. Nicola, Becky and Jo were all heading for biology which Ronnie also happened to take. They fell into step together.

'Take no notice of Alex,' said Jo. 'Hardly anyone likes her anyway.'

'I'm not exactly flavour of the month myself,' said Ronnie. 'And I'm really going to get it in the neck when I take my report home. Baggy Bagshaw is sure to put that I'm always messing about in class and never do any work. Now half the form hates me as well.'

'They don't hate you,' said Becky. 'They're more likely jealous because you're funny and popular and they're not.'

'It's people like you who make life here worth living,' agreed Joanne. 'Whereas people like Alex just make me want to puke.' In a different tone she continued: 'I'm going to be in real trouble with biology when the exams start in a couple of weeks.'

'That's because you don't have any notes,' said Becky. 'And you don't have any notes because you sit in biology lessons drawing all the time and you never give in any homework.'

'Well Mrs Young is such a soft touch.'

'Yes but that's not going to get you an 'O' level in biology is it? Writing *Mrs Young is such a soft touch* on the exam paper?'

'Never mind,' said Jo philosophically. 'I expect I'll be able to make up the work somehow or other. I've still got all of next year.'

Seen as the easiest option among the sciences, biology had been far and away the most popular of the choices offered in group one. The numbers who had chosen biology were sufficiently large that they had been split into two classes of twenty each and the class entrusted to Mrs Young comprised entirely of girls who were reluctant biologists. Any teacher might have had their work cut out and Mrs Young, who had the air of a person whose thought processes were occupied somewhere in the next room and was easily the most disorganised member of staff to hold a teaching post at Eleanor Vaux, became easy meat for a class bent on mischief.

Her pupils soon discovered that a simple experiment

involving acidity levels in soil could be extended indefinitely. 'I simply cannot understand how you have obtained those results,' a bewildered Mrs Young would say. At which point one of the girls would pipe up helpfully, 'Shall we do it again Miss?' and before Mrs Young could make herself heard, a small contingent would be off out of the lab to collect more soil samples: an errand from which they would not return until the end of the lesson.

One photosynthesis experiment in the school grounds went horribly wrong when a group led by Rebecca Addison wrapped silver foil around every leaf of one of the flowering cherries which grew along the front drive. Mrs Young could not understand how they had managed to so comprehensively misunderstand her instructions.

Then there was the bench tease. One day Mrs Young walked in to find that instead of spreading themselves out among the various lab benches as usual, every girl had carried her stool to one of the four benches at the very back of the lab, leaving the front half dozen benches completely empty. At this point Mrs Young committed the serious tactical error of objecting to this arrangement and asked them to move forward. They made an enormous meal of it, taking nearly half the lesson to transport stools, bags and text books, pretending to fall over one another and generally creating chaos out of what should have been a perfectly simple, orderly operation.

After that Mrs Young decided that if the class adopted any other unorthodox seating formations she would ignore them and simply get on with the lesson, but on the following day she arrived to find that the whole class had taken up their positions at the four front benches, from which close proximity they proceeded to goggle at her alarmingly for the full double period. It was true that she had often requested them to pay more attention, but the level of close-up, intensive scrutiny to which she was now being subjected was a bit too much.

Their next lesson together immediately followed the morning break and Mrs Young walked in to find that four benches had been mysteriously stacked on top of four more, leaving only two remaining useable benches at which all twenty five of her pupils were crammed together.

'What on earth has happened in here?' she asked.

Voices piped up from all around the benches:

'We just came in and found it like this miss.'

'We thought you'd done it.'

'Perhaps it was a typhoon?'

Mrs Young had struggled through the lesson as best she could, conscious that she had been in error in not locking the lab door as she should have done before leaving the room unattended. She dared not instruct them to lift the benches down for fear of someone getting injured in the process (clearly the caretaker would have to be summoned later to put the furniture back to rights) and how on earth had they managed to get those benches lifted up there in the first place? Every one of the little wretches must have been in on it.

Hardly surprising then that Mrs Young had come to dread fourth form biology. They were up to something all the time. She knew that they would not have dared behave the way they did if Mrs Venables or Miss Harkness had been taking the class. Well at least it was only a single period this morning. Only half an hour before she could drive away and find somewhere nice and quiet to park up and eat her sandwiches.

'Now then,' she said, facing the class with the thin smile which she still vainly hoped would encourage them to like her and be merciful. 'Let's start with a little revision of the topic from last lesson. Do you all remember the experiment with the potato?'

'Was that when we made chips?' enquired a voice from the back.

'No silly that was in D.S.,' a second voice responded.

'Now then, now then,' said Mrs Young. 'No shouting out. Hands up if you have something to say. We did an experiment last lesson with a potato. I'm sure you all remember...' she looked about desperately. 'Charlotte Young can you tell me why the potato went black?'

'No miss,' Charlotte responded cheerfully. She appeared to be cutting up a piece of paper. Mrs Young could not imagine why. It certainly had nothing at all to do with the lesson.

'Now somebody must have been paying attention.' She spotted Gail Foster's raised hand and hoped for the best. 'Yes Gail?'

'May I ask a question?'

'Of course.'

'Where are you going for your holidays this year?'

'Now really Gail, don't be silly. We are discussing osmosis not holidays.'

'I wasn't,' said Gail, just loud enough to be heard although Mrs Young pretended not to have done.

Another hand went up.

'Yes...er..'

'Jasmine,' Ronnie identified herself.

'Yes Jasmine.'

'Can I ask a question?'

'Is it relevant to osmosis?' asked Mrs Young suspiciously.

'Not exactly.'

'Then no, you can't.' She had a distinct feeling that the girl's name was not Jasmine. That if she checked her list, she would find that there wasn't a Jasmine. The name game was another torment they had invented for her. She had had the class for almost a year but she still had not got to grips with *all* their names. They kept on changing their names and shifting where they sat and she simply couldn't keep track of it.

Teaching was not what it had once been. If only Mr Young's mother would hurry up and die so that they could inherit Brackenfields. They would be absolutely made and she wouldn't need to worry about her pension. They could both just take early retirement and move down to Dorset as they had always planned. She thought wistfully of all those lovely botanical walks they would be able to take together... except that the wretched old woman was never going to die. She obviously intended to live forever just to spite everyone.

Chapter Fifty-Four

1985

As they drove out of the gates of Cliveden Nicky asked hesitantly: 'Would it be O.K. if I came home with you? I'm sure your mum is lovely, but I can't face the idea of total strangers at the moment.'

'Of course,' he said. 'You'll be all right at my place. There's no one there but me.'

She realised that she had no idea where his 'place' was. He drove the van steadily south, further and further away from the city. The vehicle was rather noisy and the seats were hard. The bumps and jolts provided an occasional sharp reminder of her bruises but she didn't care. After a few minutes she suddenly thought of something else. 'Why did you call me Mrs Cliveden?' she asked.

'Well I assumed you weren't Mrs Aston and I don't know your first name.'

Nicky was astounded. 'I'm sorry,' she said. 'I never realised. It's Nicola. People mostly call me Nicky… and my surname's Christie. That's my maiden name. I went back to it when I got divorced.'

After that they travelled in silence for perhaps ten minutes before she announced, 'I think I'm going to be sick.'

He screeched into a lay-by and she dismounted from the van but it was a false alarm.

'When did you last have something to eat?' he asked.

'Yesterday night.'

'No wonder you feel sick,' he said. From under the seat he produced a battered Adidas bag from which he extracted a flask and a plastic sandwich box with a warped lid held on with a large elastic band.

'I can't,' she protested. 'It's your lunch.'

'Won't need it,' he said. 'I'll be at home for lunch now. Come on. I'm not driving any further until you've had something to eat.'

She thought she wouldn't be able to manage food but she was wrong. They sat in the van with the windows wound down, watching the birds flitting about in the adjacent hedgerow while she consumed cheese and pickle sandwiches and drank sickly sweetened tea. There was an other worldliness about the whole experience. She began to wonder if she would shortly wake up in bed with Clive beside her and the T.V. buzzing where they had fallen asleep without switching it off.

But I won't ever wake up next to Clive again, she thought, because I've run away with the gardener… who up until about ten minutes ago didn't even know my name. The notion made her want to laugh hysterically. A fly droned into the cab then out again, as if on a mission to inspect the passing mad woman and her rescuer the gardener. Strange travelling companions temporarily stranded in the lay-by of life.

After she had finished this unorthodox late breakfast they set off again.

'Not too far now,' he said reassuringly. 'It's just the other side of Evesham.'

'You came a long way to do our garden,' said Nicky.

'Only since I moved out here,' he said. 'I had been living at my mum's in Yardley Wood. We'll be there soon. The nursery is in a really good location. It's close to the main road so once I get up and running there'll be plenty of passing trade. It's a bit of a mess just now…' He trailed off mid sentence. With every passing mile he felt more and more uncertain about bringing her there. He had never been inside Cliveden but he could imagine what it would be like. What on earth was she going to make of the cottage? He glanced across and saw that she appeared to be deep in thought. Regretting her decision to come with him, he guessed.

In fact she was thinking about what she had just said. '*Our* garden'. Because of course it was not her garden at all and never had been. It was Clive's. And now she was going to move on to somewhere else which didn't belong to her. Into the home of some other man. It was all very well letting Rob whisk her away, but didn't it just serve to underline how pathetic she was? How she could never manage to do anything for herself?

She had begun to feel ill again in spite of the recently consumed tea and sandwiches. The pain and fear and shame had left her exhausted. As if from the far end of a deep tunnel she realised that Rob had put on the indicator and was turning in between a pair of brick built pillars, each of which had a broken down top.

'This is it,' she heard him say in a rather worried voice.

It was a brick built cottage with a small, single storey, white washed extension at one side. They entered through a door in the extension which led directly into the kitchen, a room Nicky barely had time to register before Rob, like an anxious sheep dog, had ushered her into the other downstairs room which extended the full width of the main building. There was a fireplace facing the door which still had an old fashioned, brown and white tiled grate. The wall to their left had a window which looked out onto the tangle of neglected rose bushes which stood between the house and the road and in the wall to their right there was another window and a half glazed door from which you could step straight into the rear garden – an area which looked only marginally better tended than the small wilderness at the front. Beyond this Nicky could see several glasshouses which even from a distance were obviously in a poor state of repair. The living room itself appeared to have been furnished with cast offs from someone's attic, which had been saved en route to a jumble sale.

'It's a bit of a challenge,' Rob started to say, then stopped when he saw her face. 'You're knackered,' he said. 'Why not have a lie down? You can go upstairs if you like.' He indicated the steep wooden staircase in one corner of the room. 'Or maybe you'd just like to sit here for a bit.'

Nicky sank gratefully onto the sofa. It was old and battered but surprisingly comfortable.

'Put your feet up,' he encouraged her. 'I'll get us a bite

of lunch in a bit. You just have a rest. Don't worry about taking your shoes off. You're in shock at the moment. Try to relax and put everything out of your mind.'

She put her feet up as instructed. The sofa seemed to fold around her in a vaguely welcoming way and she rested her head on its broad, squashy arm while he went back into the kitchen. A few minutes later she sensed rather than saw him opening the window an inch. Good idea. Get rid of that slightly musty smell. A little while later she was vaguely aware of being covered with something: a quilt or a blanket. She half opened her eyes but someone said 'Shh,' in such a reassuring way that she dozed again.

When she finally woke up she could tell from the reflected yellowish-brown tint on the chimney breast and the way the birds were tuning up that she had been asleep for most of the day. Her neck was stiff and her legs felt as if they had been clamped in irons. She moved into a sitting position by means of a series of uneasy jerks, whimpering softly as she put weight on sore flesh, rubbing her calves and nervously twisting her neck from side to side. From somewhere in the distance she became aware of the faint sounds of hammering: three taps then a pause, over and over like a sort of bird call. She hesitated for a moment then stood up and tried the door which led out into the garden.

The fresh air met her like a soothing tonic. The only hint of another human presence was the hammering, which seemed to be coming from the direction of the greenhouses. On slightly uncertain feet she made her way through the small area of garden which was still cultivated and on into the neglected weedy realms beyond it, following the sounds which she knew must be made by Rob. Grass and nettles grew up between cracks in the concrete path. Bindweed had strangled everything in its path and then incestuously embraced itself. The noise of the hammer was louder here, almost like an appeal for help from someone who had become lost in the miniature jungle.

She found him at work in one of the greenhouses. He hadn't heard her approach so she stood watching for a minute or two as he meticulously worked his way along the section of shelving that he was repairing. Eventually she said nervously, 'Hello.'

He stopped work at once. 'Hello,' he said. 'I popped in a couple of times but you were fast asleep so I didn't disturb you. How are you feeling?'

'Not too bad,' she lied. 'Don't let me stop you.'

'I was going to stop anyway.' He hesitated a moment then said, 'Do you feel up to a little walk? Just to see around... before I get something to eat? Not that there's much to see yet.'

Nicky, whose mouth was as dry as a sawdust pit, feigned enthusiasm.

Rob's guided tour of the broken down greenhouses, weed strewn raised beds and the area of waste ground which he said he was planning to turn into a parking area, left her feeling even more depressed. He planned to do most of the renovations and improvements himself, he said, which seemed to her as ridiculous as someone announcing his intention to rebuild the Forth Bridge single handed. The best of the glasshouses, he assured her, was almost ready to be up and running and he would be starting off in a small way, selling some bedding plants which had been raised by a friend of his grandfather and when they came into season, some strawberries grown locally. He had also made arrangements with a chap who needed an outlet for his home made bird tables and an old school friend, Gareth, was due to come down at the weekend and rebuild the broken gateposts so that the place wouldn't look so run-down from the road. He intended to open for business in a modest way within the next six weeks.

Nicky did her best to nod and make encouraging noises, while trying not to register her true level of dismay at the shabby desolation all around them.

He's obviously completely mad, she thought sadly.

Chapter Fifty-Five

1972

With only two years to go until she was eligible to vote Becky was taking her democratic responsibilities seriously. She quite often listened to the news and read the Sunday papers. Once or twice she had even watched 'Panorama'. It was hurtful therefore when Stan dismissed her opinions on the Vietnam war by saying, 'What would you know about it at your age? '

They had also crossed swords about conscription. Stan was all for it. There should be no refuge for draft dodgers in Britain, he declared. Furthermore he thought that the re-introduction of national service was just what Britain needed. According to Stan it was the cure-all which would solve unemployment, strikes and inflation at a stroke, with the entirely pleasing side effect of forcing all these blasted hippies to get their hair cut.

'A few years in the services makes a man of you,' Stan said.

He was very proud of his time with the Desert Rats and

would have been driven to apoplexy had he known that his step-daughter and her friends' nickname for him was The Gerbil.

Becky knew that she couldn't win with Stan. On the one hand he disagreed with everything she said on principle, apparently not so much because he was at odds with her opinions as on the grounds that he did not think she was entitled to hold opinions at all. But keeping quiet was not the answer either. Silence was a fast track to accusations that she was sullen or else elicited tooth grinding queries about whether the cat had got her tongue.

He got on her nerves and she got on his, that was the top and bottom of it, she thought. When they quarrelled or the atmosphere became particularly tense, her mother invariably sided with Stan and told her off for being difficult. Neither of them want me here, Becky thought. They're just biding their time until I'm old enough to leave.

She felt much the same way herself. She tried to stay out of their sight as much as possible but there were some things she had to come downstairs for. Meals for example. Every evening her mother raised one leaf of the table for them sit around. Stan and her mother sat facing each other while Becky sat in the chair which faced the wall. She knew every inch of that piece of wall. She knew exactly how many ivy leaves were draped around each section of trellis which ran diagonally in an endless series of criss-crosses all over the walls (surely the most boring wallpaper pattern ever devised?) She knew just where there was a tiny wrinkle in the paper because the wall was slightly out of true. She knew every detail of the framed oval embroidery of a little girl wearing a poke bonnet and carrying a basket of flowers, which had apparently been a favourite with Muriel.

Having so many of Stan's first wife Muriel's things about would not have been so bad if Muriel had had any taste, Becky thought. The shops were full of trendy decorating ideas in oranges and browns, but Muriel's colour scheme was predominantly green and grey. The three piece suite had nylon stretch covers in battleship grey with a pattern of tiny black shapes dotted over it. Becky hated the stretch covers and in particular the way every little thing, shoe buckles, watch straps, everything… caught against the nylon and snagged it. Worse still the covers did not fit properly. Gaps at the bottom exposed the original dark red upholstery where the ties failed to meet. It looked so impoverished, covering the old suite because you couldn't afford a new one, though Stan didn't look at it like that. He said there were years of wear in it yet. As for Muriel herself, she still watched from her place above a bow fronted glass cabinet full of knick-knacks, looking well pleased, Becky thought, that no one had presumed to alter any of her arrangements.

One Sunday lunchtime when Stan was at the British Legion having his weekly pint, Becky took advantage of his absence to sit at the table and read the Sunday paper. With her mother in the kitchen getting on with the cooking, Muriel had only got Becky to stare at. The offending photograph was a black and white studio pose. A head and shoulders shot which had obviously been taken a long time ago, when Muriel had still been young. The mounting was very old fashioned: a plain sheet of glass secured to the backing by a quartet of rounded silver studs without an enclosing frame. It was obviously heavy because it was hung by a metal link chain.

Becky tried to ignore the picture but it kept on catching her eye and distracting her from the piece she was trying to read in the newspaper about the Baader-Meinhof gang. It wasn't right to resort to violence but every so often people had to strike a blow against tyranny… Her action followed her impulse so swiftly that she almost shocked herself. Reaching up as far as she could she managed to unhook the still smirking Muriel. She took a short cut through the French windows to avoid her mother in the kitchen and carried Muriel out to the shed at the bottom of the garden. A single blow with one of Stan's hammers was all it took.

Stan noticed the picture was missing as soon as he returned. 'Rita,' he called. 'What's happened to Muriel's picture?'

His wife came in from the kitchen, wiping her hands on her apron, looked at the lighter patch on the wallpaper and said she didn't know.

Becky looked up from her reading. 'I've taken it down,' she said, a touch more loudly than was necessary.

'What for?' asked Stan.

'Because I'm fed up with looking at it,' said Becky. 'I thought it was about time we all had something else to look at.'

Stan's face turned puce. 'You just get it put back up there,' he said. 'And let's be having no more of this.'

'I'm afraid that won't be possible,' said Becky, looking him straight in the eye. 'The glass is broken.'

'You've broken Muriel's picture?' He was beside himself. 'Where is it?'

She had never seen him so angry. Slightly scared now she said, 'It's in the shed.'

As Stan charged off down the garden path her mother exclaimed, 'Becky what have you done?'

'It's only an old photograph,' said Becky. 'Why should we have to keep on looking at it? We didn't know her and she's been dead five years.'

Stan returned almost immediately, holding the damaged picture out in front of him, balancing shards of broken glass on top of it.

'Look at this,' he said. 'Look at it. Damaged beyond repair. You did this on purpose. This is no accident. Look how the photograph's been damaged where something's gone into it.'

'Becky,' said her mother, twisting her fingers in her apron. 'What did you do?'

'I hit it with a hammer. And I'm glad it can't be mended. That way there's no chance we'll ever have to sit here looking at it again.'

'You unspeakable little witch,' Stan raged. 'How dare you speak to me and your mother like that? Have you no sense of gratitude? You wouldn't have a roof over your head if it wasn't for me. You've got it very comfortable here and don't you forget it. On the breadline you and your mother were, when I picked you out of the gutter. I must have been mad taking you on. You're barmy… stark staring barmy, taking a hammer to a photograph. That's mad that is. You'll end up in the loony bin you will my girl.'

'I'm sorry Stan,' her mother began.

'You don't have to apologise Mum, you didn't do anything,' Becky began, but Stan cut her off.

'Of course she has to apologise. She spends half her time apologising for you. For your rudeness and behaviour and ungratefulness. And now this…' he looked down at the shattered remnants in his hands. 'This is the worst thing yet.'

'Go up to your room and stay there,' said her mother. 'Why do you always have to rock the boat?'

Becky did as she was told, still wondering at herself for daring to smash the picture in the first place. She had experienced an almost frightening sense of power and pleasure in the actual moment of destruction. Perhaps as Stan suggested, she really was going mad.

She usually minded when Stan moaned at Mum about the things which she – Becky – had said and done but today she didn't feel sorry for Mum at all. It was her own fault for marrying Stan. I didn't choose to live with him, Becky thought. Mum must have known that he didn't like me, but that didn't stop her marrying him. She didn't bother to think about what it would do to my life at all.

When she got home from school the following afternoon she discovered that Stan had taken his revenge. Every poster had been taken down from her bedroom wall, ripped into tiny pieces and piled neatly on the middle of her bed, together with the new blouse she had saved up for weeks to buy from Chelsea Girl. The sleeves had been unevenly removed with pinking shears and the front and back slashed through. It had never been worn.

For a moment she wanted to go downstairs and smash everything in sight: the glass fronted cabinet, the china dogs on the mantle shelf, everything. Scalding hot anger coursed through her until she felt out of control and a shriek began to rise in her throat. She put a hand over her mouth to pen it in. If she went downstairs now she might do something terrible. She might even get the hammer and kill Stan, she felt so angry. Then she would be put in prison. Her whole life would be ruined. He and Muriel would be able to laugh at her from beyond the grave. She wouldn't give him the satisfaction. She wouldn't say anything about what he had done at all. He was beneath her contempt.

She gathered up all the pieces of paper and fabric and packed them into a cardboard box which she put inside the bottom of her wardrobe. She would not give him the satisfaction of seeing her carry the wreckage out to the dustbin.

When they sat down to tea she said nothing and focussed straight ahead as if intently studying the embroidered girl in the poke bonnet. Eventually Stan could not resist saying, 'You saw what I'd done to your things?'

'Yes,' said Becky. She turned glittering eyes upon him but said no more than that. Out of the corner of her eye she was aware of her mother concentrating on her food, chewing and chewing at a piece of lamb chop until it must have all but disintegrated in her mouth.

'That's taught you a lesson, then,' said Stan with some satisfaction.

Becky said nothing.

'While you're under my roof you'll learn to behave yourself.'

When Becky still remained silent he continued, 'Not got so much to say for yourself now, have you?'

'No,' said Becky.

This did not seem to satisfy him. 'Haven't you got anything to say?'

'Nothing at all,' said Becky. 'Excuse me I've had enough.' She pushed her plate away and retreated upstairs. I have to get away from him and out of this house, she thought, otherwise I really shall go mad.

Chapter Fifty-Six

1972

It seemed symbolic that 'School's Out' which had been the joyous anthem of the summer holidays, was knocked off the number one spot a couple of days before they returned to school. Their new form teacher was Mrs Badham. She gave them a pep talk on their first morning back, reinforcing the message that it would be an important year for them all. Becky, in spite of her missing school tie and forbidden eye make-up, listened attentively and reminded herself that she was resolved to try harder. Staying focussed on her work was easier these days. She was seldom distracted by Mum or the telly because if Stan was in the living room she stayed out of it and there was now a predictable, if stifling, domestic routine. The nights of cheap sherry and costly weeping were a thing of the past. Life had gained stability... at a price.

For Paula Mrs Badham's lecture was the second in as many days. Her own parents had spent most of the previous evening setting out their expectations and laying down the law. There was to be no more 'messing about' backstage with school productions. 'West Side Story' and then 'The Pied Piper of Hamelin' had been too much of a distraction from her studies. Distractions which her marks made it perfectly evident she could not afford to indulge in. There also needed to be a change of Attitude. Paula instinctively sensed the capital A. If her Attitude did not change for the better, her mother said in her we-know-what's-best-whatever-you-may-think voice, then serious consideration would have to be given to whether she was being Influenced (another capital Paula was sure) by the Wrong People.

Mr and Mrs Morrison had run into Paula's friends' parents on a number of occasions during the previous four years and concluded that they were not really their sort of people. The Christies while well meaning were obviously not very bright. Mrs Addison (or whatever she called herself now) had a very common accent and frankly looked like a tart, while on the one occasion when Mrs Morrison had caught sight of Mr Embury she had immediately categorised him as 'rough'.

'I'm not a snob,' she had confided in her husband – who might have been expected to know this one way or the other after twenty years – 'But I do wonder whether girls like that don't find it difficult to fit in at Evie's. From what little Paula tells us they seem to delight in bucking authority. That sort of attitude will inevitably rub off on Paula and it cannot possibly do her any good.'

In the earlier years Mrs Morrison had been prepared to accept Paula's funny little friends, because she thought that Paula might prove to be a good influence on them. After all one didn't want to be elitist. But now that Paula would clearly never get an A in geography and showed no inclination whatsoever to compete for the Senior Tennis Shield, Mrs Morrison had begun to question her egalitarian principles.

Nicky was not really listening to Mrs Badham. She was looking at the desk which would be hers for the rest of the year and wondering who had carved and inked the intricate pattern of swirling shapes which covered more than a third of its lid. It must have been the work of months, occupying someone lesson by lesson as they revisited the desk at the same regular point in the weekly timetable for a full school year. Or maybe it had been the work of more than one person? Two or three separate artists working together yet never meeting, their composition growing week by week while its progress was observed by everyone who sat there, including the owner of the desk who would extract and replace her books each day, never knowing who was responsible for the embellishments which steadily appeared.

These anonymous artworks were to be found on rear desks all over the school and it seemed to Nicky that they emphasised the insignificance of each individual's passage. Someone might try to make her mark but in the end they were as nameless as the rest, just one more blue clad component who was part of a much bigger machine which moved relentlessly onwards, taking in the raw and shiny girls in their first year, processing them through desk after desk, form room after form room, until they were spat out at the other end. They might be changed but the school would not be. The machine would trundle on its way and the individuals would be forgotten.

Nicky was reflecting upon all this not least because

she knew that the time when she would be spat out of the school machine was drawing nearer. She hadn't really thought about it until a few days ago when her mother had unexpectedly said something about her school days coming to an end. It was taken for granted that she would leave at the end of fifth year and although it made her feel a bit sad, she hardly saw it as some kind of tragic injustice. She never came better than half way up the class in anything. It was not as if she was really clever like Michael.

Jo wasn't listening to Mrs Badham either. She was trying to, because she did not want to think about last night when Dad had been on the pop again and had hit her mother after a ferocious row. It ripped her up inside when she heard them going at it, though she tried not to care. She had understood since primary school that not everyone's family life was played out on a battlefield and long since ceased to wonder at the unfairness of the way these things were ordered. If it happened to be your lot in life, then the best thing was to block it out if you could. To a lesser extent that was also how she made sense of Eleanor Vaux: an inward acknowledgment that she did not really belong there and never would, coupled with the consolation that it would not be forever.

For their first lesson of the new school year Paula headed off to wrestle with Latin in Room 11. It was a very small class. Hardly anyone had chosen Latin but at least, Paula thought, the others had probably chosen it because they wanted to do it whereas she'd had to do it because her parents had told her to.

In geography Nicky was somewhat disheartened to learn that in Mr Tresham's opinion, the syllabus set by the

Joint Matriculation Board was so huge that they would not be able to cover it all in the time remaining. They had to hope, he said, that the exam paper would include a sufficient number of questions on the topics they *had* covered to enable them to answer enough questions to attain a good mark. Nicky was incredulous that the geography paper was apparently a sort of lottery, in which if they happened to be unlucky they might not be able to answer enough questions to get a pass, however hard they had worked in the preceding two years.

In R.E. Becky and Jo buckled down take notes about miracles.

That's what I could do with, Joanne thought. A miracle to transform me into a different person in a different place.

Chapter Fifty-Seven

1985

Becky glanced down her list of morning appointments agan. She was expecting a Mrs Addison at 10.00 but the exact nature of Mrs Addison's business was unknown. Sadie, who had made the appointment, said that this Mrs Addison had been most insistent that it was Becky she wanted to see but had flatly refused to divulge the nature of her business, insisting that it was a private matter. Sadie had pointed out to Mrs Addison that Miss Addison (as Becky continued to be known professionally, despite being Mrs McMahon these three months past) only took criminal work, but Mrs Addison had still persisted that it was Miss Addison she wanted to see.

Becky had an instinctive suspicion that it was going to be a waste of time. Mrs Addison might easily have picked her out because of her name, having convinced herself that because a solicitor shared her surname, she must be just the person to deal with a bit of conveyancing or a disputed will. People were like that sometimes: blindly, determinedly irrational when it came to making important choices.

Opening the drawer of her desk, Becky spotted the Mothercare catalogue peeking out from under some other papers. She did not much care for the black pinafore dress on page 4, with its horrible box pleats which made it looked like a gymslip designed with Bessie Bunter in mind, but it was the only thing she had seen so far which would be remotely suitable for court wear, once she could not get into her dark suits. She wondered what the hell was wrong with people who designed maternity clothes. Did none of them stop to consider that an enormous red and black check table cloth complete with sailor collar just wasn't the sort of thing a professional woman would want to wear in the run up to maternity leave – or for that matter at any other time? Nor did a smock in cutie-pie pink which had *IT STARTED WITH A KISS* emblazoned across the bosom seem quite the thing in which to argue a bail application.

These ruminations were interrupted by the internal phone. It was Sadie to let her know that Mrs Addison had arrived and was waiting in reception.

'You can bring her straight up,' Becky said.

When Becky stood up to greet her prospective client she noticed the way Mrs Addison appeared to hesitate before taking the proffered hand. There was something slightly unnerving in both this and the swift look of appraisal which the woman gave her. A great many new clients quite blatantly gave you the once over, but there was something about the way Mrs Addison looked her up and down which made Becky feel oddly as if Mrs Addison had been expecting something or someone quite different.

Having briefly grasped hands and invited Mrs Addison to occupy the chair on the opposite side of the desk, Becky resumed her seat and said, 'Now Mrs Addison how can I help you?'

'I'd better come straight to the point,' Mrs Addison said and then proceeded not to. Embarking instead on a long rambling account of how when she had originally made the appointment with one of the girls in reception, she had thought it better not to tell the girl to whom she had spoken just what her business concerned. Becky noticed the nervous way Mrs Addison fiddled with the strap of her handbag while she was talking. She would be in her sixties, Becky guessed, and was dressed in a smart brown coat and hat and gripping a handbag in a lighter shade of brown. It was an outfit which made no concession to the warm summer weather beyond the window. Becky also noted the way she had come alone, not resorting as did a lot of older female clients, to the support of an adult child or a husband or even friend. Perhaps it was a criminal matter after all and one which she wanted to keep from reaching the ears of even her nearest and dearest. Becky wondered if she had been charged with shop lifting or writing poison pen letters.

'So what exactly is it that you would like me to help you with?' she asked patiently, after Mrs Addison had covered all possible ground relating to the making and attending of the appointment, including her anxiety that the tardiness of the 33 bus had almost caused her to be late.

Mrs Addison swallowed hard. 'I knew that you wouldn't want to see me,' she said. 'That's why I wouldn't tell the girl what it was about. Only I'd made up my mind you see. I was determined to do it. For him. He always thought so much about you. He was so proud of you...' Her voice cracked. 'I hoped you might see the announcement in the 'Mail'. Although I guessed you wouldn't come.' She shot Becky a sudden bitter look. 'Anyway I still wanted you to have something of his... because that's what he would have wanted.'

She unfastened the central clip of her handbag and produced a small, slightly battered black box from inside. She handed it across the desk to Becky who opened it in a state of some bewilderment.

'Cufflinks,' she said, her eyes going from the contents of the box to the woman opposite and back again.

'He never wore them,' Mrs Addison said. 'They were his father's. I don't suppose *he* wore them either but they're a family heirloom and you're his only family.'

Becky was conscious that the skin on her arms had turned to gooseflesh in spite of the warmth of the office. She stared down at the cufflinks, a pair of polished tortoiseshell discs set in some kind of metal surround.

'My father's,' she murmured. It was difficult to get the words out because her lips seemed to have suddenly gone dry. 'They're my father's and you're his wife. That's what you're trying to tell me, isn't it?'

'I'm Stella,' the woman said. 'Your father's widow.' When Becky still said nothing she continued, 'I'll go now shall I?' She made as if to stand up.

'No, no.' Becky found her voice again. 'Please don't go. I'll get Sadie to bring us up some coffee. Or perhaps you'd rather have tea? You say my father's dead?'

'Five weeks ago.'

'I'm sorry...' Becky was at a complete loss. For more

than twenty five years her father had been a non-person, a distant shadow of whom it was tacitly understood that one did not speak. Now she was being unexpectedly called upon to speak of him with a woman she had never met before. Feelings she did not normally allow herself to acknowledge were at risk of being laid bare before a total stranger, the situation made worse by the rawness of a bereavement from which this stranger had recently suffered. 'That must be very hard for you,' she said at last. 'Had you been married long?'

Stella regarded her with something bordering contempt. 'We'd been married for twenty two years,' she said. 'You obviously didn't take much notice of his letters.'

'I never got any letters,' said Becky. 'My mother never talked about my father and I never heard from him directly at all.'

Now it was Stella's turn to look uncomprehending. 'But he wrote every few months,' she said. 'And he sent you a birthday card with money in it every year. He used to spend ages picking out the cards. I know they went to the right address,' she added darkly. 'Because your mother would have soon been on to him if her money hadn't arrived.'

Becky stretched out her hand in an unconscious, involuntary gesture of supplication. 'You have to believe me,' she said. 'I didn't even know he used to send Mum money. I never got any of the letters or cards. I never saw the money he sent for my birthday. My mother must have intercepted it all. I don't know how she managed it, but she did.'

Her disbelief was all the greater for the fleeting thought that this long term subterfuge must have called for a level of sustained organisation of which she could scarcely conceive her mother capable.

'It hurt him,' said Stella. 'The way you never replied.'

'I never knew where he was. He just disappeared completely from my life, when I was about three or four years old and I never saw him again.'

'He saw you,' said Stella quietly. 'He saw your name in a newspaper report or something. That's how he found out what you were doing. He came to watch you in court a couple of times. He just sat and watched from up in the public gallery. That proud of you, he was, when he came home. "That's my girl," he said. "She's really made something of herself."'

Becky found that tears were running unbidden down her cheeks. She fumbled to extract a tissue from the box on her desk. 'Why didn't he come and make himself known to me? I would have been so glad to see him. You have no idea…'

'He didn't want to make a scene. He wouldn't have upset you for the world. He thought you didn't want him. All those letters never answered. Not so much as a thank you for your birthday money. Can you wonder that he wasn't going to walk up and introduce himself out of the blue?'

Becky stared down at the cufflinks. 'I can't believe it,' she said. 'I just can't believe it.'

*

When she got home, Becky she could think and talk of nothing but her unexpected visitor and the secret she had revealed. 'I can't forgive my mother's part in this. I'll have to confront her with it. She had no right.'

They were lying on the couch together. Sean's head so close to hers that his auburn hair mingled with wisps of her contrasting deep brown. He squeezed her shoulder in the hope of imparting some consolation.

'She had no right,' Becky repeated. 'All those years when she allowed me to think that he'd just abandoned us… when I thought he didn't care what happened to us… and all the time he was writing me letters, sending money, trying to stay in touch. He wrote regularly right up until I was eighteen, Stella said. After that he gave up on the letters but by then he'd been writing them for more than twelve years… and all the time thinking I didn't want him in my life.' Her voice quivered. Sean gave her upper arm another squeeze, this time a little harder. 'I could have had a relationship with him. He could have been part of my life but that woman denied me it. I hate her for this. Of all the cruddy things she's done to me this is the worst of all.'

With his free hand Sean sought and found hers. 'We can't undo the past,' he said. 'We have to keep moving forward. That's pretty much our motto Becks. I know how you feel, but you mustn't let the bitterness eat you up.'

'You don't know,' she said, not angrily but with a touch of impatience. 'When your father was taken from you, at least you had an anonymous lorry driver to blame. It's different for me. I could have had a father but my mother excluded him from my life, cynically and deliberately. I feel so angry that I want to tell her just what I think and then never see her again. I keep on thinking about him watching me in court – wanting to be proud of me – which is more than she ever did. And all the time him believing that I'd rejected him. And now it's too late to do anything about it. He's gone to his grave believing it.' She stood up abruptly, crossing the room to straighten a picture which did not need it.

'Sometimes stuff happens. Nothing can change what's gone already,' Sean said. 'There's this too… your father made his choices, based on what he wanted. He left your mother to be with Stella. Fair enough he wanted to keep in touch with you, so he wrote every few months and sent money on your birthday, but surely what you wanted was a real live dad. You wanted someone who was living under the same roof as you, not a pen pal…'

'But it mightn't have been like that…' Becky began.

Sean had listened patiently while she vented her feelings but he decided it was time to put forward a counter point of view.

'And then again it just might,' he said. 'You might not even have liked him. His being a blood relation isn't an automatic guarantee, you know. It's very easy to build up an idealised picture of someone. My mum likes to think that my dad would have stayed with her and that your mum was just a passing fling. But I'd bet you anything that your mum thinks just the opposite. Neither of them think of him as the guy who was cheating on one woman or maybe even on both women, depending on your point of view. Meanwhile I have to live with the knowledge that he never bought me and my brother a record player, although he bought one for some little girl whose mother he was sleeping with. I could be angry about that and wonder whether he loved you more than he loved us, but what difference would it make? Much better take the good things and carry them forward. Keep going forward and don't look back.'

'It's hard to forget that she did so many awful things to me,' said Becky. 'I can't help but look back and remember the way I was subjected to a string of her fancy men and then a step-father I hated, when all the time my real father was wanting to be a part of my life and she wouldn't let him.'

'You might take some consolation from the fact that he knew what you'd done and that he was proud of you. He knew you were a fighter. You're a tough, successful, independent woman. Has it ever occurred to you that maybe you wouldn't have been so driven, if you'd had the cosy family life you always dreamed of when you were a kid? Maybe life with your mum – and without your dad – was good training?'

Becky could never resist his smile. It acted as a damper on her smouldering anger. 'Kids from dysfunctional homes do better? Now there's an interesting notion for the sociologists to get their teeth into.' She rejoined him on the sofa, gratefully leaning against him while he retrieved her hand.

'Nothing like a ground breaking theory to grab a few headlines,' he said. 'That one would certainly upset the Moral Majority and disconcert all those po-faced, middle class couples who are staying together for the sake of the children.'

'She was still wrong to do it,' Becky persisted. 'You know, sometimes when I'm with her, I just feel so upset and angry that I wish she was out of my life completely and I never had to see her again. Especially when she's being whiney and wallowing in self pity… even though I know it's wicked to think like that about your own mother. Whether or not I confront her with this, I know about it now and that will only make those feelings worse. Nothing gave her the right to stop me from seeing my father.'

'Becks my love, if you don't mind me saying so you are uncharacteristically guilty of missing the point.'

'Which is?'

'Your mother didn't rationalise it in those terms at all. She wasn't stopping you from seeing him. She was stopping him from seeing you. It was the only weapon she had at her disposal. Something to punish him for abandoning her for another woman. It was her one asset and she used it. She didn't stop to think that the person who would suffer most probably wouldn't be him at all – it would be you.'

'That would be absolutely typical. Not to think about me at all.'

'She would have seen the issue wholly in terms of her versus him.'

'Selfish cow.'

'Maybe so. But not such a difficult mistake to make. Before you decide to shut her out of your life for good – purely as a punishment, because it won't alter anything that's gone before – you have to think of every single person who'll be affected.' The hand which had been holding hers gently disengaged itself and came to rest as if by chance on the rounded part of her which was already straining the fabric of her skirt.

'You mean our baby.'

'Both grandfathers already dead. Are you going to take one of the grandmothers out of the equation too?'

'Some grandmother,' Becky snorted.

'You mother probably didn't set much store by your father's qualities for parenthood either, but you still resent her for robbing you of the opportunity to make up your own mind.'

'Damn it!' she exclaimed, half laughing half crying. 'Why are you always so darned clever?'

'Oh, I don't know,' he said, pretending to gaze around for inspiration. 'Maybe it's because my dad never bought me a record player or something. C'mon Becks. Forward, always forward and no looking back.'

Chapter Fifty-Eight

1972

Paula had come to the conclusion that the best way to deal with her parents was by adopting a policy of subterfuge. Subterfuge sounded so much better than lying. Lying was an ugly word, lacking in any kind of sophistication. Telling small children that presents were brought by Father Christmas was not true but no one ever called it lying. Besides which she considered that subterfuge was entirely justified where her parents were concerned, because it seemed to be the only recourse in the face of their continually unreasonable demands.

Paula's failure to mention the existence of the school production of 'The Mikado' had ensured that her parents were unaware of this potential distraction from her studies. In this particular case she had assuaged her conscience with the thought that she had not actually told any lies at all… she had merely omitted to tell the whole truth. Mrs Heslop and Mr Sinton seemed to have forgotten about the old embargo on involving 'O' and 'A' level year pupils in school productions. Helen Staveley was singing Yum Yum and Mrs Heslop looked to her trusty team of regulars to keep things right backstage. With initial rehearsals taking place at lunch times, Paula's scheme to keep her parents in the dark about the whole thing had not faced any serious handicaps so far.

Colleen Bell's party presented a very different sort of challenge. Paula knew without even asking that she wouldn't be given permission to attend. Her parents always made a big song and dance about her going anywhere and she knew that if she mentioned the word 'party' they would be on the phone to Colleen's parents like a shot, asking all sorts of ridiculous questions. Once they found out that Colleen's parents were going to be out, there was absolutely no way they would let her go, so the only answer was to pretend to be going somewhere she *was* allowed to go. Here she was able to reconcile her conscience to some degree by saying that she was going to Nicky's house and only neglecting to point out that from Nicky's they would all be going on to Colleen's party.

The invitation had come as a pleasant surprise because Colleen was not a particular friend of theirs, but it wasn't all that flattering once they realised that she had asked half the class, only leaving out scary people like Gail Foster's crowd and the truly stuffy ones like Alex and Norma, who were too stuck up to go to parties anyway.

Colleen had a twin brother called Gary who went to a boys' grammar technical school. ('Imagine,' said Nicky. 'We've been at school with her for four whole years and we never knew she had a twin.') It was their joint sixteenth birthday party and their parents were laying on food and drink and then leaving their offspring to enjoy themselves. Everyone in VB was very impressed that Colleen's parents were so enlightened.

Mrs Christie was an enlightened parent too, Paula thought. She knew they were getting ready for a party, but she didn't fuss or ask a lot of tedious questions or pump Nicky for information or criticise the length of people's skirts.

It had taken them a long time to get ready but fortunately Colleen Bell didn't live very far from Nicky: just a short walk through almost deserted streets, damp under a heavy November sky. They stopped en route to buy an alcoholic offering because Colleen had told everyone that it was 'bring a bottle'. When Becky queried whether one bottle between them was enough they pooled their remaining cash under the patient gaze of the woman behind the counter and increased their purchase from one large bottle of Woodpecker cider to two.

The moment they turned the corner of Colleen's road it was obvious which house was home to the Bell Twins. Lights were burning brightly behind every curtained window and as they got nearer they could hear a dull throbbing beat emanating from inside the house.

Two boys were approaching from the opposite direction, wearing Crombie overcoats and Oxford Bags which flapped around their shoes like seal flippers gone mad. It was a close run thing but the boys reached the Bells' gate first. The four girls followed them up the path to the front door, where they were admitted by a blonde girl they didn't recognise.

The hall was so crammed with bodies that Becky, who

was last in, had to press herself flat against the wall so that the blonde girl could get the front door shut. There were teenagers standing all the way down the hall and teenagers sitting on the stairs. The noise was indescribable, with everyone shouting to be heard above what sounded like two competing record players.

'Booze in the kitchen, coats upstairs,' yelled the door keeper, before taking a long drag on a cigarette and immediately exhaling smoke all over everyone in the vicinity.

'I'll take the coats up,' Becky offered, wriggling out of hers with some difficulty due to the confined space and then holding out her hand to relieve the others of theirs.

As she ascended the staircase, clambering over complete strangers, Becky realised that they would all be able to see up the very short skirt of her purple pinafore dress. She eventually made it to the first floor with her dignity in tatters. All the upstairs doors were shut. The bathroom door had an oblong china plaque screwed to it, bearing the word *Bathroom* surrounded by a wreath of puce roses. On an adjacent door a similar plaque proclaimed it to be *The Smallest Room* the words this time surrounded by roses in pale tangerine. Annette Maudesley and Naomi Wiseman were standing on the landing.

'Come on, Penny,' Annette shouted while banging on the toilet door. 'I'm getting desperate.'

'Where should I put these coats?' asked Becky.

'Well not in there,' said Naomi, indicating one of the doors which led to a room at the front of the house. 'Because Charlie Young's just gone in there to have it off with some lad from St Luke's. I should use Colleen's bedroom.' She indicated the door to their right.

'*Hurry up*, Penny,' yelled Annette, banging on the door again.

Becky opened the door which Naomi had indicated. Heaped on the bed were afghans and Crombies, plum coloured maxi coats and fur hooded parkas, some of which were spilling onto the floor. Becky decided to initiate a new pile on the floor, choosing a spot just inside the door which she thought would have the advantage of enabling them to locate their coats again relatively easily.

Out on the landing Annette was now on all fours, apparently holding a conversation with Penny under the door. 'Well I know he's a bastard,' she said. 'But if you stop crying and come out of there you can go downstairs and give him a slap – and her as well.'

Becky exchanged a nervous smile with Naomi while privately feeling that she was somewhat out of her depth.

'Hello darling,' said an older looking boy, grabbing one of her thighs as she re-negotiated the stairs. Pulling herself free so violently that she nearly tumbled down the remainder of the flight, she saw that the blonde girl was admitting yet another group of youths. Paula, Nicky and Jo were nowhere to be seen. She scrambled down the remaining stairs as best she could, mumbling apologies to the people she actually trod on, then threaded her way between the bodies in the hall until she found her friends standing just inside the door into the front room.

The furniture had all been pushed back against the walls where it had been monopolised by necking couples. A group of eight or nine lads with shoulder length hair were sitting on the floor, passing a Party Seven between them and drinking out of holes which someone had punched in the top. A good deal of beer was finding its way onto the mustard coloured carpet. In one corner of the room a record player was being solemnly attended by a youth dressed entirely in black apart from some love beads around his neck and an embroidered head band. He had his eyes closed and was nodding gravely as though in deep spiritual communion with the music. The track was unfamiliar to Becky and was in any case rendered little more than a discordant noise by the interference from a rival record player in the next room which was belting out Slade with the bass turned up to max. The scent of joss sticks weaved its way stealthily between clouds of tobacco and Brut aftershave.

'Where's Colleen?' asked Becky.

Jo, who was nearest, cupped a questioning hand to her ear.

'Where's Colleen?' Becky repeated more loudly.

'She's in the next room having a row with her brother,' said Joanne, speaking directly into Becky's ear.

They stood in a line against the wall wondering what to do next. There was no question of dancing with space at such a premium, while the prospect of conversation was equally limited. Then Paula saw something which made her utter a little yelp of amazement.

'It's Ralph,' she exclaimed. 'Ralph from my cousin's wedding.' She pointed just in time for them to see the youth in question before he disappeared from sight.

'He hasn't seen you,' shouted Nicky. 'He's gone straight into the back room. You'll have to go after him.'

Paula hesitated.

'Go on,' Jo encouraged her. 'It's no use us all trying to get through. Much easier for one.'

Paula nodded. After going on and on about Ralph to the others it was like a dare that she could not refuse to take. With a fixed smile she began to work her way through the crowd. She oughtn't to be scared after all. It was fate. Her first ever proper party and he was there. It was so unbelievably romantic... as good as anything she could have written in a story.

Tonight, she thought, edging her way past someone she now recognised as Kay Fenton, who was engulfed in the embrace of a huge youth in a combat style tee shirt, tonight she would be kissed, properly kissed, by the gorgeous handsome Ralph. She would be kissed at a party in the home of a mutual friend, which was a location far superior for such a momentous event than alongside the entrance to the loos in a primary school.

She struggled as far as the doorway of the back room from which vantage point she attempted to spot Ralph. There were an awful lot of people crammed inside and it was even noisier than the room she had just come from, not least because Colleen was shouting at someone who Paula assumed must be her twin brother. Colleen looked to be on the verge of tears and as her voice rose Paula thought she caught the words '...out of control.'

Just then she turned and spotted Ralph in the kitchen where he was part of a small group who were apparently engaged in searching the kitchen cupboards.

'I've found some cups and mugs,' she heard someone say. 'If there's no more glasses I suppose they'll do.'

Paula recognised their two bottles of Woodpecker still standing unopened on the kitchen table. In the face of the glasses shortage Jo and Nick had left the bottles there, unclear about the protocol for obtaining a drink. Paula noticed that a can of beer had fallen on its side and was steadily gulping its contents onto the red formica table where it formed a brown bubbling pool, which in turn became a waterfall trickling steadily onto the floor. Without thinking she stepped across and stood the can upright, noticing as she did that someone had stubbed a cigarette out directly onto the table.

In the meantime Ralph and his three friends were pouring generous slugs of Smirnoff into willow pattern tea cups.

'Hello,' said Paula, as calmly as she could. 'Remember me?'

Ralph – who had come on from the pub – focussed on the thin, blonde girl and tried to remember when and if he had ever seen her before.

'Who's the chick?' enquired one of his companions (who having had the misfortune of being saddled with the name Fred had to talk in an extra cool way to make up for it).

'Dunno,' said Ralph, gesturing none too politely in Paula's direction with his tea cup. 'What's your name, babe?'

Paula, smouldering with embarrassment, felt that she had little alternative but to plough on. 'I'm Paula,' she said. 'We met at a wedding about a year ago.'

'Oh yeah. *That* freak show.' Ralph laughed heartily enough to ensure that his friends would get the point that he only attended uncool events such as relatives' weddings under sufferance.

The music seemed to be making the floor pulsate. Paula wished it would rupture the chequerboard tiles and create a big enough hole to swallow her up. He evidently remembered both the wedding and her. The dismissive words 'freak show' echoed around her head. Completely crushed she said, 'I just thought I'd say hello.'

She turned too quickly and narrowly avoided a collision in the doorway with someone who was trying to get past the enormous guy who was up to his armpits in Kay Fenton's tee shirt.

Waking up to the possibilities of a ready made introduction with a not bad looking girl, Ralph was about to call out after her when he was distracted by a shout that someone had started a fight out in the back garden.

Biting back tears, Paula returned to the others who were still standing exactly where she had left them. 'He didn't remember me,' she said in answer to Jo's enquiry, then watched miserably as Jo relayed this on to the others. It's a horrible party, Paula thought. The most horrible party ever.

Above all the other noise there now seemed to be a lot of shouting in the hall. The girl who had been letting people in abruptly marched into the front room and yanked the needle from the record that was playing, initiating cries of protest from the boy in black.

'Everybody get out,' she shouted above all the other noise. 'The police are coming. Fuzz. Pigs. One of the neighbours has rung them and they're on their way.'

The boy in black had taken his record from the turntable and was tilting it against the light. 'You've scratched my Dr John album,' he yelled indignantly.

Discovering that their beer tin was empty the group on the floor had begun to toss it from one to another, like a rugby ball.

Although not many people seemed to be taking the threat of the police seriously, Paula needed no second prompt. 'Come on,' she said. 'Where are our coats?'

'I'll get them.' Becky had already started to struggle through the mélee in the hall.

'I'm going to get our cider,' said Joanne. 'We're not leaving that. We haven't had a drink or got anywhere near the food.'

'Where is the food?' enquired Nicky.

'My point exactly,' Joanne shouted over her shoulder as she pushed past Kay Fenton and the youth she was still entangled with.

Paula and Nicky threaded their way along the hall until they reached the front doorstep where they stood waiting for the others. One or two other people had decided discretion was the better part and were drifting away. In the meantime two boys with hair cut short enough to have won Stan's instant approval were coming up the path against the current of departing revellers.

'Don't say the party's over already?' One of them addressed Nicky.

'Afraid so. One of the neighbours has called the police.'

'Sod it,' said the other youth. 'I told you we should have got here earlier.' He turned to Nicky, who was about two inches taller than he was. 'The night is still young. What are you ladies going to do for the rest of the evening?'

'Nothing which requires your assistance thanks,' said Nicky, turning away at just the right moment to see Jo emerging empty handed.

'Some blighter's nicked our cider,' said Jo. 'Bloody cheek.'

'Forget it,' the other newcomer said to his friend. 'They're a three.'

'A four actually,' said Nicky irritably. 'So just buzz off.'

'I wish Becka would hurry up,' said Paula, who was fidgeting from one foot to the other. 'We must get away before the police come.'

'Colleen's crying in the kitchen,' Jo told them. 'She says everyone is just going off and leaving everything in a mess and she wants people to stay behind and help clear up.'

Now that the short-haired boys had been repelled Nicky was back to her usual, generous self. 'Do you think we should stay?'

'We can't,' said Paula desperately. 'If the police come and my parents get to hear about it I'm dead. I'm not supposed to be here at all, remember?'

At that moment Becky finally appeared, clutching an armful of coats. She too was on the premises without parental knowledge. 'Anyway,' she said, when they put the point to her, 'It's not as if we made any of the mess.'

This seemed to be an eminently reasonable excuse for not sticking around. Anticipating the imminent arrival of a squad of panda cars and black marias, Paula insisted that they run most of the way back to Nicky's. Fortunately the art of running in platform heel shoes was one which they had all long since mastered.

Chapter Fifty-Nine

1985

Nicky found redemption through sheer hard work. It cleansed, purified and ultimately empowered her. There was no alarm clock in the front bedroom of the cottage where Rob had directed her to sleep, but she usually managed to wake early enough to hear Rob descending the stairs shortly after 6.00 each morning. By then her room was already light because the unlined cotton curtains were wholly inadequate to the task of keeping out the sunshine. It was a sparsely furnished room. The double bed – though new and comfortable – did not enjoy the luxury of a head or footboard and the wardrobe, which was missing its door handle and had to be wedged shut with a square of corrugated cardboard, only boasted half a dozen hangers, so most of Nicky's clothes remained in the bin liners in which they had travelled, which didn't really matter because she kept recycling the same sets of faded jeans and old tee shirts through the wash.

On her first full morning she had tentatively offered to

deal with the housework and after making a token protest Rob had been grateful to accept. His priority since moving in had been the business side of the premises which meant that apart from routine washing up and laundry nothing much had been done inside the house at all. Nicky threw herself into the task, leaving only the second bedroom where he slept untouched, hesitating to intrude upon to his privacy. By the third day she had moved on to helping him outside.

'You don't have to slave like this,' Rob said rather anxiously, on encountering Nicky staggering behind a barrow load of wilting weeds and other rubbish.

When she insisted that she didn't mind he'd initially looked at her doubtfully, but passing her later that same afternoon and noticing the determined glint in her eye as she hacked at a recalcitrant thistle, he decided to leave her alone. It quickly became clear that dragging out and burning the weeds in readiness for Rob to dig over and replenish the beds gave her a sense of purpose and achievement.

Nicky returned to the house ahead of him each evening, dishevelled and dirty, needing to scrub her hands thoroughly before preparing their meal on a gas stove older than herself. He would work on until she called him in to eat. She had never known anyone like him: so driven, so determined to meet his own challenges. Nothing seemed to defeat him. Each night she fell into bed and slept in a way she had not done for months, perhaps even for years, maybe not since she was a child. She kept herself so busy that there was no time to worry about the future.

During her first weekend at the cottage, Rob's friend Gareth turned up and rebuilt the brick pillars at either side of the gateway. He returned the following weekend, bringing three friends, an earthmover and a lorry load of gravel, which Nicky helped to rake all over the new parking area. Gareth had also collected the wooden board which Rob had commissioned from a firm of sign-writers and he helped Rob to set it up on the roadside verge. *Grafton's Nursery* it said, in huge blue lettering. They fixed a smaller, removable notice on the front of it, advertising the opening date in just four week's time. Every so often Nicky caught Rob going out into the lane to admire it. He's like a big kid, she thought.

As the days went by she actually began to think he might make his deadline. The parking area was ready. The sales area was all but complete with four rows of long slatted benches, all built by Rob, where the plants would stand for sale once they arrived. The beds which were visible from the road had been replanted and the old roses bushes which had previously robbed the sitting room window of half its daylight, had been replaced by newly planted bushes which were already displaying buds and blooms in a range of pinks and creams. The bird table man arrived one afternoon with a good selection of tables and feeders and soon after that Rob embarked on a series of forays to gather more stock. Travelling first to his grandfather's friend, Teddy, who had been devoting his garden, greenhouse and allotment to Rob's project since Christmas and then to the specialist growers from whom Rob had arranged to take fuchsias and clematis. He tried to persuade Nicky to accompany him on these trips but she said she preferred to stay behind and carry on the work of titivating the place, sanding down and repainting the old front gates in a handsome deep blue to match the sign and writing price tickets until she thought her hand would drop off. Watching the sales area as it gradually came alive with plants was like seeing the coloured areas growing larger and larger on a painting by numbers, she thought.

Then a salesman called offering various sizes of wooden tubs and troughs. Rob looked them over and agreed to take a few and when the man had gone, Nicky, who had been speculatively regarding these new acquisitions ventured: 'Why don't we plant a couple up with something bright and put them out on the verge under the big sign… and maybe have another couple at each side of the gate posts?'

'What a smashing idea.' Rob beamed at her. 'Will you do them? You've got a really good eye for that sort of thing.'

Nicky mumbled something about not really knowing what she was doing, but secretly she felt pleased. Hardly a day went by without Rob saying that she shouldn't feel obliged to do anything and how badly he felt to see her slaving for no pay. She kept on reassuring him that she wanted to do it. Although she could never have explained it to him, there was a wealth of difference between repaying him because she felt that she had to and repaying him because she wanted to.

On the night before opening day they had worked so late that it was almost dusk when they finally sat down to eat. After dinner he shared the washing up as he always did. Apart from the odd occasions when she put her weight next to his on a pick axe handle or held something in place while he knocked in a nail, standing side by side at the kitchen sink was the closest proximity they ever achieved.

He was absolutely punctilious about never touching

her. He also took care to avert his eyes if he met her still in her dressing gown en route to the bathroom. He did not even sit next to her on the sofa, always choosing to occupy a separate armchair several feet away and on the rare occasions when they found time to talk about anything unconnected with the practicalities of the business, he kept the conversation safely away from anything personal.

She had wondered but did not ask, how he had explained her presence to Gareth and his other visiting helpers. Perhaps he had simply left them to draw their own conclusions. It was the same when his sister Lorna called in on them. Nicky assumed that she had been tipped off in advance not to ask any questions. She had received no visits from friends or relations at all. When she'd phoned her dad to let him know that she could no longer be contacted at Clive's, she got Vi instead. Vi had taken down her new address and phone number (which Nicky told her were only temporary and not to be passed on to Clive in the event of his ringing) but had seemed almost absently disinterested. Vi had not enquired how it was that Nicky came to be living in rural Worcestershire nor for that matter with whom she was living. She did confirm that Clive had not been in touch at all. Although Nicky didn't ever want to see Clive again it still came as a painful jolt to discover that he had not made the slightest attempt to locate her. Felling lines of nettles which stood like so many ranks of enemy soldiers, helped to push these uncomfortable thoughts from the forefront of her mind.

This evening however, as she reached up to replace a saucepan on the rack above the cooker, she suddenly thought about how alone she was. There was still a lot of work to be done here of course. She was pretty confident that Rob would continue to welcome her efforts around the place for some time to come… but what would happen after that? What about when he stopped needing her? Or when he started a relationship with someone and she was in the way? (He was four years younger than her so it was only a matter of time.) The cottage was tiny. There was no scope for privacy or space for lodgers.

'You're looking very pensive all of a sudden,' he said.

'I was just thinking… you know… that it's opening day tomorrow and one day soon everything will be up and running and you won't need me anymore.'

'You're not thinking of leaving are you?' His tried to make light of the question but his eyes were serious and his brow furrowed in an expression which she had learned to recognise as denoting a problem to be solved.

'No,' she said, folding the tea towel and placing it neatly across the edge of the sink. 'I was just thinking that I suppose…well… one day… you won't be needing me anymore.'

'Don't say that,' he said earnestly. 'I could never have done this without you. You're a part of it now. I thought you felt that too.'

Nicky had never dared to hope as much. The nursery had been a bit like playing with Dennis's train set. You might be called upon to help fit the track together but there was no question of being allowed to work the switch which controlled the trains.

'Thanks,' she said in a small voice.

'As for not needing you anymore,' he said. 'I've never needed anyone so much in my life.'

Nicky tried to smile. 'I'm not that useful,' she said.

'That wasn't what I meant.'

They were only a foot apart. The kitchen was hazy with the scent of the honeysuckle which grew just outside the door.

'What did you mean?' she asked.

He shook his head. 'Better leave things as they are,' he said abruptly. 'I'm just going to have a last look round.'

'Rob…'

He turned back, hesitating in the doorway but she could not find any words to say.

'Won't be long,' he said.

She stood beside the sink, watching through the window as he disappeared round the side of the cottage. Even when he went out of sight she could still hear his footsteps on the newly laid gravel, the distinctive drag of his damaged leg growing fainter until there was nothing but the fussing of the birds, the faint sounds of the encroaching night.

She felt thoroughly dispirited. After all these weeks of easy friendship there was now an awkwardness between them. She should never have opened her big mouth and made him say those things about needing her. He was regretting it now. She had spoiled everything. They would become self conscious and embarrassed and sooner or later she would have to leave.

She decided that for tonight at least the best thing would be to keep out of his way. It was getting late, so he would think nothing of it if she had gone up to bed by the time he came back in. He'd probably only gone outside to create some space between them. She mounted the steep, carpet-less stairs without bothering to put on the light. You couldn't go wrong, even in the dark, because the staircase rose straight between two walls and ended in a small square landing across which the two bedroom doors faced one another. They always kept the bedroom doors closed in an unspoken agreement to preserve each other's privacy, so the windowless landing was normally dark but tonight as she climbed the stairs she realised that there was light entering the stair well from the top as well as the bottom. For once Rob had left his bedroom door ajar.

She had never seen inside his bedroom although she'd guessed from the layout of the house that it must be a mirror image of her own. When she reached the landing she stopped dead, completely arrested by what she saw. There was no bed in his room at all. Just a sleeping bag spread out on the floor. He'd given up his bed to her and had been sleeping all these weeks on the hard bare floorboards. The only furniture in the room was a couple of cane dining chairs on which various items of clothing had been stacked. Forgetting all previous reservations she pushed the door open to its full extent, at which point the absence of clothes hangers from her wardrobe was explained. Hangers bearing Rob's clothes were arranged on a variety of nails driven into the walls. She thought of all the nights when they had worked to the point of exhaustion, only for him to retire to this bare little cell while she luxuriated in the double bed next door.

Just then she heard him returning via the kitchen door. Closing and latching his bedroom door, she retraced her steps downstairs. He was standing in the living room looking very unhappy.

'Rob,' she said. 'There's something I've got to say to you.'

'No... don't,' he interrupted. 'I'm sorry Nicky. I shouldn't have said anything. I kept telling myself to keep quiet and not put you under any pressure. Please don't go. I won't say anything like that again.'

'Anything like what?'

'Anything about needing you or wanting you. I know you've had a terrible experience... Promise me that you'll forget what I said...'

'Perhaps I liked it.' She regarding him steadily. While he continued to look at her doubtfully she took a couple of steps forward and kissed him. 'I think it's about time you stopped sleeping on the floor,' she said.

Chapter Sixty

1972

At Monday morning registration no one was talking about anything except Colleen's party. Every member of VB had something to say on the subject whether they had actually been there or not. Some versions of the event were wilder than others but the picture which emerged was of an over-large original guest list which had been more than doubled by the involvement of friends of friends and a vast crowd of gatecrashers, many of whom were entirely unknown to either Colleen or her brother. One point on which there seemed to be no divergence of opinion at all, was that once Colleen's parents saw the catastrophic post-party disarray, their fury rendered the volume of those earlier Slade records positively subdued by comparison.

Colleen was deeply resentful of just about everyone who had been there, feeling that in widely publicising the party and then subsequently failing to help clear up, they had all contributed to the terrible trouble she was in at home. Only Penny (who had been staying the night anyway) had stuck around until Colleen's parents got home. (Mr and Mrs Bell had discovered Penny on her knees upstairs, attempting to unblock the loo through a brandy and Babycham induced haze.)

The party goers had contrived to do a fearful amount of damage in a relatively short space of time. Ornaments and glasses had been smashed, carpets stained beyond repair, furniture had sustained cigarette burns and out in the garden two of Mr Bell's miniature conifers had been uprooted. The cordial neighbourly relations which had previously existed with surrounding households, established over years of amicable garden tool loans and mutual plant watering during holiday absences had been soured over night.

'What happened when the police came?' Paula wanted to know. However it transpired that the police had never arrived – only Colleen's parents – whose wrath had probably been infinitely more terrible. The Bells not only blamed their own offspring but in almost equal measure the other participants and decided that their parents ought to be fully appraised of their children's behaviour and called to account for the damage done. Colleen and her brother had been instructed to provide a list of the names and addresses of all those known to have attended the party, so that their parents could be written to, with a view to them disciplining the culprits in whatever way they saw fit (to say nothing of hopefully feeling obliged to help foot the bill).

Paula was reduced to a state of panic at the mere threat of such a letter. 'For God's sake Colleen, don't give them my name,' she pleaded.

'I've got to tell them everyone who was there,' said

Colleen, stubbornly. 'I can't start looking out for anyone in particular. I'm in enough trouble already.'

'But they would never know if you didn't include me,' Paula protested. 'Besides which I was hardly there any time at all.'

'That's what everyone's saying.'

'Yes but in my case it's true.'

Opinion was divided on the best way to exert influence on Colleen. Sympathising with her predicament might encourage her to feel hard done by and think that she was entitled to name names: something she was inclined to do anyway in the hope of getting herself back into her parent's good graces. On the other hand threatening to cold shoulder her if she shopped you might backfire too, because then she might well name you out of pure spite.

There was no 'Mikado' rehearsal that lunch time and as it was raining Paula and the others were able to sit in their corner of the form room and discuss the situation in conspiratorial tones.

'I don't see why she has to give her parents *everyone's* names,' said Paula. 'It's not as if they can possibly know exactly how many people were there or who they were.'

'If they knew they wouldn't need a blinking list would they?' agreed Jo.

'She could easily leave some people out,' said Paula, casting a covert glance towards the middle of the form room, where Colleen, Penny and a couple of others were sitting in a similar huddle. 'Her parents would never know.'

'Colleen isn't noted for logical thinking,' said Becky.

'And the trouble is that everyone wants to be left out,' said Nicky. 'Even people whose parents had given them permission to go don't want their mums and dads getting a letter saying that everyone went wild and asking for money to buy a new carpet.'

'If Colleen leaves everyone who asks her to off her list,' agreed Jo: 'There will hardly be anyone left on it… and her parents aren't completely daft.'

'And if she does decide to leave anyone off it's going to be her best friends isn't it? Not the likes of us,' said Becky.

'I wish we'd never gone,' said Paula. 'It was a crap party anyway. The worst party ever.'

'You don't suppose this letter will say anything about people doing stuff in the bedrooms do you?' asked Nicky. 'My mum and dad will go bonkers if they hear about that.'

'Colleen's parents won't know about it will they? Surely she's not been stupid enough to go and tell them?' asked Becky.

'Naomi told me in art, that Colleen's mum went upstairs as soon as she got home and she could tell straight away that people had been in the bedrooms, so she asked Colleen and Penny about it and Penny went and told her that one of the girls was Charlie Young,' said Jo.

'Flipping heck! Suppose they write to Charlie's parents telling them that!'

'I shouldn't think that's going to happen,' said Becky. 'Parents don't go around talking about sex to one another. I mean what do you think they would say? Dear Mr and Mrs Young, did you know that your daughter Charlotte was having it off with someone at Colleen's party last Saturday? P.S. Kindly send £5 by return, to cover the replacement of our defiled sheets.'

Whatever subjects might be off limits between parents, VB had no such scruples and speculation was rife as to who had been doing what and with whom in the Bells' bedrooms. This included a good deal of wild conjecture as to the identity of the girl alleged to have aided Colleen's brother's best friend to break his duck behind the locked bathroom door.

Paula noticed that she and her immediate friends were not included among the candidates under consideration. This was only half pleasing, because while no one wanted to be labelled cheap or easy, nor was it flattering to be dismissed as not attractive enough to be involved in any lustful acts committed in someone else's bathroom. Much more important however, was the awful possibility that Colleen's parents would get in touch with hers. Colleen had become extremely evasive about whose names she had already provided and those which were yet to be revealed.

Becky and Jo were united in the hope that the letters were no more than an idle threat.

'They're just saying it to frighten people,' Becky said. 'They won't really do anything.'

'And anyway,' said Nicky. 'They must realise that people didn't do any damage just by being there. Surely they can't just write accusing people of doing stuff because they happened to be there? It wouldn't be fair.'

'Since when have parents worried about being fair?' asked Jo.

'They probably won't write to everyone,' said Becky. 'Think how long it would take. There must have been sixty people in that house... maybe more.'

In spite of these reassurances Paula was aware of a little knot of fear in her stomach each day as she got off the bus and took the short walk home. The post hardly ever came before she set out for school. So far no one had reported that their parents had received a letter and Colleen was unable or unwilling to confirm whether any letters had actually been written, so Paula figured that with each passing day the prospect of a letter grew a little more remote. Parents often blew up and said things and made threats and then did not carry them out. Well maybe not her parents… they did tend to follow through… but from what she heard in school other people's parents did that sort of thing all the time.

It was on Friday afternoon that the blow fell.

'Paula, come in here please.' Her mother had evidently been waiting for her because she called out from the sitting room, the moment Paula entered the house.

Paula knew that kind of imperious summons and she obeyed it at once, not even pausing to stroke Ophelia on her way. In her heart of hearts she knew what it must be about, even as she tried to keep alive the faint hope that it might be something else. She found her mother sitting forward on the edge of the armchair which faced the bay window. In her hand she had a couple of used sheets of Basildon Bond. Paula wondered how long she had been sitting there, letter in hand, tipsy with outrage. Perhaps ever since the arrival of the post that morning.

'Where were you last Saturday night?'

This opening prelude induced a profound sense of irritation in Paula. Her mother had read the letter so she must by now be perfectly well aware of her daughter's whereabouts on the evening in question.

Paula adopted an unexpected counter attack: 'Why?'

'Don't cross question me young lady. Just answer,' her mother snapped back.

Paula had recently noticed the way some very unattractive wrinkles were starting to appear on her mother's face, including crows feet at her eyes which were much more noticeable when she was displeased about something.

'I was at Nicky's house,' said Paula. 'We were invited to go to a party round at Colleen Bell's, so we went round to have a look but when we arrived there were dozens of people there already and as it was standing room only we didn't stay more for than a few minutes. After we left we went straight back to Nick's.'

'Back to Nick's,' her mother repeated derisively. 'Back to Nick's. The girl has a name Paula, why don't you use it instead of all this nasty, slangy talk? And for the umpteenth time why aren't you wearing your school tie? You walk about the streets in such a slatternly state, carrying your books in that scruffy plastic bag when you've got a perfectly good satchel. I feel ashamed to admit that I've got anything to do with you. And now this!' She flapped the sheets of note paper angrily. 'You didn't have permission to go to this Colleen Bell's house. You lied to us – pretending you were going to Nicola's house.'

'No I didn't. I did go to Nicky's. I told you that a minute ago.'

'Don't butt in. You went to this party at Colleen Bell's house. You had planned to go all along hadn't you? Don't try to pretend it was all decided on the spur of the moment. And even if it was, you know you are not allowed to go anywhere without us knowing in advance where you are going. And you knew we wouldn't have given you permission to go to something like this so you didn't ask.'

'Logically enough,' Paula muttered under her breath.

‘What was that?’

‘Nothing,’ said Paula in a voice scarcely louder.

‘Do you know what this is? It’s a letter from Colleen’s parents, asking us to pay something towards the damage. I can’t believe you could have been so stupid as to get yourself involved in something awful like this. What do you have to say for yourself? What am I supposed to say to Colleen’s parents? Have you any idea how ashamed I am that you could be involved in doing damage to someone else’s property?’

‘Mum,’ Paula almost shouted. ‘If you would just stop for a minute and give me a chance to speak…’

‘How dare you interrupt me like that? Who do you think you are talking to? I will not have you raising your voice to me like that. I’m not one of your common little friends at Colleen’s party, you know.’

‘Please may I speak?’ Paula spoke through gritted teeth. Discussions like this – well hardly discussions really, with her mother going on and on, demanding answers but never allowing an opportunity to provide any – always made her want to scream. ‘I wasn’t involved in doing any damage. I didn’t damage anything and we don’t owe anyone anything. Not even an apology. I told you. We went to Colleen’s house and when we saw how crowded it was and what a mess everyone was making, we went straight back to Nicky’s.’

‘Well that’s not what Mrs Bell’s letter says. She says that you *were* there and that everyone who was there was equally responsible… smoking… drinking… and…’ her mother shot Paula a dark look. ‘Generally going wild.’

‘How would she know who was there or how long for?’

exclaimed Paula. 'When she wasn't even in the house at the time. As I keep on trying to tell you we walked round from Nicky's house, stayed about ten minutes and then came away again. There were dozens of people in that house. A lot of them were people Colleen didn't even know. Mrs Bell is just trying to make believe it was all the fault of the people whose names she does know, so that you'll chip in and help replace her carpets. If you want to know how long we were out, you can ring Nick's mum and ask her. *She'll* tell you. I don't suppose we were gone for more than half an hour.'

Paula noticed the way her mother completely ignored this latter suggestion. It's as if she doesn't really want to know the truth, Paula thought angrily. She just automatically disbelieves anything I say. She wants to believe I've done something wrong because it gives her an excuse to stamp me down and control me.

'If you weren't one of the people involved then why would Mrs Bell be writing me a letter, saying that you were? She sounds like a perfectly respectable person. I've got no reason to disbelieve anything she says.'

'What does she actually say?' Paula demanded. 'Just tell me that. What does she actually say that *I* specifically am supposed to have done?'

'Don't challenge me like that.'

'Well I think I have a right to know. Some woman I've never met writes to you accusing me of things and you believe her not me. I think I've at least got a right to know what I'm supposed to have done.'

'I've told you,' snapped her mother. 'You were one of the people at the party. It's perfectly obvious that Mrs Bell hasn't just written to people at random. Only to the ones who misbehaved.'

'And you believe her,' Paula shouted. 'You believe her even after I've told you that I didn't do any damage in her blasted house – or any smoking or drinking or – or anything else for that matter.'

'Well I certainly can't be expected to believe anything you say because you can't be trusted to tell the truth.'

It seemed to Paula that her mother derived a strange sense of satisfaction from this. She was like a detective who was triumphant at finally getting proof of a long held suspicion.

'You lied about going to Nicola's because you were intending to go to this party all along, so you can hardly expect me to believe anything you say about it now. You had better go up to your room and stay there until your father gets home and we decide what to do about this letter. What I can tell you is this: there will be no more parties because from now on you won't be going out in the evenings at all. You'll be staying in every night because we can't trust you to tell us the truth about where you are going and stick to it.'

Paula longed to make some sort of defiant gesture but nothing came immediately to mind. She considered ignoring the banishment to her room but since the alternative was to stay within her mother's orbit downstairs, she really much preferred to go upstairs. She left the sitting room with as much dignity as she could muster, hoping her demeanour would convey that it had been her intention to go upstairs all along and had nothing to do with her mother's edict. She pretended not to see Ophelia on the landing, shutting the bedroom door before the cat could come sidling in, purring and demanding affection which Paula felt too full of bitterness to give.

I hate them, she thought. I would run away if I had anywhere to go.

Chapter Sixty-One

1985

Nicky lay in bed watching the dust motes dancing in the sunbeams, part of an undulating sea of happiness which filled the cottage bedroom. It was just past 6.00 and Rob was dragging on a pair of jeans. No lie in for him on today of all days. Even if the doors didn't officially open to the first customers until 9.30. From nowhere in particular she found herself remembering some lines from 'Lili Marlene' of all things. Something about creating a world for two… just them and no one else. It no longer mattered how it had come about, by whose initiative or why. The important thing was that they had found each other.

As he opened the bedroom door Nicky suddenly thought of something else and clapped a hand in front of her mouth. The movement caught his eye and he turned to find that her eyes had widened, like a six year old who has just spotted a couple of Daleks making for Dr Who.

'What's up?' he asked.

Nicky removed her hand and gulped in some air. 'I'd

better get myself registered with a local doctor,' she said with a touch of hesitation. 'I've run out of pills and because I wasn't sleeping with anyone I didn't bother.' Her blue eyes scanned his face anxiously. 'And we didn't use anything. I never thought. Oh flip…' She trailed off into incredulous silence. Not getting pregnant was always, always, always the first thing you had to think about unless you were specifically trying for a baby. He would never believe that she had genuinely forgotten. He would think that she was trying to trap him. All this flew through her mind in the split second it took him to raise both hands in a breezy gesture of enquiry.

'So what?' he asked cheerfully. 'I thought you said you'd always wanted marriage and babies.'

Nicky regarded him with disbelief. Her eyes were now so wide that her eyebrows had disappeared behind the tangle of blonde curls which she daily attempted to tame into a fringe.

'Marriage?'

'Well I don't want our children born out of wedlock. What would my Granddad say? He's a lay preacher you know… Hey, hey… don't start to cry.' He was at her side in a heartbeat, taking her in his arms. 'I didn't realise that marrying me was such an awful suggestion as to bring tears to your eyes.'

'Not crying because of that,' Nicky mumbled into his shoulder. 'Crying because I'm so happy.'

He said nothing but hugged her more tightly. .

Later he always liked to say that Jonathan was conceived the night before the nursery opened – making it well and truly a family business from the very first day.

Chapter Sixty-Two

1972

Opinion on Colleen Bell had split into two distinct camps. The pro-Colleen camp included a number of girls who had not originally been invited to the party and might well have been far less complimentary if they had been asked to give their views about Colleen during the week before the event. However from the safe position of non-attendees they could not only sympathise with her stance that she had no alternative but to supply the names and addresses of those girls who *had* been there, but also enjoy the frisson of watching other people getting into hot water from a safe distance.

Classmates on the receiving end of various levels of parental censure saw things rather differently.

'You should have explained that some of the people who came had nothing to do with the trouble. You shouldn't have let them just write to everyone's parents, tarring us all with the same brush,' raged Paula.

'I can't control what they do,' Colleen retorted. 'Why

don't you just tell yours that you didn't do anything? If you think mine will take any notice of me, then you must think yours will take notice of what you say.'

Reaction to the letters had varied from household to household. Nicky's parents had taken the whole thing reasonably calmly. They knew that on the night of the party the girls had not been out of the house for very long and on their return Nicky had mentioned the extremely crowded house and developing chaos as the reasons for their speedy return. The Christies therefore found Nicky's explanation entirely plausible and went so far as to describe the Bells' letter as 'a bit of a cheek'.

'That Mrs Bell wants to get her facts straight before she starts writing to girls' parents, stirring up trouble,' Mrs Christie declared, before emphatically consigning Mrs Bell's missive to the orange plastic pedal bin in the kitchen.

'It's got Paula into terrible trouble,' Nicky said. 'Couldn't you ring Paula's mum and tell her that we weren't away from here for very long? I'm sure it would help.'

Mrs Christie immediately looked troubled. 'I couldn't do that love,' she said. 'I can't just go ringing up someone I hardly know and interfering in their private family business.'

'But she wouldn't believe Paupau and I know she'd believe you Mum.'

Mrs Christie hesitated before saying, 'I can't go poking my nose into other people's business.'

'But it's so unfair…'

Mrs Christie vanished into the pantry, returning a moment later with a net of sprouts in her hand.

'Please Mum,' Nicky wheedled.

'No Nicky. I can't. Now stop hanging about in here or I'll find you a job to do.'

Nicky tried one final shot. 'If Paula's mum rang you, you'd tell her what really happened then, wouldn't you?'

'Well yes of course I would. But I'm sure Mrs Morrison won't ring,' she added quickly. Mrs Morrison made her nervous, what with her posh way of talking and always going on about when she had been at Eleanor Vaux. Mrs Christie had been to Saltaire Street Secondary Modern.

Nicky had done her best but the ploy was doomed to failure. Paula's parents had refused to budge an inch from their initial decision. In future there would be no leaving the house in the evenings except on bona fide school trips to the theatre or in the company of one or other of her parents.

'It's ridiculous,' Paula shouted at them. 'I'm nearly sixteen years old.'

'You're just a school girl Paula and you know very little of the world,' her father said.

Paula would have liked to point out that this was hardly surprising and moreover unlikely to change so long as she was prevented from ever going anywhere or meeting anyone, but she could hardly ever get a word in and anyway they never listened.

'What you fail to realise Paula is that we have got your best interests at heart. One day you will see that we were right. Perhaps when you have children of your own, you will understand how important it is to nip these dangerous situations in the bud.'

'What dangerous situations?' asked Paula.

'Situations such as the party at the Bells' house.'

'We are protecting you Paula, until you have acquired enough experience and common sense to protect yourself.'

Fat lot of experience and common sense I'm going to acquire, sitting upstairs with Ophelia for company, Paula thought.

'And by staying in more you will have the time to concentrate on your school work and get the best possible marks. I'm afraid you've let too many distractions get in the way of your work these past couple of years.'

They argued round and round in circles until her parents eventually refused to discuss the matter any further. No one else was facing a complete ban on any kind of social life. My parents don't think I'm a person at all, she thought. They think I'm a sort of robot to be programmed and controlled so that I can accomplish their set plan. Ophelia gets more leeway than I do.

The Bells' letter had dropped through the Emburys' letter box on a Saturday morning. Joanne had expected an eruption of volcanic proportions but her father took an unexpected line.

'Bleeding cheek,' he said, screwing the missive up after a cursory read.

'What is it?' asked Mrs Embury, to whom the letter was jointly addressed.

'Some people whose daughter had a party last week. Writing to everyone whose kids were there and asking for money to replace their carpets. What a scam! Sounds like an excuse to get a new carpet at somebody else's expense to me.'

'What are they saying?' Mrs Embury was confused. 'Why do they want money off us?'

'They're saying,' Mr Embury spoke slowly, as if to an imbecile. 'That a lot of stuff in their house got damaged on account of this party and now they think the parents of their kids' friends should send them some money to make amends. Must think we're a right soft touch. If there's any damage then it's only themselves to blame. What sort of fools go out and leave a house full of teenagers to have a party anyway? Must need their heads examining if you ask me.'

Stan's take on the situation was not entirely dissimilar. He pontificated at some length about how Becky needn't expect him to ever let her have the run of *his* house for a party, condemned the Bells roundly as irresponsible and declared that anything might have happened. However in spite of his general lack of sympathy with the Bells, who he said had made their bed and must lie on it (fortunately their letter contained no mention of anyone else having lain on it) he did feel that the young people involved ought to be taught a lesson. He therefore proposed, he said, to send them five pounds through the post which he would stop out of Becky's pocket money.

Although inwardly wincing at the prospect of no pocket money for five whole weeks, Becky gave no sign. The penalty was hard to take but at least it had a strictly defined duration and wasn't so awful as what had happened to Paula.

'What have you got to say to that?' Stan asked.

'Just as you wish,' said Becky, in the specially disinterested voice she had recently perfected for use on Stan.

It was a phrase she frequently employed because she

knew that he found it particularly annoying but could do very little about it. The first time she had responded with: 'As you wish,' Stan had spluttered with annoyance and asked her what she meant by it.

'As – you – wish,' Becky had repeated, slowly and carefully enunciating each word with only the faintest detectable hint of sarcasm. 'It means that I am agreeing with you. It means that you can have whatever it is you want. As – adverb – you – second person pronoun singular, meaning the person addressed – wish – verb meaning what you want or desire.'

'Don't be so bloody cheeky,' Stan had exclaimed, almost hopping up and down with annoyance. 'Don't try to be clever with me. I know what it means.'

'Then why did you ask?' Becky said. She had moved so that she was standing right next to the stairs which enabled her to get the last word in before scooting out of earshot.

Chapter Sixty-Three

1985

The cream teas had begun entirely on Nicky's initiative. In the first days after the nursery opened several customers had asked directions for the nearest place where they could buy refreshments of some kind and this had given Nicky the idea of serving tea and coffee as an extra money spinner. Though concerned that she might have been biting off more than she could chew, Rob gave way in the face of her enthusiasm and conceded to a trial run. They had invested in a trio of circular plastic tables, each with its own quartet of matching plastic chairs and equipped each table with a little brass hand bell with which to summon Nicky's attention from wherever she might be.

The scale of the operation soon increased from the original modest plan to provide tea and coffee. By the end of week four Nicky had instituted a menu on a chalk board, which included canned soft drinks and various items of confectionery obtained from the cash and carry and by week six this had graduated to whatever home made cakes

Nicky had found time to produce in the kitchen. ('I can whizz up a few scones and a Victoria Sandwich in no time,' she had assured Rob when he half-heartedly attempted to demur.) The incorporation of locally made strawberry jam and cream seemed a natural step and before long Rob discovered that people were stopping off specially to sample the apricot and sultana bread without having any interest in the plants at all: a development he pretended to be cross about while secretly rejoicing at the success of her enterprise and her obvious pride in it.

'You're wonderful,' he said, pausing to deposit a kiss on top of her hair.

He was glad to find her for once taking full advantage of a lull in trade, sitting in one of the white plastic chairs with her bare feet resting on another while she read a couple of pages of 'The Jewel in the Crown'.

Ezekiel the cat was sitting on her lap. Ezekiel had come from the animal rescue centre, where Rob's sister Lorna worked. He had been the victim of some terrible accident in one of his past lives and this had left him with a badly damaged ear and only one eye, but anxious to prove himself in spite of his apparent disabilities, Ezekiel was now the Official Greeter (self appointed) in respect of the entire catering operation and often undertook a night shift on Mouse Patrol as well. Observing that Nicky was the recipient of some affectionate attention, Zeke as he was known in off duty moments, made a prutting noise and lifted his black and white head expectantly so that Rob could tickle him under the chin.

Ezekiel had worked out so well in respect of the mouse problem that Lorna had had no difficulty in persuading them to take on Esther, a silver tabby, who unfortunately turned out to be far too grand for menial work such as mouse catching and preferred to sit in sunny spots, looking important and soaking up admiration from customers. ('That cat is definitely management material,' Rob said of her darkly.)

While Rob moved on to tidy up and re-stock in the herb section, Nicky reached down to continue petting Zeke, while covertly resting her other hand just below her waist in the vain hope of detecting movement, although she knew it was really far too early for that. The baby was still no more than a tiny secret, undetected by anyone who had not been told about it. She still had to get past the thirteenth week – the point at which her previous pregnancies had ended.

How happy I am, she thought. How happy small things make me. Well… not just small things, she conceded as the sun caught Rob's ring sitting proudly on her third finger and made it wink at her. A baby and getting married were not exactly small things… but if those bigger things had not made her so contented, then perhaps the smaller things, the passing bees and butterflies, the exquisitely lovely roses blooming at her elbow, the friendly presence of Zeke in her lap, would not have had quite the same sheen.

Chapter Sixty-Four

1973

Miss Carling paused alongside the table where Joanne was working. The standard in the 'O' level art classes this year was generally high, but whereas some pupils were merely good technicians who approached their projects in an able but slightly mechanical way, Joanne Embury had a genuine talent coupled with good draughtsmanship. She was a funny girl in some ways, Miss Carling thought, rather quiet and self contained, by no means the most communicative of pupils.

Jo had been concentrating fully on her work: an arrangement of driftwood and sea shells which had been set up on a central table in the art room, but after capturing the essence of the subject in a series of swift sure strokes, she happened to lean back just as Miss Carling reached her.

'That's very nicely done,' said Miss Carling. 'Of course with 'O' level we do an awful lot of still life work and you may sometimes find that a bit restricting. I plan to include as much fieldwork as possible when we start 'A' level, next year.'

It had not escaped Miss Carling that Joanne never offered any response when she mentioned the 'A' level course. Miss Carling naturally assumed that any girl in possession of Joanne's talent (and very few of the girls she had ever taught could hold a candle to Joanne Embury) would specialise in art. It would be a criminal waste for them not to. Yet Joanne's non-committal silences had started to worry her. They had become too obvious to be merely coincidental. Surely Joanne had not been wooed away into the arms of a different area of the curriculum? (You had to watch some of the staff, who were inclined to sideline art as being strictly for the non-academics.) Could it be that her star pupil had been seduced by languages or science? The time had come when the question could be put off no longer.

'You will be taking art 'A' level?' she asked.

Joanne turned in her seat because it would be rude not to face Miss Carling when talking with her. 'I'm not staying on,' she said.

'Why ever not?' gasped Miss Carling, rather more loudly than she had intended, thereby attracting the attention of everyone else in the room.

'My parents want me to get a job,' Joanne said in a voice shamefaced enough to imply that the career they had in mind was at best embezzlement or prostitution.

Miss Carling hesitated. Joanne's embarrassment and unwillingness to elaborate were plain to behold so for the time being she merely said, 'I see,' and continued on her perambulation around the room. By the time she had done another full circuit enough chit chat had broken out again for her to be able to say quietly to Joanne, 'Would you pop along here at lunch time so that I can have a word with you?'

'O.K.,' said Joanne. She liked Miss Carling but she didn't like the sound of 'having a word'. If Miss Carling thought anything to do with her taking an art 'A' level would be solved by having a word, then she was barking up the wrong tree altogether.

At lunch time Miss Carling herself began to appreciate the scale of the problem. She was forced to accept that her willingness to talk with Joanne's parents would do no good whatever, swiftly picking up on the way the prospect of such an offer conjured a look akin to fear in the girl's eyes. 'It would only end up in a huge row,' Joanne told her.

All this worried Miss Carling considerably. For a brief period after graduation Miss Carling had become Mrs Webb. It was a part of her life unknown to all but her oldest friends and a completely closed book to anyone at Eleanor Vaux, but a drunken, bullying spouse had opened Miss Carling's eyes to a side of life she had previously never suspected and her suspicions had been alerted less by Joanne Embury's words, as by the expression in the girl's eyes, artificially magnified by her big round spectacles.

'There's nothing I can do to persuade him,' Joanne had told the art teacher. 'Nothing anyone else can do either. And I can't stay on if he won't let me. You can get a grant and a job in a bar or something once you get to university. But you can't make enough money to pay your keep while you stay on at school for two years to get your 'A' levels. We're not even supposed to have part time jobs while we're still at school: it's in the rules. Although a lot of people do have Saturday jobs on the quiet.'

Miss Carling nodded. Only the previous week she had elected not to have her lunch in a cafe in the Burlington Arcade, because at the last minute she had spotted a familiar face and realised that going in would have unavoidably brought to her attention the fact that one of her sixth form pupils was waiting tables in there.

'Well I agree it is a very difficult situation,' Miss Carling said. 'All I can suggest at this stage is that you carry on doing your best and in the meantime I'll give it some more thought.'

If anything this interview made Joanne feel even worse. She had achieved a grade one in her art mock exam a few weeks before… the only girl in the year to do so. Miss Carling reminding her about it and saying what a waste it would be if she left… well when she left because there was really no *if* about it, didn't help at all. It might be unusual and flattering to have a teacher taking a personal interest, but in the long term it wasn't actually any use at all. Miss Carling's thinking about it was not going to help. If merely thinking could do any good – or even prayer – because although she didn't really have much faith that there was a God, Jo had tried that too – then her father would have had a change of heart long ago.

When Jo rejoined the others she found them trying to jolly Paula up a bit. Paula was in one of her mopey moods. She had done quite poorly in her mocks: disastrously according to her mother. She hadn't actually managed to fail anything. (She had even managed to scrape a grade five in biology). But of course just getting a pass wasn't good enough for Paula's parents, who seemed to operate on the principle that whatever Paula did she could always have done it better. Nothing short of a straight run of grade ones was going to satisfy them, Paula said, which was totally unrealistic. No one was expected to do that. Even people like Alex and Norma would not expect to get more than a couple of grade ones: it was unheard of. Paula had joked grimly that even a whole bunch of grade ones would probably only raise the familiar spectre of her mother's distinction in geography – something which Paula couldn't possibly emulate as there was no such thing any more.

'If it wasn't that it would be the bloody Senior Shield,' Paula said.

'What about the Senior Shield?' Nicky asked.

'My mother won the blasted thing when she was here.'

'So?' said Becky. 'What's that got to do with the price of fish?'

'Absolutely nothing,' said Paula emphatically. 'But it's dragged out and tossed across the dinner table – metaphorically speaking – along with the distinction in geography whenever they need evidence of my general uselessness and failure to achieve anything.'

Feelings of gloom and despondency were not confined to Paula. As the real exams drew close a sense of depression settled over the fifth years. Even Mrs Young's biology classes were no longer the junkets they had once been now that a core of students had belatedly settled down to work in the hope of scraping a pass. The efforts of Ronnie and her allies to create a series of fun filled diversions during biology were not welcomed by this newly studious minority. Other members of the biology class, having accepted that it would take a minor miracle for them to get a pass, just resented the waste of five periods a week on biology when they could have been putting the time to more productive use on another subject.

Running in tandem with the approach of the exams was a sense that things were about to change. Whatever might be happening beyond the school gates and however much they might have resisted it, Eleanor Vaux had been their world for almost five years, but only two thirds of them would be coming back for sixth form in September. The sand was running through the egg timer faster than they had ever thought possible. Fifth form study leave would begin in May. Their last lessons together were fast approaching. One day soon they would all line up and walk into assembly together for the last time.

Chapter Sixty-Five

1986

Becky gazed down at the small goldy pink face, encircled by the cellular hospital blanket, which was acting as a shawl. She knew that it was really a touch of jaundice but it did look remarkably as if Madeline Lucy McMahon had been born with an attractive sun tan. Now that Sean had gone home and everyone else in the ward had gone to sleep, she had carefully lifted Madeline out of her Perspex cot and taken her back to bed, where she sat cradling the sleeping baby in the dimly lit alcove, occasionally transferring her gaze from the unbelievable sight of the sleeping baby out through the hospital windows at the black January sky.

She knew she was supposed to be tired but it was too exciting to sleep. Her own child. Her child and Sean's, but principally – just at that very moment – hers and hers alone.

All my own work, she thought, smiling. Well… perhaps that was not entirely true… but she had done well today and could allow herself a few minutes of selfish, solitary pride.

Throughout her pregnancy she had entertained a secret irrational fear that once her baby was born, she might not be able to differentiate it from all the others in the hospital. This had preyed on her mind to such an extent that she had even had a couple of nightmares about it. Looking down at her daughter now she could laugh at such foolishness. If they were to put Madeline in a room filled with hundreds of babies, she would still be able to pick her out. Apart from anything else Madeline was beautiful. Sean said so too. Even the midwife who had helped to deliver her had remarked on it.

Of all the things I've done in my life, Becky thought, of all the memories I shall have, I will always remember this. Sitting here alone with Madeline who isn't quite twelve hours old.

How could the other mothers possibly sleep, Becky wondered. How could they pass up the opportunity to sit here, watching something so fresh and absolutely brand new? It was a whole new life beginning.

I'm going to do my best to be a good mother to you, Becky promised, silently. I haven't got much of a role model to go on but I really will try. You have a wonderful daddy too, who loves you and will always be there for us both and never leave us.

Madeline Lucy McMahon received these solemn assurances with a tiny snuffle, as if her upturned baby nose had just been tickled with a feather.

Chapter Sixty-Six

1973

'In London?' said Sonia. 'But where will you live?'

They were sitting in the living room of Sonia and Mick's flat. Radio One was on in the background, playing 'Tie A Yellow Ribbon Round The Old Oak Tree', which Joanne thought must rate as one of the most irritating records ever made.

'With this Burgoyne woman,' said Joanne. 'Miss Carling knows her. She says it's all right, because she often has students and... and artists lodging with her.' She hesitated over the word artist because she didn't want Sonia to think that she was being pretentious or getting any big ideas.

'Dad'll never go for it.' Sonia shook her head.

'I know. That's why you've got to help me.'

'Let me look at the letter again.'

Joanne obediently reached the letter out of her brown and green Greek bag and handed it over. It confirmed that Joanne had been offered a place at Chesney School of Art in Wimbledon to undertake a two year course in 'A' level art, together with other subjects of her choice which had yet to be chosen from the curriculum. According to the letter all her fees would be met by a scholarship awarded from the Percival Burgoyne Trust.

'I don't get it,' said Sonia. 'How can you get a scholarship without sitting an exam or something? Surely you had to fill in some application forms?'

'Miss Carling approached them and showed them some of my work,' said Joanne. 'She borrowed my art folder a couple of weeks back without telling me what she wanted it for. She took it to London and showed it to the people who run this Burgoyne Trust Thingy and they got me a place at art school.'

Although Joanne would never know it, the fact was that the trustees in the plural had not seen her work at all. The Percival Burgoyne Trust was administered by three trustees two of whom, Sir Rupert Heatherington-Wilcox who had been a friend of Percy Burgoyne himself and was now in his nineties and Miss Lucille Bertram, a wispy mouse of a woman who never disagreed with anything anyone ever said to her, were entirely subordinate to the third trustee, Percy Burgoyne's only surviving daughter Eleanor. Nell Burgoyne, as her friends knew her, often exercised sole discretion and had done so in this particular case.

Moreover, contrary to the impression which Joanne had derived, Miss Carling had never met Eleanor Burgoyne until in mounting desperation she had begun to discuss the 'Joanne problem' with some old friends from her university days and one of them had said, 'Why not try Nell Burgoyne?' At which point Miss Carling had vaguely recollected Nell Burgoyne – an eccentric figure who flitted about in the background of the London art world – someone she had occasionally seen from afar at shows and openings in her student days. It was therefore with some trepidation that she had obtained Miss Burgoyne's telephone number, contacted her and outlined the problem.

Miss Burgoyne had taken the call mostly in silence, asking no questions, so that Miss Carling initially wondered whether she was taking the matter seriously. Only when Miss Carling had pretty much run out of things to say did the rather loud, somewhat masculine voice of Miss Burgoyne come back at her down the phone. 'I see, I see. Well I can't promise anything but if you'd like to come down on Saturday and bring some of the gel's work with you – not her, just some samples of her work – I'll take a look.'

Such a vague arrangement hardly sounded very promising and Miss Carling had a nasty suspicion that she was about to waste the price of a return ticket to Euston. However when she arrived at the address Miss Burgoyne had given her on the telephone, a tall Victorian house not far from Wimbledon Park, she was relieved to discover that her hostess (who offered tea, coffee, or cocoa at eleven in the morning) appeared to have her eye very much on the ball. Miss Burgoyne examined every piece of work in the folder, pausing a particularly long time over the primroses done in chalks and then the painting of the dark woodland interior.

'This was her own interpretation,' Miss Carling said eagerly. 'I gave them a photograph to look at, something I'd cut out of a magazine and everyone else just pretty much reproduced it, you know, leafy glades and bluebells…'

'Interesting,' said Miss Burgoyne thoughtfully, without taking her eyes off the picture. 'I like the way the faces are suggested... just a hint here and there, very atmospheric. Mature and well executed for someone so young.'

Miss Carling was about to burble something about Joanne having simply oodles of talent, but Miss Burgoyne did not give her the chance. In fact what came next floored Miss Carling completely. The payment of fees by the Burgoyne Trust... 'no problem getting her a place at Chesney's,' Miss Burgoyne boomed cheerfully. 'Because I'm on the Board of Governors... free bed and board here for two years...' Miss Carling was completely taken aback but Miss Burgoyne, a professional Bohemian, thought nothing of it. 'Oscar Lewis lodged here for years on and off until he made it in America,' she said. (Miss Carling looked him up when she got home and found out that he was a sculptor who now worked in Los Angeles providing modern pieces for the rich and famous.)

'You say she talked about trying to work her own way through university? Well she'll easily find a little job round here on Saturdays to earn herself some pocket money while she's at Chesney's.'

When Miss Burgoyne took her on a tour around the house, specifically in order to inspect the studio space in the attic and the bedroom which she intended to assign to Jo, Miss Carling found herself wondering what Joanne Embury would make of a house where the walls had not been re-papered for thirty years or more because it would entail moving just too many pictures, and where books not only filled their yards of allocated shelf space but also marched into every other nook and cranny, including the stairs where they formed up into neat piles on every tread. Books had even encroached half way along the enormous oak dining table, the other half of which was still substantial enough to accommodate whichever seven or eight waifs and strays happened to have dropped in at meal times. Miss Carling had never seen the Embury's house but she did not suppose that it would be much like this one.

As for Miss Burgoyne herself, with her dangling pendant earrings of Whitby jet and her shapeless green velvet dress, its fashionable length entirely accidental, Miss Carling hardly knew what Joanne would make of her either. She wondered where the Burgoyne money had come from in the first place.

'I heard it was tea,' said the friend who had originally suggested initiating the contact. 'Someone once told me that the Burgoyne family had some sort of plantation in India or Ceylon, which Percy Burgoyne sold so that he could come back here and be a patron of the arts in a modest sort of way. There were three children originally – two brothers and Nell – but she inherited everything because one of her brothers caught some awful tropical disease while he was abroad and the other one was killed in the Great War.'

'Do you know how old she is?' asked Miss Carling, who had privately placed Nell Burgoyne somewhere in her late fifties or early sixties.

'Well no one knows exactly, but she once told me that she remembers being in London for the coronation and being taken to watch the procession by her father.'

'Which one?'

'Edward VII.'

Chapter Sixty-Seven

1973

Though a section of the form were attracted by Ronnie's idea of obtaining a pair of huge bloomers, marking them on the rear with a large E and V and then hoisting them up the flagpole above the front entrance doors, nothing actually came of it. To begin with there were practical difficulties to be overcome such as getting up onto the roof. Secondly no one was sure how the bloomers were to be secured in place. The flagpole had not been used in the five years they had been there and did not appear to have any ropes attached to it. Finally Mrs Carpigo was thought quite vicious enough to be capable of suspending the culprits, not from the flagpole, but from school itself and thereby preventing them from sitting the exams which they had all worked so hard towards.

In the end there was no major prank playing on the last day before fifth form study leave began and only a few half hearted gestures made in acknowledgement that for some of them it would be their last ever day of normal school.

Joanne tried to symbolically smash her tennis racket at the end of P.E., but useless and decrepit object that it was, the thing must have become so toughened with age that it would not break. She had to content herself with consigning it to the school dustbins so that no one could ever be tortured with it again.

Gail Foster invited everyone to autograph her school shirt while she was still wearing it. Even people she had not spoken to for years were invited to join in. Apart from this there was a disappointing absence of excitement.

This is the way the world ends, thought Paula. Not with a bang, but with a whimper. Nicky and Becka were both going to look for jobs once their exams were finished and Jo was going away to study in London, so she would be returning for the sixth form without them. As the months had passed, Paula had come to feel increasingly isolated. The others tried to include her as much as they could, but if they went out in the evening she was not allowed to accompany them and although they had tried to make her feel part of the preparations for 'The Mikado' it had all been a farce really, because of course she had not been allowed to stay behind after school and work backstage during the week when the production actually took place. So long as term lasted they could all be together every day in school, but from September she would not even have that. Ronnie and Adele had already let it be known that she was welcome to hang around with them at lunch time and free periods when sixth form began, but she knew that it could never be the same.

Paula was still undecided which 'A' levels she wanted to do. English obviously, because she needed that for her writing and would presumably be taking it at university, although she was not sure that reading English at university was particularly essential to writing bestselling novels. University still featured in her plans because apart from marriage it looked like the only sure fire way of escaping from her parents, though she thought it would be pretty horrible not knowing anyone when she got there and probably never managing to make any friends. She had already decided that she would have to spend all of her free time outside lectures writing her first book.

She knew that Becky had a quite different plan for achieving independence, part of which entailed a cardboard box kept on top of her wardrobe and misleadingly labelled *Old School Books* in green felt tip. In reality the box contained a hoard of tinned food and packet soups which Becky had been filching from the kitchen cupboards when her mother and Stan were not around. Becky intended to get a place of her own as soon as she could, but Paula thought the reality of this sounded scary and precarious. If the advertisements in the 'Evening Mail' were to be believed the cost of bedsits was enormous in proportion to the amount a female school leaver could expect in wages.

As their last day on the premises approached, the girls had been gradually clearing out their desks in order to lighten the final load, but in spite of this there was still an awful lot left to carry.

'We would have to have P.E. on the very last day,' grumbled Jo, as she tried and failed to cram her P.E. bag into a plastic carrier before dumping it back on top of her desk, resigned to carrying it as a separate item.

'At least you've got rid of your tennis racket,' said Paula, who had wedged the head of hers into her P.E. bag then tightened the drawstring which left the handle sticking out, ready to get in the way at the first opportunity. 'I daren't go home without mine. There'd be hell to play.'

'Jo's got the right idea,' said Becky. Picking up her own P.E. bag she marched to the front of the classroom and dumped it on top of the green enamel waste paper bin, which was already so crammed with paper that Annette Maudesley had been lifted on top of it earlier in a vain attempt to stamp it down.

'You can't just throw your stuff away,' gasped Paula.

'Why not? I'll never use it again. None of it fits me anyway. Those hockey boots are at least two sizes too small. They're the ones Mum bought for me in first year.'

'We ought to make a ceremonial bonfire of the whole lot,' Ronnie commented when she saw what Becky had done. 'I was going to get some scissors from the needlework room, cut my tie into thirty pieces and give everyone a bit to remember me by, but then I remembered that we're supposed to turn up in uniform to take our exams and I thought it would be just like Cow-Pig-Oh to be standing on the door turning anyone back who wasn't wearing their tie, so I decided I'd better hang on to mine and have it in my pocket with me just in case.'

'Won't it be bliss being able to wear our own clothes instead of uniform in sixth form?' said Adele.

'Only no jeans or trousers,' Paula and Ronnie chorused in perfect unison. 'No skirts more than an inch above or below the knee and no low cut or revealing tops.'

Becky made no comment. Privately she had realised long ago that the sixth form dress code would have been yet another bar to her staying on at school. She had been making do with an increasingly shabby uniform, which like her hockey boots had been purchased in Rackhams on that original far distant summer day. Only her school shirts – which absolutely would not stretch in the wash the way her sweater had – were replacement items. Everything else had just had to do. The state of her uniform had become a source of permanent embarrassment, but nor did she possess enough clothes to wear approved non-uniform skirts and tops five days a week and she knew that the constant recycling of her tiny wardrobe would soon have attracted comments from girls like Alex Dunston, whose parents could seemingly afford to let her buy new things from Dorothy Perkins every other week.

They finally set off down the lower drive laden with bags in each hand and were half way to the gates when Nicky exclaimed: 'Hold on! I know what we've forgotten.'

'What?'

'We can't just go off like this without doing our theme tune.'

There was no need for discussion. In spite of being so heavily encumbered they managed to link arms and carry off the overlapping walk without tripping each other over, while giving a rather breathless rendition of 'Raindrops Keep Falling on my Head'.

Chapter Sixty-Eight

1988

Having sorted out the altercation in the sand pit in such a way that both Jonathan and Madeline were happily occupied again, each digging with their brightly coloured plastic spades instead of batting each other over the head with them, Nicky returned to her chair.

As she watched her friend settle back against the patchwork cushions, Becky smiled at the way she looked cheerfully, rosily pregnant. Nick was one of those women who really glowed under the mantle of maternity. In a funny, superstitious way she had taken the news that Nicky was pregnant again as a sort of good omen for herself and Sean. They had been trying for another baby themselves and since she and Nicky had produced babies within five months of one another last time around, an irrational, superstitious part of her saw a significance in it, so that although the mathematics were increasingly against them being simultaneously pregnant again, she was still optimistic that they would get lucky before Nick's second baby arrived in about ten weeks time.

From somewhere on the other side of the cottage a small brass bell tinkled for assistance. They caught each other's eye and Nicky grinned and stretched ostentatiously. The business was going so well that there were staff on hand to run the catering when Nicky needed a break. Operations had advanced a long way since the days of cakes produced from the cottage kitchen for consumption at white plastic picnic tables. A newly constructed, detached, brick built pavilion housed half a dozen tables and its own kitchen area, and there were some more tables under parasols outside.

'All your doing,' Rob had said, resting his arm proudly around Nicky's shoulders when they stood surveying the new facility on the day when it had finally opened.

From modest beginnings Grafton's Nursery had enjoyed phenomenal success. Their turnover had doubled and then quadrupled and they now had several employees. Job creation was something to be proud of, Nicky thought. And these days when she completed forms she had to put down her occupation as company director, which invariably made her laugh because she still only had one smart suit which had to do for weddings, funerals and visits to the bank manager.

In the meantime Becky was now a partner in her city centre practice. Madeline was looked after by a nanny while her parents were at work, but Becky had recently cut down her hours, which allowed her the luxury of driving out every so often to spend an afternoon with Nicky, catching up with each other's news while their offspring played amicably together, give or take the occasional spat over a plastic spade.

It was the children that had brought them back together. Prompted by Rob, Nicky had eventually dialled her old friend's number and let her know that she too had joined the ranks of the pregnant and the married. After such a long silence she had been rather doubtful of her reception but pregnancy had provided the common bond which instantly bridged the time when they had barely spoken. Two years down the line it was as if that awkwardness had never happened.

As Nicky relaxed into the chair she said, 'I had a letter from Jo yesterday.'

'I haven't heard from her since she had that one woman exhibition,' said Becky. 'But that's because I owe her a letter. I really must get round to writing. Did she have anything exciting to say?'

'I don't know about exciting. Do you remember Miss Burgoyne, the funny old stick that Jo lived with when she went to art school in London?'

Becky nodded.

'Well Jo says she has died. She was a good age though. Ninety two. She'd been in an old people's home for the last couple of years.'

'Do you remember when Jo used to tell us about that house? All the things that went on there? All those weird arty types coming and going? I couldn't believe it was real life. It sounded just like an Iris Murdoch novel come to life.'

'You always were reading stuff like Iris Murdoch,' said Nicky. 'I think I was still on the Famous Five at that stage.'

'You were not!' exclaimed Becky. 'You used to read

exactly the same as the rest of us did. We all read the same books because everything got passed round between the four of us.'

'I was never as bright as you three.' Nicky spoke with a complete absence of envy or resentment.

'What rubbish. You know the trouble with the Eleanor Vaux ethos of never praising anyone who didn't come first with ten out of ten and a gold star, was that we none of us saw ourselves as exceptionally bright. If ever a group was set up to under-achieve it was us. Hardly anyone made it through that school with any appreciation of how bright they really were. We started off going in as the top kids from our primary school classes and they spent the next few years grinding us down until we felt utterly useless. I met a woman who used to work in the Education Department and she told me – seriously – that you had to get an eleven plus pass in the top 5% in Birmingham to get a place at Eleanor Vaux in those days.'

'Crikey,' said Nicky. 'No one ever told me that.'

'Of course they didn't,' said Becky, a touch bitterly. 'When I look back I can see that they spent far too much time putting us down and not nearly enough time building us up. Kids who came from homes like mine needed a bit more carrot and a lot less stick.'

'They never allowed for kids coming from homes like ours,' Nicky reminded her. 'Apart from darling Miss Carling who stepped in and rescued Jo, it never seemed to occur to any of them that not everyone had a dad who went to work every day in a collar and tie, then came home at night and listened to a Beethoven symphony before reading a chapter of Trollope or Dickens at bedtime.'

They were both silent for a few moments.

'Have you heard anything from Dennis since we last spoke?' Becky asked.

'Yes. He sent some photographs,' said Nicky. 'He doesn't do letters as you know, but there were a few cryptic notes on the backs. I'll go inside and fetch them in a minute. I must say she looks quite pretty – this Raylene.'

'Hmm,' said Becky. 'I've always thought sensible is what Dennis needs. Not pretty.'

'Oh don't be mean.' Nicky laughed indulgently. 'She must have something about her, because she's managed to tie him down to marriage, which is more than any of the others have done. The pictures are mostly taken round their swimming pool. Do you suppose it's quite common for people to have swimming pools in their gardens in Australia or does it indicate that they're filthy rich?'

'No idea,' said Becky. 'You say he works for her father?'

'Yes. They own a fish canning plant. That doesn't *sound* illegal.'

They both burst out laughing.

'You have no idea how relieved I was when he went to Australia,' Becky said. 'Because it significantly reduced the risk of me ever meeting him professionally. I could never have taken Dennis as a client you know. One look at him doing that butter wouldn't melt face in the witness box and I'd have just cracked up, thinking about that time when he broke the kitchen window with his cricket ball. Not that his story about the bird wasn't good…'

'How's Sean?' asked Nicky. 'Have they managed to get that skin problem sorted out yet?'

'No,'. A faintly anxious look crossed Becky's face.

'It definitely isn't eczema and it isn't any of the obvious measles or chicken pox type rashes. The doctor is going to refer him to the hospital because he thinks it might be some sort of allergy… though we just can't imagine what he's suddenly become allergic to.'

'It's a funny time to start being allergic to something… in your middle thirties.'

'Early thirties if you please,' laughed Becky. 'Sean reckons that anything the right side of thirty six is early thirties. Do you know I've started to go grey? I keep finding little grey hairs and I'm not thirty two until November – it's a disgrace!'

'Gosh,' said Nicky. 'Thirty two. We've been out of school longer than we were in it. Where has the time gone?'

Chapter Sixty-Nine

1973

It was so quiet in the examination room that the noise made by a chair leg scraping on the floor rasped around the room like a chain saw starting up. Every June since coming to the school they had been greeted by strategically erected blackboards at various points in the corridors bearing the message:

SILENCE
EXAMINATION IN PROGRESS

and each year they had dutifully observed the edict, diverting along alternative routes to lessons in order to avoid passing the hall doors at all. Now it was their turn to sit in the hall, fenced around with an almost holy silence, protected by the unseen blackboards. There was a magnificence about that silence: a sense that it was wrought by the collective efforts of the entire school. Even the electric bells nearest the hall had been disconnected so that when bells rang out to mark the passage of lessons they sounded distant, like the ghostly echoes of church bells from villages long drowned beneath deep reservoirs.

Joanne had made sure that each of her two fountain pens were filled to capacity before the start of every paper, not least because the reservoirs made a loud sucking noise whenever this operation had to be performed and if she had to replenish them during a paper it would be a wonder if Alex Dunston didn't complain about it. It was just the sort of thing Alex would complain about and as they were allocated places alphabetically, Alex was sitting immediately in front of Joanne.

The weather had been very hot all through the exams. Fortunately the windows were set so high in the walls that the body of the hall did not get much direct sunlight, but even without direct sunlight the hall still tended to get stuffy when it was full of breathing perspiring bodies. It was not so bad, Joanne thought, in non-compulsory subjects where a lot of vacant desks gave the semblance of more air to be shared between fewer pairs of lungs. The worst subjects were the ones like maths, when there was someone occupying every seat on the fifth form side of the room.

On this particular morning the paper was biology so Jo had plenty of time to ruminate on these matters. For once there hadn't been any point in getting nervous before the paper, because she knew she would fail whatever happened. The worst part about it was the boredom of having to sit there for hours because until time was called, no one was allowed to leave the examination room.

She forced herself to read the multiple choice section slowly and carefully in order to kill the maximum amount of time before selecting answers at random from the choices offered. ('I ticked box B for everything,' Ronnie said later. 'I figured that way I'd have to get one or two right on the law of averages.') When she had completed the multiple choice questions Jo considered the remainder of the paper. She had half hoped for something on the reproduction of a rabbit because she could have made a stab at that. (The class had affected great interest in this particular topic since rabbit reproduction was the closest the syllabus ever came to any reference regarding sexual activity.) Disappointed by the examining board's lack of interest in rabbits, Jo revenged herself upon them by decorating her answer sheet with drawings of rabbits, one of whom she depicted in a white lab coat, wearing a pince nez and holding a test tube aloft in its paw.

Cow-Pig-Oh's chief henchman Miss Harkness, herself a science teacher, stood for some time alongside Jo's desk while she was putting the finishing touches to her lab rabbit. Jo knew perfectly well that Miss Harkness was there but she did not glance up or desist from her drawing. It gave her a pleasurable sense of victory to know that Miss Harkness could do absolutely nothing about it. She wasn't cheating or disrupting anyone else's work and Miss Harkness could not bawl her out. No… however hopping mad Miss Harkness might be, she could only watch in impotent silence. The thought of her being hopping mad inspired Jo to fill the final space on her answer sheet with a picture of a rabbit whose face bore a suspicious resemblance to Miss Harkness.

The clock on the wall told her that there was another whole hour to go. Another whole hour. Alex Dunston didn't take biology. In fact all three desks between herself and Nicky were empty. Nick appeared to be doing *something*. Possibly covering her blotting paper with slowly widening circles of ink. That was always good for whiling away a bit of time until the sheet – having absorbed as much liquid as it could take – turned from pale green to purplish blue and the ink began to leech out in a watery puddle underneath it.

Two rows away she could see Deborah Reed methodically colouring each of her finger nails with felt tip pen, using a different colour for each nail. Across the aisle Colleen Bell was staring into space. Joanne reconsidered her paper. The only area of her answer booklet which had been spared the lapine decoration was the first section where she had written her name, exam number and school. She toyed with the idea of writing a succinct message about the futility of forcing people into compulsory subjects that they neither wanted nor needed to learn, but eventually decided against.

The trouble with having an hour to fill was that it gave you a lot of thinking time and however much you tried to take an interest in the progress of Deborah's nails or to remember your answers from geography and wonder whether you had written tropical climate when you meant to put temperate, your thoughts invariably landed back on the thing which was worrying you most. In Joanne's case this was not her 'O' levels – although passing them was obviously important. It was the letter from Chesney's School of Art.

Her three best friends were in on the secret, but none of her other classmates, as she feared the possibility of gossip reaching multiple families and spreading out along the mysterious, unseen channels of communication wrought of workplaces and relationships until it reached her parents. She still had not breathed a word about the letter at home.

It was folded up and back inside the envelope in which it had arrived, addressed to Miss J. Embury care of the school and she had hidden it under a pile of old sketch books in the bottom drawer of her dressing table. She took it out each night and read it, just to make sure it was real.

Her father had already been getting on to her about finding a job, though he had half-accepted her protest that she wanted to concentrate on doing her best in the exams. (He had now decided that it had been all his own idea for Joanne to stay on and get some qualifications, so he could hardly find fault when she focussed on the task in question.) But soon the exams would be over. He wasn't likely to take the same line as Nicky's Mum, who had told Nicky to enjoy a few weeks break before she started looking for work.

The trouble was that Miss Burgoyne was not expecting her until a couple of days before the term started at Chesney's and that was not until the second week of September which was an age away. She couldn't go to live with Auntie Maggie the way Sonia had done, because Auntie Maggie had given up her house in Acocks Green and moved to Stockport, where she now lived with her old friend who had been widowed. Nor could she stay with Sonia and Mick because their flat was tiny and only had one bedroom and anyway Mick didn't like getting involved in family rows, Sonia had said. Miss Carling, the only person whose help and advice she might have sought, was off sick with shingles.

Jo had pretty much decided that the best thing to do would be to go along with what her father expected and start looking for a job. The snag with that was that jobs were so easy to get. There was no way you could hang out the process of looking for more than two or three weeks at most, but if she got a job she would only be there for a few weeks before she had to give in her notice, which she thought would probably make her employers pretty mad. Specially if they found out that she had never intended to stay in the first place. At least, Jo thought, if I do get a job my wages will pay my train fare down to London.

Chapter Seventy

1988

The nurse who called Sean's name took them to sit in a small ground floor room, where they awaited the arrival of the consultant in silence. Apart from the usual examination couch and allied paraphernalia there was nothing to look at. The window looked out across the hospital car park where a thin October breeze was playing tag with posses of dry brown leaves.

Becky desperately wanted to say something but she could think of nothing to say. She glanced across at Sean and he gave her a brief encouraging smile before becoming engrossed in the leaves and the parked cars again. He obviously could not think of anything to say either.

They seemed to have travelled a long way in a short time. It was a mere seven weeks since Sean had been referred to the dermatologist about his rash. While they were waiting for the dermatology appointment to come through he had discovered the lump. It wasn't a dramatic lump, not a grapefruit sized lump, not even golf ball sized lump. Just a pea. A large pea immediately below the surface. Innocent and innocuous, so small that it needed to be pointed out to the doctor before he could find it. But with its discovery things had started to move much faster. Their G.P. had telephoned the hospital who said they would send an appointment right away and when Sean was instructed to report to the hospital only four days later, a powdering of ice had settled on Becky's heart. No one got seen that urgently unless they thought it was something serious.

He had been listed for a lumpectomy. A simple procedure everyone kept saying and the lump might turn out to be nothing at all. But N.H.S. waiting lists did not evaporate before you for nothing at all. Lumps were sinister. All the bright smiles and optimistic words in the world could not alter that. And now they were awaiting the results of the biopsy. The very fact that they were going to hear the results from the consultant himself and not a mere underling seemed to Becky an omen of bad tidings.

As soon as the consultant walked into the room and shook their hands she knew. While he talked she felt the room start to spin, the way a room had spun once before when she was expecting Maddy. It was the only time in her life when she had fainted. She made a conscious effort to overcome the giddiness, sit still and concentrate on what the consultant was saying. As if from a long way off she heard Sean asking quietly, 'What is Hodgkin's Disease?' and then having received the consultant's reply, saying very calmly: 'So it's a kind of cancer then?'

'Well we don't like to use that word…'

After that came more explanations about the insidious creeping nature of the disease, how it tiptoed from one set of lymph nodes to the next, secretly travelling around your body while you remained blissfully unaware of it and put the series of minor illnesses which your immune system had failed to counter, down to a run of coincidence and bad luck. Becky looked sideways at Sean and saw that he was listening with interest. Concentrating. Applying himself as if to a logic problem. She wanted to reach out for his hand but she was afraid that if she touched him her emotions might take over. It was important to stay calm and listen.

'Is it curable?' Sean posed the question with a smile, as if the answer hardly mattered one way or the other.

The consultant was instantly reassuring. Treatment had advanced enormously. Twenty years ago pretty much everyone diagnosed with Hodgkin's had died whereas now the survival rates were very good… though of course it all depended on how far the disease had progressed. Catching it early – that was the key thing. Sean would need to have a full body scan in order to assess how far advanced his case was. After that they would look at treatment options. The scan would be arranged in a mere matter of days. The hospital had a new state of the art scanner and he would be among the first patients to use it.

'How are you feeling?' she asked, as soon as they were out of the consulting room and negotiating the maze of hospital corridors again.

'Well it's still a bit sore where they made that incision under my arm,' he said with an idiot grin.

'Don't be daft. I mean, how are you *feeling*?'

'To be absolutely honest not bad. A little bit as if it's someone else we're talking about. I mean I keep thinking that it can't be me. I'm never ill. I don't get ill. How about you?' He squeezed her hand. 'Are you holding up?'

'I feel sort of the same,' said Becky. 'As though it's not quite real. What do you think we should do about telling people?'

Sean hesitated. 'Just be open and up front I guess. It's not something to be ashamed of after all. We'd better tell people and then try to get on with life as normally as we can, I suppose. We'll have to be a bit careful what we say in front of Maddy, but luckily she's too young to understand very much about it.'

Sean had said it so casually but Becky found telling people very hard. The distress and discomfiture which friends could not quite manage to hide was a strain on her resolve not to get upset in public. Not that she could allow herself to get upset in private either, while Sean stayed so relentlessly cheerful and up beat.

People said such silly things. Well meaning but silly. 'Everything will be O.K.,' they said. She heard it so often that in the end it made her want to scream: 'You don't know that. How can any of us know?'

Then there was the refrain which became her particular pet hate. How Sean would be O.K. because he was a fighter who would not give in to cancer. It was a ridiculous affront to her logical mind. If cancers could be beaten by mere fighting spirit and strength of will, how was it that anyone ever needed medicines and drugs? Why did anyone ever die of cancer at all?

She went with him to the hospital for the body scan. She was not allowed into the actual room where the scanner was, but she sat beside him in the little waiting room while he drank a jug full of something which looked (and he assured her also tasted) like white emulsion paint. They had to wait a week for the results. It was a different consultant now because they had been transferred from the surgeon who had removed the original lump to a specialist in Hodgkin's Disease and allied disorders, whose name was Mr Gregory.

Mr Gregory explained things slowly and carefully. Hodgkin's Disease was sub-divided into four levels he told them. Sean had level three which was worse than level one or two but not so bad as level four. He had considered Sean's results and decided to attack the disease with chemotherapy. Initially, he said, he was putting Sean on a series of six treatments staged over a period of six months.

Becky listened with a kind of disbelief. Sub-division into four groups irrationally reminded her of being graded for French and maths with a place in group 3 not as good as being in groups 1 or 2... Sean thanked Doctor Gregory and accepted the sheaf of information they were being given to read. Since receiving the diagnosis Becky had already secretly read every medical reference book she could lay her hands on, but none of them could answer the really big question in her mind.

They read through all the latest information together when they got home. Sean immediately discarded the sheet giving details of a local support group. It smacked too much of being a victim, he said. He wanted to spend his time productively, not sit around exchanging symptoms. As far as it was possible to do so, he said, he wanted to carry on as normal.

And yet, Becky thought, we have already been sucked

in. We have become a part of that hospital world of half dressed people shuffling about in bedroom slippers, people I scarcely know stopping me in the off licence to ask how Sean is and friends all but bursting into tears at the sight of us. We have already become the kind of people who while away hours at a time reading last year's 'Country Living' or someone else's discarded newspaper, while we sit around in a series of waiting rooms. And this is just the beginning. Six months… initially…

The night before Sean's first scheduled dose of chemotherapy, he carefully collected together a Wilbur Smith book and some tapes for his walkman. They had already learned that serious illness and its treatment was like fighting a war: bursts of unpleasant activity interspersed with long interludes of boredom.

Late in the evening Becky made one more attempt to insist on accompanying him to the hospital but he was adamant that she should go to work instead. 'Everything as normal as possible.' That was his new motto. Becky tried not to believe that his real motive lay in safeguarding her earning power, because one day soon she might become the sole breadwinner.

At ten o'clock they retired to bed and made love with a frantic urgency. Outside the rain pattered softly against the house, leaving the windows streaked as if by thousands of tears.

Chapter Seventy-One

1973

Joanne saw no harm in ringing work and telling them she was sick on the day of her 'O' level results. Other people seemed to do it all the time and anyway she would be giving in her notice in a couple of days. She set out from home as if heading for work as usual but then diverted to Nicky's house, stopping to call work from a phone box along the way.

'You seemed all right yesterday,' her section head said doubtfully.

'It came on suddenly,' Joanne lied. 'I've got to go. My money's running out.'

They met Paula at the usual place and walked the last bit together, just as they had done on hundreds of previous mornings except that today Becky was missing. Becky, who was saving hard, had flatly dismissed the idea of taking a day off work, so they were going to collect her results and hand them over to her at cafe near her offices at lunch time.

On a normal school day the pavements would have

been teeming with girls, but today the streets seemed oddly empty as if everything had fallen asleep for the long summer holidays.

'I don't know whether I want to hurry up and get it over with or put off the awful moment,' said Paula.

'You will have done all right,' said Nicky. 'You always panic and then get perfectly good results in the end.'

For the auspicious errand of collecting G.C.E. examination results, pupils were allowed the singular honour of walking along the front drive and entering school via the front doors. Miss Pentland and Miss Hardiker were sitting at a table in the entrance hall, handing out the little cards which had the results written on them.

'I daren't look,' said Paula, taking hers and holding it against her chest.

'Can we have Rebecca Addison's results too please,' requested Nicky.

'Is she away on holiday?' Miss Pentland enquired as she sorted through the cards and selected the right one.

'No,' said Nicky. 'She's at work.'

'At work?' Miss Pentland looked puzzled.

'Yes,' said Nicky. 'She's got a job in an insurance office in Kings Heath.'

'But surely… she'll be coming back for 'A' levels at the start of term?'

'No,' said Nicky. 'She's not coming back.'

'Well she should be,' said Miss Pentland. 'With grades like these. I have to say that I assumed she would be joining my history class.'

Nicky looked down at the card Miss Pentland had handed to her. Forgetting their own results for a moment the others crowded in to read over her shoulder. Becky had achieved grade one passes in history, R.E. and English lit. All her other subjects were grade twos except biology which she had managed to pass with the lowest grade possible – a five.

'Crikey,' said Joanne. 'Those results are bloody fantastic.'

Miss Hardiker gave her a glassy look but at that moment both she and Miss Pentland were distracted by the arrival of a whole posse of VT, all nudging one another and pretending to be scared of asking for their results.

After admiring Becky's results they stood comparing notes about their own. Nicky had averaged grade threes and fours with the inevitable fail in biology. Paula had done a bit better with mainly twos and threes and the longed for grade one in English language, which may have been a reward for an essay which had run to ten sides. Like Becky she had managed to sneak under the wire with a low pass in biology. Jo's grade one in art was pleasing if no more than she expected of herself. She greeted her eight in biology – the lowest grade it was possible to get – with a wide grin. 'The Joint Matriculation Board just don't like rabbits,' she said.

As they were about to leave they met Adele coming into the building on her own. (Ronnie was on holiday in Bournemouth until Saturday.) 'Wait for me,' Adele pleaded. 'My heart's in my mouth.' But she emerged from the building a couple of minutes later, grinning broadly.

In spite of dire predictions from the staff throughout the year, alleging lack of effort and universal stupidity, it seemed that everyone had done well. The only real exception was Penny Lynch, who had registered several failures, achieving only grade sixes in geography, biology and maths. No one knew what to say to her. In spite of all that had been said beforehand, people did not fail things at Eleanor Vaux. It was not expected. It simply wasn't done. The dismal performance of Mrs Young's biology group was exceptional and even among them only a handful had actually missed out on a grade five.

At The Silver Grill in Kings Heath they indulged in a celebratory lunch of beef burger and chips while conveying all the morning's news to Becky.

'Miss Pentland said you should be taking 'A' levels with your results,' said Nicky.

'Easy for her to say,' Becky said through a mouthful of chips.

'I haven't heard of anyone else who's got three grade ones,' said Paula.

'What about Alex? I bet she has.'

'No she hasn't,' said Jo. 'We met Kay Fenton while we were waiting for the bus. You know what Kay's like… she knew *everybody's* results. She said Alex only got two grade ones. French was one of them of course… and Norma didn't get any grade ones at all.'

'Was history one of the things you would have taken if you had been staying on?' asked Nicky.

'I don't know,' said Becky. 'I hadn't really thought about it.'

In truth she knew exactly what she would have taken but talking about it was only a bitter reminder of how much more interesting 'A' levels would have been, in contrast to the way she had just spent her morning, filing fire insurance policies into numerical order. Like Joanne, Becky was about to hand in her notice. She had found a new job in town which paid the same but had the added benefit of luncheon vouchers. Luncheon vouchers meant having to spend less on food when she got her own place. Her starter box of groceries was now full to capacity and her savings account was growing steadily, if not quite as fast as she had originally hoped because she had not anticipated having to hand over quite such a large proportion of her wages in housekeeping money.

There had inevitably been an argument about this, during which Stan had informed her that when he first went out to work he had handed his weekly wage packet over to his mother unopened and she had handed him back some pocket money. His expectation was that Becky would do the same. Becky had faced him out, saying that she would not. She intended to give her mother housekeeping money of course, but she had no intention of handing the whole of her wages over in the way he suggested.

He had then subjected her to a long lecture about understanding the value of money. Having struggled to manage on pathetically inadequate amounts of money for years, denying herself break time crisps so that she could replace laddered tights, Becky thought that she had a pretty good idea of the value of money already but she bit her tongue.

Stan and her mother had debated for some time over how much of her wages Becky should be allowed to keep. She was only going to be earning thirteen pounds a week, but Stan's initial idea was that she should hand over ten pounds. Becky protested that their entire weekly shopping bill was never more than fifteen pounds and that she certainly didn't eat more than half the total amount of food coming into the house. Stan countered that there was also the electric to be considered and that ten pounds would still leave her with twice the amount of pocket money she had previously been used to. Her mother had demurred at this, saying that now she was working Becky would need extra things. She would need more clothes than she had done for school and she might make new friends and want to go out with them occasionally.

Stan muttered something about people junketing around enjoying themselves and leaving all the upstairs lights switched on, but he allowed himself to compromise at seven pounds – making it clear that he thought Becky should count herself lucky in the face of such munificent generosity.

Becky handed over her seven pounds a week without further argument, although she knew that it was double what any of the other office juniors gave their parents. When topics like this were discussed over lunchtime sandwiches she only listened and never joined in, fearing ridicule if she revealed to her colleagues that she gave just over half her weekly wages to her mother. As she listened enviously to their tales of Saturday shopping sprees in town and nights out in town, she wondered if she would ever be able to take part in life on the same footing as everyone else.

Chapter Seventy-Two

1973

'You can't just run away to London,' Sonia said.

'It's not really running away.'

'Whatever you call it, you can't just go off to London without a word,' Sonia insisted. 'Anyway it would look like running away. Think how upset Mum's going to be. And plus you're not landing me with the job of telling *him* where you've gone.'

The sisters had engaged in variations on this conversation throughout the summer until Jo was finally persuaded that she would have to tell her parents where she was going, because otherwise they would report her missing and as Sonia pointed out, if the police tracked her down to Miss Burgoyne's house there would be an embarrassing scene and perhaps her scholarship would be withdrawn. Having persuaded Jo that something must be said, Sonia had promised to be on hand when Jo finally spilled the beans.

Jo had settled on making the announcement on the

Sunday afternoon before she was due to travel to London. She had already secretly packed most of her things and put away the money to pay for a taxi to the station. Travelling by taxi was normally an unheard of indulgence but she could not possibly manage to carry everything as far as the bus stop and she did not know anyone with a car who would be available or willing to help.

On the appointed afternoon Jo had helped her mother to wash up after lunch while she nervously awaited Sonia's arrival: conscious of a nasty feeling that the roast lamb, peas, roast and mashed potatoes, onion sauce, gravy, treacle turnover and custard might be about to reappear at any moment. When the washing up was finished and she could find nothing further to detain her in the kitchen, she followed her mother into the living room.

Her father was half dozing in his chair. After 'Star Soccer' had finished he'd turned the volume down, so that the old Deanna Durbin musical which followed the football was scarcely audible. Mrs Embury, who quite liked Deanna Durbin, pretended to herself that she could hear it well enough and got on with the sweater she was knitting. Brian was out somewhere, probably playing football with his friends, his brief summer flirtation with cricket having come to an end the moment the teams kicked off in the Charity Shield. Although he had been at a rugby playing grammar school for two years now, Brian's love affair with football was undiminished and his bedroom walls were covered with pictures of Villa players. He had stuck a big one of Brian Little (given away free with 'The Sports Argus') in his bedroom window until his mother had told him to take it down.

'What will the neighbours think?'

Brian's response – 'That I'm a Villa supporter,' had earned him a clip round the ear and a sharp, 'Don't be so damned cheeky to your mother.'

Joanne wished that Sonia would hurry up. She perched on the edge of the sofa and flicked through 'The Sunday Mercury', not actually reading it. Finally she heard Sonia coming in at the front door. Sonia greeted her mother with the usual peck on the cheek, saying that she had decided to drop in and yes please she would love a cup of tea. She looked so casual and ordinary that Joanne found herself half wondering if Sonia had forgotten what it was that had brought her there. Then it occurred to her that a lifetime of pretending that everything was normal, hiding what you really thought and papering over the cracks, turned you into a consummate actress by the time you got to twenty two.

As soon as Sonia had been given her tea in the tangerine crock mug with the purple flowers all round it, Joanne slipped upstairs to retrieve the letter. She took it out of the envelope in which it had been hiding for so long and returned to the sitting room.

'Mum and Dad,' she said. 'I've got something to show you. I've been given a scholarship to study 'A' levels, so that I can carry on with my painting and... and... go on to university.'

She shoved the letter at her mother who unfolded it and began to read. Joanne sat down alongside Sonia on the sofa.

'What are you talking about?' her father demanded. 'You're working now aren't you?'

‘I’m going to give it up,’ said Joanne, who had actually worked the last day of her notice on Friday.

‘Don’t talk so bleeding stupid,’ said her father. ‘Here – give me that letter,’ he demanded, extending an imperious hand in his wife’s direction.

As Mrs Embury handed him the letter, she was looking not at him but at Joanne. ‘This is in London?’ It was a question, not a statement.

‘That’s right. All my fees are being taken care of and they’re paying for me to lodge in London with a woman called Miss Burgoyne, who is something to do with the Trust that are paying for it all.’

‘Aren’t you proud of her?’ Sonia attempted to thrust a shaft of sunlight between the gathering storm clouds.

Her father had been reading the letter in silence. Now he glared at her over the top of it. ‘What’s the idea of going in for a scholarship behind our backs?’

‘I didn’t...’ Joanne began.

‘Oh yes you did. You never said a word to me or your mother about it. This letter’s dated last May. It didn’t take three months to get here. Where’s it been since then, eh?’

Sonia said, ‘She didn’t apply Dad. It was something the school put her in for.’

‘Don’t try that line with me. I see you know all about it. I might have known you’d be in on it. Anyway...’ he returned his attention to Joanne, ‘you’re not going so you can just forget all about it.’

‘Why shouldn’t she go Dad?’ asked Sonia. ‘She’s won her place. It’s not costing you anything. It’s a great opportunity.’

‘A great opportunity to get mixed up in sex and drugs and goodness knows what. I’m not letting any daughter of mine go off down to London. She can stay here where I can keep an eye on her.' He held the letter up level with his chin and tore it into small pieces, letting them flutter unchecked onto his trousers and the carpet around his feet. 'Finished,' he said. 'That's the end of it.'

Joanne winced at the fate of her precious letter, but the sight of its destruction helped her to find her voice. 'I don't need the letter,' she said. 'You had no right to tear it up but it doesn't matter. It's not some sort of admission ticket. Tearing it up doesn't change the fact that I've got a place... and I'm going to take it.'

'Weren't you listening?' her father demanded. 'I've already told you. You're not going.'

'I *am* going.' Joanne spoke with steady determination. 'I've got my place and I've got somewhere to live. It's all sorted out.'

'Don't talk back to your father like that,' Mrs Embury put in. 'You're only sixteen you know...'

'Exactly,' her husband shouted triumphantly. 'You're sixteen years old. You're a minor. You can't just go off and live in London without my permission. If you go I'll fetch you back. I'll come and fetch you back myself and I'll have the police on anyone who tries to stop me. There's laws, you know. I'll have this Burgin woman. She can't keep you in London against my say so.'

'For crying out loud Dad!' exclaimed Sonia. 'What is wrong with you? Can't you see this is Jo's big chance? Do you want to ruin her life or what?'

'You keep out of this and stop talking such bloody rubbish,' he shouted. 'She's not going to London and that's final!'

Joanne stood up. In a voice which shook she said: 'I hoped you'd be pleased for me but I should have known better. I'm sorry you don't trust me not to get into sex and drugs while I'm in London. If you think that's what I'm like then you're wrong. Actually you're wrong about a lot of things. Principally about my future. I'm going to study and I'm going to have a career involving art. I hope one day that you'll be proud of what I've done. I *am* going to take up my place at art school. My things are all packed and I'm going tomorrow.'

Her father was on his feet too. 'We'll see about that,' he said and grabbed her wrist. Joanne looked down fearfully. His hand completely encircled the fine narrow bones and she could feel the power of his grip. It was her right wrist and she was right handed. She thought how horribly easily he could snap it.

'Please let go,' she said quietly. 'You're hurting me.'

Out of the corner of her eye she was conscious that Sonia had fled, quick as a cat into the kitchen. Her mother began to wail something about everyone calming down and not doing anything silly.

Jo looked up directly into her father's face, something she rarely ever did. There was a pale tracery of red showing under his skin and across the whites of his eyes. It was always more pronounced when he had been drinking or was angry, one of which conditions generally followed hard upon the heels of the other. Red for danger. 'Let go,' she repeated.

He was blocking her view of the kitchen door so she didn't see Sonia re-appear, but she heard her say, 'Let her go Dad or I swear I'll do for you.'

Taken by surprise he relaxed his grip and Joanne sprang away into the corner of the room from where she had a clear view of Sonia, who was standing white and frightened in the kitchen doorway holding a knife. Jo recognised it as the one Mrs Embury had used earlier to carve the lamb.

'You put that knife down,' her father snarled. 'Or I'll hurt you my girl.'

'Maybe you will,' said Sonia. 'But I'll hurt you too. Mum, get the police on the phone and tell them he's threatening us. Go on.'

'You stay where you are.' Mr Embury's words were directed at his wife but he did not look her way as he spoke, evidently deeming it politic to keep most of his attention on Sonia. 'Put that knife down,' he commanded. 'Have you gone bleeding barmy?'

'No,' said Sonia. 'I've just come to my senses. If you do anything to stop our Joanne, I'll take this knife to you and what's more if I ever hear you've gone down to London causing trouble for her, or laid a finger on Mum or our Bri ever again, I'll go down the pub… I'll go round all the pubs in fact and I'll tell every landlord and every bar fly and drinking pal and every barmaid you imagine's got her eye on you, that you're a wife beater and a bully. What do you think they'll think of that?'

There was a short silence. The air prickled with tension. Then Mr Embury made his move. Jo saw Sonia sidestep in expectation of an attack but he did not go for Sonia. He went back to his chair where he paused to flick a couple of the remnants of Joanne's letter out of his way before sitting down.

'You're round the bleeding bend the lot of you,' he said.

'Your mother's crackers, so it's no wonder the pair of you have turned out the way you have. You get off to London if you want to – but don't get bringing any trouble home here. I wash my hands of you.' He picked up 'The News of the World' and opened it with a dismissive shake, as if to demonstrate his contempt for them all.

'Get your things together Jo,' Sonia instructed. 'I'll ring for a taxi and you can stay the night at ours.'

'What about your Mick?' Joanne asked, as they climbed the stairs together.

'What about him?' said Sonia 'It's my flat too and if I want my sister to stay for one night then she shall. I've had enough of being pushed around.'

While they were cramming the last of Joanne's things into a carrier bag, their mother joined them in her bedroom.

'Oh Joanne,' she said. 'I wish you weren't going off like this.'

'So do I,' said Joanne.

Which was true, she thought sadly. There was no triumph in it. No feeling that she had got what she wanted or was at the start of a great adventure, because deep down what she really wanted was to be getting into the train tomorrow and waving goodbye to her smiling family, while they stood on the platform blowing her kisses and wishing her good luck.

Chapter Seventy-Three

1988

Nicky woke up gradually. She had been deep asleep. Dreaming. It must have been something to do with school because Paula had been there and Jo. In fact for a confused moment she had imagined that she could hear Becka laughing, but when she listened properly all she could hear was the wind in the big trees on the other side of the lane and Rob snoring rhythmically beside her. A lot of wives complained about their husband's snoring but when Rob snored it was a steady peaceful sound which quite often sent her to sleep.

Whatever the dream had been about it was completely gone and now that she was fully awake she became conscious of several things, the most important of which were that firstly she appeared to be sleeping in a puddle and secondly there was a low familiar pain in her back, familiar both because she somehow felt that she had been aware of it in her dream, but also because she recognised it from past experience and knew what it meant.

‘Rob…’ she began quietly, but a different sort of pain interrupted her. It wasn’t bad, she reassured herself, but it meant not saying anything for a few seconds until it had passed.

‘Rob…’ She had to shake his shoulder. ‘Rob. The baby’s coming.’

Once awake he became marginally more useful. ‘Are you sure?’

By way of an answer Nicky raised the duvet so that he could see the mess her breaking waters had made of the sheets.

‘O.K. Don’t worry. I’ll go straight down and ring for an ambulance.’

Nicky nodded. She had to nod because there was another contraction coming. Rob put off the trip downstairs and held her hand instead.

‘How long between contractions?’ he asked.

‘I don’t know. Not long. Go and ring.’

He still didn’t possess a dressing gown so he put on his jeans before going downstairs. An entirely unnecessary operation in Nicky’s view, given that they lived in the middle of nowhere and all the curtains were drawn anyway.

It had got to be an ambulance ride this time, because Rob would have to stay at the cottage with Jonathan. She would have liked Rob with her, because she thought the hospital staff were less inclined to bully you if your husband was on hand to stick his oar in, but there was no one else to have Jonathan at short notice so it couldn’t be helped.

Her principal emotion at finding herself in labour was one of surprise. Jonathan had been ten days late so they had sort of assumed that the current pregnancy would run a similar course, but instead here she was going into labour (in a rather purposeful, determined fashion – ouch that one was stronger) two whole days before the date she was due. She had only seen the midwife a couple of days ago and she hadn't indicated that she thought the birth was imminent. With Jonathan they had been telling her for what seemed like weeks beforehand that everything was poised for action and she could expect to have him any day.

It's all guesswork, she thought. For all the emphasis on high-tech, childbirth was still a bit of a mystery. Women had been giving birth for thousands of years and most of them had managed pretty well without scans and foetal heart monitors and women being wired up like so many Frankenstein monsters all round the delivery wards. Except of course that sometimes things went wrong ... she mustn't think about that. Oh, owww... that was bad... she must relax and try not to think about things going wrong because that made the contractions seem far worse.

Rob's distinctive approach sounded on the stairs, making much more noise than usual as he clambered up to rejoin her as fast as he could. Fortunately Jonathan had inherited his father's ability to sleep through an earthquake.

'I want to push,' she gasped, shoving the quilt to one side. 'Can you have a look and see what's happening?'

Rob obliged. 'I think it's the top of the baby's head,' he said, with a substantial degree of wonder. 'Can you hold on until the ambulance gets here?' Then seeing her expression. 'No, no, of course not. Well don't worry. We'll manage.'

He tried to remember everything about last time. The whole business was a blur of people in green coveralls and Nicky sobbing with effort then crying with joy. What should he do? Hold her hand? No... no... rub her back between contractions? Tell her she was doing really well. Encouragement, that was the ticket.

'You're doing really well,' he said. 'The ambulance will be here soon... but you're managing fine anyway. That's right... that's good.' He wondered about returning downstairs to seek advice on the phone, but that would mean leaving her. 'You're doing great,' he said again. 'Just tell me if there's anything you want me to do.'

Nicky, very red faced, managed in spite of everything the ghost of a smile. 'Get ready to catch the baby,' she said.

The ambulance crew arrived in time to cut the cord. All parties – except perhaps Baby Rose whose face was rather scrumpled and sulky – were looking very pleased with themselves. Nicky adamantly refused to go into hospital. 'I'm fine and the baby's fine,' she said. 'Someone can come and check us out tomorrow and once Rob's got this bed stripped and changed I can get back in it.'

When the ambulance crew eventually departed, Nicky said, 'You know what? I've got a feeling they think we did it on purpose. I expect they think we're one of those funny, back to nature couples, who planned to have a D.I.Y. home delivery all along. We're probably going to get a right telling off from the midwife and Doctor Sykes.'

'Well I did think you should have gone in the ambulance,' Rob began.

'Rubbish,' said Nicky. 'Home is obviously where we belong. Oh look... she's opening her eyes.'

Chapter Seventy-Four

1988

Jo was in a sombre mood. The good news that Nicky and Rob had a daughter was uneasily tempered by that saying of her mother's that a birth always brings on a death. For a woman born in the twentieth century her mother had been remarkably superstitious and although Jo had tried to expunge these fetishes and fallacies from her adult thinking, old habits died hard so that when she first heard the news about Sean she could not help but remember her mother's belief that deaths always came in threes. First there had been Nell Burgoyne, then her Auntie Mary, which according to her mother's theory meant that she was sure to hear of the death of some other close acquaintance before very long. As her mother would have said, those other two would be waiting on a third to keep them company. (A sinister phrase which had helped to inspire a painting of which she was rather proud).

Since first hearing of Sean's illness, Jo had made a point of keeping in regular touch with Becky by the phone. In spite of these fancifully gloomy portents of the Grim

Reaper's proximity, news bulletins from Becky had initially been very hopeful. The doctors said that Sean was young and strong and extremely fit, all of which stood him in good stead to make a full recovery. And although the first lot of chemotherapy had made him very ill (he had joked about the cure being worse than the disease) the medics and therefore Becky too, had still seemed optimistic.

The picture had darkened since those early days. Lately, although Becky was still attempting to sound cheerful when they talked, Jo was not fooled. She had known Becky long enough to read between the lines. Moreover she had called in on a recent visit to Birmingham and observed for herself the way all that health and strength and vitality which she associated with Sean had already leaked away. The changes wrought by the drugs might not have been obvious to everyone but to Jo – the trained observer – they were dramatic and frightening. Even the shape of his face seemed to be different: puffy and permanently flushed as if he had just come in from a run, although the poor guy could hardly make it unaided up the stairs.

This evening when she had spoken to Becky on the telephone, the update seemed even more depressing. After the latest session of treatment Sean's immune system had taken such a knock that he was currently hospitalised. Becky was hopeful that he would be allowed out for Christmas but until his blood counts improved, she said, the hospital couldn't contemplate another dose of chemo. 'It's a mixed blessing, poor love,' Becky said. 'On the one hand the chemo makes him feel so rough that's he sort of glad of a respite, but on the other it drags out the timescale and leaves him with another lot still to get through.'

It had been very hard to find something upbeat to say in the face of such tidings and as if talking with Becka had not been depressing enough, when Ant switched on the evening news they heard that a jumbo jet had crashed near a place called Lockerbie and everyone on board was believed to be dead.

'I'm going to pop outside for a breath of fresh air,' Jo said, after the news had finished.

'You're mad,' Ant responded. 'It's freezing out there.'

She left Ant in the sitting room, watching a trailer which was plugging the Christmas television schedules. As she fetched her boots from the kitchen Jo could hear the trilling festive muzak, followed by clips from the forthcoming shows which she already knew by heart even though they did not watch a lot of television. The British Broadcasting Corporation doing its bit to get the nation into a cheery mood.

She grabbed a warm jacket from the row of pegs alongside the door, dragged it on and thrust her hands into the pockets without bothering to fasten it up properly, heading out of the back door almost at a run. When she rounded the corner of the house she could see the lights on Hugh and Mary's Christmas tree, which stood in the bay window of Holme Lea. Hugh and Mary were their nearest neighbours and had become some of their closest friends. Hugh was a mine of information about the local area. He knew all the best walks and exactly the place to go if you wanted to see a dipper or hear a woodpecker, while Mary was full of solid common sense and what she did not know about cooking was not worth knowing.

After looking directly at the tree lights it took a minute

or two to adjust her eyes for the stars. The longer she could bear to stand out there, stamping her feet and emitting clouds of steamy breath, the more pinpricks of light she would be able to see. A share in these celestial treasures could be anyone's in exchange for no more than patience on a clear night like this, with nary a street light for miles. The sky was carpeted with stars. It was breathtaking.

Then she saw that one of the lights was moving. It was an aeroplane, very high up, tracking its way across the cold winter sky. It reminded her of the crashed plane which was nothing but a cargo of misery for hundreds of people now. Every lost life would have been precious to someone and the whole thing was made worse somehow by the tinsel, the schmaltzy sentimentality, the inescapable festivities of the season.

Now she came to think about it she had never really liked Christmas.

Chapter Seventy-Five

1973

Although instructed by Nell Burgoyne to make herself at home, Joanne was navigating the big house in Wimbledon on tiptoe. She had arrived at Ivydene three days before. The very fact that the house had a name – which people used as if they were referring to a person, Ivy Dean, was outside the ordinary run of her experience. She had never known anyone who lived in a name rather than a number. Miss Burgoyne's directive, 'call me Nell,' was equally unsettling. Jo thought of Miss Burgoyne as a figure on a par with teachers and other grown-ups. Someone she hardly knew. She was not accustomed to dealing with adults who were so much older than herself on first name terms.

As for Ivydene, it did not seem like a house where ordinary people lived at all. It was enormous in comparison with the house where she had always lived, completely detached from the surrounding houses, with strips of garden running down both sides and for some distance at the rear. It had both cellars and attics. The sheer size of her dwelling, coupled with Miss Burgoyne's loud plummy voice, meant that she must be rich and therefore posh and Joanne had been brought up to regard posh people with suspicion. Posh people looked down on the likes of families such as the Emburys and tried to catch them out. You had to be on your guard all the time and try not to put a foot wrong.

If any further confirmation of Miss Burgoyne's poshness were needed, it came in the form of Clara who seemed to be a sort of ancient family retainer. Clara lived in a bed sitting room on the first floor, did all the cooking and occasionally flicked a duster about. Miss Burgoyne had taken Joanne into the kitchen to meet Clara within half an hour of her arrival and since Clara spoke with a disconcerting foreign accent, Joanne had struggled to understand her which was embarrassing and led to misunderstandings.

It would be several weeks before Joanne discovered that Clara's initial reaction on meeting anyone was to shyly withdraw, regressing into a semi-incomprehensible accent which would gradually disappear once Clara and the newcomer had become more confidently acquainted, thereby making perfectly intelligible conversation possible.

Clara always cooked enormous quantities of food in expectation of company. In the event that fewer than six or eight people sat down to dinner, the remainder would be spooned into waxed cardboard containers and placed in the chest freezer (an appliance which Joanne had never seen in a domestic setting before). Miss Burgoyne had informed her that first day that the freezer had been purchased as a remedy against waste, because Clara was distressed by the thought of throwing food away and lived in perpetual fear of hard winters and shortages. As Jo would later discover, although the theory of the freezer was splendid, the practice was rather less so because Clara, who was deeply suspicious of consuming food which had been frozen, cooked something fresh every day and never drew on the stocks in the freezer at all, so that after a few months of use the chest freezer was full. In order to maintain the system without upsetting Clara, Nell Burgoyne regularly removed frozen food and pressed it on departing guests and acquaintances when Clara was not around and in extremis even sent Jo to deposit the odd carrier bag full in the rubbish skip at the back of the shops in Wimbledon village. These subterfuges ensured that there was always enough space for Clara to consign leftovers to her bottomless store chest, against theoretical hard times to come. Of course Jo knew none of this in the initial days after her arrival.

On the first day of Jo's stay in London, Nell Burgoyne had explained that she had a number of what she called 'engagements' which would entail her being out for most of the next few days, so with the term yet to start Jo was left to her own devices. She found her way to Wimbledon Common (in a falsely cheerful letter to her friends she wrote that she had not spotted any Wombles) and she also walked past the gates of the All England Club which she discovered on peeking in looked just as it did on the telly. (She put that in her letter too. Paula had a bit of a thing about a young Swedish player called Bjorn Borg so Jo knew they would be interested.)

She also ventured into the garden at the back of Ivydene, which was rather neglected except for some carefully tended pots of herbs near the kitchen door. Blackbirds and robins bustled about and the birdsong was sufficiently loud that if you closed your eyes it gave the illusion of being out in the country.

Inside the house she browsed enthusiastically among the books. Miss Burgoyne had made a point of telling her to borrow anything she wanted, so she chose a book full of arresting illustrations called 'The Pre-Raphaelite World' which she took up to her bedroom. On opening a page at random she was startled to be confronted with a picture she knew well, which had hung for as long as she could remember on the stairs of the museum and art gallery in town. From the caption she discovered that it was quite a famous painting called 'The Last of England' by someone called Ford Madox Brown.

Miss Carling had taken them there a couple of times and Jo and her friends had often gone in there of their own volition to mooch around the galleries on Saturday afternoons – not least because admission was free. Now she found herself wishing that she had paid a bit more attention to the paintings. She had probably walked past 'The Last of England' a hundred times without ever taking very much notice of it, not even registering what it was called and now here it was, important enough to be mentioned in a book while she, a supposedly serious student of art, knew nothing about it at all.

It was just the sort of thing she was afraid she might get asked about at the meal table. She had only eaten three dinners at Ivydene so far and there had been visitors present on every occasion – all of them alarming people, holding conversations about things she did not fully understand – the sort of people she imagined were perfectly likely to turn to her and say something like, 'You're from Birmingham aren't you? What do you think about 'The Last of England'?' And she wouldn't know how to reply. So she'd sat with her eyes on her plate, perpetually in fear that her ignorance be ridiculed or her table manners found wanting.

On the first evening a man (called Hector of all things) who had a bristly beard and paint on the sleeve of his jacket, had asked her what mediums she preferred to work in. The query had thrown her into a panic because Joanne could only associate the word medium with the séances her mother had sometimes attended secretly with Auntie Pat and Auntie Maggie, to see if they could get a message from the Other Side. Then the man Hector had babbled on about acrylics, which until then Jo had not realised was a type of paint used by artists as well as something printed on the labels of clothes. Art 'O' level at Eleanor Vaux had been no preparation for anything like this.

I can't cope, she thought. It's all a huge mistake. I don't belong here with people like this. I'm too ignorant and stupid… a dwarf trying to keep pace with giants. Several large tears plopped onto the serious faces in 'The Last of England'. She scrubbed the sleeve of her cheesecloth shirt across the picture, hastily shutting the book for fear of damaging it. Nell Burgoyne chose this moment to rap sharply on the outer panels of the bedroom door calling: 'May I come in?'

'Yes,' said Jo, who would never have dreamed of asking Miss Burgoyne to wait a moment in her own house and thereby forfeited the opportunity to take a minute to compose herself. With no hankie in reach there was no time to do more than give her face a cursory wipe on her sleeve.

She attempted a smile of welcome but Nell Burgoyne was not fooled.

'I've been sent by Clara to order you downstairs for some cake. She's made sachertorte, which I can assure you is well worth coming down for. Now then,' she flopped down hard next to Joanne on the bed, making it bounce like a trampoline. 'What's this? A touch of homesickness?'

'No,' Jo shook her head, looking confused and uncomfortable. 'I don't want to go home.'

Her hostess, perhaps remembering something of what Miss Carling had told her, nodded thoughtfully. 'Something else then. Can you tell me about it?'

Jo took a deep breath. She never normally confided in anyone, but there was something in Nell Burgoyne's eyes which compelled her. 'I don't belong here,' she blurted out. 'I haven't even started at the art school yet and I'm already out of my depth. People talk about things here that I've never even heard of.'

'But my dear Jo that's what you've come here for. The opportunity to learn. If you knew everything already you wouldn't need to go to school.'

Although this seemed reasonable it did not really go far enough. 'It's not just that,' Jo said, wondering how she could ever get the point across to someone so rich and self assured and clever as Miss Burgoyne, who had probably never experienced a moment of doubt or uncertainty in her whole life. 'I don't fit in here. I don't fit in at home either, if it comes to that. I'm not like other people – in all sorts of ways – I don't really fit in anywhere.'

'But my dear girl…' Nell Burgoyne's normally ringing voice was muted. 'Of course you don't. Interesting gifted people are always misfits. Do you suppose Leonardo or Vincent fitted in?' (Miss Burgoyne always referred to Leonardo Da Vinci and Vincent Van Gogh as if speaking of personal friends.) 'Of course they didn't. Only the boring common or garden people fit in. Anyone with talent or imagination or the power to think for themselves always feels they are an outsider, at odds with the common herd of humanity. It's what sets them apart and makes them interesting, but it's also a burden to bear… especially when we are young and feel that it would just be so much nicer and easier to fit in and be like everyone else.'

Jo regarded her with considerable surprise.

'I've been a misfit all my life,' Nell Burgoyne continued cheerfully, much in the way that other grand old ladies might confess to having always voted Tory. 'No mother, a thoroughly eccentric father, brought up by a succession of governesses, most of them chosen for their looks rather than their methods. I always suspected that because I had the looks of a horse my father felt he had to compensate by bringing pretty women into the house on aesthetic grounds. I've never fitted in anywhere I can assure you. The thing is that in the end you have to be true to yourself. Don't be ashamed to be yourself. It's what people want you know, in the long run. The genuine article… not a fake or a sham.'

Jo could only regard her with wonder before nodding slowly as if in response to the revelation of some great new idea.

'Come downstairs and have some of Clara's cake. Clara's sense of belonging is only derived from believing that we need her to feed us. She survived the Warsaw ghetto you know, so when she hoards things or sometimes behaves a little oddly we must make allowances. She plays the piano like an angel when she thinks no one is listening.' Seeing Jo's look of surprise she added, 'Never underestimate anyone my dear. All of mankind is capable of surprising one.'

Chapter Seventy-Six

1989

Children were remarkably resilient, Becky thought. Madeline was only three but she seemed to cope better than any of them with the changes in domestic routine. She had accepted with surprising poise and dignity, the news that because Daddy was ill he would not be able to come to her birthday party and would have to stay upstairs instead, then watch it all afterwards on the video being shot by Uncle James.

'Because Daddy gets tired,' Madeline said nodding wisely, as if these arrangements were no more than what any sensible person would have expected.

'Yes,' said Becky. 'Daddy is very tired today.' It was no use trying to explain to Madeline that Sean must also be protected from all the innocent little germs which were liable to arrive with a dozen little imps from play group.

Becky had paid Cherie, their nanny, to come in for the day of the party and Sean's brother James and his wife Jill were also on hand to help. All the same it was a relief to see the last of Madeline's friends depart, clutching their party loot bags filled with assorted sweets, a plastic whistle and a slice of the jammy, sticky iced sponge cake, wrapped in a paper napkin with My Little Pony on it.

Sean's mother had baked and iced the birthday cake. Her own mother had advised against a party. 'You're trying to do too much,' she said, but Becky knew that the party must go ahead for all their sakes, even if her internal elastic band was stretching thinner and thinner with every passing day.

She did her best to hide it but she became very angry with her mother at moments like these. Could she not see how much worse Sean would feel if Maddy didn't have a party? Or what a bitter blow it would be to a three year old if the long promised rituals of musical bumps and blowing out the candles had failed to materialise?

Of course she can't, Becky thought angrily. She never sees any point of view but her own. When told of Sean's illness her mother's first reaction had been floods of tears, prompted not by the predicament of Sean and Becky but by memories of the illness and loss of the men in her own life. She inevitably saw herself as a needy recipient of sympathy, Becky thought, rather than someone who might be expected to give it.

On receiving her mother's advice to abandon the birthday party, Becky had been sorely tempted to let fly. The urge to have everything out with her mother was getting ever stronger, but on another level she knew that she could not cope with such a monumental confrontation at the moment. She must not let herself go or the elastic band would snap.

At least Sean's family had been supportive. James and Jill organised their lives around helping out and Win let it be known that she was entirely at their beck and call whenever required. She had given Sean a rosary. It had been specially blessed she said, brought back by a member of her church who had been on a pilgrimage to Lourdes. Sean had promised to keep it with him. He carried it in his pocket and had it on his bedside cabinet during hospital stays. Becky understood that he was only indulging his mother and anyway what harm could it do?

The fourth session of chemotherapy had gone better than the third one but even so she could see that he was weaker. Outwardly most people scarcely saw a change. His hair was only a little bit thinner (the notion that chemotherapy automatically made everyone's hair fall out had turned out to be a myth). His face was sometimes flushed and puffy thanks to the steroids, but his smile was as bright as ever. Those were the things that other people saw.

In the meantime his life had become a strange half way house between illness and the real world. Normal everyday things seemed to be more and more of an effort. He slept for short bursts then often stayed awake all night, listening to the radio downstairs, using an earpiece so that he would not disturb the rest of the household. Unable to concentrate on books or newspapers anymore, he absorbed information via the airwaves. There seemed to be nothing he did not know about, from the political situations in distant countries to the latest advice issued on 'Farming Today'.

'You've become the Trivia King,' said Becky. 'When you get better you'll be in constant demand for pub quiz teams.'

Occasionally, though not very often, their conversation turned to more serious matters. On the day before the party Sean had suggested rather hesitantly that in the event of his dying it would please his mother to have a proper requiem mass.

'Not that it's going to come to that,' Becky said. 'But if that's what you want then of course, that's what we'd do.'

It was then that Sean had told her he sometimes felt he was drawing strength from the rosary beads. 'It's probably just a faith healing thing,' he said, trying to weigh up her reaction.

'Good,' said Becky quickly. 'That's good. Anything that works is good. It doesn't matter what it is or why. And you don't have to sound so damned apologetic.'

Sean grinned sheepishly. 'I thought you'd be saying, "once a Catholic"...'

Later she had reflected on how strangely people's minds worked. You might have expected Sean to turn further from his God... to rage against Heaven and say 'why me'? Instead he had swallowed the pill whole, accepted it with a calm and uncomplaining shrug. 'Stuff happens,' he said. 'It's no use being bitter. It won't help or change anything.' Several times he had said that he could not wish it away so why waste time trying to. Once when he and Becky were sitting alone, he had said that maybe there was a purpose in it. Maybe by him having this illness someone else was being spared. He had looked at the photo of Maddy when he said that, the one where she was sitting on a white fluffy photographer's rug, taken when she was coming up to her second Christmas.

Becky had not said anything to that. She could see how

it might help someone in his position to endure what he was going through if he could hold onto the idea that it was all part of some greater purpose, even entertain the notion that by his own suffering he was saving someone else.

In the meantime, she thought, if she could do anything... anything to get him cured she would do it. As for belief in God, well if He would make Sean better here and now then she would willingly dedicate her whole life to believing in Him. But God didn't do bargains, Win said. It did not work like that. And how am I supposed to believe in a loving God, Becky asked herself, when I'm faced with losing the one thing that's made me happier than I've ever been, after only having him for four years?

Chapter Seventy-Seven

1974

'She'll soon be back,' Stan said to the empty living room. These youngsters didn't know when they were onto a good thing. It was ridiculous, Rebecca imagining that she could manage a place of her own on her wages. She would soon get tired of living in one room in Moseley. That wouldn't suit her hoity toity ideas one little bit.

'You will come back and see me won't you?' Her mother watched tearfully as Becky struggled past with a hefty box labelled *Old School Books.*

'Of course I will,' Becky said, trying to partially balance the box on one upraised knee while she struggled to open the front door, which of course her mother made no attempt to help her with.

Chris was waiting patiently outside, tapping his fingers on the steering wheel of his car in time to the Allman Brothers track which was playing on the little battery operated cassette tape which he kept on the floor of the passenger side. The one really big advantage of going out with Chris was that he owned a Ford Anglia in two tone grey and rust.

'Is there much more?' he asked.

'Only another couple of things,' said Becky. 'I won't be long.'

Her mother met her as she re-entered the house, beckoning conspiratorially. Becky followed her into the kitchen. 'Here,' said her mother, reaching down the old tea caddy and opening it. 'Take this... just to help you out a bit.' She pushed a twenty pound note at Becky's hand.

Becky hesitated. The box of misappropriated groceries pricked her conscience.

'Go on,' her mother urged. 'You never know when you might need it. I don't know how you're going to manage as it is.'

'Thanks.' Becky stuffed the note deep into the pocket of her jeans.

'Don't let on to him.' Her mother indicated the direction of the living room with a quick sideways tilt of her head.

'No of course not,' Becky said.

'You're not in any sort of trouble are you?'

'No! Of course I'm not.'

'You're not just going off on your own so's you can sleep with that boy? That's what Stan thinks you know.'

Becky reddened. 'Well Stan's got a dirty mind then hasn't he? Anyway I should think he'll be glad to see the back of me. He's always moaned enough about me.'

'Now Becky, that's not fair.' Her mother's tone developed a whining note. 'It was me that suffered... always caught in the middle between the two of you...'

I haven't got time to listen to this, Becky thought. 'I'm

sorry Mum,' she said briskly. 'I'll have to get going. I can't expect Chris to wait out there all day.'

When she descended the stairs with the final load she heard her mother sobbing dramatically in the kitchen. She knew that she was intended to hear but she pretended not to.

At least when they got to the other end Chris was able to help her upstairs with her various bags and boxes. He would have given her more help at the point of departure, but one of Stan's embargos covered friends being allowed to go upstairs. Not that there was anything exciting or different about upstairs, but it was just one of those things that was not permitted and Stan's rules were not to be relaxed even if there had been a baby elephant to be transported out to the car.

Having assisted in the deposition of all her worldly goods Chris seemed inclined to hang around, but Becky made it clear that he was not required by saying that he could pick her up at half seven. She was starting to get bored with Chris, in addition to which his hints that he would like to take things further were going to be much harder to deflect now that she had got her own place which they could go back to at any time, with no possible interference from parents.

It did not take very long to organise her possessions. It was not as if there was very much scope. It was a small room with a single bed up against the wall, a sort of kitchen cupboard affair with sliding doors on the wall above the bed, a single wardrobe and a chest of drawers with a splotchy mirror in front of the sash window which looked out onto the street. The good part about it was the price. The landlord was letting her have it for seven pounds a week. The room she had originally enquired after was bigger but someone had already taken it by the time she rang up – which was lucky because that had been eight pounds a week. The extra pound made a significant difference, not least because it reduced the six weeks in advance down from forty eight pounds to forty two. She had lied about her age when she signed the rental agreement. She knew that you were not really supposed to sign things like that until you were eighteen.

Gas and electric was included and there was shared use of the kitchen. Not that she would be doing much in there. She didn't eat breakfast and she had found a place near work where she could get a pretty decent meal in exchange for her luncheon vouchers. At weekends she could live on spaghetti hoops or baked beans or the occasional Vesta beef curry if she was feeling flush. The house was not in a particularly nice bit of Moseley but so what? She had lived in some not very nice places before and survived.

There was still a good hour to go before she needed to think about getting ready for Chris. Pulling out her library book she lay full length on the bed and pretended not to mind about the funny smell.

Chapter Seventy-Eight

1989

Sean's face lit up as soon as he saw Becky appear at the door of the side ward where he had placed in isolation again. Before levering himself into a slightly more upright position he removed his headphones, taking care not to get the wire entangled with the drip going into his arm.

Becky kissed him on the forehead (she was no longer allowed to kiss him on the lips) and fussed about with his pillows, plumping and re-stacking them against the sloping metal bed rest. It helped to feel that she could do some small thing for him. She noticed without comment that they had managed to get the latest drip into his left wrist. The battle to find a vein was getting more and more difficult.

She gave him the run down on her not very interesting day. However dull it was he always wanted to hear about it. The boredom of the long hospital days and nights alone on a side ward made him grateful for any news of the outside world.

When Becky had been there for a few minutes, Velma,

his favourite ward assistant, brought his dinner in. If Becky had not been there Velma would have paused to help him get his table pushed to the right angle and tell him the joke she had heard in the canteen earlier, but his wife was there to give him a bit of company, so Velma decided the joke could wait until cocoa time.

All the staff liked Sean. They popped into his side room whenever they could to spend a few minutes with him. He always managed a smile – not like some patients who were far less ill, but moaned all the time – or the ones who were as sick as he was and seemed to feel a particular duty to share the suffering around, making little dramas out of everything and keeping their families perpetually on the rack.

Sean managed a few small, slow mouthfuls of his dinner while Becky pretended not to notice how difficult it was for him. She would not patronise him by exhorting him to eat although she mentally willed him to.

'I heard a really nice song on the radio this morning,' he said. 'It's by The Bangles.'

Becky's brow wrinkled. She did not really keep up with pop music anymore. 'Are they the ones who did 'Walk Like An Egyptian'?'

'That's them. But this is completely different. It's a ballad. 'Eternal Flame' it's called. The words are lovely.'

'I'll listen out for it,' said Becky.

It was Valentine's Day later that week. The usual nine red roses were delivered to her office. She wished he had not done it. It was totally unexpected and made her cry so hard that she had to completely re-do her make up and was late for her next meeting. Naturally she told him none of this when she visited that evening.

'How on earth did you manage to arrange it?' she asked.

'They do have telephones in here you know. And I can still read the numbers off the bottom of a credit card. The other bit of your present was more difficult. I had to bribe Velma to go out and buy it for me.'

'What other bit?'

'You'll see. I'm going to save it until you're ready to go.'

It was a copy of 'Eternal Flame' by The Bangles. She played it as soon as she got home then wept so hard that she thought she would never stop.

He contracted pneumonia a few days later and within a fortnight he was dead.

Chapter Seventy-Nine

1974

Paula was lounging in one of the armchairs in the sixth form common room, pretending to read her Chaucer. There was no one around to talk to but she could not be bothered to get out her pen and make some notes about 'The Nuns' Priest's Tale'. At times like this she still missed the others horribly.

In some ways the sixth form had not turned out so badly as she had expected. It had been very strange getting off the bus on the first morning of term and not having anyone to wait for, but she found that the general atmosphere of sixth form was different to that which had prevailed further down the school. Girls who had hardly spoken to one another in previous years, now found themselves thrown together during shared free periods and gathered around the same tables rather than sitting alone. People offered to make each other mugs of coffee or shared the cost of the loaves and tins of baked beans which were a lunchtime staple. Old rivalries and ancient feuds were forgotten, while divisive exercises such as choosing sides in P.E. were a thing of the past. Moreover Ronnie and Adele had particularly looked out for Paula, making sure that she was not left out or on her own.

There were other changes in the school. Baggy Bagshaw had become Mrs Abel – a source of wonder to everyone – for who would have thought she would ever find a man willing to take her on? Mr Tresham and Miss Prior had retired. Mrs Young had moved (or been moved) on to a post in another school. The domestic science block had been repainted and a new board had been erected at the main gates, which did not look much different to the old one except that the school coat of arms was a little bit more prominent.

Some things however could not be changed. Cow-Pig-Oh's attempt to modernise by trying to institute the English words of 'Oh Come All Ye Faithful' into the carol service, had been an embarrassing failure for when the organ struck up every girl in the school (save for the recent intake of first years who knew no better) had ignored the printed words on their carol sheets and reverted to the habitual Latin. As the final resounding Venite Adoremus Dominum rang around the church Mrs Carpigo recognised that for once she had been beaten.

In some ways the winter term had been particularly dismal. With the annual miners' dispute and power shortages in full swing, the restrictions on heating sometimes meant studying in coats and gloves. The sixth form held lunchtime debates about the political situation and if the nightly news was not moaning on about strikes and the Troubles in Northern Ireland, it was talking about Watergate which was something (no one seemed to quite know what) which had happened in America. As if all that was not bad enough the school was plagued with phone calls purporting to be from terrorists who claimed to have planted a bomb on the premises and although everyone knew they were hoax calls, the whole school still had to get their coats on and assemble on the netball courts until the fire brigade had been summoned, examined the premises and confirmed that it was safe to re-enter the premises. ('When I do plant a bomb,' said Ronnie darkly, 'I'm certainly not going to ring Cow-Pig-Oh and warn her.')

In the midst of it all a determined, graveyard humour prevailed. Paula thought that perhaps it was experiences like these which she could build on to write her book. Books about writing books invariably advised the would-be novelist to 'write what you know'. These days when she looked back through the pile of uncompleted manuscripts in her bedroom she was often embarrassed by their immaturity. Her flights of fantasy had included numerous unintentional howlers – invariably when she strayed into territory with which she was unfamiliar – whereas life at Eleanor Vaux... well that was something she really did know about. Sitting in the sixth form common room, watching the breeze and the sunshine play shadow puppets on the wall with the branches of the flowering cherries, she pondered on possible titles. 'Inky Fingers and Laddered Tights' ... 'The EV Girls' ... or maybe 'How Not To Educate Young Women'. Contemplation of this project preoccupied her for the remainder of the afternoon and all the way home, but was temporarily driven from her mind when her mother met her on the doorstep with a studiously composed, sorrowful countenance.

'I've got some bad news darling.'

'What?' asked Paula bluntly.

'I'm afraid we've had to have Ophelia put to sleep.'

Paula felt a lump rise in her throat. 'Why?' she asked.

'We took her to the vet this morning. You know how she's been off colour for a while. He said there was nothing he could do for her. She *was* fifteen.'

'So you had her put to sleep,' said Paula angrily. 'Without even telling me that you were going to. Without giving me the chance to say goodbye.' She knew that she had to stop talking or she would start to cry and she didn't want to show weakness in front of her mother.

'We didn't intend to do it like that,' said her mother, with a shade less sympathy in her tone. 'Honestly Paula, you make it sound as though we deliberately went behind your back. Once we knew how ill poor Ophelia was, you wouldn't have expected us to let her suffer surely – just so that you could say goodbye?'

Paula could see the direction the conversation was going in. Her mother was twisting things around to make her feel guilty, making it seem as if she were the sort of person who would force the cat to suffer in sheer gratification of her own petty wishes. Instinctively she knew that if she went into her mother's handbag and checked her diary, she would find an entry saying *Ophelia to Vet*, together with a note of the time. That appointment would have been made days ago but kept from her with the express purpose of concealing the state of the cat's health and the imminent likelihood of her despatch to the Happy Hunting Ground. It was all part and parcel of their misguided ideas about protecting her. The same sort of protection which entailed them hardly ever letting her out of their sight. Instead of replying Paula marched into the kitchen, grabbed a handful of custard creams from the biscuit tin and marched out again, ignoring her mother's indignant voice as it followed her upstairs.

At least these days it was only her mother's voice which followed her and not her mother in person. Just after Christmas Paula had purchased a small metal bolt complete with fixings, borrowed a screwdriver from the tool box in the garage and not without difficulty – this being her first foray into D.I.Y. – she had fitted the bolt to the inside of her bedroom door. When her mother discovered it and threatened that her father would take it off, Paula vowed to keep on replacing it and confronted with the possibility of even more damage to the internal paintwork Mrs Morrison had reluctantly let the matter drop.

When they sat down to dinner that evening Mrs Morrison attempted to build bridges by saying, 'We can easily buy you another cat.'

Paula glared at her contemptuously. 'How can you talk about replacing Ophelia like that, as if she was just a… a… thing. If Granny dies are you going to offer to buy me another grandmother?'

Mrs Morrison affected outrage but Mr Morrison, (who privately thought replacement mother-in-laws – some sort of trade-in arrangement perhaps – might not be a bad thing) began to chuckle, something which did not go down at all well with either of his womenfolk.

Paula went straight back to her bedroom at the conclusion of the meal. Ignoring the prior calls of her homework she idly jotted down a few ideas for 'Inky

Fingers and Laddered Tights'. She also planned to spend part of her evening writing to Jo, whose last letter from London had arrived a couple of days previously. It always took Jo longer to reply to Paula's letters than vice versa, which did not matter because it was understood between them all that for Paula writing was a natural extension of living and breathing, so that she could happily fill sides and sides of paper with her funny, unformed handwriting which leaned first one way then another, often using more than one colour as successive biros ran out. Paula knew that writing did not come so easily to the others and she did not expect replies to arrive at a length or speed which matched her own.

It isn't only that, she thought. I also have more time to write because I'm always stuck here on my own.

She envied Jo enormously. It was apparent from her letters that after an uncertain start Jo was really enjoying herself. She's like a bird, Paula thought, who has been kept in a cage all her life and is suddenly set free. All jail sentences were finite. That was the thing to remember. On the first day of sixth form Paula had steeled herself to remember that it was only two years. Just two years and then she would be going away to university. Somewhere very far away. Somewhere her mother could not be constantly breathing down her neck. She had heard alarm bells a few days earlier, when her mother started chattering about someone she knew who worked at Birmingham University and how handy it would be to pull a few strings. It's a plot, Paula thought, to keep me locked up here for ever and ever. Well she would have to avoid the Birmingham University trap somehow. There were university students among the tenants of Becky's latest lodgings in Selly Oak. Becka went out for a drink with them occasionally. That's what normal students do, Paula thought, but I won't be allowed to unless I can get away from here. My parents want to keep me a child forever. And in one way, she thought, they were succeeding, because she already felt left behind, socially retarded in comparison to everyone else of her own age.

A lot of the other girls in lower sixth had boyfriends. They went to concerts in town, often to hear bands that Paula was only half aware of. They talked about String Driven Thing and Rory Gallagher and whether or not Deep Purple could ever be the same now that Ian Gillan had left. Ronnie and Adele went regularly to Bogart's and the Parisienne where they sometimes bumped into Becky or Nick, who also met up in the Red Lion and the Regency, where they got chatted up and bought vodka and limes by a succession of guys called Chris or Rick or Steve. Paula had begun to suspect that if she did not manage to get onto the circuit where all these things were happening fairly soon, everyone would get so many laps ahead that she would never catch up.

Chapter Eighty

1974

By the beginning of the summer holidays Paula had temporarily abandoned 'Inky Fingers and Laddered Tights' in favour of 'Venetia', which she hoped might turn out to be the greatest romantic novel of the seventies. The Venetia of the title was a luxury liner which in keeping with the current enthusiasm for disaster movies was going to be destroyed and sunk by a terrorist bomb – but not before Philip and Helga, the doomed hero and heroine who had met one another on board, had fallen for one another, consummated their passion and made a pact never to leave one another, which would result in them drowning together in a heroic display of love and self sacrifice. In spite of sounding horribly like 'Juggernaut' meets 'Romeo and Juliet' meets 'The Poseidon Adventure', Paula had convinced herself that it was a completely original slant on the old familiar, three hankie winning formula of doomed love.

'Inky Fingers' had run into difficulties after only a

couple of chapters, because when Paula dispassionately read back the bits which were meant to be hysterically funny she could see that they were not. Incidents in Mrs Young's biology lessons which had been an absolute scream for those involved, did not translate well onto paper. She found that she had to keep including explanations as to why this and that thing was so funny… but once you needed to explain the joke all the humour went out of it.

'Venetia' was a completely different kind of material with mercifully no need for any humour at all, being a tale of drama and romance and ultimate tragedy. Yet with 'Venetia' she had run up against a different set of problems. She had never been on a boat bigger than a cross channel ferry, though that was not what really worried her because she was pretty sure that tossing in a few nautical terms here and there ought to suffice. No, the problem lay in the big scene at the centre of the story when Philip and Helga were scheduled to consummate their love in his cabin on B deck. Naturally she wanted to make this as authentic as possible but in order to do so there were some things she really needed to know which she could not get out of books. The love scene was pivotal to the whole plot so it had to be thoroughly convincing. But without personal experience it would be impossible to know just what it felt like from the girl's point of view. Worse still, Paula thought, with *her* level of ignorance she might inadvertently make some fundamental error and end up writing something which would be patently absurd when read by anyone who was sexually experienced.

She knew that Becky had done it but it was not the sort of thing you could ask for details about. And Nicky was almost certainly covertly sleeping with Mark, because they had been going out for quite a while now and the one thing necessarily followed on the other. People didn't wait until their wedding night anymore whatever her mother might think. As for Ronnie, it was well known that she had done it on a weekend away in Blackpool, because being Ronnie she had regaled the entire sixth form common room with a hilarious story about a hunt for condoms. As for Jo… well living in London and mixing with a crowd of art students it was hardly likely that she would still be a virgin.

I always knew that I'd be last, Paula thought sadly. When I get to university I'll probably be the only virgin on the campus.

Chapter Eighty-One

1997

Jonathan was sulking because he had been tipped off the computer by his father, who wanted to use it for some boring stuff to do with the business. Nicky decided it was best to ignore him. It had been a very wearing day with the nursery so busy and the kids off school for Easter and Rob distinctly tetchy because the promised extra delivery of hanging baskets had not arrived when it should have done. Never mind… she still hoped to cheer everyone up with a nice meal at 6.30, by which time the place would be transformed into the haven of peace that it became every evening when the last of the staff and customers had gone.

She switched on the portable T.V. in the kitchen, no more than half listening to it while she chopped the onions and mushrooms. It was an old episode of 'Roseanne', a programme she quite liked, not least because the children were realistically obnoxious. Like mine, she thought with an unconscious grin.

No, no, that wasn't fair. They were not that bad…

most of the time. Her eye was caught by the muddle of Sylvanian Families and their various equipage which Rose had left lying all over the kitchen table, having lost interest in them and departed to play outside on the swing which was conveniently out of calling distance from the kitchen door. Rob sometimes claimed that the sole reason for adding extensions onto the house was to facilitate the infinite expansion of Rose's possessions.

Well that wasn't quite fair either. The original lean-to housing the kitchen had been long past its sell by date when they got round to replacing it with a brick built, two storey extension. This had doubled the floor space in the cottage at a stroke, creating a huge kitchen and adjoining utility room with two extra single bedrooms above it. An essential addition because once Peter had been born in 1991 things had started to get really cramped. Last year they had added another bit onto the opposite side of the house. This gave them a second sitting room and also provided a home for the computer, the use of which had become a constant bone of contention between Jonathan who thought he should be glued to it constantly and his parents who did not.

She had been hoping that Jonathan would engage in some kind of constructive activity but when she passed the sitting room door on her way across the kitchen to the fridge, Nicky was irritated to see him slumped on the sofa, using the remote to flick through the pages of Teletext, of all things. She was about to remonstrate with him when she remembered in the nick of time that an argument was what he wanted, so that he could whine about being turfed off the computer again. Instead of saying anything she ignored him. If he wanted to waste the remnants of a sunny afternoon reading the racing results or the Recipe of the Day then let him.

She had just started to make the béchamel sauce for the lasagne when his voice floated through from the sitting room. 'Mu-um.'

'What is it?' she asked, without taking her eye off the pan.

'What was the name of that school you went to? You know... the one with the funny name?'

'Do you mean Eleanor Vaux?'

'That's it. Well there's something about it here. On the telly.'

Nicky took the pan off the heat and hurried into the sitting room, wiping her hands on her butcher's stripe apron. Jonathan had the Lost Touch pages up on screen.

'You've missed it,' he said. 'It's just gone onto the next page.'

Nicky glanced at the corner of the screen which told her it was page seventeen out of twenty three. 'Can you get it back up?' she asked.

'No,' said Jonathan. 'I keep on telling Dad that we need a better remote. One where you can move the text pages on. You'll have to wait until it comes round to page sixteen again.'

'I can't wait for that,' said Nicky briskly. 'I'm busy. What did it say?'

'Well I can't remember all of it,' said Jonathan, in the tone of an exasperated, world weary slave who has just been called upon to undertake one task too many.

'Well can you remember some of it?'

'Yeah. A reunion, it said. For the intake September 1968 I think. There was a number to ring.'

'September 1968!' exclaimed Nicky. 'That was my year. Are you sure?' She broke off suddenly, regarding him with deep suspicion.

'No kidding?' he said.

She fixed him with a look. He knew perfectly well that it was her fortieth birthday coming up. He was quite capable of working out the maths. She glanced back at the screen which had only moved on as far as page eighteen.

'Just keep it on the Lost Touch pages,' she instructed. 'When it comes back round to page sixteen put it on hold – the remote's advanced enough to manage that – then call me back in so that I can read what it says myself.'

*

In spite of collective urging by the entire family it took Nicky two days to pluck up courage to ring the phone number she had copied down from Lost Touch.

'I'm getting round to it,' she said in the face of an enquiry from Rose. 'I'll do it when I've got a minute.'

'Not now,' she said, when Rob brought the subject up again later the same day. 'It's getting a bit late. Some people don't like getting calls out of the blue after half past nine.'

She knew that he knew it wasn't really that at all. The idea of a reunion was both fascinating and at the same time scary. Did she really want to go back to school? Delving into the past and perhaps dragging up all kinds of memories best forgotten? She tried phoning Jo to see what she thought about it, but Ant said she was leading a painting course somewhere in Scotland and when offered Jo's mobile number, Nicky did not feel that she could go ringing Jo on her mobile and perhaps interrupting her when she was in the middle of ... well... doing whatever the person leading a painting course has to do. It was no use trying Becky either, because she had taken Madeline to Euro Disney, followed by a couple of days doing the sights in Paris. A compromise to accommodate the preferences of them both.

Nicky finally used the kitchen extension to ring the number when the rest of the family were all safely out of earshot. She was thrown into confusion when a man answered and could only stammer out an incoherent sentence containing the words Teletext and reunion.

'I'll get my wife,' came a resigned voice from the other end of the line.

A couple of moments passed before a female voice came onto the line.

'Hello,' Nicky said. 'I saw your number on Teletext. For the reunion. The September 1968 intake. I was in that year.'

'Oh excellent.' The disembodied female voice sounded enthusiastic. 'I've got my list here. What's your name?'

'Nicola Grafton.'

'Was that your name at school?' The voice sounded uncertain.

Nicky could suddenly visualise a woman checking down a list and of course drawing a blank.

'No – sorry. I was Nicola Christie at school.'

'Nicola Christie.' Delight registered down the line. 'Where on earth are you ringing from? According to my notes you were last heard of getting married and going to live in America.'

'I did,' said Nicky. 'But then I got divorced and came back again. I live just outside Evesham now.'

'Oh excellent. That means you'll be near enough to come. I'm Vicky Davis-as-was – Vicky Marchant now.'

Nicky experienced a rising sensation of panic. The name meant absolutely nothing to her at all. Oh God! Had she somehow gone and got the year wrong?

'Don't worry if you don't remember me,' said Vicky, just as if she had read Nicky's thoughts. 'Most of us haven't seen each other for over twenty years and have trouble recalling anyone who was in a different form.. I was in VT with Leah Huntley, Jane Williams, Charlotte Young...'

'Charlie Young!' Nicky exclaimed, grasping a familiar name with relief. 'I remember her! My God, I can't believe I've forgotten anyone's name. We used to know the names of almost every girl in the school when we were there. Certainly all our own year.'

'It's anno domini I'm afraid,' Vicky said cheerfully. 'We'll all of us turn forty during this school year. That's why a couple of us thought it was time for a get together. We're trying to contact every girl in the year. Or at least as many of them as we can.'

'How many have you got so far?'

'Thirty two,' said Vicky. 'You make number thirty three.'

'Wow,' said Nicky. 'All from Teletext? '

'No, you're only the second one from there. We got some through the Old Girls Association.'

'I didn't know there was one,' said Nicky.

'You *and* most of the rest of us. Apparently it started up about five years ago. Anyway we got two or three from that and one or two more from people happening to know where a member of someone's family is still living, things like that. Mostly though we find that one girl brings in another because most people have kept in touch with at least one friend from school, even if it's dwindled down to no more than a card at Christmas.'

'Thirty two. That's a lot. Who have you got so far?'

'I'll give you the ones from your own form,' said Vicky. 'Those are the names that will be most likely to mean something. There's Rowena Abbott, Colleen Bell…'

'Oh my God!' exclaimed Nicky. 'Colleen Bell! I remember her.'

'You didn't by any chance go to that birthday party she had?'

'Yes,' Nicky almost shouted. 'Were you there too?'

'I certainly was. When I think now how her poor mother must have felt coming back into that mess…'

Nicky found that for some reason she could not fathom she was almost crying. 'Colleen Bell's party,' she said wonderingly. 'I'd forgotten that years ago. And you were there. I wish I could place you.'

'Sue Farrell,' Vicky continued down her list.

'She used to have a terrible lisp poor girl,' said Nicky.

'She still does: I've talked to her on the phone. Gail Foster, Helen Staveley – you must remember Helen? She had a wonderful voice. She sang YumYum, the year we did 'The Mikado'.'

'I do, I do. I was one of the stage managers.'

'Well picture Helen singing YumYum and then look a bit to your left and I'm standing right next to her. I was Peep-Bo.'

'Victoria Davis – I *do* remember you,' Nicky burst out. 'You used to sing and you played the violin in the orchestra.'

'Aah, yes, the good old vile-din section. I still sing but I packed up the vile-din once I left school.'

'Go on… go on,' said Nicky eagerly. 'Who else have you got?'

'Only two more from your form so far: Adele White and Naomi Wiseman.'

'Adele!' exclaimed Nicky. 'Doesn't Adele know where Veronica Nicholls is? Those two must have stayed in touch, surely? They were inseparable all through school.'

'Apparently not,' said Vicky. 'It's sad but after school a lot of people do seem to have just drifted apart. Adele went abroad for a while and lost Ronnie's address. The first thing she asked me was whether I'd managed to trace Ronnie yet. The million dollar question is can *you* add any more names to the list of finds? Are you still in touch with anyone?'

Chapter Eighty-Two

1976

Becky had been surprised to receive the letter from Paula, asking whether she could come and stay, however when she thought about the request a bit more she could see exactly why Paula was trying to unravel the apron strings by not going back to stay at her parents' home for the Easter holidays. Fortunately Becky was able to write back in the affirmative because Maggie, her flatmate for the past twelve weeks, had recently followed her musician boyfriend to Holland and that meant there was a spare bed in the flat.

She was a bit afraid that Paula might not think the flat was up to much, because essentially, it was only a combined kitchen and living room which had two tiny bedrooms leading directly off it and a bathroom with a stained enamel bath and a hand basin with a hairline crack in the bowl. For Becky however it was a real step up from sharing a bathroom with an assortment of fellow tenants – her first self contained flat – even if it could only be reached via a dodgy looking fire escape alongside a betting shop.

The letter had at least reassured her about one thing. Lately Becky thought she had detected a change in the tone of Paula's letters. Although she could not put her finger on it, the letters read as if there was something being left unsaid and Becky had been wondering if this might be indicative of a distance developing between them. She knew that this happened sometimes when people went off to university. They dropped their old friends because they thought themselves too good to spend time with perceived lesser mortals who had not gone on to higher education. And although she could not really believe that Paula would ever be like that, the news that she wanted to come and stay had been reassuring.

In the meantime it was undeniable that some things *were* changing.

She still kept up the Thursday evening ritual of going to the Christies' house for her tea (ironic really that whereas she went to Nicky's once a week, regular as clockwork, she had no particular pattern for visiting her own mother). Nick's mum could always be relied on to provide a good feed. A cooked tea and a pudding, much appreciated by someone on a tight budget. But aside from their Thursday evenings she had seen less and less of Nicky ever since Mark had come on the scene. Their jolly nights out together at the Red Lion and the Regency (it had been on one such evening that Nicky had met Mark in the first place) were essentially a thing of the past and the rest of their social lives had steadily diverged too.

Becky knew that this was partly due to a mutual antipathy between herself and Mark. While she could see what Nick or indeed any girl might see in him, Becky had always found him just too glossily handsome and too smoothly charming to be for real and she had not been altogether surprised when a mutual friend saw Mark out with another girl and thought it her duty to let Nicky know the score. Nicky had been predictably broken hearted and initially inclined to listen to Becky's advice, which had been to finish with the two timing rat immediately. But somehow Mark had talked her round and when Becky had expressed the view that Nicky was making a big mistake, Nicky had rounded on her friend with an angry, 'You've never really liked Mark have you?'

It was the closest they had ever come to having a serious row. Becky had backed off and watched her step where Mark was concerned after that, though she had been secretly appalled when for Nicky's eighteenth birthday, Mark had presented her with an engagement ring.

*

When Paula arrived she was very complimentary about the flat. Becky had covered the walls with posters, several of them acquired from the galleries Joanne had taken her to on a recent trip down to London.

'And your own kitchen,' Paula said. 'God, how I envy you. We've only got an electric kettle at the end of our landing so that we can make hot drinks. All our meals are provided in halls and let me tell you school dinners were a gourmet banquet by comparison.'

'Never mind,' said Becky. 'You'll be able to go into a shared house next year. Only one more term in halls.'

An odd expression crossed Paula's face and she turned

to look out of the window, although there was nothing to see except the blank brick wall of a nearby building. Becky sensed the same odd hesitancy which she had first noticed when she met Paula off the train. As if some barrier lay between them. Something which had not been there when they had last met up at Christmas.

'What's the matter Pau?' asked Becky.

'I won't be going back next year.'

'What do you mean?'

'I won't be going back.'

'Are you going to Michigan with Greg?'

A student called Greg had been making regular appearances in Paula's letters for several months now. He was an American who had come to Britain on a year's exchange – a Born Again Christian whom Paula had once described as the kindest, most sincere person she had ever met.

Paula shook her head. 'I'm pregnant,' she said.

Becky stared at her dumbly.

Paula laughed nervously. 'Say *something*,' she said.

Becky gulped. 'How far gone are you?' she asked.

'Nearly six months.'

'You can't be,' said Becky. 'You're having me on.'

'I'm not,' said Paula. 'I know it hardly shows at all but I am. Look.' She stood up and turned sideways against the light from the window, pulling her loose cheesecloth dress taught against her body to outline a small but unmistakeable bump.

'Is it Greg's?' asked Becky.

'No.'

'Oh.'

There was a brief silence before Paula blurted out, 'The

father's just some guy. He doesn't know. I haven't seen him in ages... the father I mean. It was an accident.'

'Well obviously,' said Becky dryly.

'My parents don't know yet. Actually nobody knows. You're the first person I've told.'

'But surely people must have noticed? How about Greg, hasn't *he* noticed?'

Paula shook her head. 'It doesn't show if I wear all my loose fitting stuff and he doesn't see me naked. He doesn't believe in sex before marriage so it hasn't arisen.'

Becky caught her eye and they only narrowly avoided giggling.

'Don't,' said Paula quickly. 'It's really not funny.'

'No,' said Becky. 'It's not. Did you think about having an abortion?'

Paula shook her head. 'I didn't twig on at first. You know I've always been a bit irregular, so I thought I was just a bit late. Then because I didn't feel any different... I mean... I wasn't being sick in the mornings or wanting to eat coal or any of that stuff...'

'I don't think that's compulsory,' said Becky.

'... so I sort of thought I might not be. I didn't want to go to the clinic and get a test just in case I was pregnant and word got round. Eventually I sat down and worked out that I hadn't had a period for more than four months and it seemed a bit obvious.'

Becky continued to regard her friend with undisguised disbelief.

'I suppose I did try to bury my head in the sand a bit,' Paula conceded reluctantly. 'I kept thinking that I couldn't be. I mean... I'd only done it once.'

'Which is obviously all it takes,' said Becky.

'Anyway... even if I had been sure early enough, I couldn't have murdered my own child.'

'So when's the baby actually due?' Becky asked.

'I'm not sure,' said Paula vaguely. 'About July I think.'

'You think! Haven't they told you at the hospital?'

'I told you,' said Paula. 'I haven't told anyone but you.'

'But you're supposed to go to clinics and stuff.'

'I haven't really got round to it,' Paula said. 'I always seemed to have a lecture or something.'

Becky's expression had changed from disbelief to exasperation. 'Paula Morrison you cannot just drift along like this. What are you going to do when you *still* haven't got round to it and you go into labour?'

Paula grinned sheepishly. 'Panic, probably.'

'And you're going to have to tell your mum and dad sooner or later.'

'I know,' said Paula, suddenly sobering up. 'That's why I asked if I could stay with you. I'll have to tell them this holidays and I know they'll be unbearable, so I thought this would be a bolthole to escape to until the initial wrath has worn off a bit. You see I will have to go back there to have the baby. It will be awful of course, but I haven't got any alternative.'

'Why not?'

'Well I can't stay in halls,' said Paula. 'People don't have babies in halls. There's sure to be rules about it and anyway term will be finished before then.'

'Yes but why go back to your parents? You're over eighteen. You can get your own place. You've even got some money in your building society account. You haven't spent all the money your grandma left you surely?'

‘No,’ said Paula. ‘It’s still all there. But I’m not sure if I could live on my own, Becka. After I’ve had the baby perhaps but not before that. Imagine going into labour on your own. I’d be petrified.’

‘I need a flat mate now that Maggie’s moved out,’ said Becky. ‘The lease says no children but it doesn’t say anything about pregnant women.’

‘Don’t be silly.’

‘Well obviously if you’d rather live with your mother…’

‘No chance,’ exclaimed Paula. ‘If you really mean it, it’s like the answer to a prayer.’

‘Do you want me to come with you?’ Becky asked. ‘When you tell your mum and dad?’

‘Would you mind?’

‘Not if you think it will help,’ said Becky, who could actually think of few errands she would sooner avoid, but had a sneaking suspicion that if she did not go along to supervise the meeting, Paula might manage to accidentally on purpose not mention the pregnancy to her parents at all.

Since the next day was Saturday and Becky thought that striking while the iron was hot seemed the best plan they called on the Morrisons at two in the afternoon and Paula wasted no time in getting to the point.

Mr Morrison’s reaction to the news was very odd. Initially he said nothing at all, appearing to be in deep thought, but then he rose dramatically from his chair and interrupted the three women to state loudly and dispassionately that he washed his hands of Paula and hoped that he would never set eyes on her again. With that he walked out of the room. Becky was shocked. In similar circumstances she supposed that Stan would have mocked and lectured and told everyone so, while her mother had indulged in hysterics and turned the whole thing into a melodrama about herself and how she had been betrayed and let down by everyone in general and her daughter in particular. But in Mr Morrison's rejection Becky felt there was something altogether more brutal. It was as if he had adjudicated upon Paula in the great examination of life and marked her a fail, with no chance of a re-take at any point in the future. There was an awful finality about his pronouncement.

Mrs Morrison, who was in a towering rage, continued as if her husband had neither spoken nor departed, berating Paula for a fool, a trollop, an idiot and a common little slut. Paula faced her mother in silence, her white face turning steadily crimson much as their exam room blotting paper had steadily absorbed ink until it had completely changed from green to purplish-blue.

'We have given you everything,' Mrs Morrison shrieked. 'You have been given every opportunity. Some young girls would have given their right arm to have changed places with you. You've had a wonderful education and a chance to make something of yourself and your life, instead of which you have squandered it. Completely squandered it all. Every penny spent on your education was a complete waste of money. You could have done something with your life...'

'Like you did with yours,' Paula interjected quietly. 'Three years at university just so that you could meet the right sort of chap. Was that your smart career move, Mummy? Latching on to someone who was going to get a first and be guaranteed a good job after graduation? You could have left school at fourteen and been a housewife you know. But then you would have had to do some paid work wouldn't you? So all that education and playing tennis and the university debating club came in very handy for filling in the seven years between fourteen and twenty one, until you found a suitable Mr Right to latch on to. Come on Becky, let's go.'

Chapter Eighty-Three

1976

Under orders from Becky, Paula finally registered herself for ante-natal care and attended the hospital booking clinic, where she was roundly ticked off for not having sought medical care before. After several hours of being talked down to by everyone from the records clerk upwards, a midwife reluctantly confirmed that in spite of Paula's lackadaisical approach there appeared to be absolutely nothing wrong with her or the baby at all. As Paula told Becky later, she got the distinct impression that the old dragon privately hoped that there would be and serve her right too for not reporting in the moment she missed a period.

She returned to university at the end of the Easter holidays, where prodded by letters and phone calls from Becky she made enquiries and established that if she passed her first year exams it would pave the way for returning to complete her degree at some stage in the future.

She also broke the news to Greg about the baby and

though she could tell that he was shocked, they remained on very friendly terms and when the summer vacation finally arrived and he left for Michigan he kept his promise to write to her.

As soon as she heard the news Jo came up for the weekend visit, sleeping on the floor of Paula's room in halls. While she was there she drew a series of cartoons, depicting the baby listening to lectures in the womb and making pithy comments which Paula loved so much that she pinned them up on the walls of her room.

Nicky hid her perturbation that Paula was not, under any circumstances, going to fit into one of the pale blue bridesmaids' dresses which were being made by a lady down the road, to measurements which took no account of someone who was going to be eight months pregnant. She was extremely relieved when Paula raised the matter of her own volition, offering to stand down from bridesmaid duty, because as she said, a pregnant bridesmaid would look ridiculous on the photographs.

Mrs Christie, though she would not have a word said in front of Paula, was deeply shocked. 'Who would ever have thought it,' she said. 'A nice girl like that. So well brought up too. I always thought she had such lovely manners.'

Paula, who had been so well throughout the early months that she often had difficulty believing in her pregnancy at all, found the end of year exams unexpectedly trying. There had been no rain for weeks and one scorching airless day followed another. The whole campus felt as if someone had laid a giant stifling blanket over it. She began to count down the days when she could take the train home and move in with Becky. Not that it was any cooler in

Birmingham, but at least she would not have to sit in lecture theatres or examination rooms, trying to stay awake.

Living with Becky was rather like regressing several years. They often sat up late at night, just talking and talking about anything and everything the way they had in the old days, when Becky had sometimes come to stay the night. In the daytime while Becky was at work, Paula often took a book and a picnic lunch to Highbury Park where she tried to find some shade in which to escape the stuffiness of the flat. Sitting reading on the parched grass she experienced a similar sense of freedom to that which she remembered from the summer holidays long ago, when six weeks had seemed like an eternity and she could lose herself in book after book.

She looked forward to Becky returning from work each evening. She had not made many friends at university. At least not people in whom she felt she could truly confide. All her insecurities and shyness had manifested themselves on arrival, putting up a barrier between herself and the other students. Except of course for that one idiotic occasion a couple of week's after she had arrived, when in a desperate attempt to fling herself into university life she had drunk too much in the Union Bar and gone to bed with the first bloke who had ever asked her to. Something so clichéd and humiliating that she could not even begin to explain it to herself.

One evening in June when she and Becky were sitting one each side of the open window, Becky said: 'Do you feel like a grown up?'

'Me?' Paula laughed. 'You must be joking.'

'Me neither,' said Becky. 'I mean you'd think wouldn't

you, with us all doing grown up things… you having a baby, Nicky getting married on Saturday week…'

'It doesn't make any difference,' said Paula. 'I'm still about fourteen in my head. Physically too if it comes to that. I mean look at me… apart from the bump I'm still the same plain, scrawny kid…'

'Are you mad? You're gorgeous. People turn round in the street to look at you.'

'Probably just staring because I'm pregnant and not wearing a wedding ring.'

'No they are not,' said Becky. 'You are slim and pretty with the loveliest blue eyes and all that fantastic blonde hair. The blonde one in Abba's got nothing on you.'

'Don't be daft,' Paula said cheerfully. Nothing would ever convince her that she was attractive. One drunken jerk had once wanted to sleep with her it was true, but she thought it most unlikely that anyone would ever want to repeat the exercise. 'Men don't find me attractive at all.'

'Of course they do,' Becky protested. 'What about Greg for a start?'

Paula's face softened. 'He's very nice of course. But I think he probably just carried on seeing me to be kind. Because he sees me as a fallen woman or something.'

'Rubbish!'.

After a pause Paula asked somewhat hesitantly, 'Have you ever wondered about Jo?'

'Wondered in what way?'

'About men and sex and stuff?'

'Why? Has she said something to you?'

'Not directly, no.'

'I think she's kind of hoping we'll catch on without her

actually having to say anything,' said Becky. 'Which we all have… on the quiet I think.'

'Thank goodness,' said Paula. 'I thought it was only me. And I didn't want to say anything.'

Becky laughed. 'When I last went to see her in London she introduced me to this incredibly butch looking friend called Julie – Jules for short – who kept looking daggers at me until Jo said something like, "Becky's an old friend and she's straight". Well I know it sounds a bit soft but I didn't cotton on to what she meant right away. I just thought she was saying I was… well… a straightforward, honest sort of person. I never twigged on until I was thinking things over after I got back here and then it suddenly dawned on me that what she really meant was straight as opposed to bent.'

Paula laughed. 'I probably wouldn't have got it either. Until I'd almost finished sixth form I didn't think lesbians really existed. Or if I did, I probably thought there were only about three in the whole country. Lesbian was just a rude name Gail Foster used to call people back in second year.'

'I wonder how long Jo's known?'

'Maybe always,' said Paula.

'I wish we'd known,' said Becky. 'It must have been hellish for her sometimes, trying to pretend.'

Chapter Eighty-Four

1976

'Is my hat on straight?' Mrs Christie asked anxiously. 'Only the cars will be here any minute.'

'Calm down Mum,' said Nicky. 'They shouldn't be here for another quarter of an hour yet.'

Mrs Christie took a deep breath and glanced around the room, thinking that these girls did not get any tidier as they got older. Suddenly all the times she had seen it like this – with the four girls getting ready to go somewhere – came flooding back to her together with the realisation that today was the very last time. It was never going to happen again. Not here in this house at least. Exercising more self control than she had realised herself capable of she forced a smile and said, 'You look smashing in that dress Joanne. I knew that blue would suit your colouring.'

'Thanks Mrs C.,' said Jo, who privately thought the dresses, with their puff sleeves and flounces around the hems, were absolutely hideous.

'Come on Nicky,' Mrs Christie's anxiety bubbled to the fore again. 'Are you ready to get your dress on?'

'I'm leaving it to the last possible minute,' Nicky said. 'I'm going to be frazzled in that net underskirt.'

She was wafting about the room in a full length white nylon petticoat. Becky, similarly attired, was being helped into her bridesmaid dress by Jo and Paula. Paula looked lovely too, Mrs Christie thought, in a flowing yellow dress which had a print of little white daisies all over it. A motif which was picked up around the brim of her floppy hat.

'Have you got your corsage on Paula?' asked Mrs Christie.

'Mum will you stop worrying,' said Nicky. 'Nobody is going to forget anything.'

They were interrupted by a tap on the door. Nicky was nearest so she opened it a crack to find Dennis standing on the landing, looking a bit self conscious in his first proper suit.

'I just came up to say good luck,' he said. 'Me and Michael will be setting off in a minute.'

'Thanks Den,' said his sister, genuinely touched.

'Incidentally,' he added, as if by way of a genuine afterthought. 'Do you know if there's a telly at this place where you're having the reception? Only I've got a fiver on Borg to beat Nastase in the men's final this afternoon.'

Several retorts passed through Nicky's mind, but she decided that it was neither the time nor the place to enquire how Dennis had been able to get a bet on at his age, nor indeed where he had come by the five pounds with which to do so. In the end all she said was, 'I think there's a television in the bar.'

'Thanks.' Dennis favoured her with a broad grin. 'See you in church I suppose.'

'Yes,' she said.

All the older people kept saying that. It appeared to be some sort of mantra, delivered with a knowing smile as if it held some clever hidden meaning to which she was not privy. It made her nervous, the thought of the church and walking up the aisle in front of all those people. Suppose she tripped over her dress or slipped in her new sandals or her headdress fell off? It was a nerve wracking business this getting married and not half so much fun as she had always imagined it would be.

From the bedroom window they had been able to see all the various comings and goings which had occurred since they had retreated up here an hour before, ostensibly to get ready but really to have a natter and escape from all the friends, neighbours and well wishers who kept on finding excuses to pop in. The house was starting to empty out now. Once Dennis and Michael had gone in Uncle Fred's car, there were only two more car loads destined for the church. First a car to take her mother and the bridesmaids and Paula, who they had all insisted should travel as a bridesmaid, even if she wasn't actually going to be one. And finally the car scheduled to arrive after all the others which would take Nicky and her father.

'Phew,' Becky was saying. 'This must be the hottest day so far.'

'I think I've sprayed on a whole tin of deodorant,' said Nicky. 'And I'm still going to pong in that dress. To think when I picked it out, that I was worried in case we didn't have a nice day and I wouldn't be warm enough.'

The dress had been purchased from Polly of Piccadilly almost four months earlier and was now hanging self-importantly on the front of the wardrobe door. It had dozens of white sequins and pearls stitched onto the bodice and had been declared utterly beautiful by every female visitor who had been sneaked upstairs for a preview. The girls lifted it over Nicky's head as if it were made from cut glass, then did up the twenty four inches of zip and the series of hooks and eyes, like hand maidens attending on a queen. Watching at arm's length Mrs Christie gave way momentarily and had to dab her eyes.

'You look beautiful Nick,' said Joanne.

'Frabjous,' said Becky softly and the use of their old catchphrase froze the compliment on Paula's lips and set her reaching for the hankie which she had placed at the ready in her new white handbag.

Jo took charge of the headdress, securing it with a couple of pale grips which she assured Nicky could not possibly be seen among her curls.

By this time Mr Christie was calling upstairs that it was time for the bridesmaids to be going.

'Are you coming down to show your dad?'

'In a minute,' said Nicky. 'You carry on. I'll be down in a minute.'

They took her at her word and she stood where they had left her in front of the mirror, listening to their long dresses whispering as they skimmed the stairs and hearing her mother again seeking reassurance about her hat. It was only natural, she thought, to feel a little bit jittery. It was having to say her vows in front of all those people. That was enough to make anyone nervous. It was not that she had any doubts about it. Not really.

Some advice flashed unbidden into her mind. Something that an agony aunt had written, (when reading any magazine she always turned to the problem page first) to a bride who was wondering whether or not she should go ahead with her wedding. *If in doubt – don't*. That had been the advice. But surely no one would ever get married at all if everyone took that to heart? Everybody must experience a teeny twinge of doubt at some stage or another before the big day?

She hadn't got anything to worry about. Mark loved her. He wouldn't be marrying her if he didn't. He'd had a last little fling while he was still single but lots of blokes probably did. It's me he wants to marry, Nicky thought. And very soon now they would make those magical promises which would keep him faithful and bind the two of them together forever.

'Nicola.' It was her father calling from the foot of the stairs.

'Coming,' she called. With one final look at herself in the mirror she set off down the stairs on her way to marry Mark.

Chapter Eighty-Five

1976

'I'm sorry,' the nurse repeated the phrase almost as if she meant it. 'But I'm afraid the rules are very strict. Only husbands are allowed into the labour wards.'

'But my friend hasn't got a husband.' Becky was still hoping that she might be able to appeal to reason. 'I know it *says* Mrs Morrison on her card, but she's not *Mrs* Morrison.'

'We know that dear,' said the nurse, lowering her voice presumably to protect the sensibilities of the only other person in sight, a distant cleaning lady who was mopping the corridor in slow motion. 'We put Mrs in front of all the unmarried mother's names to save them feeling embarrassed when their names are called out in the clinic and so forth.'

Trying not to bridle at the patronising 'dear', Becky tried again. 'My friend isn't embarrassed about not being married. She just wants someone to stay with her. If it's husbands only that means anyone without a husband has to be on their own which isn't fair.'

'Your friend isn't on her own. The hospital staff will be there to take care of her.'

'But it still isn't fair though, is it? Letting some women have their husbands with them while they're having their babies but making other women have no one at all.'

The nurse looked exasperated. She was sorely tempted to tell this persistent young girl that it was not so very long ago that husbands in the labour ward, still less in the delivery room, were absolutely unheard of. When she had first qualified fifteen years ago, husbands had been kept in the waiting room where they belonged. Fixing Becky with a very firm look, she said, 'I'm afraid those are the rules and there's nothing I can do about it.' She banged some files on the counter by way of further indication that the discussion was at an end.

Becky retreated to the waiting room where a couple of expectant fathers were sharing an uneasy, jokey conversation about take-away meals. Husbands are allowed, Becky felt like saying to them. Why aren't you in there with your wives? Perhaps they had been unable to produce a valid marriage certificate to get them past the dragon at the gate. Or maybe they had been allowed in with their wives to start off with, but subsequently been thrown out for transgressing some secret hospital taboo.

The waiting room was absolutely spartan. There were a dozen vinyl covered armchairs with their backs pushed right up against the four walls and in the centre of the room a low table with nothing on it except a metal ashtray which had recently been emptied and wiped by the cleaning lady.

After a while Becky got up and returned to the admissions desk. There was a different nurse standing behind it. 'I'm with a patient called Paula Morrison,' said Becky. 'She was admitted about an hour ago in labour. Can you tell me how she is please?'

Before the new nurse could respond the original hatchet faced nurse appeared out of a door a little further along the corridor and frowned when she saw Becky standing there.

'This lady is asking after Paula Morrison,' said the nurse behind the desk.

'She's fine,' said the hatchet faced nurse. 'I've just seen her.'

'Do you know how long it's going to be,' asked Becky. 'Before the baby's born?'

'If I could predict that sort of thing I'd have made my fortune by now,' the hatchet faced one said briskly. 'But I should think she'll be quite a while yet.'

'Thank you,' said Becky, giving the woman a smile which was not reciprocated.

Reassured that she was not missing anything Becky went down a couple of floors to the main foyer, where she used one of the pay phones to call work and explain that she had gone to the hospital with a friend and could they please put it down as a day of holiday. Then she bought a cup of coffee and a small Kit Kat from the coffee bar run by the W.R.V.S., making them last as long as she could. Finally she bought a 'Daily Express' from the W.R.V.S. stand, which she took back to the waiting room, finding that she was now the sole occupant. She read the paper from cover to cover. Beyond the closed door of the waiting room there were occasional bursts of activity in the corridor but no one else joined her. She finished the paper and put it on the central table, thinking that if anyone else came in they might be glad of something to read. Then she thought what a neat thing it would be to keep the paper with its dated front page for the baby to have as a keepsake in the years to come, so she retrieved it and placed it an adjacent chair, ready to confirm ownership in the event that anyone else should appear and try to claim it.

After she had checked her watch a few more times it occurred to her that perhaps Paula might have had the baby and no one had bothered to tell her. They had been at the hospital for getting on three hours now so it was entirely possible.

She went back to the admissions desk but it was deserted. She did not like to ring the bell because she wasn't an admission and she might be fetching someone from doing something important in the mysterious recesses of the labour ward. She waited for some time until a member of staff appeared. Unfortunately it was her bête noire again. 'I'm here with Paula Morrison,' Becky began.

'Yes, *I know*,' said Hatchet Face pointedly. 'There's still no news for you.' Then in a slightly kinder voice. 'First babies often take their time. Your friend is in very good hands. Why not pop down and get yourself a sandwich?'

'Will I have time? I want to be here when anything happens.'

'Plenty of time.'

In spite of this Becky did not stay very long down at the W.R.V.S. She had not got much money with her so she decided she had better be careful and only have a sausage roll, which was cheaper than a sandwich and left her with enough cash for a cup of tea and a piece of cake later on if she was still waiting.

During the afternoon she was joined in the waiting room by a swarthy, silent man, who clearly did not welcome conversation, preferring to pace about the room in the traditional fashion. Becky, who had previously thought the boredom alone might be enough to send her insane, was driven almost to screaming pitch by Mr Perpetual Motion and felt like cheering when a nurse popped her head round the door to tell him that he had got a daughter and conduct him off to inspect the new arrival.

Becky thought about poor Paula and wished that she could give her some moral support. With this idea in mind she sought out Hatchet Face again and asked whether it would be possible for someone to take a note in to her friend.

'We're not here to be employed as carrier pigeons,' came the waspish reply, which Becky assumed to be a no.

The next time she ventured into the corridor there was a completely new face behind the desk. Crikey, thought Becky, we've been here so long that the shift's changed over.

The new nurse looked up from what she was writing and smiled. When she spoke it was with a soft Irish lilt. 'Can I help you?'

'Yes,' said Becky. 'I'm here with my friend Paula Morrison. She came in at about nine o'clock, this morning. Can you tell me if she's all right?'

'My word – have you been waiting here all day?'

Becky nodded.

'What a good friend you are. You hold on here and I'll go and check on her progress.'

The Irish nurse returned about five minutes later. 'I've

told your friend that you were asking after her and she says she's sorry to keep you waiting and to tell you that she loves you. She's having a bit of a tough time but she's keeping her spirits up.'

'It's been nearly twelve hours,' said Becky. 'Is that normal?'

'Well now it can be. I don't think they'll be leaving your friend much longer anyway. If she doesn't make a bit of progress soon they'll give her something to speed her up a bit.'

'So you think I've got time to go down and get another drink?'

'You won't get anything at this time,' the nurse said. 'The W.R.V.S. shuts at six. Tell you what,' she glanced conspiratorially up and down the corridor. 'I'll make you a cuppa and bring it into the waiting room. We've a kettle in our sitting room. You must be parched.'

This first cup of tea was followed by a second at about eleven o'clock. In the corridor beyond the waiting room door people came and went. Once Becky heard a woman screaming horribly, but when she rushed to look out of the little glass panel set in the waiting room door, she saw to her relief that the noise could be traced to a woman being wheeled in by an ambulance man. At one point she dozed off to sleep then awoke with a start, feeling as though in dozing she had let Paula down.

Then she heard a footstep in the corridor and saw the glass panel darken before the door was opened. It was the Irish nurse. She walked straight across to Becky and sat down beside her, taking and holding her hand firmly, in a way that no other woman had done since she was a child.

Becky stared at her in fearful enquiry.

'I have to tell you... I am so sorry... your friend Paula has just died.'

'She can't have,' said Becky, tears rising in her eyes. 'She can't have died.'

'Have you known her a long time?'

Becky nodded, overcome.

'Did you ever hear anyone saying there was anything wrong with her heart?'

Becky shook her head. The nurse leaned forward and allowed Becky to sob in her arms.

After a few minutes Becky said, 'What about the baby?'

'We tried very hard. When we knew Paula had gone, Doctor tried an emergency caesarean, but I'm afraid it was too late. It was a little boy.'

Becky nodded. 'She was going to call him Philip,' she said.

'I have to ask you... Can you give us Paula's next of kin? Her records don't seem to have been filled in properly.'

Becky recited the address mechanically.

'Would you like me to ring someone to fetch you?'

'No thank you,' said Becky. 'I'll be OK.'

She walked down the stairs to the foyer in a dream. The W.R.V.S. shop was shuttered, the clinic waiting areas deserted. She walked out into the still dark night and headed for the bus stop. Women didn't die in childbirth anymore. They just didn't. At the bus stop she remembered that it was well after midnight. There was probably no night service on this route. As she started to walk through the empty streets, she thought of Paula's message. Tell her I love her. They never said that. They had never said it before anyway. Although love was what it must be, because otherwise the pain would not be so bad as this.

Chapter Eighty-Six

1997

Madeline took a gratifying interest in the contents of the box. She fingered the scarf and the old exercise books and wanted her mother to identify everyone on the photos. Madeline knew that the things in the box had belonged to Paula and all about how her mother came to have them because Paula had brought them to her mother's flat just before she died and Paula's parents had not wanted them back.

Madeline knew all about the reunion too – although she could not understand how people could ever lose touch with any of the friends they saw every single day. It sounded suspiciously like carelessness. She could not imagine a time when she would not see Katie and Hannah who were her absolutely best friends in all the world.

They were still looking through the box together when Nicky rang. Madeline slid off her mother's bed and drifted downstairs to put 'Nickelodeon' on, because she knew that when it was Auntie Nicky on the phone the calls tended to go on a bit.

'Now don't forget that we're going to park up and meet around the corner,' pleaded Nicky. 'I'll never do it if I have to walk in there on my own.'

'I've told you,' said Becky patiently. 'Everyone will look older. Lots of people will have put on weight.'

'You and Jo haven't.'

'I have,' said Becky. 'Believe me I have.'

'Well not as much as me. And they'll all have had sparkling careers,' wailed Nicky. 'Half of them will be rocket scientists.'

'Come off it. Do you remember nothing about the science teaching at Eleanor Vaux? Can you see any of Mrs Young's biology class becoming rocket scientists?'

'Well… no. But we were the thickies.'

'Cheers Nick. That's made me feel heaps better.'

'Well no. Not you.'

'Not any of us,' said Becky. 'Now stop panicking. If it turns out to be hideous we don't have to stay. The three of us can bugger off to the pub.'

After an initial burst of enthusiasm, Nicky had been blowing hot and cold about the reunion for weeks. Although she tried to encourage Nick, Becky secretly felt much the same. And tomorrow was the big day.

When she returned to the bedroom and found that Maddy had gone downstairs, Becky packed the contents of the Paula's box carefully away. The things all had a dull, faded look. A reminder that some of them were nearly thirty years old. How could that be she wondered, when it was only yesterday?

Just when she thought that everything was back in the box she noticed Paula's scarf was still lying on the bed. How she had longed for one of those scarves. Unlike everything else in the box the scarf did not appear to have faded. It must have been made of some good quality, durable stuff. The silver, black and blue stripes would go very well with the blue skirt and top she was planning to wear next day and she had a sudden impulse to wear it. She decided that it was not an overly sentimental or mawkish gesture, because it was unlikely that anyone else would remember that she had never had a scarf of her own and deduce that it was Paula's.

Chapter Eighty-Seven

1997

Becky parked her car round the corner from school and waited for Nicky as arranged. It was daft in one way, she thought, but nice in another because it meant that they could walk the last bit together.

'Have a nice time,' Maddy had instructed, before being whisked away in Hannah's mother's four wheel drive.

Maddy was only a few weeks away from leaving junior school. In a matter of months she herself would be stepping onto the stage of senior school. Which is where it all began for us, Becky thought. It was like the completion of a pattern: the point where two ends of the circle met.

Remembering her friend's anxieties, she said as soon as Nicky stepped out of her car, 'You look lovely.'

'So do you.' Nicky hugged her. 'And you're wearing Paula's scarf,' she added approvingly.

Being unsure about the time of her train Jo had arranged to meet them inside, but as they turned the final corner they were hailed by none other than Jo herself, approaching the junction from the other direction.

There was another round of hugging.

When did we start hugging one another? Nicky suddenly found herself wondering. Not at school, that was for sure.

Jo was wearing black trousers and a white tee shirt with an Eleanor Vaux tie loosely around her neck, the knot coming several inches below her throat. As usual she looked at least ten years younger than she actually was and made the tie look like a stylish fashion accessory.

'Where did you get the tie?' asked Nicky.

'It's mine,' said Jo. 'Believe it or not my mum still had it. She dug it out for me and I washed and pressed it. It's come up pretty well considering all the abuse it took.'

'Joanne Embury wearing a school tie voluntarily,' said Becky. 'It will probably be the biggest shock of the day.'

'Well girls,' said Nicky, as they reached the first set of gates. 'It's the V.I.P. treatment today, entering the premises along the top drive.'

'Contendere et Vincere,' Jo read aloud from the shield on the gate. 'To strive and to overcome. Well we've each done a bit of that in our own ways. Maybe we were better at living up to the Evie motto than we realised.'

'Do you think we'll recognise anyone?' asked Nicky.

'Well we should be able to pick out Adele.' said Jo.

They had reached the front doors.

'They've put carpet in the entrance hall,' exclaimed Jo and Nicky in unison.

'And what's happened to room 17?' asked Becky. 'Good heavens, it's full of computers!'

The invitation said '*gather in main hall*' and here they

found about twenty women had already arrived. In spite of knowing that it had to be so, Becky was still momentarily jolted to realise that everyone had grown so much older. For a single awful moment, she thought that Nicky's fears would be realised and they would recognise no one. Then something uncanny happened. As people turned their faces toward her – this assortment of forty year old strangers – she knew them all.

The woman nearest to the door could not be anyone but Colleen Bell and standing next to her was Penny Lynch and there, bearing down on them, looking matronly but still with those striking dark eyes was none other than Gail Foster. She held out her arms and Becky held out hers. Gail hugged each of them in turn.

'You three,' she said. 'Still together. Oh look! Here's Annette… I must go and say hello. Excuse me.' She dashed off to greet another arrival.

'I've just been hugged by Gail Foster,' murmured Jo. 'Now there's a sentence I never thought I'd hear myself saying.'

Gail rejoined them a couple of minutes later by which time they were part of an ever widening, laughing, talking group.

'What are you doing now?' Jo asked her politely.

'I've just completed my degree with the O.U.,' said Gail. 'I know it probably doesn't sound much to you, because I expect you three all went on to university straight after school, but I never fitted in at school like you did. I was the proverbial square peg in a round hole.'

'We never fitted in,' protested Jo.

'Of course you did,' said Gail. 'You were proper Evies, the genuine article. I felt such a sense of achievement getting that degree. And do you know when I walked on stage to collect my BA, I remembered Baggy Bagshaw saying that I was the stupidest girl she had ever taught and I thought to myself, well that's one in the eye for you. Not that she'll ever know but never mind.'

'I was in her French group,' said Nicky. 'And she told me that I was the stupidest girl she had ever taught too. She obviously believed in sharing the honours around.'

'When you come to think about it,' said Jo. 'She wouldn't have been all that old when she taught us. We'll be older now than she was then.'

'They all just seemed so old,' said Becky. 'I wonder what's happened to them all? Do you remember Mr Sinton? He was a sweet old thing.'

'And the dreaded Miss Harkness? And dear old Miss Prior, shedding face powder in all directions?'

'Oh look,' said Nicky. 'Here's someone else coming. Crumbs,' she dropped her voice. 'Who on earth is this?'

The hum of conversation died away with the entrance of this latest arrival. She was a tall woman, with straggling, unkempt, black hair, who appeared to be suffering from some sort of awful skin complaint.

'Poor thing,' Gail stage whispered. 'Who on earth can it be?'

'Let's go across to meet her,' whispered Becky. 'No one's recognised her and we can't just let her stand there.'

But before they could move the new arrival startled them by raising a hand to her neck and jerking off the rubber mask complete with attached wig, which had covered her whole head.

'Ronnie!' chorused several voices at once.

‘Sorry guys,’ said Ronnie cheerfully, as she smoothed her own short, dark hair back into place. ‘My son got it last Halloween. Couldn’t resist, I’m afraid.’

Jo grinned. ‘It’s good to find some things never change,’ she said.

Contrary to Nicky’s fears, no one confessed to being a rocket scientist. Adele was now a successful accountant and Colleen a social worker. Rowena had become Dr Abbott and lectured at various universities around the country. Alex sent greetings from New Zealand where she and her Kiwi husband ran a hotel. Norma was a translator in a London publishing house. Naomi Wiseman taught in a local primary and Debbie Reed was a full time mother. Like Paula, Kay Fenton was missing – a victim of cancer at thirty seven. Ronnie confessed to having discovered a vocation. She had been ordained the year before.

Their tour of the school produced laughter and some surprises.

‘Look at this!’ exclaimed Helen Staveley. ‘A room full of tools for woodwork and all that boys’ stuff. I hope they’re being taught how to mend a fuse and wire a plug, too. And how to use a plunger to unblock a drain.’

In the dining hall the menu drew forth more exclamations. ‘Cheese burgers!’ said Jo. ‘What’s happened to lamb hot pot and spotted dick?’

‘I don’t know how we were ever allowed anything so risqué sounding as spotted dick,’ said Norma, who happened to be standing nearby. ‘I can only assume that Miss Forster wasn’t aware of the potential double meaning.’ She turned to Becky with whom she had not yet had a chance to talk. ‘Did you have far to come?’

'I never went very far away. I live in Sutton Coldfield now with my daughter. Do you have any children?'

'No,' said Norma. 'We tried for three years with never so much as a whisper. Then my husband walked out. He's got two kids with his new partner.'

'I'm sorry,' said Becky.

'Don't be. I'm actually very happy. Although I'll admit I was terribly nervous about coming today. I might have chickened out altogether but I knew that Alex would be furious if I wasn't able to write and tell her all about it. I was afraid it might be horribly competitive like school was, only instead of how many marks you got in your test, it would be how many kids have you got and how big's your house.'

In the light of Norma's well remembered participation in past competitive exercises, Becky was too surprised to reply.

'It hasn't been like that though, has it?' Norma continued. 'It's turned out to be a really positive experience. We weren't exactly a united group at school, but today it feels as if there's a really strong bond between all of us. And knowing about Paula and Kay makes you count your blessings. Reading between the lines I think most of us have been through the mill a few times since we last walked out of those gates. Perhaps that's what we've all got in common. We've survived life.'

'Contendere et vincere,' murmured Becky.

A set of back doors had been unlocked so that they could go outside and look out across the hockey pitches.

'I wonder what Miss Leopold's doing now?' mused Adele.

'Ten year's hard labour if there's any justice,' said Annette.

'Look,' said Nicky. 'They've taken out all the rosebushes and grassed the beds that used to be along the bottom drive.'

They strolled in that direction to see what else had changed. Paula's scarf slipped and Becky had to adjust it, flicking the longer end over her shoulder. There was no mention of a school scarf on the list which had been issued to Maddy by her new school. Very soon they would be going into town together to buy the uniform. It would be a fun day with the usual larking about in the shops and probably lunch in McDonalds – never Becky's first choice but always her daughter's.

'It's different for you, of course,' her mother often said. 'With your job you can afford nice things. You don't have to struggle like I did.'

But that wasn't the difference, Becky thought.

They had reached the edge of the school buildings and were at the point where the drive led down to the bottom gates, which because it was a Saturday were closed and padlocked.

Suddenly Nicky said, 'You know what we've got to do, don't you?'

'We can't,' protested Jo. 'We haven't done it for years. We'll get out of step and end up falling over.'

'Rubbish,' said Nicky. 'Come on.'

Laughing at one another, looping their arms around each others' shoulders, crossing their feet slowly at first until they found their timing, the trio headed towards the gates giving perhaps their most tuneless rendition to date of 'Raindrops Keep Falling on My Head'.

Matador